Cath Weeks has been writing since she was a child, winning a national writing competition aged nineteen which spurred her on. She lives in Bath with her husband and two sons.

Also by Cath Weeks

Blind
Mothers

The Wife's Shadow

Cath Weeks

PIATKUS

First published in Great Britain in 2018 by Piatkus

1 3 5 7 9 10 8 6 4 2

All characters and events in this publication, other than those clearly in the public domain, are fictitious and any resemblance to real persons, living or dead, is purely coincidental.

A CIP catalogue record for this book is available from the British Library.

TPB ISBN 978-0-349-41870-4

Typeset in Bembo by M Rules
Printed and bound in Great Britain by
Clay's Ltd, Elcograf S.p.A.

Papers used by Piatkus are from well-managed forests and other responsible sources.

Piatkus
An imprint of
Little, Brown Book Group
Carmelite House
50 Victoria Embankment
London EC4Y 0DZ

An Hachette UK Company
www.hachette.co.uk

www.littlebrown.co.uk

For my brother, Rob

And hereupon it was my mother dear
Did bring forth twins at once, both me, and fear

Thomas Hobbes 1588–1679
English philosopher

PROLOGUE

My friends used to tell me that I had it all. And I used to say that that was a matter of opinion. To which they would roll their eyes and tell me not to be so modest – that it was plain to see that my life was charmed, like living inside a snow globe or a doll's house.

Often on such occasions, and increasingly so that winter, I would fall silent.

Even snow globes and dolls' houses were made by someone, I thought to myself. Behind the luxury, shimmer and plastic, there was labour.

I had worked so hard for everything. My friends knew this, which was why they could tease me about my gains. They had known me since school. Not the cleverest or the prettiest, I had always had my hand up, my head down, my ponytail screwed on tight. I had even kept a scrapbook – an eighties version of the modern vision board, where I stuck pictures of my life goals as a way of manifesting them.

I still have that scrapbook. It is somewhere in storage, out of sight. Perhaps if I had heeded it sooner, had turned its glue-wrinkled pages to see what it had been trying to tell me, then everything would have been all right.

But I didn't. The scrapbook stayed where it was, and in my stomach that January there grew a sense of unease.

It was strongest when my friends were gathered, perhaps because this was the only opportunity that I had to stop and ponder. I found myself drifting in and out of focus, catching fragments of the conversation. My head was turned towards the world outside, watching the skeletal trees twitching in the cold afternoon wind. It felt as though something were about to happen, as though life were about to lose its balance and tip over.

During those reflective moments, I often thought of something my mother used to say about not making the gods jealous. I had never known what to do with this piece of advice. It didn't seem very progressive or positive. It felt intrinsically female, the fear of being seen to have too much. Yet it had been repeated so often to me as a child that the warning had been heeded.

Or so I thought.

Had I known what was about to occur, I would have put down my coffee cup and run straight home. I would have turned the key in the lock and held my children close. I would have nailed the roof tighter and shuttered the windows and barred the door.

That's the thing about dolls' houses.

Anyone can reach inside.

PRELIMINARY MEETING

Monday 27 March, 2017

From outside, the building is daunting. I hesitate at the foot of the steps, but then the large door swings open and a man appears. It is clear, even without my staring, that he is devastated. His face is ashen; he is holding a tissue to his nose.

I stand aside for him, gripping the handrail, feeling myself become brittle with emotion.

I hadn't thought that there would be others here like me. So personal, so life-changing, the experience feels unique. Like weddings or funerals, you don't expect anyone else to be going through the same thing, let alone on the same day, in the time slot before or after yours.

I glance at my watch, my stomach shifting nervously. Behind me, normal life goes on – shoppers with designer bags, tourists taking selfies. I don't want to leave them; even though it's an illusion, for their lives are no more normal than mine. Still, I eye a passing shopper with envy. She isn't having to do this.

Or maybe she is. Maybe she just doesn't know it yet.

I turn back to the door, tell myself that I am being cowardly. I must go in.

I ascend the steps. The brass door knob is worn yet shiny. I push it and the door gives. Inside I am swallowed up by the warmth – by smiles, leather chairs, fresh orchids, brochures.

It's not the receptionist's fault, but I know that I will regret the day that I first saw her.

'How can I help you?' she says pleasantly.

'My name's Suzy Taylor,' I say. 'I have a twelve o'clock.'

1

The February morning that we buried my mother was so cold, the six-foot hole awaiting her was laced with frost, like a greedy mouth rimmed with sugar.

I gazed up at the sky, yet its white glare made my eyes throb. There was nowhere else to look but at the elm coffin. I had opted for *The Chiltern* – simplistic, white gown, white satin interior. The brochure wording had sounded oddly bridal to me.

As they lowered her down, tiny snowflakes appeared, tumbling on to the elm casing as though a flower girl were scattering rose petals after my mother, another poignant echo of her wedding day.

I sniffed and Mike drew me closer, tipping me slightly off-kilter. I balanced myself against him, grateful for his being there. He was my tall, handsome rock in his black pea coat, not that anyone would have noted this. There were too few of us: Mike and I, and half a dozen of my mum's elderly neighbours – white-haired, arthritic, dewdrops on noses.

The reverend began to speak in a quiet voice. The graveyard was silent, as though the deceased were listening in. One of the mourners was cupping his hand to his ear, his hearing aid whistling forlornly.

'Our eyes, dear Lord, are wasted with grief, as we remember the life of Annie Stone. And we pray for her only kin, Suzy Taylor ... ' The reverend raised his hand towards me in acknowledgement. ' ... That she may find comfort in You ... '

I was her only kin and never before had I been so painfully aware of the fact.

I had tried hard to bolster the numbers for the funeral, but there just hadn't been enough people to invite. And now it was clear for all to see: my mother's life had been small, insignificant.

I took a gulp of air and reached for my tissues, finding that Mike had beaten me to it and was unfolding a baby-blue handkerchief. I held the handkerchief to my face, inhaling the comforting scent of laundered cotton.

I was thankful then that my children were at school. Some people believed that children belonged at funerals. Perhaps I did too, just not today, not here. My distress would have scared and disturbed them. I had been doing my best to contain my grief at home, limiting it to after lights out; keeping it all together had been the hardest part of everything I'd experienced of late.

My mother would have done the same thing. I had learnt from the best.

I pressed the handkerchief into the sockets of my eyes, catching the tears before they fell. I was trying not to picture my mother inside the coffin – her floral socks, oversized knickers. No one ever talked about the details, forewarned you. It had come as a shock that I was to decide what to dress her in. Bra or no bra? That one decision had floored me. In the end, I had chosen no bra. Above all, I wanted my mum to be comfortable.

As the reverend said his closing prayers, I was thinking of the list of wording suggestions for the headstone. It was another awful choice, one that I had been advised to postpone. Yet it was bothering me nonetheless. I was convinced that the first item on the list of suggestions wasn't even legitimate but planted there just for me.

Resting where no shadows fall.

I was being paranoid, I knew.

'All right, my love?' Mike squeezed my hand. He looked cold, his lips tinged lilac. I glanced about me, saw that the ceremony was over. The mourners were beginning to shuffle away. We had organised a wake of sorts in the village hall – tea and biscuits.

'Do you need a minute?' Mike said, reaching down to wipe a tear from my cheek.

'Please,' I said.

I'm not sure how long I stood there with Mike beside me. I wasn't looking at the hole in the earth, but at the yew trees lining the graveyard. They were utterly still, sentry-like. My mother had loved trees. She used to say that trees and children were the most beautiful things in the world, that they made it all worthwhile.

'Bye, Mum,' I said, my throat swelling painfully. I didn't stop the tears now, couldn't have caught them had I tried.

If there was something else that I could have done to offer her comfort, I would have done it then. If I could have slipped the sun beside her to keep her warm or sprinkled her with stars to give her light, I would have.

But there was nothing more I could do.

I was turning away, when something caught my eye. I stared at the dark corner of the graveyard where the yew trees grew. The area was overgrown, with headstones leaning amongst the long grass as though bending back to talk to each other.

I had thought that something or someone was there. But it was nothing; a cat perhaps, or someone tending to a grave who had vanished through the back gate.

We left, our feet clipping on the concrete path. Each step

felt as though I were being pulled away from my mother. It felt unnatural, like deliberately going in the wrong direction.

I could see her waiting for me by the school gate, stirring supper on the stove. I could see her tickling me, tucking me into bed.

I could see her thin wrists, her freckles, the telltale salty streaks of dried tears under her eyes.

'You were a good daughter, Suzy,' Mike said. 'That must have meant a great deal to her.'

I nodded, too heavy-hearted to reply.

We walked the rest of the way to the village hall in silence, Mike's arm around me. As we pulled open the door and a gust of warmth air-kissed our cheeks, I felt my stomach churn once more with doubt, misgivings.

I hadn't wanted a burial for my mother. We hadn't discussed the subject in the past. I had just assumed that she would want to be cremated as it felt like the softer way to go. Her written request for a burial had surprised me.

I didn't have to adhere to it, could have overruled it. Yet I hadn't wanted to do that either.

So, a burial it was. But why? My mum hadn't been a traditionalist, a church-goer. Why would she have wanted to be incarcerated in the cold, deep earth?

This question had niggled at me throughout the funeral and the grey days that followed.

And then, within only a handful of weeks, the answer came to me.

You had to be truly frightened in order to understand the appeal of burial. To my mother, going underground must have felt like the safest place to be.

2

My four-year-old daughter liked to play with her vintage paper doll set just inside our front door. On that particular Wednesday morning, I slipped ungracefully on a paper dress.

'Mum*mee*!' Ruby said. 'Look what you've done!'

'Sorry, poppet,' I said. 'I'll iron it later.'

'Iron it?' Ruby said, wrinkling her nose.

'Yes. You can iron anything.'

'Even snails?'

I smiled. One week after the funeral, my smiles were still tight, pulled on my eyes. 'No. Not snails . . .' I raised my voice: 'Jakey?'

'Are you painting today?' Ruby said.

'Yes.'

'Can I help after school?'

'P'raps not,' I said, tugging her skirt straight. 'You don't want to get paint on your uniform, do you?'

'No,' she said. 'Maybe just a flapchat then.'

Flapchat was Ruby's way of saying *flapjack*. *Valinna* was her favourite cupcake at my deli. I sometimes made them just so I could hear her say it.

'Jake?' I called again, buttoning up my coat. I hadn't looked outside yet, but it seemed very dark.

There was a rustle in the doorway and Jake appeared, eyes downcast. When he was lost in a book, heaven help the rest of us.

'I've got to go,' I said. 'Can you watch Ruby whilst Daddy's in the shower . . . Jake?'

'Huh?' He gazed at me, blinking. He was tall for eight years old and dark like his father. Ruby was fair, like me. My friends said that we looked like a catalogue family.

'Please watch Ruby for a moment,' I said, kissing his forehead. 'I'll see you later, sweetheart.'

'OK,' he said, but was reading again.

'Well, I'm off,' I said, picking up my work holdall which was bulging with Tupperware and paperwork.

Mike appeared then, calling out to me. 'Wait a sec, Suzes.' He was coming down the stairs, towel around his waist, steam rising from his shoulders.

He halted before me. 'Let me know if you need anything,' he said, kissing me on the lips.

'Will do,' I said. 'Bye then, everyone.'

And I left the house, going out into the jaundiced fog that had been hanging around the street for several days now.

That morning, as I walked down the hill to work, I didn't feel entirely alone.

I didn't believe in ghosts, not even now. There were things that I would have asked my mother were she to appear, but I didn't think that was going to happen. I was forty and the years had somehow passed in silence, with my questions unspoken.

All the administration work surrounding her death had been completed, aside from clearing her apartment, a job that I would defer as long as possible. Everything about my mum was contained in that tiny space, as though she were homeless at heart.

I shivered, glancing about me as I continued on my way. It

was so quiet, so still, I could hear a milk float purring along a neighbouring street, out of sight, bottles softly clinking. A rural city in the main, Bath was set in the base of a valley. It wasn't unusual to encounter moments of silence within it, even in the centre, in its deepest pouches. At this hour, you could easily find yourself alone.

As I turned the corner on to the high street, I caught sight of my shop and felt my spirits lift. A beam of sunshine had struggled through the fog and was highlighting the new sign: THE BIG LITTLE DELI. It used to be just THE LITTLE DELI, two doors down. The old place looked lonely now, windows whitewashed, sign removed.

As I unlocked the door of the new premises, pausing on the threshold to take in the sight of the dust sheets, paint cans and cardboard boxes, I realised that for the first time in weeks I felt hopeful, happy.

That night when I arrived home, I was weary, my body aching.

I was just unlocking the door, pushing it open with my hip, when I stopped. I could smell smoke.

I set my bag down on the floor, looking about me. Mike and the children weren't back yet from Ruby's ballet class. The house was silent, a freeze-frame of activity, Jake's sweater spreadeagled on the floor, Ruby's paper dolls by my feet.

As I crouched down to pick up the doll set, I noticed something lying on the floor underneath the sideboard. Reaching forward into the cobwebs, I pulled out a red Rizla wrapper.

I set the wrapper on my palm and stared at it.

A sudden draught made me shiver. I had left the front door open. Behind me, the fog was yellow, shifting underneath the street lights.

I closed the door, lost in thought. How had the smoke and the wrapper got there?

Perhaps someone had been smoking whilst making a delivery earlier. They had dropped the wrapper and it was swept indoors by feet or the wind.

I didn't have time to dwell on the matter. Mike was going out tonight with old friends from the police force. I scrunched the wrapper up and went downstairs to the kitchen to start making dinner.

When Mike and the children arrived home, it was later than expected so our meal was rushed. Mike kissed us goodbye and headed out again, telling me not to wait up.

Naturally, I did wait up. I always found it hard not to.

After settling the children down for the night, I got into bed with a cup of tea and a bundle of paperwork.

By the time Mike returned, I was yawning over my diary.

'Did you have a good time?' I asked, putting the diary aside to look at him. I liked watching him undress. Ten years of marriage hadn't changed that.

'Not bad,' he replied, unbuttoning his shirt. 'Just the usual.' He noticed then that I was watching him. 'What?' he said, tossing his jeans onto the chaise longue.

'Nothing,' I said, smiling.

He had recently turned fifty but didn't look it. Forced to retire from the police seven years ago because of a leg injury, relegation had kept him young, determined as he was to stay in shape.

He pulled back the bedcovers, got into bed. 'How come you're so awake?' he asked.

'Not sure.' I glanced at the diary. 'Did you know it's . . . ?'

'Mufti day tomorrow?' he said. 'Yep.' He yawned. 'All sorted.'

'Thanks, honey,' I said, kissing him.

I felt like welling up with gratitude but didn't. If I had cried every time Mike did something without my asking, I'd have been crying all the time. I knew how priceless he was as our stay-at-home dad. And if I ever forgot this, my friends would soon remind me.

''Night then, love,' he said, kissing me before rolling over, taking a handful of duvet with him.

''Night.' I lay still for a moment, gazing at his back. 'Mike, did we have any deliveries today?'

'No,' he said into his pillow.

'No one called round? Not a door-to-door salesman, odd-job man or anyone?'

'No.' He rolled over to face me again. 'Why?'

'Just that I found a Rizla wrapper. And I smelt smoke.'

'Smoke? Where?' He rested his head on his elbow, frowned.

'Inside the hallway.' I gazed at him. 'Have you been smoking?'

He laughed. 'What? I've never smoked in my life!'

'Then who?' I said.

'I dunno. Jake?'

'Jake?' I said. 'He's eight!'

'Not *Ruby*,' he said, in mock alarm.

'Glad to see you're taking it seriously then,' I said, hitting his arm lightly.

'There's nothing to take seriously. It's just a freak incident. The wind changed direction ... some kid having a sneaky smoke in next door's garden ... It's nothing.' He patted my waist. 'Get some sleep.'

I sighed, reached for the bedside lamp, then lay down, staring into the darkness.

Mike was probably right. It was a freak incident. So why was it troubling me?

I changed position in agitation, the mattress bouncing.

That was one of the biggest challenges of grief – the way it addled the heart, stirred up the past until it was cloudy. Since my mother's death, I had replayed almost every moment that I could recall spending with her, going back to my early years.

And in those early years, I could see the red Rizlas, my father's fingers dexterously rolling cigarettes, his eyes screwed up against the smoke.

I had used the smoke as my official reason not to draw near, rather than confess to the dread and revulsion that I had felt just being in the same room as him.

'You still thinking about that Rizla wrapper?' Mike said.

''Course not,' I said.

And I closed my eyes.

PRELIMINARY MEETING

Monday 27 March, 2017

'Take a seat, Mrs Taylor,' the receptionist says. 'Mr Cassidy will be right with you.' She turns back to her screen and begins to type impressively quickly.

I look about me. There are four leather tub chairs in a row, each with their own small table. The set-up feels both intimate and alienating, suggesting that many people come through this way, yet the experience is acutely solitary.

You have your own table, your own chair, your own turmoil.

I sit in the nearest chair and pick up a magazine with no intention of reading it.

The typing noise is agitating me. It's so fast, so clicky. I wish it would stop.

I consult my watch. Mr Cassidy is running late. I keep my eye on the white door that will surely open any minute now.

No one comes or goes. I tap my foot, flick through the pages of the magazine.

The door doesn't open until twenty past twelve. When I see Mr Cassidy coming towards me, I feel perspiration break out on my top lip.

Am I sure about this? I glance at the front door, wondering if it's not too late to slip back outside with no harm done.

But Mr Cassidy is standing before me.

He will be used to shaking clammy hands; I need not worry about this.

He shakes my hand so heartily that the motion jangles my shoulder. He is tall, with a bald head and glasses so thick that his pupils are tiny dots. The effect is menacing, but he cannot help this. He is smiling, doing his best to reassure me.

'Shall we?' he says, pointing to the white door.

3

On the Friday, three days before the deli was set to open, I went into work early to meet with a new supplier.

The day ahead was easy enough, but I was feeling jittery. My mother's death had unsettled me in ways that hadn't materialised yet. It was like waiting for something to hatch from an unidentifiable egg.

My friend, Helen, would have said that grief had knocked my chakras out of alignment. I wasn't sure that I knew what chakras were, but I did feel vulnerable and my inclination was to slow down and keep my children close.

Doing the latter would be easier now. I had installed a book corner in the new deli with Jake and Ruby in mind. They had helped me to furnish it and now whenever I caught sight of Jake's rowing boat bookcase, I felt a pang of happiness.

Part of the reason for upsizing was to incorporate children – mine and others – into the business more effectively. Not only would I be able to spend more time with Jake and Ruby, but hopefully the move would also prove profitable given the amount of families that came this way every day just after three o'clock.

The new supplier that I was meeting with that morning made vegan quiches from home. We had been talking for some time when I realised that I hadn't asked her how she proposed to make her quiche vegan.

The secret was chickpea flour mixed with water to make the fluffy filling. Evidently, I wouldn't be able to tell the difference. This sounded terrific, so I agreed to a trial run.

I saw the supplier out and was just crouching down to undo a cardboard box, when someone tapped me on the shoulder.

I gasped, jumped up. Nicole was standing there, trying not to laugh.

'Crikey,' I said, hand to heart. 'You gave me a scare!'

'Sorry, hun,' Nicole said. 'I didn't mean to.' She pushed her dark hair from her eyes to gaze around the room. 'Wow. The place looks amazing.'

'It's getting there,' I said.

She went to the book corner, picked up one of the velvet cushions and held it to her face. 'These are cute. Did Ruby choose them?'

'Yep,' I said.

'And Spiderman,' she said, pointing at the wall motif. 'For Mike?'

'You've guessed it.' We both laughed.

Sometimes it felt as though I had spent my whole life laughing and mucking about with Nicole. We had met on our first day at senior school and had got on well from the outset. I was more studious than her; she was prettier than me – beautiful. Together, we were the perfect woman.

'Got time for a coffee?' I asked.

'Better not,' she said, glancing at her phone. Then she smiled at me excitedly. 'Nervous?'

'A little,' I said.

'Well, you're bound to be. But really, it's the same as before, just bigger ... Isn't that your motto in life anyhow?'

'Yeah, right,' I said, rolling my eyes.

Nicole often made little jokes about my have-it-all lifestyle. I let her get away with it, didn't mind, because she had had a hard time of it over the past decade. She was a single mum to nine-year-old Zack and didn't suit the role too well, like an extrovert being forced to work in solitary confinement. A property valuer for an estate agent, she liked being part of a team – still missed her serial-cheating ex-husband.

Seen through her eyes, I did appear to have rather a lot, especially given the fact that I had Mike close at hand to help. I did feel guilty about this sometimes, until I reminded myself that it had taken a horrific car crash and several complicated leg operations to bring this good fortune about.

Still, when the subject arose with Helen and Donna, our two other friends from school, they agreed with Nicole: I was blessed indeed.

There was no use arguing. Besides, it was just a bit of fun – the sort of banter that only old friends could get away with.

'You'd better get going,' I said, kneeling on the floor to undo a box of cappuccino cups. 'Leo will be here in his shorts in a minute and won't want you ogling him.'

Nicole, along with many of my customers, fancied handsome Leonardo. Hailing from Florence, he was working for me before moving on to something more ambitious. I was making the most of my time with him because he was a gifted baker and nonchalant. I was calm under pressure, but Leo's composure was celestial.

Yeah, Nicole liked to say – calm, celestial. That's what most springs to mind about Leo.

'And here he is . . . ' she said, as the doorbell tinkled and Leo appeared in his running gear, his forehead glistening with sweat.

'Morning, ladies,' he said, going straight downstairs to shower.

Nicole was smirking at me. Then she consulted the time on her phone again. 'Whoops. Gotta go ... You sure you're all right?'

''Course,' I said. 'Why wouldn't I be?'

'I dunno ...' She gazed at the box in my arms, as though the answer lay in my chinaware. 'Well, look after yourself. I'll be in on Monday to toast the new place.'

'Thank you,' I said, kissing her goodbye.

Then I went outside to the back of the shop to break boxes down. I was in the middle of doing so, was lost in stamping and snapping cardboard, when someone spoke from behind me.

'Oh, my goodness!' I said, swinging round to see Leo standing there. 'Leo! You scared me.'

He shrugged. 'You want this where?' he said, a painting of David Bowie propped on his hip.

'In the side room, please,' I said. 'Next to Blondie.'

'Righty-ho.'

Within several minutes, he returned. 'And this?' he said, holding up an angel figurine on a silver thread.

'Above the front door, please,' I said. 'It's to protect us ... Just a silly little superstition of mine.'

'I understand,' he said coolly. And disappeared.

By five o'clock, our work was done. Leo had left for the day and I was on my own. We had aired the building to banish paint fumes and now it was chilly inside. I wrapped my arms around me and walked through the rooms, taking a moment to admire the details.

Lit only by the string of fairy lights behind the counter, the deli felt enchanted. The book corner was waiting for its tiny visitors; the row of high chairs was waiting for even smaller guests. In the adjoining room, the regulars would eat in peace, whilst still enjoying the busyness of the main space. And in the front side room, with its oak dining tables and glass ceiling lamps, the workers who had dashed in formerly for takeouts would now be able to sit down with clients to do business.

The Big Little Deli would be many things to many people, not least of all to Mike, my children and me.

And the thought of my family made me want to lock up and start the weekend.

As I hurried up the hill to home, I barely noticed the steep, habitual incline. On my left were Georgian apartments with door wreaths still in place from Christmas and front rooms where televisions were talking seemingly to themselves.

The road evened out now and our house came into view.

From this distance, the house looked toy-like, as though the roof and shutters could be fitted on and off with a satisfying click of plastic. It was a Grade II listed building with original fireplaces and vaults – uncannily similar to the dream home that I had glued wishfully into my scrapbook as a teenager.

Our front gate had been left open. Ruby normally liked to close it with a loud twang. Tonight, she wouldn't have bothered because she would have been stroppy about having to go to Jake's football training.

I was smiling about this, when I spotted a toy on the railings of a neighbour's house several doors along from ours. A child must have dropped the toy and someone had set it on the railings for safe keeping.

As I drew parallel with it, I stopped, stared.

It was a knitted monkey in blue and white, with a chunky red '1' that looked like a squashed heart on its chest. My father had brought me back an identical toy from a business trip to France many, many years before.

I had never liked that monkey. Not only had it seemed male and unrelatable, but my father had gifted it to me in compensation for an especially rough episode at home.

How could there be a toy – so unique, so loaded with meaning – just sitting there on the railings like that, near my house?

I continued to walk slowly, distractedly, glancing back at the toy. I couldn't get over it, was trying to explain it to myself in a way that sounded plausible. But really, it was just a coincidence.

I glanced over my shoulder and then all around me to check that I was alone. It certainly seemed that way and, as if to exaggerate the sense of loneliness, from somewhere above me a bird began to caw plaintively.

Opening the front door of my home, I saw that there was a piece of junk mail lying on the welcome mat. I bent to pick it up, my scarf swinging in front of my face. Pushing the scarf aside, I peered at the leaflet.

Experience the Lake of Lights at Talkin Tarn Country Park, near Carlisle, Cumbria.

I gazed at those last two words in disbelief. Then I turned the leaflet over, read the other side.

Talkin Tarn will be transformed with hundreds of lights on the surface of the lake. Why not come along and personalise a light to remember a deceased loved one?

What on earth was this doing here, so far from home?

I set the leaflet down on the sideboard, catching sight of myself in the hallway mirror. I was gaunt from grief, my cheekbones angular in the gloomy light.

I took a moment to inhale deeply, to pull myself together. There was no need to be melodramatic. So, I had found a Rizla wrapper, and a toy that looked like an old one of mine; and now a piece of junk mail that happened to originate from my childhood home.

So what?

Grief was turning my head backwards, that was all.

I decided not to think any more of it.

I went to the kitchen to make a cup of tea, which I took

back upstairs to the sitting room, with its magnificent view of the eastern slopes of the city. I couldn't see much at this time of night, only a multitude of lights in the dark, but it was surprising how comforting seeing all those lights could be.

I tried to relax on the sofa, grabbing a few precious moments of rest. Yet I couldn't shift the sense of unease that was creeping across my skin, as though I had just watched a horror film.

My tea became cold and the night sky blackened as my thoughts grew darker.

So, when I heard a sudden movement behind me, I jumped, spilling my tea.

It was the children. They came running into the room, jumping on to my lap, full of chatter about goals, KitKats, Radio 1 tunes – talking all at once, smelling of winter, their noses red, Ruby's hair crackling with static.

I asked them to go upstairs and start running their bath, whilst I went to find Mike, who was kicking off his boots in the hallway.

My gaze fell on the junk mail, which was lying where I had left it on the sideboard. 'How did it go?' I said.

'Good,' he said. 'Jake's really coming along.'

'That's great,' I said.

As Mike moved away to hang his coat up in the cloakroom, I plucked up the leaflet and slipped it into my pocket.

'Just going upstairs to bath the kids,' I called out.

'OK, love,' he called back.

In the bathroom, I ripped the leaflet up and dropped it into the bin. The bin squealed as I took my foot off the pedal and then snapped shut.

4

The next day, Saturday, was one of those sunny days in winter that couldn't go to waste. We decided to make the most of it and go for a walk along the canal, setting off from our house on foot. As we passed our neighbour's railings, I noted with some relief that the toy monkey had gone.

We walked down the hill to the high street, towards the deli. 'Is it ready, Mummy?' Ruby said, skipping alongside me.

'Yes, sweet pea. It is,' I said, glancing in the deli windows as we passed by.

'It looks so pretty,' Ruby said.

'Mummy's clever, isn't she?' Mike said, taking my hand.

'Are we going to be multimillionaires?' Jake asked. He was kicking a tennis ball along the pavement, unable to see the point of walking without a ball.

'No, Jake,' I said. 'Not selling quiche we're not.'

'Just well fed,' Mike said.

When we had gone some twenty yards along the canal path, Ruby pulled on my arm and stopped. 'Is this going to be a long walk?' she asked.

'Yes, it is,' Mike said frankly.

I pulled a foil packet of brownies from my pocket. 'Would this help?'

'Yes, Mummy!' Ruby said, jumping up and down. Jake stopped kicking his ball, looked over in interest.

'You shouldn't have to bribe her,' Mike told me.

'No,' I said. 'But it makes for a nicer walk. Want one?'

He sighed, took a brownie and we continued on our way, chewing, the afternoon sun on our backs.

There were no tantrums, tears or fights that day. Everything went smoothly, as it did every once in a while. I could not have been more rested by the time Mike and I headed up to bed.

'Wasn't today just perfect?' I said, as we settled down to sleep.

'Yep,' he said drowsily, putting his arm around me. 'Love you.'

'Love you too.'

I nestled against his chest, the faint scent of sandalwood from his cologne lulling me to sleep, when a sudden noise made me jump.

It was Jake, coughing upstairs. He suffered from asthma and was prone to a winter cough that, left unchecked, would morph into a nasty chest infection.

I threw off the bedcovers. 'Where are you going?' Mike said.

'Jake's coughing,' I said. 'Didn't you hear him?'

'No,' he said. 'He's fine.'

'I'll check on him, just in case.'

Mike yawned, plumped his pillow. An excellent father, it still amazed me – his ability to be so blasé about his children's well-being, especially if sleep were being compromised.

I opened the door, entered the darkness, grappling for the light switch before ascending the narrow staircase to the children's room.

I pushed open their bedroom door and stood looking about me. After a few moments, the toadstool nightlight afforded me enough light to see the children's faces.

Jake began to cough again and I glanced about for his inhaler, recalling that it was in the kitchen, three flights of stairs down.

I set off downstairs, flicking on light switches as I went.

By the time I was in the kitchen, barefoot on the cold floor, the wind rattling the window panes, I didn't feel quite so brave. I was intending to turn out the lights and run back upstairs, when I noticed something lying on the counter by the back door.

I approached hesitantly.

I could read the words even though they were upside down, could see the image of the lake with its floating candles.

'Mike!' I called.

He wouldn't be able to hear me. I picked up the leaflet and hurried upstairs, taking two steps at a time, still calling for Mike.

By the time I got to the next floor, he was coming down the stairs. 'What's going on?'

We met on the landing. I held the leaflet out. 'Did you put this in the kitchen?' I said.

'What is it?'

'A tourist flyer . . . for Cumbria.'

'Cumbria?' He frowned. 'Why–?'

'It came through our door yesterday and I ripped it up and put it in the bin. So, why's it still here?'

He scratched his head. 'Does it matter?'

'Well, I think it's a bit strange, that's all.'

'I see,' he said. 'And is that it?'

He meant – was there anything other than a piece of junk mail that we needed to discuss in the middle of the night?

'Um,' I said. 'Yes . . . Sorry.'

He stared at me for a moment, before heading back upstairs.

'I'll ask the children if they know anything about it,' I said, following him.

He stopped, turned to look at me. 'Not now?'

'No, silly,' I said. 'In the morning.'

Back in Jake's room, I shook his shoulder, eased him upright. His eyelids were heavy, but he sounded wheezy. I had done the right thing, waking him up to take his inhaler.

For one moment, I was tempted to ask him about the leaflet. But I didn't. And I was proud of myself for that.

I was the first to rise the next morning. I put a pot of coffee on and whisked up a pancake batter, watching the bubbles pop as I fried spoonfuls in a griddle pan. Like most of the rooms on this side of the house, there was an attractive view from the kitchen of the surrounding hills. Spring wasn't with us yet, but there were signs in the garden of its imminent arrival. It was raining lightly – very straight rain, since there was little wind. One hill beyond was lit with an intense patch of sunshine.

Ruby appeared on the kitchen steps, sniffing the air. 'Are you making pancakes?'

'Yes,' I said, before kissing her good morning.

'How super!' Ruby had picked up this phrase from school and had been saying it a lot lately. She sat down at the table, her hair flicked neatly over her shoulders. She always looked immaculate, even in her nightie.

'Rubes . . . ' I said, picking up the leaflet and holding it before her. 'I don't suppose you put this in the kitchen yesterday, did you?'

She cast an eye over it. 'Nope,' she said.

Jake appeared then in his Liverpool FC pyjamas, hair stuck on end.

'How about you, love?' I said, showing him the leaflet. 'Have you seen this before?'

He rubbed his eyes. 'No,' he said. 'Why?'

'It's nothing,' I said, returning to the stove.

Mike came up behind me. 'Happy now?' he said, kissing the back of my neck.

'No,' I said. 'Still no idea how the leaflet got there.'

'One of life's little mysteries. Let it go. We've got too many other things to worry about.' And he turned away, satisfied that the matter had been dropped.

I would have left it at that too. As a working mum, a business-owner, I didn't have time to overanalyse things.

But then I went outside with the food scraps for recycling and came to a sudden halt.

There, in front of me, on the railings that fenced off the patio area, was the toy monkey.

'Mike?' I called.

He appeared, blinking at the bright light. 'What?'

'Look,' I said, trying to point to the toy with my chin. Mike didn't follow the gesture, took the food parcel from me instead and dropped it into the bin.

Jake poked his head out of the back door. 'When are we eating, Mummy?'

'I'll be there in one sec,' I said. He retreated indoors.

'What's up?' Mike said, returning.

I stared at the toy. 'Someone's messing with me.'

'Hey? What do you mean?'

'Leaving things lying around, things that only mean something to me.'

'Like what?'

'Like that,' I said, pointing to the monkey.

Mike turned to look. 'That ugly thing? What is it?'

'A stuffed toy. It was out in the street yesterday. And now it's here. How do you explain that?'

'Mummy!' Ruby shouted from the kitchen. 'Can we start the pancakes?'

'Be right there!' I shouted back. 'It's not just the toy,' I said, lowering my voice. 'There was the Rizlas and the smoke and that junk mail from Cumbria ... What if someone's creeping about the house?'

'What?' he said. 'Why? How would they even get in?'

'I don't know. But my father used to smoke red Rizlas and I used to live in Cumbria, plus I had a toy monkey just like that one. You've got to admit – that's quite a few coincidences in the space of a—'

'Your father? What's he got to do with this? When did you last see him, even? Thirty–?'

'Thirty-four years ago.'

'Well, then I'm confused,' he said, folding his arms.

'Maybe someone wants me to think about him, Mike. All these clues lead to him.'

He smiled sympathetically then, placing his hands on my shoulders. 'Look ... Maybe you're the one who wants to think about him. You've just lost your mum. It's only natural to be a bit sentimental.'

'No,' I said. 'It's not that. I don't feel sentimental at all. Especially not about him.'

'And why is that?' he said.

I looked back at him, opened my mouth to reply and hesitated, my cheeks colouring.

Beyond Mike, I could see the monkey gaping at me, taunting me behind his back.

'Because he left us,' I said. 'I hated him for that.'

He nodded. 'Then there's no reason to believe that anyone would want you to think about him, is there?'

My face flushed a deeper red.

If that version of events were true then yes, that would have been a fair assumption to make.

But it wasn't true. My father hadn't left my mother and me. Far from it.

I would have loved to have told Mike the secret then that I had kept all my life and throughout our marriage. But when you had stayed silent about something for so long, it became easier to maintain the silence rather than shatter it and possibly everything else around you in the process.

Mike had always looked at me with love. Even now, with my eyes squinting horribly in the sunlight, he was looking at me as though I were beautiful.

I couldn't bear for him to ever look at me differently.

Nothing would take his love from me – not a stuffed monkey, a Rizla wrapper, or junk mail about a morbid lake.

'You're right,' I said, looking up at Mike. 'It's my grief, playing tricks on me . . . Come on.' I took his hand, led him indoors. 'The pancakes are getting cold.'

Later that day, when we were outside in the garden enjoying the sunshine, Jake decided to shoot the monkey with his Nerf gun. When he upgraded to stoning the toy, trying to dislodge it from the railings, I didn't stop him.

Eventually it took a fist in the belly from Jake to topple the monkey from its perch and down into the wintry rose patch where it remained, unsolved, unclaimed.

PRELIMINARY MEETING

Monday 27 March, 2017

The white door leads to a corridor. We pass half a dozen closed doors. Underfoot, the antique floorboards creak. I could do without the creaking, the dim light, the stuffy air.

'This is us,' he says, outside a closed door.

This isn't us, I want to say.

This isn't me at all.

Forget you ever saw me here.

He opens the door, allowing me to enter the room first. He slides a tab on the door, setting the sign to PRIVATE; MEETING IN PROGRESS.

'Have a seat,' he says.

There are three chairs. He pinches his trousers at the knees before sitting down in the chair furthest from me, as though we have an invisible guest between us. I know who will be sat in that empty chair soon, the thought of which makes me feel faint.

'I'm Daniel Cassidy. But please, call me Dan.'

I nod.

'So, thank you for coming in today. I know it's not easy, but it's my job to make this as painless as possible for you.'

Painless.

I think of the ashen man, my predecessor, going down the front doorsteps earlier, crushed.

'Today is really all about fact-finding, about getting to know you and what it is that has brought you here.'

He smiles, crossing one leg over the other. He's wearing a shirt, suit trousers, and has removed his tie, but I'm guessing that it's not far from here; maybe it's even in his pocket.

He is opening a leather file in which there sits a notepad. It's the sort of fancy accessory that men of a certain status like to use instead of a Pukka pad.

He can remove his tie, call himself Dan, but the leather file is a dead giveaway.

There is nothing casual or painless about this.

He pulls a silver pen from his top pocket, holds it on the paper pad and sets his tiny pupils on me.

5

The Big Little Deli opened at nine o'clock on Monday 13 February.

There was a queue to enter, a line of people trailing down the high street. 'Welcome, everyone!' I said, trying not to sound shrill in my excitement.

The customers bustled into the deli, lively and loud, especially the regulars. They were gazing about them in awe, commenting on the decor; and they made such a fuss over the pies, even though we had always sold wild mushroom and truffle oil, and lamb and chorizo.

I had hired three more staff to help with the increased business. The hardest thing that day was learning to find our way around each other behind the counter. It would take a few weeks, I told one of the new staff after she slopped a glass of milk down my back. I soon dried off – we were all overheating. The weather was fine, so we propped the front door open. But after the tablecloths began to flutter and a few people blew their noses, we closed it again.

None of us took a lunch break. It wouldn't always be this way, I said to my staff during a quieter spell that afternoon. Leo smiled knowingly at this and I flicked my tea towel at him. 'Get back to work.'

'You slave driver,' he said.

'You wouldn't know hard work if it bit you on the arse,' I said. And I swung round to see Mike standing behind the counter with the children.

'Oh, hi!' I blushed a little, but Mike didn't appear to have heard my comment about Leo's arse, or at least was playing deaf and dignified.

I moved to the other side of the counter, bending down to address Jake and Ruby. 'So, do you like the deli?'

'Yes, Mummy,' Ruby said, kissing me gustily. 'It's super!'

'It's awesome,' said Jake, nodding. Then he pointed to the Smarties cookies in the counter jar. 'Can we have one?'

'Only if you give me a huge kiss,' I said.

Mike and the children didn't stay for drinks, just long enough to say hello, before letting me get back to work.

I didn't stop again that day.

At five o'clock, I flipped the OPEN sign on the door to CLOSED. The deli fell quiet, save for the sound of Leo's whistle as he cleaned the coffee machine and the sound of my broom as I slowly swept up.

But then the doorbell rang defiantly and in came my friends, waving bottles of Prosecco. I had forgotten about our get-together.

Leo raised an eyebrow at me as if to say good luck. He was not only calm, but discreet. When the time came for him to leave me for a better job, I wouldn't be above begging him to stay.

Helen was the first to approach. She liked to kiss both cheeks whilst holding my hips, and often smelt of plasticine and baby food, given that she worked as a nursery assistant. 'How are you doing?' she said, stepping back to assess me.

'Good,' I said.

'You look tired,' said Nicole. 'Did it go all right?'

'Yes,' I said. 'It went really well.'

Leo had untied his apron and was standing patiently to one side, waiting to be dismissed.

'You can go, Leo,' I said. 'Thank you for all your hard work today.'

'Aww,' said Nicole, sticking out her bottom lip as he headed downstairs. 'He's so well trained. Can't he stay and play with us?'

'You're sick,' said Donna. 'You can get tablets for that, you know.'

'Prescription or over the counter?' said Nicole.

Donna tutted. A chartered accountant, she was the quietest, most orderly of the four of us. I liked her for that. She tended to calm our group down, like an Alka-Seltzer.

'Let's uncork this beauty,' Nicole said, holding up a bottle. 'Where are the champers glasses, Suzes?'

'We don't have any,' I said. 'I don't have an alcohol licence.'

She frowned at me. 'You need to get right on that.'

'Ordinary glasses will do,' Donna said.

'Here,' said Helen, pulling a chair out for me. 'Park yourself down. Have a rest.'

'Can we have some quiche?' Nicole said from underneath the counter. 'There's half a ton of it here.'

As the conversation rattled on, I nodded wearily, saying little. My friends were handing around plates of food, clinking glasses together. Items on the agenda were Donna's boy-racer son passing his driving test, and Helen's teenage daughter's fluorescent dental braces.

And then Nicole mentioned Tim.

It caused an awkward pause in the conversation, the way it did when married people mentioned exes, as though discussing the dead or disgraced.

'He was in town, near Krispy Kreme's,' Nicole said. 'Not that he looks as though he eats there. He looked really fit, Suzes. When did you last see him?'

I held my glass to my lips, kept it there. My instinct was to pretend that Nicole hadn't said anything at all.

'Anyhow,' she continued, 'I told him about the deli and that he should stop by sometime to see you.'

'And why would she want him to do that?' Helen said.

Nicole sighed. 'He won't actually do it, *will* he? I was just being polite. I didn't know what else to say. It was awkward.' She winked at me. And I winked back to show that I wasn't bothered.

Then Donna diplomatically changed the subject to trainer bras.

But the prior subject was too weighty for me to shake off so easily. As the others discussed teen lingerie, I drifted off, sifting through the debris of my past with Tim. I could see his Roman nose, the dimples that appeared either side of his mouth when he smiled; and I didn't feel at all comfortable imagining such things.

Love, when axed, was like an open plant root that didn't know what to do with itself. It just sat there, unsure whether to grow, seal over or die.

It still felt like that with Tim, even after all these years: a sticky mess that I didn't like to touch very often in case it hadn't healed but was raw, weeping. Better that Tim – the man who had broken my heart – ceased to exist.

I hadn't seen him for years, nor had I thought of him much – had purposely not done so. After our break-up twelve years ago, I had stuck coded Post-it notes on my computer at work and on the bathroom mirror at home to remind me not to think about him.

It was difficult, not thinking about him, since we had both been working for the same IT company in Bristol at the time. I was marketing director; he was operations director. For the four years that we were dating, we were, I suppose, a power couple, although we would have found that label funny at the time.

Power couple or not, we were headed for marriage, so I had thought.

I picked up my glass, half listening to my friends' conversation, whilst backtracking through my old role at JB Alliance: a six-figure salary, a BMW, company shares, a seat on the board of directors.

It was exactly what I had set out to do, was all there in my teenage life goals scrapbook. Driven, ambitious, nothing could have knocked me off course. During that time, I was supposed to have been getting married and had been expecting Tim to propose at any moment.

And then he had announced that he was leaving me for the receptionist at his gym.

I had met Mike not long afterwards and was engaged to him within a year. If my friends had thought *rebound*, they hadn't said the word out loud.

I loved Mike, quickly, wholeheartedly. And no one who had ever set eyes on him would have described him as a consolation prize.

We dealt with the mess of my heartbreak by never mentioning Tim again, a method that worked not only for Mike and me, but for the millions of couples worldwide who got married in white with no romantic history in view and – in cases such as mine – no history to speak of whatsoever.

The obliteration of my immediate past made it easier for me to fudge some of the details from my formative years. In many respects, I had become a different person when I had married Mike. And wasn't that one of love's greatest gifts: the promise of new beginnings?

I think I read that on a Valentine's Day card once.

'Top-up, hun?' said Nicole, holding the bottle towards me.

'Please,' I said. I was watching the fir trees outside of the window, on the opposite side of the road, jostling in the wind. It was a rough night, dark already. The trees were swaying violently, as though set on a seafront, with spray about to hit the windows any moment.

I sipped Prosecco absently, slipping back to my thoughts.

Everything had been wonderful for the first couple of years, even during our first year as new parents to Jake. But then Mike had suffered the fateful car crash that had ended his career.

I had already been struggling to manage my workload, given the lack of flexible working arrangements at JB Alliance at the time. So, when JB was acquired by a larger organisation, I took my chance to leave, cashing in my shares.

Once Mike had recuperated, I had used the cash lump sum to open the deli – something manageable, near home. Mike had become Jake's main caregiver, and all ties with Tim were cut.

'Oh!' I said, slamming my glass down, slopping Prosecco on the table.

'What is it?' Nicole said.

I could see a dark shape underneath the fir trees – someone with their back to the wall, watching me.

I tugged on Nicole's arm, pointed to the window. She frowned, gazed in the direction of my hand. 'What are we looking at, hun?' she said.

The trees were flailing wildly. Litter and leaves scurried along the pavement like rats.

'I can't see anything,' she said.

'What's wrong, Suzy?' Helen said, touching my knee. 'You look like you've seen a ghost.'

I swallowed hard, blinked, looked at Helen and then back at the road, but the shape had gone. In its place was a black bin with a carrier bag flapping out of its mouth, like a waving hand.

I was seeing things.

I bowed my head, moaned.

'Get some camomile tea on,' Helen said to Nicole.

'Sure,' said Nicole, not sounding sure at all. She went to the counter, pulled a cup down and began to pour hot spluttering water from the coffee machine.

I could feel my friends' eyes on me.

Helen reached for my hand. 'Sweetheart ... is this about your mum?'

I thought about that.

Was it?

I shook my head. I was trying to stop myself from crying, didn't want my first day here marked with tears. My mum wouldn't have wanted that. She would have wanted me to be celebrating with my friends, not dwelling on old stories, cowering from anything that moved in the dark.

Nicole set the camomile tea down before me, the scent meeting my nostrils. I had never liked the smell. I gazed at the yellow liquid, at the particles of herbs that had escaped the gauze bag and were swirling round as though lost.

Donna spoke then. 'You miss your mum,' she said bluntly.

That was it. She didn't say anything else. She didn't need to.

The gathering never really recovered its cheerfulness after my outburst. We said our goodbyes quite soon after and Nicole gave me a lift home.

'Suzy,' she said, as we pulled up outside my house. 'You seem ... ' She swivelled in her seat to look at me. She looked so pretty in the dusky light, her silver earrings glinting against her olive skin. ' ... On edge,' she said carefully. 'I wish I could do something to help.'

'I'm fine,' I said. 'It's been a long day, that's all. I just need a good night's sleep.'

'If you say so,' she said. 'But I'm here if you need me.'

''Course.'

'Well, I'd best go pick up my little man,' she said.

I got out of the car, balancing my work bag in my arms. 'Thanks for the lift,' I said.

She lowered the window on my side. 'You really need an accessory upgrade,' she called out.

That made me laugh. She hated my graceless holdall, had said so on many an occasion.

She drove off and I walked towards the house, picturing the scene ahead.

Jake and Ruby would be full of energy, bombarding me with questions. *How'd it go? How'd it go?*

They would tell me all about their days and I would tell them about mine: the toddler who had left chocolate handprints on the windows, and our regular customer – whom we secretly called Mr Hum – who always hummed whilst eating dessert.

Ruby and Jake loved these stories, always begged me to tell them, and so I would. And then Mike would tap his watch and we would bundle the children upstairs to bed.

But that night, as I cleaned the children's teeth and brushed their hair, I would feel a prickle of guilt about what I hadn't told them.

What I would remember most about my first day at The Big Little Deli wasn't the chocolate handprints, Mr Hum, or even the dark shape in the street outside, but that by the end of it I wasn't sure that I could trust my own eyes any more.

6

The deli remained hectic, but by the end of the week our new team of four had found a way of working around each other and we were up and running.

I was in the middle of cling-filming a pie on the Friday morning, when the phone rang behind me. I swivelled on my heel to answer it.

'Mrs Taylor?' a man said. 'It's Ifor Owens.' I couldn't place him. 'From the stonemasons',' he added.

'Oh, my goodness. I'm so sorry.' I eyed my diary that was lying open underneath the counter. There it was in bold: *stone-masons, 11 a.m.* I glanced at the wall clock. It was eleven thirty. 'I completely forgot.'

'Not to worry,' he said, his tone sympathetic, light. 'Do you want to come now?'

'That would be perfect,' I said. 'Thank you. I'll be right there.'

I hung up, asked Leo to mind the shop for me and set off along the high street, putting my coat on as I ran.

When I got home, I called for Mike. 'Just taking the car!'

He appeared from the sitting room, leaning on his cane. 'What for?'

'The stonemasons'. I should have been there half an hour ago,' I said. 'I can't believe I forgot.'

'I'll drive,' he said, unhooking his coat from the rack. 'You're not driving whilst stressed. And that's that.'

I didn't argue. I pretty much always drove whilst stressed though.

The stonemasons were based a twenty-minute drive away. On the way, I kept glancing at my watch, muttering to myself. I hated forgetting things, was often to be found with diary in hand, studying its contents as though about to be tested.

Put that thing down, Mike would tell me. What's the worst that could happen?

I don't know. What *was* the worst that could happen? This? Feeling breathless, on edge?

Forgetfulness meant – according to weekend newspaper supplements – the onset of menopause, senility, or both.

Great.

I gazed out of the window. 'So, what have you been up to this morning?' I asked.

'Not much,' he said. 'Bit of job hunting.'

'Oh?' I said. It always saddened me when Mike said this. His being at home hadn't ever been a long-term solution; we just couldn't find an alternative. Unable to run, or even drive for longer than half an hour at a time, Mike wouldn't be able to work for the police again, nor could he come up with another career that he might love as much. 'Anything good?'

'Not really.'

'Sorry,' I said, reaching for his hand, glancing at him. He was shrugging with his mouth, the way he did whenever he missed his old job.

After the accident, Mike had been granted an injury award and an ill-health pension, but the police couldn't give him what he had really wanted. He had just been promoted to chief inspector at the time. That was what he had wanted, not a pension.

But we tried to focus on the positives. He was able to spend time with the children now, something which he wouldn't have been able to do before.

'So, about the headstone ...' he said, squeezing my hand. 'Are you going to be all right?'

'Yes,' I said, smiling thinly.

He let my hand go, took the wheel with both hands, watched the road ahead as it narrowed. Within moments, the sign for the stonemasons' appeared in view.

'Here we go,' he said, pulling into a driveway and stopping the car, the engine humming, creaking.

I looked about me. We were in a workman's yard. Nearby, a grey-haired man was sawing a piece of wood. The sight threw me a little – a stonemason sawing.

'Best foot forward,' Mike said, reaching for my hand.

Ifor Owens wore chalk-stained clothes and his hair was grey not with age but dust. He led us into a Portakabin, where we all sat down.

'Sometimes you need to wait for settlement of the grave,' he told us. 'But in your mother's case there's a concrete beam along the ends of the graves, so you can go ahead right away.'

'Oh,' I said. 'Well, that's good.' I opened my diary, ripped a page from it, handed it to Ifor. 'That's what I'd like on the headstone, please.'

He read my notes, scratching his beard, fragments of dust cascading down. 'Would you like to look through a brochure to—?'

'I've already chosen the style that I'd like. It's written further on down the page.'

'Ah,' he said. 'Got it ... Well, you seem to know what you want, so there's no need to take up your time. Standard production time's ninety days. I'll give you a bell when it's ready.'

We stood up, shook hands and he saw us out.

The sun was shining now. It made the yard seem dustier than ever. 'Well, at least that's done,' Mike said, putting his arm around me. 'I expect he thought we were a bit quick.'

'Yes,' I said.

We didn't say much on the way home. Mike put the radio on and I listened to it, closing my eyes in the sunshine.

I didn't feel guilty about being decisive, efficient at the stonemasons'. I had spent as long there as I could cope with.

When Mike dropped me off outside the deli, I leant in through the car window to kiss him goodbye. 'Thank you very much,' I said.

'Do I get a reward?' he said, his eyes twinkling.

'If you carry on being a good boy.' I smiled then turned away.

'Take it easy this afternoon,' he called after me. 'And make sure you put your feet up tonight when we're at footie.'

I had forgotten it was football training night. Nothing seemed to be sticking at the moment.

The idea of being on my own in the house as darkness fell didn't really appeal. I thought then about telling Mike about the dark shape that I had seen outside the deli on Monday. I had gone to tell him several times, but had stopped myself, reasoning that it had just been a carrier bag flapping in the wind. No one else had seen anything, after all. I didn't want to sound delusional.

But then I caught sight of Leo inside the deli and so hurried inside to relieve him.

'That was quick,' Leo said as I joined him, tying on my apron.

'Yes,' I said. 'Thanks for covering. You're a lifesaver.'

'My pleasure,' he replied. 'You're happy ... I'm happy.' He was putting the finishing touches to his Italian cream cake, smoothing the frosting with a spatula, tea towel hanging from the back pocket of his jeans.

'Wow, Leo. That looks amazing. Just the job.'

It was warm inside the deli. We propped the door wide open. There was no icy wind today to lift cappuccino froth from cups, so everyone was comfortable. And Leo's cream cake sold out within the hour.

That evening, I had trouble getting to sleep, which was unusual for me. I was on my feet all day, did such a physical job that ordinarily I fell asleep within minutes of turning out the light and didn't wake until my alarm told me to. Yet that night, my mind was so active, I found myself going back through the day's drinks to tally up how much caffeine I'd had. It was easy to get carried away when you worked with an industrial-sized coffee machine behind you, like life support. Yet, I hadn't drunk any more caffeine than normal. Why was I so wired?

Mike seemed to be sleeping more soundly than ever. I eyed him in the gloomy light, envying him.

After an hour of mental drivel, involving cream cake recipes, till receipts, pie orders, my mind grew even less lucid.

Past midnight, my thoughts became coated in stonemasons' dust until I couldn't tell them apart. I could hear marble being chipped, could see yew trees swaying in the wind, headstones in graveyards half lost in fog.

By one o'clock, I was light-headed with exhaustion. Cross with myself for being so daft – I had work tomorrow afternoon and would be dead on my feet – I plumped my pillow determinedly, resolving to fall asleep, which I did. Only to wake again what felt like moments later.

I couldn't think what had disturbed me. I listened; Mike was snoring ever so softly. It couldn't have been that. Was Jake coughing? I listened again. Nothing.

Something had woken me though. I was sure of it.

I held my breath, listened, watched.

A sudden smattering of rain hit the window panes, like a

handful of gravel being tossed against the glass. It was this that had woken me.

I felt appeased, was relaxing back into the duvet, when I heard the smallest sound in the dark. It could have been the rustle of clothes, a faint intake of breath.

I opened my eyes. There was something at the foot of our bed. I sat up, squinted. And then my heart began to pound.

Someone was there ... *in our room.*

I thought I was going to pass out with terror. Instead, I screamed. There was a shuffling of feet, a sudden movement.

And then it was gone.

PRELIMINARY MEETING

Monday 27 March, 2017

'Before we begin, it's important for you to know that I'm taking notes purely for my own convenience. Nothing that you say in this room will be transferred outside. Everything that you tell me will be in the strictest of confidence.'

I shift position on the chair, glance about the room. It is tastefully, purposefully decorated: a green palette for calm, potted peace lilies on the shelves, a bronze wall clock. Just above Dan Cassidy's head there's a poster of a stick figure parent and child holding hands, with keyboard teeth smiles and a rainbow arching over them.

The poster makes me think of the children, as it is surely intended to do. I look away, watch as Dan writes my name at the top of the page and underlines it twice.

'So, Suzy,' he says. 'Tell me about yourself. How many children do you have?'

I smile briefly. 'Two. A boy and a girl.'

'Lovely,' he says.

I look at the poster again, at the stick figures behind Dan's head. It seems to me that the figures are getting smaller. Either they are moving away, or I am.

It doesn't matter who is moving. The end result is the same.

I think of the parable about the frog in the pan – how the frog will leap out of hot water, but if placed in tepid water that is gradually heated to boiling, it remains, not realising that death is imminent.

'What are their names?' he says.

'Jake and Ruby.' I wipe my hands on my trouser legs, a trickle of perspiration running down the side of my ribcage.

'Jake . . . Ruby,' he says, writing this down. 'Great.'

Just seeing their names on the pad makes me feel tearful.

I wish with all my heart that I wasn't here.

7

Mike checked all around the house. I waited for him in bed, hugging my knees to my chest.

When he returned, he looked at me regretfully. 'I'm sorry, love, but I can't see anything,' he said. 'No sign that anyone was here.'

'Oh,' I said, putting my head in my hands.

I knew what I had seen. I was certain that Mike would find smashed glass, evidence of forced entry.

'Are you sure you saw something?' he asked, peeling off his fleece and dropping it down.

I looked at him. 'Not something,' I said. 'Someone. Right there.' I pointed to the end of the bed.

'And can you describe them?'

'No. Other than the fact that it was a man,' I said. 'He wasn't there long enough for me to see more than that. It was pitch black and I was half asleep. All I know is that he disappeared when I screamed.'

'What do you mean, *disappeared*? Did you see him leave?'

I shook my head. 'Not really. I mean, I heard footsteps. But I was too frightened to take it in.'

'OK.' He sat down on the side of the bed, picked up the bottle of brandy that he had brought with him from downstairs and unscrewed the top. 'Here ... have a drop of this.' I listened to the soothing glug of brandy as he poured it into a tumbler. 'It'll help.'

I took the drink, quivering as I drank it. Mike always kept a bottle in the house, a habit from his police days when he had offered brandy to shocked families. Rather ghoulishly, I used to want to hear those stories: *What did she say when you told her both her children were dead?* But now that I was a parent, I couldn't imagine why I would have wanted to know what that poor mother or anyone else in that position would have said.

Dejectedly, I pushed my legs out flat onto the bed. 'I don't know what's wrong with me,' I said. 'I don't feel like my usual self at all.'

Mike sat with his back against the headboard, his hand on my knee and yawned loudly. 'Give yourself a chance to heal, love. You only just sorted the headstone today.'

I glanced at him. 'Do you think I imagined this?'

He hesitated. 'I think you had a nightmare.'

'You don't believe me?'

''Course I do. I'm just saying that you've been through a lot lately. The obvious conclusion is that—'

'This isn't the first time I've seen someone,' I said.

He shifted position in bed to face me. 'You what?'

I put the brandy tumbler down on the bedside table. 'I saw some-one outside the deli on Monday night when I was with the girls.'

He looked at me in surprise. 'Why didn't you tell me?'

'Because I wasn't sure what I saw. But now I think that it was the same person.'

'I see,' he said, frowning.

'I knew you'd react like this,' I said. 'It's why I didn't say anything.'

'React like what? I've barely said a word.'

'You don't have to. There's no evidence of a break-in. So, I'm obviously imagining things.'

‘Not at all,’ he said. ‘I’m just trying to take it in.’

I picked up the brandy glass again, drained the last drop before speaking. ‘I think that this might be connected,’ I said.

‘To what?’

I turned the empty glass on my lap, watching the circular indentation that it made on the duvet.

‘To the Rizla wrapper, the toy monkey, the junk mail from Cumbria.’ I held the glass still, gazed at him. ‘I think someone’s watching me.’

‘OK . . . ’ he said, his chin dipping into his neck as he thought about this. ‘So, let’s suppose that they are. Who could possibly be doing that?’

My stomach fluttered disconcertingly. ‘I don’t know.’

‘You mentioned your father the other day,’ he said, stretching his leg out with a wince. ‘Why was that?’

‘I’m not sure . . . Just that it felt connected to him.’

‘Could it be him?’

I looked away. ‘I . . . ’

‘Suzy,’ he said. ‘I know there’s something you’re not telling me.’

The silence felt so thick, it hurt my ears.

I ran my finger around the rim of the glass on my lap, feeling its sharpness, wondering how it didn’t cut when drinking. ‘I haven’t seen him for such a long time,’ I said. ‘He left me and Mum, and—’

‘Is that true?’

I glanced at him. ‘Yes?’ I said feebly.

He laughed lightly. ‘Come on, Suzy . . . There’s more to it than that.’

‘Is there?’ I said. ‘How can you know that?’

‘Call it a copper’s hunch.’

I didn’t see any way round it. There was nothing I could do other than tell the truth, or at least the part of it that I dared to. If I was right and somehow someone was gaining entry into the house, then our children were at risk. Nothing was more important to me than keeping my family safe – not even keeping the old one safe.

I began to speak, feeling as though the game were over.

When really, it had just begun.

'My father was violent,' I said.

Mike's body tensed. He sat up straight. 'In what way?'

'Is there more than one way?' I asked.

'You'd be surprised. So, what are we talking here?'

I paused, saying a mental apology to my mother before turning to look at Mike, hoping that nothing was about to change between us.

'Domestic,' I said.

He stared at me without blinking. 'Did he hit you?'

I shook my head.

'Sexually abuse you?'

'No,' I said. 'It wasn't like that. It was . . . '

'What?'

I shrugged. 'Aimed at my mum. He used to knock her about, not me.'

'Jesus, Suzy,' he said. 'Why wouldn't you have told me about this before now? Why make up a cock and bull story about him abandoning you?'

'It wasn't cock and bull,' I said.

'Then how would you describe it?'

He sounded exasperated, hurt: just the way I had imagined he would.

'Mike,' I said, reaching out to touch his arm. 'Maybe we should get some sleep and—'

'No,' he said sternly, standing up. 'We're doing this now . . . When did you last see him?'

'You already know that: thirty-four years ago,' I said.

'So, what happened? Did you and your mother run away?'

I nodded, my throat hurting at the thought of my mum.

'Suzy . . . ' he said, his tone mellowing a fraction. Yet he still kept his distance. I hated that distance – wanted him to come back to bed. 'Your mum's gone. You don't have to keep her secrets now. You can tell me. It's OK.'

I began to cry.

He sat back down on the bed. 'I'm sorry to upset you,' he said. 'But we have to talk about this . . . You left Carlisle and you came, what, straight here to Bath?'

'Yes,' I said, holding my hands to my face.

'And your father never found you. But you were always afraid that he would.'

I nodded.

'Could it be him?' he asked.

'I don't know,' I said. 'It seems unlikely.'

'How old would he be?'

'Sixty-six,' I said. 'Five years older than Mum.'

He fell silent for a moment.

'Makes sense now, really – how withdrawn your mum always was,' he said. 'I always thought there was something odd between the two of you, but I just put it down to you being abandoned by your old man.'

He sounded almost relieved to have finally solved an old puzzle. And I thought that perhaps the subject was over, that I had somehow escaped unscathed.

But then he said something else.

'Did you change your names? Were you born Suzy Stone?'

I peeped at him from between my fingers. 'No. I mean: yes, we changed our names; no, I wasn't born Suzy Stone.'

He paused.

'What was your name?'

Such a simple question – not one that you would expect to ask your wife ten years into marriage.

I couldn't bear to look at him. I scrunched my hands into fists, pressed them to my eyes.

'Faire,' I said.

'Faire?'

'Yes,' I said. 'With an "e".'

He simply nodded. He seemed quietly sad – possibly the worst response.

'Why couldn't you tell me?' he asked. 'Were you ashamed?'

'Yes,' I said, grabbing his explanation.

Thankfully, he didn't question me further.

'I get it,' he said. 'I really do. I used to come across a lot of this sort of thing at work – women feeling guilty or ashamed about abuse as though they'd done something wrong.' He looked at me solemnly. 'I'm sorry you had to go through that. But I'm even sorrier that you felt you couldn't tell me.'

I gazed at him in dismay.

He stood up, went to turn out the main light.

'Mike . . . ' I said, reaching out my hand to him. 'I'm really sorry. I didn't mean to be secretive or to hurt you. It was just . . . complicated.'

He suddenly seemed very tired. 'OK,' he said. 'Let's get some rest.'

I could almost touch his disappointment, it was so apparent.

'Can we talk about it again in the morning?' I said, sounding desperate.

'If you want,' he said, lying down, closing his eyes.

At that moment, I felt as though I had lost him.

I turned out the bedside light and lay watching him, listening to his breathing. A lone tear tickled my nose. I flicked it away.

And then he reached for me, pulled me into his heavy arms, kissed my forehead.

We didn't speak again. We just lay there like that.

I wouldn't, couldn't sleep.

But the next thing I knew, it was daylight.

8

I couldn't remember much about my early childhood, but there were several incidents that I couldn't forget, no matter how hard I tried. One such occasion was the night that my father had hit my mother so hard that I hadn't recognised her afterwards.

When she had come in to wake me the next morning, I had recoiled in dread. There was a scarf wrapped around her face, even though it was a balmy autumn morning with the sun warm on the window pane. One of her eyes was so puffy it was closed, with the hint of a watery blue iris within. It had reminded me of the eye of an animal – something like a rhinoceros or an elephant, with damaged, wrinkly skin and a mere dot of life in its eyes, just a glimpse that it had feelings.

I couldn't remember what I would have said, what she would have said in turn. I could remember the scarf though. That morning it was colourful, with paisley swirls. I only saw it that one time. She tended to wear each scarf once. I supposed that after it had served its purpose, it was spoilt.

Her bedroom in our old home in Cumbria, Carlisle, had been full of accessories: scarves, hats, sunglasses. We used to have a cleaner – a stubby woman with short arms who couldn't reach very far up the walls to dust. She used to ask about those accessories, why my mother had so many. And then one day, she was gone, sacked. I had assumed that it was because of the short arms. But now, I doubted that.

That autumn morning, after the beating, my mum had worn the paisley scarf to the end of our driveway and then stood there, head bowed.

She waited until a group of schoolchildren passed by our front gate and then prodded me forward, gesturing for me to go with them.

At the age of five, I was to make my own way to school. Of everything that had taken place, she would have hated that most of all.

Our lives changed after that.

It had been apparent to me – even then, so young and uninformed – that things couldn't have gone on the way they were, that something bad would happen and soon, maybe even before Christmas.

It was funny how intuitive children could be.

'Did you think of anyone for my presentation, Mummy?' Jake asked at breakfast the following day. I didn't work Saturday mornings, went in to the deli at one o'clock for the afternoon. These spare mornings had become precious family time, or, in other words, homework and laundry time.

I put my spoon down. 'For what, love?'

'You know – someone famous who inspired me.' Jake was chewing toast, a blob of jam on his chin. Sometimes he seemed so grown up; other times, less so.

I glanced at Mike, who was at the other end of the table, eating granola, reading the paper.

Things were tense between us, but better than I had imagined during the many times in the past when I had pictured this scenario. I had woken him up early to talk about my father, having sensed that given the option he would have shut off communications. I had hurt him and he wouldn't want to dwell on that or deal with it, but I couldn't afford for us not to. I hadn't done anything wrong, aside from try to protect myself and our marriage. He had to understand that. And after our talk, he seemed to – or at least, he showed signs of getting there.

There wasn't much that we could do for now, we had concluded. There wasn't enough information to act on. We would just have to remain vigilant.

'So, did you . . . think of someone?' Jake said, his brown eyes boring into me. He was wearing a beige sweater that made his skin look pasty and was torn on the shoulder. I made a mental note to put it out for recycling.

'I uh . . . ' I could vaguely remember his having asked me about this last week. I looked at Mike again. 'Isn't Daddy helping with it?'

'You said you'd do it, Mummy,' Mike said, lowering his newspaper, 'that it was your sort of project.' He was raising his eyebrows at me, torturing me.

'When's it got to be in for, Jakey?' I asked.

Ruby, who was sitting beside me, sighed. She was fishing alphabet cereal out of her bowl, setting them on the table to spell her name, but was struggling to find a 'Y'.

'RUB', it said.

'Monday,' Jake said, scooping more jam on to his toast. No one could get through jam like Jake.

'As in two days away?'

'Yep.'

'Oh great,' I murmured.

'Hey?' said Jake.

'Nothing,' I said.

'Can we go see Granny Annie today?' Ruby said, pressing her fingers into my bare arm, leaving traces of milk.

Hearing the name sent a shock wave of sorrow through me.

'Can we, Mummy?' Ruby said. 'Pullease?'

'She's dead, stupid,' Jake said.

Everyone stopped. Ruby looked as though her face had been slapped. She dropped her spoon with a clatter. I gazed at Jake in dismay; Mike stopped chewing.

There was an awful silence. And then Ruby began to cry.

I thought she was crying because of my mother. But it was because Jake had called her stupid.

'I'm not stewpit,' she said. 'I'm not stewpit. You're stewpit. I *hate* you.'

I tutted, pulled Ruby on to my lap. She had overheated instantly, her breath warming my neck, her tears tickling my chest.

Mike was looking at me compassionately. Yet his frown seemed to be saying that we needed to explain death to Ruby more effectively.

And it occurred to me then that I always did such a good clean-up job, was so efficient, determined not to drag my children through my sorrow, that I hadn't given them the chance to grieve.

'Granny Annie died last month,' I said, stroking Ruby's hair. 'We can't see her – not today, or any day.'

'But we see her on Sattydays,' said Ruby.

'Yes,' I said. 'We did, poppet. But I'm sorry to say that we can't do that any more because she has passed away. Do you remember me telling you a few weeks ago that Granny Annie was gone? Do you remember: Mummy and Daddy went to her funeral?'

Ruby pulled away from me then, setting her blue eyes on me. Her eyelashes were spiky, clumped with tears. 'Where has she gone?' she asked, placing her hand flat on my face as though trying to scan my feelings and inner vibrations. It was a strange thing to do, but I had learnt not to read too much into children's actions. She was probably seeing how big her thumb was compared to my nose.

Sure enough, she added, 'You have a big nose.'

I laughed. And then grew serious again. 'She's dead, my love,' I said. 'Everyone dies. It's a sad fact of life. That's why we have to make the most of our time on earth whilst we're here.'

'Oh,' Ruby said, assessing my nose further by prodding it. Then she got down from my lap and continued her breakfast.

Throughout this conversation, Jake hadn't stopped eating. He was either famished or didn't miss his grandmother that much.

But after breakfast, as I was clearing up I heard a noise and saw that Jake was sitting on his own at the table, crying.

I hurried to him, pulled him into my arms. 'I'm sorry, Jake,' I said. 'It's sad, isn't it? I know you miss her.'

'It's not that,' he said, sniffing, rubbing his eyes. 'It's my presentation.'

In truth, the children hadn't seen my mum all that often. We had gone to her flat on Saturday mornings occasionally or had sometimes met her at the park. She had preferred the latter, not liking the children to be cooped up in her small apartment.

She had lived in a rough area of town by Bath's standards. It wasn't all that bad though. I had grown up there on the second floor of a cheese-coloured block opposite a vacant airy park. My walk to primary school had taken four minutes, but Mum had always gone with me, holding my hand protectively, seeing me to the gate and waiting there until I entered the classroom.

It had been the same after school. The bell would go and Mum was there again in a black coat for winter, beige for summer. Never any bright accessories. She was a blur on the horizon – in the winter, a black blob against the railings; in the summer, she disappeared against the creamy background of the wall behind her. On such occasions, my heart would skip a beat, but then I would spot her and run towards her, my plaited ponytail thumping my back.

She was always there, at every concert, play, prize-giving. It would take me a while to spot her in the audience. It was like *Where's Wally*, except that there was no stripy hat and jumper to help me. I tended to look at the seats nearest the door and there she would be, smiling. But over the years her smile had become ghostlier, until sometimes it was barely there.

Your mum's a weirdo.

I had sometimes heard this at primary school.

I hadn't let it bother me. I had known exactly who and what my mum was. No one could have changed that for me.

At senior school, parents were less visible. This had suited my mum far more. She had allowed me to have friends over – Nicole, Helen and Donna, in the main – but it was normally on special occasions and Mum had made herself scarce. Had my friends thought her weird, they wouldn't have been unkind enough to say so. Mum and I hadn't had a lot of money compared to them; I think my friends had felt sorry for us.

Sometimes I had wondered why they even hung out with me, especially Nicole, with her crimped hair, lace gloves and Duran Duran LPs. But Donna said years later that I had been like a high-speed train that was heading somewhere where everyone would want to be. So maybe my perception of myself was a little off.

All I knew was that our old flat was so well known to me, so loaded with emotion, that returning to it as an adult was to step back to childhood, to a time when I had lived underneath my mother's watchful eye. Some people reverted to old stereotypes when gathering with the family at Christmas; I just had to turn the key in the lock of a door some ten minutes from home. For a high-speed train, I hadn't gone very far.

It was hard for me to convey my feelings about my mother to my children, difficult to give them a sense of her true meaning to me without telling them precisely why.

Despite considerable effort on my part, Jake and Ruby weren't all that close to her, not as close as I would have liked. She had loved them but kept them at a distance. So much of what my mother and I had shared was intuitive, non-spoken. But children weren't like that. They liked to prod and poke, explore, stimulate. My mum was like a trampoline that wouldn't bounce, a book that never opened.

'What about Narnia?' Mike said, ruffling Jake's hair.

Jake stopped crying, looked up. 'What about it?'

'For your presentation. You could make a poster about the author, how he's inspired you, how you've done all those sketches about Aslan and—'

'Yes!' Jake said, pushing back his chair. 'Where are my sketches, Mummy?'

'In the drawing room,' I said, smiling thankfully at Mike. 'Come on.' I held my hand out to Jake. 'I'll show you.'

'Why do you call it the drawing room?' Jake asked me on our way upstairs. 'Is it because we do drawing in there?'

'No, Jake, although that's as good a reason as any. But really, it's because that's what it was called on the original floor plan. I like the old names. I think history matters. Don't you?'

'S'pose so,' he said.

As we began to sift through the box of sketches, Jake chattering about Prince Caspian and the White Witch, my mind drifted back to my mother, back to her small apartment in a humbler pocket of town.

I had paused at her front door, catching my breath before turning the key in the lock.

It was ten o'clock in the morning, Friday 20 January. I had brought chicken soup in case my mum was poorly. It was the only explanation I could think of as to why she hadn't answered her phone since yesterday.

It took a while for my eyes to adjust to the gloom. The curtains were shut. There was a funny smell: wheat, cereal, dairy.

My mother's holdall was on the chair next to the door, crammed with dusters and detergents, ready to take to her next cleaning job. She couldn't drive, went on foot to homes in the area. I had bought her the bag – in the same style but fancier than mine, with shimmery charms. Nicole would have cringed.

I flicked on the light.

On the table in front of me was a bowl of puffed wheat. The cereal, floating in milk, was obscenely swollen. I shuddered at the sight of it.

Mum? I called, setting my holdall containing the flask of soup carefully down on the floor.

I was making for her bedroom, when I stopped. Something was poking out from behind the sofa. It looked like hair.

I approached, dropped to my knees.

My mother was lying on the floor, eyes open, her face a grey-blue hue.

I reached for her hand. It was so cold, it shocked me. I placed my hand on her chest, feeling for her heartbeat. There was nothing.

I sat back on the floor, my mind blank.

Mike. I would call him. He would know what to do.

I could barely use my phone, my fingers stabbing at the screen.

He answered immediately.

It's Mum, I blurted. She's dead. Please come. Please come here as soon as you can.

Suzy, he said calmly. Take deep breaths. Are you at the flat?

Yes.

I'm on my way. All you have to do . . .

I was moaning, rocking.

Suzy, listen. *Listen.* All you have to do is call the doctor. Do you have the number?

I considered that, my eye falling on the tiny address book that my mother kept by the phone.

Yes.

Good. Then as soon as I hang up, you must call the doctor and report this. OK?

I nodded.

OK? he repeated.

Yes, I said.

Good. I'm leaving now.

Please hurry, I said.

On my way, he said.

We hung up and I remained kneeling on the floor, staring at my mum, my limbs jolting involuntarily. Then I picked up her hand and held it in mine.

When Mike arrived, I hadn't yet rung the doctor. He phoned for me. I remained kneeling on the floor, holding my mother's hand.

Then he put his arms around me and hugged me from behind, but I barely felt his presence.

My mum had been lying there for just over twenty-four hours. She had got up, poured milk onto her cereal and then had suffered a fatal heart attack.

The doctor was in no doubt and promptly issued the death certificate. She was sixty-one years old. The doctor had been treating her for high blood pressure for two decades, he said.

This I had not known.

Mike took me home, where I spent the rest of the day in a state of shock.

I had only returned to the flat once since to pick up paperwork to register the death. I had known exactly where Mum kept the required documents. There was so little in her flat, so few hiding places.

I hadn't been able to bear looking at the names on the marriage certificate, at the long loopy handwriting. It seemed so poignant, that someone in the church – the vicar or other executor on the day – had entered this information in good faith, in a place of worship, and had probably thought that they were doing a good thing.

'Mummy?'

I came to, looked at Jake. 'What, sweetheart?'

'What do you think?' He frowned, shook the two sketches that he was holding.

'About what?'

He tutted. 'Weren't you listening? About Aslan or the White Witch?'

'Um,' I said, taking the sketches from him and making a show of considering them.

'Do you think,' he said in the annoyed tone of someone who was having to repeat himself, 'that I should make it mostly about Aslan or the White Witch?'

'Definitely Aslan,' I said. 'Always concentrate on the good people and make it about them.'

'Like you,' Jake said. 'You're good.'

'I like to think so . . . ' I began. 'But—'

''Course you are,' he said happily. 'You're Mummy!' And he began to cut out his Aslan sketch, the scissors snipping, his tongue poking out in concentration.

It was so simple for Jake, for many children up and down the country.

Aslan, White Witch.

Good, bad.

No use wondering why it hadn't been that way for me. I wasn't the only one, never would be alone in that respect.

We were the children who fell today, tomorrow, yesterday from the building blocks of life. Dislodged, we were trapped, lost in dust and minutiae, where no one could hear us.

There was nothing anyone could do about that now. All we could do was grow up and try our hardest to stop our own children from falling.

'What do you think, Mummy?' Jake asked, holding his Aslan sketch out proudly before me.

I gazed at the picture, taking in its flaws with my adult eyes.

'It's perfect,' I said.

PRELIMINARY MEETING

Monday 27 March, 2017

'Tell me about Jake and Ruby,' he says. 'How old are they?'

I clasp my hands together, sit up straight. 'Jake's eight. Ruby's four.'

He is writing this down. 'Lovely ages.'

'Do you have children?' I ask.

He looks at me, a hesitation registering on his face that he doesn't vocalise. 'Yep.'

That's all I get. He isn't here to tell me about his kids. It's fair enough. Yet, still, the abruptness offends me.

I must not be so sensitive. He is just doing his job.

'What does Jake like to do?'

'He . . . well, he loves reading,' I say. My voice wobbles. I clear my throat. 'And football.'

'Great stuff. Does he support a team?'

I smile. 'Liverpool.'

'Good man,' he says. 'And what about—' he glances down at his notepad '—Ruby?'

At the mention of her name, I well up. I love them equally, but there is something about one's youngest child.

I look away, down at the floor, willing myself not to cry in front of him.

Once the wave of emotion has passed, I gaze at him, waiting for the next question, before realising that he is still waiting for an answer to the previous one.

'She's very cute,' I say. 'She says valinna.'

I break off, unable to say anything more about my Ruby.

9

The rest of the weekend passed peacefully and life almost began to feel normal again. Whilst performing our Sunday night kitchen shuffle, as I ironed and Mike packed the lunch boxes, I noticed him watching me with a thoughtful, speculative expression. I put the iron down and it hissed sulkily. Without speaking, I went to Mike, put my arms around his waist, held my head against his chest, listening to his heart beat. He stopped what he was doing and hugged me back, his muscles relaxing, his breath dispelling in a long sigh.

That sigh was of great comfort to me. It was a sigh of acceptance, of ease, of love. I couldn't begin to tell Mike how much it meant. Instead, I kissed him. And then I returned to my ironing, and the peaceful rhythm of domesticity and routine resumed.

The next morning, I was serving a customer, when the doorbell rang and I glanced up to see a man in a suit enter the deli and become lost amongst all the people. We were still experiencing a lack of seating and customers were having to stand up to drink their coffee, leaning on the counter, on shelves – wherever an elbow could be supported.

The suited man approached and took off his sunglasses to survey the menu board. When Leo asked for his order, the man said, 'I'm waiting for Suzy, if that's all right.'

I gave him my full focus then and saw immediately that it was Tim.

I turned away, my face burning. Mortified, I grabbed the empty ciabatta basket and hurried out to the kitchen, where I stood with my back to the door, barring entry.

What was he doing here?

Surely this was because Nicole had bumped into him recently.

Oh, my goodness.

I looked down at myself. I was wearing a dowdy apricot-coloured shirt that should have been slung out years ago.

Why had he chosen today to rise from the dead? On Saturday, I had worn a black dress that hugged my hips just right. Why couldn't he have come in then?

I crossed the room to look in the mirror, peering forward to examine my wrinkles.

It was not good news. The light was not generous in here.

Putting lipstick on would be too obvious. Instead, I smoothed my hair, pinched my face to give it a little colour, before realising that I was being a fool.

I couldn't stay hiding in the kitchen. I refilled the basket and returned to the counter, where I pretended to look surprised.

'Tim! Wow! It's been *ages*.'

He smiled broadly. And there were the dimples in his cheeks. I tried to ignore this – tried also to ignore his fitted white shirt. He looked tanned. Was he deliberately wearing white to offset his colour?

I was nervous, rambling mentally.

'Great to see you, Suzy Floozy,' he said.

I glanced about me. No one needed to hear his old nickname for me. I didn't have time to explain that it was ironic – an allusion to how serious and unflirty I had been at work. I hadn't believed in office relationships, especially not with co-board members. It had taken Tim many months to get me to agree to a date, no matter how green his eyes and handy his IT skills.

He nodded towards an empty table. 'Got a minute?'

''Course,' I said, wiping my hands on my apron.

As we sat down, I began to predict what he was about to say: he loved me, he had made a terrible mistake, he was—

'Sorry to hear about your mum.'

'Oh,' I said. 'Thank you.' Then I thought about that. 'How did you know?'

'Nicole mentioned it.'

'Ah.'

'So how have you been?' he asked.

I gazed down at the table surface, flicking away a crumb. 'Not so bad,' I said.

He nodded. 'I hope you don't think it's weird, me coming in here after all these years.'

'It is a bit weird,' I said.

'But I know how close you were to your mum.'

I didn't have a reply to that. I just blinked rapidly, hoping that I wouldn't cry.

'How rude of me,' I said, going to stand. 'Would you like a drink?'

'No, thanks.' He touched my hand very lightly. 'Just sit here with me a minute. I've got to go to my next meeting shortly.'

'Are you still with JB Alliance?' I said, gazing at his expensive suit.

'Yep. Still am. Sad, eh?'

I wasn't so sure about that. There seemed nothing sad about being successful at something and sticking with it.

'So, Suzy . . . I just wanted to say something,' he said.

If it was that he shouldn't have chosen the gym receptionist over me then he was over a decade too late.

'Your mum came to see me once,' he said.

I stared at him. 'She did?'

'Yep. She met me in Bristol.'

'When?'

'In my lunch hour.'

'No,' I said. 'Which year?'

He glanced up at the ceiling to think. 'I dunno. When did I . . . ?'

'Dump me?' I said.

He looked sheepish. 'Uh, yeah. That. Well, when was that?'

I folded my arms. 'Twelve years ago. The nineteenth of March 2005 . . . Not that anyone's keeping a record.'

'Well, it was just before that.' He hazarded a smile, the dimples appearing then vanishing. 'Your mum was worried about you. She thought it was time for you to move out, that she was getting in the way of you living your life.'

'She was?' I said, trying to think back. I couldn't recall her ever saying anything of the sort to me.

He smoothed the front of his tie; it was mauve, silky, reflecting the lights of the deli. 'She said that if I was ready to take the next step, then she would approve.'

'The next step?'

'She gave me her blessing to marry you.'

I laughed then – a clumsy blurty laugh. 'But that was the last thing you wanted. Right?'

I expected him to laugh too, but he fixed his eyes on me rather too seriously for my liking. 'I'm sorry,' he said.

There it was: sorry.

For a moment, I remembered what it had felt like in the first few days when he had ended things. And then I told myself that old pain was simply that: old.

'It's OK. Really.' I picked up the salt shaker, fiddled with it. 'Did she . . . well . . . did she scare you off?' I asked, trying not to sound as though the answer to this question mattered. 'Did her talk of marriage make you end things with me?'

He looked down at the table, frowned. 'I don't think so. I think it just made me realise ... you know ... '

'I know,' I said resignedly.

'Look,' he said. 'I'm not here to dig up the past.'

'Then what are you doing here?' I set the salt shaker down, folded my arms.

'Your mum made me promise something strange that day,' he said. 'She asked me to keep you safe.'

'And how's that strange? I'd have thought that was pretty normal as far as parental requests went.'

He shrugged. 'Normal enough, I suppose. But when I heard that she had passed away, I thought it would be nice to come and see you – to check you're all right.'

'Well, as you can see,' I said, 'I'm fine. And,' I added somewhat childishly, 'I'm married to a policeman.'

I didn't mention Mike's injury and retirement. There was a good chance that Tim didn't know about that.

'Great,' he said. 'I'm pleased for you.' He pushed back his chair. 'Well, I'd better be off. But you take care of yourself. And take this.' He handed me his business card. 'Just in case.'

'Of what?'

Back in the day, we would have said in case of sexual urges or doughnut cravings or ...

'Anything,' he said.

The doorbell tinkled and he was gone. I looked down at his card. He was now company CEO.

I went back behind the counter. Leo was looking at me inquisitively. 'Suzy Floozy?' he said.

'Yeah and you can forget you ever heard that,' I said, grimacing.

I'll admit that on my way home, I was lost in thought about Tim.

I loved Mike more than him – then, now, for ever. Yet exes were powerful beings. My friends and I often said that exes were far more attractive in memory – flawless, in fact. An ex never contacted you innocently, was the general view. Any communication was to be greeted with suspicion and caution, in much the same way as you would treat a message received via a Ouija board.

I was still reeling from the news that my mother had approached Tim behind my back. It was brave of her, given that she hadn't liked to venture far. The thought of her going to Bristol and meeting with Tim to try to lock down my future . . . I found the idea poignant, painful.

She had always wanted so much for me, in her quiet way. I was a 28-year-old BMW-driving marketing director still living with her at the time of her meeting with Tim. She had had a point.

So I was thinking, when I remembered that Mike had rung earlier to say that we were out of milk for the children. I couldn't face returning to the deli and unlocking the doors again, so decided to go the long way home, via the grocery store.

I turned back on myself and went the length of the high street, still thinking about Tim.

As I rounded the corner, about to go up the main road to the store, I felt suddenly as though someone were following me.

I quickened my step, glancing over my shoulder. A fat cat was behind me, hiding in the shadows of the wall. I pressed on, satisfied.

Inside the shop, it looked as though it had been looted, with the shelves standing empty. There was no milk left, aside from an extortionate bottle of creamy milk. It would have to do. I paid and set off again.

The traffic was heavy; horns were beeping. Someone was

swearing from their car window, as drivers jerked their way across the four-exit roundabout. I was glad to be on foot.

I turned into the alley that led up to our house. I didn't often come this way. I hadn't expected it to be so dark. Still, I kept up my pace, made my footsteps sound loud and purposeful, as though I were the last person whom anyone would want to mess with.

It had just been a cat following me, I thought. Just a silly fat cat.

I glanced over my shoulder again, clutching my holdall tighter. It was bulging, a lever arch file knocking against my leg.

I was beginning to wish that I hadn't come this way, was wondering whether to turn back, when I saw something ahead of me and came to a halt.

I couldn't see to the end of the alley. Undergrowth was leering over the walls, blocking the light.

Levitating in the darkness was a red pinprick of light.

I thought at first of Jake's laser-beam key ring – that perhaps Mike and the children had somehow come this way to meet me.

Then I saw the red light fall in a trail of sparks like a miniature firework and heard the sound of a foot grinding on gravel and I realised exactly what I was looking at.

I couldn't see him, but I knew he was there, putting out his roll-up cigarette, waiting for me.

I did the only thing that I could do: I turned and ran back down the alley.

On the main road, the traffic had come to a standstill. I ran alongside the cars, my coat flapping open, my hair straying into my eyes and mouth. I wasn't thinking about where I was going, was intent only on escape.

As I turned onto the high street, I bumped into a man who was looking down at his phone.

'Sorry,' he said congenially.

This small human touch reassured me a little. Yet I didn't slow down. I continued running along the high street, passing the deli, my chest burning as I inhaled the night air.

I looked back only once, seeing nothing but pavement, car headlamps, stone walls.

I turned onto the hill, my breath rasping as the incline increased. Someone beeped at me as they drove past – a neighbour or customer perhaps. Two teenage boys thumped into me with bulky rucksacks. A group of army cadets poured past in single file.

When I reached home, I ran up the pathway and hammered on the door. I had my house keys but didn't want to stop and look for them. I was fixated with entering the house, kept shouting for Mike.

When I heard voices beyond the door, my sense of urgency became magnified.

'Mike! Hurry! *Mike!*'

The key was turning in the lock. And then the door was open and Mike was standing there in a haven of light.

I ran forward, stumbling into his arms. He didn't react immediately, didn't embrace me – was too taken aback. Ruby was approaching with a look of curiosity on her face. Jake was beyond her, book in hand.

'What the heck . . . ?' Mike said, holding me at arm's length to look at me.

I realised that my fingers were sore from gripping the holdall, so I let it go.

I had forgotten about the bottle of milk. There was a smash as it hit the ground. Milk glugged across the floorboards, trickling between shards of glass.

'Wow!' said Jake, eyes widening.

'Quick. Get a cloth, Jake,' Mike said. 'And a dustpan and

brush, please.' Then he turned back to me. 'What the hell's going on?'

For a moment, all I could see and feel was fear.

I wondered whether I was insane, if this was what it felt like.

I glanced at Ruby, who was watching me, sucking her finger noisily.

I looked back at Mike. 'I saw him,' I said.

'Who?'

'The same man that I saw before. He was there, tonight.'

'Where?'

'In the alley at the back of our house.'

'What were you doing there?'

'I went that way to get milk.'

He glanced at the smashed bottle on the floor, ran his hands through his hair.

Jake appeared then, cloth in hand. 'Where shall I put this, Daddy?' he said.

'Drop it down there,' Mike said. 'Got the dustpan?'

'Whoopsie,' Jake said. 'Forgot.' And he disappeared again.

'Did you get a good look at him?' Mike said.

Ruby frowned up at me. 'Did you, Mummy?' she asked pleasantly.

She had no idea what we were talking about, was just joining in, in the way that she liked to. But I didn't want her to.

I bent down to her level, tried to sound like I usually did and not witless. 'How was your day?' I asked.

'I sit next to Tilly now,' she said. 'She has jawbills.'

I frowned.

'They are wodents, Mummy. Don't you know them?'

Gerbils.

I smiled weakly. 'OK,' I said, standing up, smoothing my clothes, composing myself. 'Go on upstairs and start running your bath, please, my love. I'll be there in one minute.'

'OK, Mummy,' Ruby said, starting up the stairs.

I watched her go, looking at the back of her school dress that was full of creases like cabbage leaves.

'We need to talk,' Mike said.

'Yes, but please can we get the kids to bed first.' This wasn't a question.

He gazed at me for a few moments, before turning away. I took a deep breath then hung my coat up and headed upstairs.

Once Ruby was in the bath, bobbing about in the bubbles, I sat down on the closed toilet seat in order to watch over her.

I noticed then that she was looking at me, sitting sideways in the bath. 'Why are you scared, Mummy?' she asked.

I held my hands out before me, saw that I was trembling. 'I . . . I don't know,' I said. 'But there's nothing for you to be frightened of, all right, sweetheart? Mummy's fine. I'm just tired.'

'Mmm,' she said. She had already moved on.

She scooped up a handful of bubbles, held them to her face. 'Look, Mummy,' she said, 'I've got a beard.'

I stared at Ruby, my pulse racing. I had remembered something.

The man that was in our room on Friday night had a beard.

I had seen the outline of it in the glimpse of light spilling from the bedroom windows.

10

It was hard to imagine someone who hadn't existed for most of your life. I couldn't even picture my father's face any more.

Once we had left Cumbria, Patrick Faire had vanished from our life – or us from his.

My memories of him were probably unreliable, distorted. Yet I could recall his violent episodes with sickening clarity. I could see his hands, hear his voice. I just couldn't see his face.

I didn't even know what he had done for a living, beyond being a 'Sales Agent', as noted on my parent's marriage certificate. I could remember that he had been given a big promotion at work in the autumn of 1982 and that things had deteriorated rapidly from there. I had known then that one way or another our time in Carlisle was coming to an end.

My mum hadn't told me so. It would have been too risky. But at the library, I had noticed her returning a book about Bath. I had asked her about it and she had urged me not to mention it again, especially not in front of Father.

I did as I was told.

It was during these days, in the build-up to leaving, that I began to feel sick-to-my-stomach afraid. My mother had gone quiet on me. Looking back, I suspect that she had been busy stashing money in socks, memorising transport timetables.

Silence became a way of life for us. After the move, we didn't talk about my father, about the world we had left behind. Yet now I wished that I had asked more questions, had pressed my mum for answers.

That awful autumn in Carlisle, I had had no idea how she was going to pull off an escape. She had had no money of her own – no job, no driving licence. Like many women of her generation, she was at the mercy of the man in her home and the laws made by men in the society around her.

Yet she had done it: she had escaped and had taken me with her.

Until then, my father was tense because of the promotion, my mother was silent, watchful; and the pressure was hanging in the air for us all to smell.

Some people say that they can smell a storm coming. They ascribe it to changes in airborne molecules, the earth's metabolism and atmospheric chemicals.

To me, imminent danger was just a smell. And it meant *run*.

'Tell me exactly what you saw,' Mike said.

We hadn't turned the lights on fully in the sitting room, just the twin table lamps. Mike's face was full of shadows, his voice low. The children had been asleep for half an hour or so.

I drew my legs up underneath me in my armchair, picked up a cushion and hugged it. 'A figure in the dark,' I said. 'He was smoking.'

'And you think that's somehow connected to the Rizla and the smoke in the hallway from before?'

'Maybe,' I replied.

'And this man, this figure – he didn't speak to you? You didn't see his face?'

'No. But I think he has a beard. I remembered earlier that I caught a glimpse of hair on his face when he was in our room.'

'OK,' he said. 'Well, that's something at least.'

'Look, I know what I saw, Mike. I know it sounds insane, but—'

'Forget how it sounds,' he said. 'This will be one of two things. Most things in life are logical. There are patterns, explanations. And it's no different with this.' He moved to the edge of his seat, hitching his trousers at the knees. 'Either this is grief playing with your mind. Or there's someone out there trying to scare you.'

'So, what do we do?'

'Let's go with the second explanation, because you seem so sure about what you've seen … Can you think of anyone – anyone at all – who might want to get at you? A vendetta of some kind. Or someone with a soft spot for you?'

I shook my head. 'I can't think of anyone who—'

'Your father?'

'No,' I said. 'It doesn't feel right. It feels … '

'What?'

'Well, like I said before … it's like someone wants me to think about him.'

Mike sat back in his chair, scratched his stubbly chin. 'Let's do that then.'

'Do what?' I said.

'Focus on him.'

My stomach dipped unpleasantly. 'How?'

'We could find out where he is, what he's been up to. Sounds like the sort of bloke who'd have a criminal record. Wouldn't be hard to find him.'

I wriggled in my seat, shifting position. 'No,' I said. 'I don't think that's such a good idea.'

'Why not? I'd be discreet, ask a few friends. Nothing formal.'

'No,' I said. 'We can't involve the police. We don't have enough to go on.'

'What happened tonight isn't enough?' he said. 'What are you waiting for? Violent assault?'

I shuddered. Surely that wasn't going to happen?

'Seriously, Suzy – not speaking up about these things early enough is one of the worst things you can do.'

'But we haven't got anything solid,' I said, picking at a stray thread in the cushion on my lap. 'I just don't know . . . '

He frowned. 'You can't keep saying, *I don't know*.'

'But I *don't* know!' I said, standing up in my agitation, the cushion toppling to the floor. As I bent down to pick it up, the mauve colour of the embroidery reminded me of Tim's tie.

I had forgotten about his visit to the deli earlier.

As I stood upright again, my head rushed with indecision. The timing of Tim's visit was strange, yet I wasn't suspicious of him. Mike, however, would think differently. His learning about Tim's reappearance would serve no purpose other than to bring jealousy into the mix. I wanted – needed – Mike on my side, not warring with me about irrelevant details.

He rose from his chair, standing with his back to the log burner. It wasn't very warm in the house, yet we had been too distracted earlier to light the fire.

'Why didn't you and your mum tell me about your father right from the start, when I first met you?' he said.

I was still standing in the middle of the room, clutching the cushion to my chest. I felt trapped, didn't know how to reverse out of this.

'She . . . we just didn't want to talk about it.'

He shook his head. 'I was in the police. I could have protected you. You must have both been well aware of that. Why, really?'

I squeezed the cushion, trying to think of what to say.

'Suzy, you have to tell me the truth.'

'I have.'

'All of it.'

I didn't react for a few moments.

'Come on,' he said, moving towards me, stooping to look me in the eye. 'You can tell me anything.'

'Please,' I said. 'Don't do this. Don't make me.'

'Don't make you what?' He laughed reassuringly, yet his expression betrayed his doubt, insecurity. 'I don't understand. What is it?'

I turned away from him, pulled open the curtains a few inches either side, yanked the stiff window frame up an inch, paint splintering in its wake.

I could feel the cold air, like frosty hands on my shoulders. Dots of rain were set on the glass before me.

'We couldn't tell you about him,' I said.

'Why not?'

I paused, reached forward to touch a raindrop. I couldn't do so though. It was on the other side of the pane.

It felt at that moment as though all my life I had always been on the other side, the wrong side.

The only way out, across, was to tell the truth.

'The night that we ran away from Cumbria, we left him for dead.'

'What?' Mike said, pulling on my arm to get me to turn around.

I looked up at him but couldn't quite meet his gaze.

'I didn't mean to do it,' I said. 'It was an accident.'

In the kitchen, Mike was moving wordlessly around, keeping his back to me, filling the kettle, rinsing mugs. He hadn't stopped fiddling. It was past ten o'clock. We had already gone through the facts twice and were on a loop now, repeating ourselves: Mike was shocked; I was sorry.

Finally, he stopped, set a mug of tea in front of me and sat down at the opposite end of the table.

'How could you keep this from me?' he said. 'We've been married ten years.'

I thought for one terrible moment that he was going to cry. He seemed to be struggling to control his emotions, grinding his jaw, his hands clenched.

'I'm truly sorry,' I said.

'Sorry doesn't cut it,' he said. 'Not even close.'

'I know. But, Mike – what else could I have done in the circumstances?'

He stared at me, incredulous. 'You could have told me! And I could have investigated it to find out if your father was dead or alive.'

'But that would have just drawn attention to what I had done,' I said. 'The police would have arrested me.'

'No, they wouldn't have,' he said, smiling unhappily. 'It was an accident. It wasn't premeditated, it was self-defence. And you were just a kid.' He folded his arms high, his hands tucked underneath his armpits.

'We weren't to know that,' I said. 'My mum didn't trust the police, didn't trust anyone to help us or do the right thing by us. Look at how the system had let her down so far. She just did what she thought was best, to protect me. She sacrificed everything when we left Carlisle. She left her whole life behind. She wasn't about to start blabbering about it to anyone who walked once we got down here.'

'Anyone who walked?' he said angrily. 'I'm your husband!'

'Yes. And I can understand why you're reacting like this,' I said. 'But don't you think there were times when I wanted to tell you? It would have been so much easier to unburden myself. But I couldn't. We had to stay quiet. I promised Mum.'

'You promised Mum,' he echoed. 'That says it all.'

'Why?' I said.

'Because you put her before me.'

'Oh, that's not true. I loved my mum and I would have done anything for her. But it wasn't a case of choosing her over you. It was a case of trying to keep out of danger.'

'And to hell with the effect it would have on our marriage ... I mean, why me, Suzy? Why did you marry a copper?'

'Because I fell in love with you,' I said.

He gazed at me and there was so much sadness in his eyes, I had to look away.

The fridge was humming erratically, jangling my nerves. I stood up, opened the fridge door, slammed it shut and it fell quiet.

I sat back down. 'I just wanted a chance at happiness, the chance of a normal life. You've no idea what it was like growing up in a house like that. It either drags you under and ruins your life, or it makes you determined to leave it all behind and start afresh. And that's what I chose to do. Isn't that a good thing?'

He slurped his tea in response, his shoulders hunched miserably.

'He'll win if this spoils things for us,' I said. 'Don't let him win.'

'Don't let him win?' he said. 'I don't even know the bloke. I don't even know you. Was there ever even a Suzy Stone?'

'Of course there was,' I said. 'It's me!'

He shook his head. 'It's not what you did,' he said. 'I can appreciate what you were going through.' He looked at me. 'But the lying? I don't think I can ... '

'You can't what?' I said. 'You can't forgive me? We can't move on from this?'

A silence fell.

I felt so defeated at that moment that I put my head in my hands and cried.

Mike, who ordinarily couldn't bear to see me cry, didn't say a word. He simply finished his tea and rose to wash the mug. When he was done, he left the room, limping markedly. He tended to feel the pain of his injury more at night.

'So that's it?' I called after him.

I stayed up for another two hours, thinking. I made a cup of tea, did some work on the laptop. And then I went to bed.

Mike was still awake, lying with his eyes open, the bedside light on. 'Why aren't you asleep?' I asked as I undressed.

He turned his mouth down in response.

I slipped into bed, lay on my back, staring up at the ceiling. 'I know this has been a horrendous bombshell,' I said. 'And I know you're feeling cheated and hurt. I'd be feeling exactly the same. But my life will be awful if this changes things for us. I can't let that happen. I've come too far and I've worked too hard.'

He didn't reply.

'I've been going over and over what to do to fix this and I think there's only one thing that I can do: I have to go to Carlisle,' I said.

There was a rustle of bed sheets as he turned to look at me. 'What? Why?'

'Maybe running away and pretending the past didn't happen only served a purpose up to a point, and now I've crossed that point. Maybe now I need to know what happened to my father.'

'So, you've ... what ... changed your mind? Do you want me to make a few phone calls, ask—'

'I want to go up there in person, on my own,' I said.

'That's insane, Suzy,' he said, lying flat on his back again. 'No way.'

'It's not insane. I can get there and back in a day – fly to Glasgow, train it to Carlisle. It only takes a few hours.'

'No,' he said. I knew this voice; it was his *this is non-negotiable* tone.

'But what if doing this helps us, helps our marriage?' I said. 'Come on, Mike. I need to know the truth.'

'And what if you don't like it? What if you walk into a dangerous situation? You'll be far from home, vulnerable. Have you thought about that?'

'Yes,' I said. 'OK ... no ... But I can't see how else to do it. I need information and I don't want the police involved.'

'Then we'll all go,' he said.

'No. We're not dragging the kids up there. It's too much. And it'll cost a fortune.'

'I don't care about the money. All I care about is your safety.'

'And the kids',' I said. 'This is about them too. And that's why they shouldn't go. They're better off staying in their routine, with you, whilst I go there quickly.'

'You make it sound like it's just up the road.'

'Well, it is, in a way,' I said.

There was a pause.

'Get one of your friends to go with you,' he said. 'Ask Nicole.'

'No,' I said. 'I'm not involving her. She's got enough on her plate. And I'm not asking Helen or Donna either. It makes things too complicated.'

He sighed, rubbed his face.

'Mike ... ' I said, placing my hand on his arm. 'I got us into this, whatever it is. Let me have the chance to sort it out my way – quietly, no fuss.'

He frowned, turned on his side to look at me again.

'*Please*,' I said.

'Where would you start to look for him?'

'In our old street.'

'You know where that is?'

'Yes. It was eight Rose Lane.'

'And what will you do when you get there?'

'Ask around – see if anyone remembers Patrick Faire.'

'What if no one does?'

'Someone will. We lived in a large house on a fancy road. I've Google-mapped it. It's still very exclusive-looking. I don't think he lived in obscurity.'

'Will you disclose who you are?'

'I'm not sure.'

'Well, you need to be sure, Suzy. Before you go, you need to have all this worked out . . . When would you go?'

'This Sunday. There's nothing in the diary. The trains and planes run as usual – I've checked.'

'Well,' he said dryly, 'it sounds like you've got everything worked out.'

'I have, almost,' I said. 'I just need your blessing.'

'I can't give you that. I'll just have to look the other way.'

'Good. Then it's settled,' I said, reaching out to turn the light off.

There was nothing settled about it. Nothing about our life was settled now.

In the dark, I doubted myself – doubted my ability to return to Carlisle alone and the wisdom of my plan. I thought of the shadow at the foot of our bed and in the alley blocking my path and I trembled all over.

Mike misinterpreted the movement, thinking perhaps that I was crying.

'I'm sorry about what happened to you,' he said. 'No little kid should ever have to go through that.' He kissed my forehead, pressed his chest close as he folded his arms around me.

'And I'm really sorry that I hurt you,' I said. 'I didn't—'

'Shush,' he said, smoothing my hair. 'I've got thick skin. I'll get over it. You just have to do what you've gotta do to move on.'

'Do you think I'll be all right in Carlisle?'

'Yes. Like you say, you can get there and back in no time . . . Besides, nothing bad will ever happen to you. Not while I'm alive.'

His gentle words and the warmth of his strong body soothed me into slumber.

That night, lying there, I felt completely safe.

I wished it could have stayed that way.

PRELIMINARY MEETING

Monday 27 March, 2017

'So, you have two beautiful kids. And do you have a husband or partner living with you?'

'Yes, a husband.'

'And he's the children's father?'

'Yes.'

'Of both children?'

'Yes,' I say again.

'Sorry,' he says. 'Have to ask . . . And your husband's name?'

'Mike.'

'OK,' he says, writing the name down. 'And what does Mike do?'

'He was a policeman. But he was injured so now he's the children's stay-at-home dad.'

Dan nods. 'And he enjoys this role?'

'Yes,' I say. 'Very much so.'

'Good,' Dan says. 'And what about you?'

'Do I enjoy being a mum?'

He smiles. 'Do you work?'

'Oh. Yes.'

He nods, encouraging me with his eyebrows to be more specific.

'I own a deli.'

'Sounds fun,' he says. 'And hard work. I assume that's a full-time occupation?'

'Yes, and a bit more.'

'I'll bet,' he says. 'Do you find it hard to spend quality time with the children?'

'Not really. I mean, obviously it's a challenge. But it's one that I'm happy to meet and I think I get it right. I'm always there for my children, even when I'm not in view.'

'Great,' he says.

I don't feel uncomfortable about this, not even here. I have worked very hard to be a good mum. I will not squirm in my seat.

I think of all the times I have traipsed upstairs in the middle of the night to give Jake his inhaler, the knee scrapes I've patched up, the name badges I've sewn into clothes, the cakes I've made for school sales, the PTA meetings I've attended, the lunch boxes I've packed, the consent forms I've signed, the papier-mâché I've moulded, the fungi I've cultivated for science projects.

All this comes to me in such a rush that I suddenly feel warm, indignant. I watch Dan as he scribbles on his notepad, his silver pen catching the light.

I wonder – when he takes my file out later, when he puts his tie back on, removes his smile and looks at my profile – what he will make of me?

11

When the day of my trip finally arrived, I rose at four in the morning, stepping into clothes that I had laid out the night before. I even woke before the alarm, as though I had been waiting for that wake-up call my whole life.

Mike came downstairs with me and made me a Thermos mug of coffee which he carried outside, leaning his head inside the car window to kiss me goodbye. 'You're going to be fine,' he said. 'Call me as soon as you land.'

I didn't dwell on leaving, didn't look at Mike as I drove away. Had I done so, I would have turned the car around and gone straight back home to him.

As I left the city, the sky was beginning to show signs of brightening, leaking berry-coloured light on to the horizon.

I could do this, I told myself, gripping the steering wheel. I had often taken business trips during my old role at JB Alliance – had thought nothing of doing so, alone, or with company, in the UK or all over the world. This was nothing.

I arrived at the airport in less than half an hour. It was very quiet, still dark. I drove to the car park, deposited the car, locked up.

My plane was leaving for Glasgow at six thirty. Inside the

airport, I headed for the departures board along with all the other travellers who were consulting phones and watches.

I didn't know, standing there on the forecourt, looking up at the board, what I was going to find in Carlisle that day. But I wasn't scared any more.

I was doing this for Mike and for our children. I was ready for anything.

Except for what it was that I actually found that day.

The flight to Glasgow was a small plane with few passengers. I wasn't a nervous flyer but I could have done without the man opposite me who had his fist in his mouth and was biting it so hard, he appeared to be drawing blood. I concentrated instead on applying my make-up, no mean feat on a bumpy flight.

Mission accomplished, I gazed out of the window, hoping that the hour-long journey would pass quickly.

I couldn't remember having ever flown with my parents or going away with them on holiday. We must have, I supposed, but the memories were lost.

Memories, so I had once read, were most powerful when loaded with emotion. It was why everyone could recall where they had been when they had heard that Princess Diana had died, or when the Twin Towers had been attacked.

It also explained how I could remember the night that we had left Carlisle – the night of my sixth birthday, in 1982 – so clearly, even that there was a pumpkin on our front lawn that my mother had carved. It was just after Halloween. The pumpkin was already starting to sink and gape.

My father had forbidden me to have a birthday party. I was to have jam sandwiches and jelly, by myself.

But that morning before school, my mother told me that

my father had changed his mind and I could have some friends round after all.

Something about the way she said this made me think that she wasn't quite telling the truth. Then at the school gate, she told three mums that their daughters were invited to ours and if they could please be picked up at five o'clock *sharp*.

I knew then that my father hadn't changed his mind, that the girls had to be out of the way before he came home. If this was supposed to be a birthday treat, it didn't feel that way. It felt risky, daring.

That day at school, as the clock edged closer to home time, I felt my stomach wriggling with nerves and my armpits dampening with fear.

At three o'clock, when I saw the three girls waiting for me at the school gate, I felt hot all over.

I didn't speak much, was too anxious for words.

When we got home, my mother had decorated the dining room with balloons. There was a lime jelly on the table that had been made in a mould. We played a short game of pass the parcel. And then we sat down to tea.

We had only just started eating when I heard the front door slam. I thought I would choke on my crisps.

There, in the dining-room doorway, was my father.

I waited for the look of anger, but it didn't come. He was carrying a package under his arm and moved forward to kiss my mother and then me, and to say hello to the girls.

This threw me off. It was a decoy. Besides, he never sounded off in front of other people. We would catch hell later.

I continued to eat furtively, listening to the conversation that was taking place out in the hallway, which was very difficult to do whilst eating crisps.

That's fantastic, Patrick, my mother was saying.

I groaned internally. It was something to do with work.

My father poured a glass of beer and joined us at the table, talking to our guests, who answered him as politely as they could whilst eating as much party food as possible.

Sure enough, their mothers arrived at five o'clock *sharp* and I watched as the girls said thank you and their mothers led them away down the path. And then I waited for the explosion.

But instead my father led me to the lounge where he handed me the package.

I opened it. It was an Etch A Sketch, which wasn't so bad, and a brown envelope.

I opened the envelope with a sinking feeling. My father was hovering expectantly. Inside, there were three tickets.

We're going to the Carlisle Market Hall tonight, Suzy, pet, to see a Celtic folk group play live.

I looked at my mother for guidance as to how to set my face. But she wasn't any help because she was looking cross and was shaking her head.

Not on a school night, Patrick.

My father scowled. But our chairman gave these to me, for Suzy's birthday. He went to a lot of trouble to get them for us. And he'll ask me tomorrow how we got on.

Maybe you can go on your own then and I'll stay here with Suzy.

But he very kindly gave us three tickets, Annie. It's rude not to go.

He stood up then. I remained seated, gazing at the Etch A Sketch on my lap.

I didn't want any of this to happen – hadn't wanted the girls to come to tea, hadn't wanted the Etch A Sketch or the Celtic folk group tickets. I had just wanted to eat a few chocolate fingers for my birthday and go to bed.

And now we had to go to see a live concert at the Carlisle Market Hall with its giant iron and glass roof tonight, whether we liked it or not.

I braced myself, knowing what was coming next, not knowing what to do about it.

'Thank you for flying with us, ladies and gentlemen. Don't forget to take your personal items with you and we wish you a safe and pleasant onward journey.'

I looked about me. We had landed. The man with his fist in his mouth had already gone, leaving a shredded newspaper behind him.

I picked up my belongings and left the plane.

I caught a taxi to Glasgow Central, where I then got on the quickest train to Carlisle, taking only an hour and ten minutes. We would be travelling down through the Scottish Lowlands, crossing the border into England. A leaflet lying on the seat beside me said to look out for the Belties en route – the black and white cows of Galloway – and the glimpses of the stunning Nith Valley and of Gretna Green.

Again, there were few passengers around me. I was able to stretch out my legs, close my eyes. I didn't mean to sleep. I had fully intended taking in the scenery, but my four o'clock wake-up was taking its toll on me.

When I opened my eyes, I was in Carlisle.

The taxi driver knew where Rose Lane was and took off without further ado. I asked him how far we were going and he said 1.2 miles from the station. I then asked him what he could tell me about the area we were going to and he said absolutely nothing, other than that it was north of the city and where posh people lived. He sounded tetchy, so I didn't ask him anything else, but looked out of the window instead, hoping to see something familiar.

We went down the high street, which was red-bricked in the main, with several shops bearing to-let signs. As we joined a faster road, the sun came out, hitting a glass-fronted building to blinding effect. After several minutes, we came to a long road alongside a park. We then crossed a river, before turning up a small almost concealed road that was thick with shrubbery on both sides.

This felt different. The road was manicured, the garden walls of the residences were high. The lamp posts were ornate, Narnia-like; Jake would have liked them.

There was something about the straightness of the road, the very length of it, that stirred a memory within me, but it wasn't distinct.

We continued along, not seeing anyone; it was too early, Sunday. We passed a sign at the side of the road that said: PRIVATE ROAD. NO PARKING.

It seemed to go on for ever, that road. And then in a wooded area, there was a fork in the road and we turned right on to Rose Lane.

I recognised it immediately – the oversized willow tree on the corner, the cherry blossom trees set on a strip of lawn that ran down one side of the street.

I held my hand to my mouth, stared around me in wonder.

The taxi driver was watching me in the rear-view mirror. 'Where do you want me to stop?' he asked.

'This will do, thanks,' I said.

We were outside number eight. I looked up at the large house. And then I spotted the two yew trees in the back garden. They had been there in my childhood – had outlasted us all.

I paid the driver, got out of the car. He lowered the window. 'Want me to wait for you?' he said.

'No, thanks,' I replied.

'Suit yourself,' he said, then pulled away.

It was just beginning to rain. I stood gazing at the yew trees, thinking how pleased my mum would have been to see that they were still there.

She had loved those trees, telling me once that they were female, that our ancestors had thought of the yew as a female deity or mother goddess. I hadn't understood that entirely at the time but had sensed that it had meant that the two trees were like Mum and me. So, I had grown to love them too.

The problem was that a lot of the components of a yew tree, especially the seeds, were poisonous.

I could remember one of our neighbours shouting vehemently at my mother to cut the trees down in order to safeguard her pet puppy. My mother had refused politely to do so, saying that the yews were ancient, couldn't be uprooted – that there were many things in a garden that were potentially toxic to animals, not just our yews.

And then, not long after, the puppy had died.

We hadn't told my father. But when he inadvertently found out, my mother paid dearly for her loyalty to those old trees.

I glanced about me, up and down Rose Lane, wondering whether anyone would recognise me now. Surely not. I wouldn't appear the same at all.

Yet to me, it was obvious who I was as I stood there, outside my old home.

I was Suzy Faire, just turned six years old.

I did my coat up, lifted my chin resolutely, but somehow my legs wouldn't move.

I thought of everything that my mother and I had been through inside that affable-looking house – all the things she had endured on my behalf and that I had endured on hers.

But my musings were cut short then because I heard a noise and saw that the front door of number eight had opened and that someone was coming out.

12

The woman was in her late fifties, I would have guessed. She was well dressed in a toffee-coloured coat and was going to her car, but when she saw me at the foot of her driveway, she stopped.

'Can I help you?' she said, coming towards me, fixing her bag on her shoulder. I saw that she was wearing a wedding ring.

My first thought was that I could be looking at my father's second wife. He hadn't divorced my mother, would be committing bigamy were that to be the case.

'Are you lost or looking for someone?' she asked.

I glanced warily past her. There didn't appear to be anyone joining her from the house though. She had locked the door after her, I recalled then.

'I'm not lost, no,' I said, looking at her. She was attractive with very blue eyes and bright red lipstick. 'I used to live here.'

'Oh,' she said, smiling at me. 'And when was that?'

'A long time ago,' I said, straightening my coat. I was dressed all in black, in an effort to seem professional, impersonal. Glancing down at my feet, I saw that Ruby had chalked an orange heart on the toe of my left boot. Curiously, it had lasted all the way to Carlisle.

I pointed to the heart. 'Look at what my cheeky little girl's drawn on my shoe. I've only just noticed!'

The woman laughed. 'You have a little girl?' she said. 'I have three ... They're big girls now though.' Then she hesitated, cocking her head at me as though weighing the suitability of what she was about to say next. 'I was just popping out to get the paper, but if you'd like to come in and look at the house for a wee while, you're more than welcome to?' I could hear the Scottish accent in her voice then.

'That's very kind of you,' I said. 'Maybe just for a moment.'

It was exactly what I had wanted her to suggest. Ruby would never know the power of her chalk doodle.

The woman waved her keys at her car to lock the doors, then led me up the driveway.

'Do you live here alone or with ... ?' I asked.

'My husband?' she said, then laughed. 'Yes, but I'm on my own most of the time. My husband's always away on business. And my daughters left yonks ago, off to uni and whatnot.'

As she opened the door, a cat appeared from inside, squashing past us, running off down the steps with a tinkle of its collar bell.

Inside the house, an immediate change came over me, my heart compressing uncomfortably. I gazed about me in disbelief and dismay. No one liked to be confronted with change, not even when they didn't like the old version.

The floorboards were bare, not brightly carpeted; the walls were painted a discreet magnolia, not 1980s Power Peach; gone were the swirling patterns on the plastered ceiling and the overpowering chintzy curtains.

It would have smelt of hairspray back then and my father's tobacco. Now there was a citrus scent wafting from a stylish bottle of reeds labelled 'Italian Florals' on the hallway table.

But it was the staircase that arrested me – the fact that it looked exactly the same, with its spindly banisters and abrupt twist halfway, like a broken neck.

Suddenly, I didn't want to be inside the house any more, didn't want to look around.

'When did you say you lived here?' the woman asked.

'Early eighties,' I said.

'Well before my time,' she said. 'I wasn't even living in England then.' She pointed through to the kitchen. 'Would you like to go take a look? I really don't mind.'

I shook my head. 'I'm a bit short on time actually and I don't want to intrude. I'm happy just to have seen this much.'

'As you like,' she said. 'But one thing I am curious about . . . what was your family's name?'

I tried not to look bothered. 'Faire,' I said. 'I'm Suzy.'

'And I'm Shirley Cook,' she said. Then she put her hands on her hips, her eyes shining. 'Well, I can tell you something interesting: Faire was the name of the man we bought the house from.'

'Really?' I said. 'Did he . . . was he . . . ?'

Her face clouded. 'We never actually met Mr Faire,' she said. 'We bought the house because he had passed away.'

'Oh,' I said, feeling faint.

She moved forward, touched my elbow. 'Have I said something stupid? I've a habit of doing that, I'm afraid. It doesn't get any better with age either . . . Here . . . Come and sit down.'

She was steering me through to the lounge, the furniture and floorboards a blur. It was often said that the past came flooding back when stimulated, implying a flow. But for me, the experience was unstable, broken, with memories darting at me like a panicking bird that was trapped, circling the room.

'I'll get you a drink. You look pale. Would you like tea? Water?'

My mind was saying so many things at once, I couldn't concentrate on what she was asking me.

There was a momentary silence.

Then she said, 'I think tea's best. Do you take sugar?'

'Please,' I said, mostly to get her to leave the room. I needed space to think.

So, my father was dead.

When had he died?

I perched on the edge of the sofa, my arms wrapped around me.

How long had Shirley been living here? Had she told me how long just now? I couldn't remember.

I looked about me, trying to take in the fact that I was sitting in the lounge that I had grown up in, where so much strife had taken place. You would never have been able to tell now. The house was so civilised, genteel, it belied its true nature.

No one, aside from the yews, knew otherwise. Through the French doors, which hadn't been there before, I could see the loyal trees with their evergreen needles, defying winter and time.

I gazed at them, tears forming in my eyes. Those precious yews were the only living members of my old family and history. No wonder my mother had fought for their right to survive.

'Here you go,' the lady said, returning with a china teacup on a saucer.

I took the cup from her, held it on my lap.

She sat down beside me, albeit at a polite distance. 'You didn't know that Mr Faire had passed away then?' she said.

'No,' I said.

'Was he . . . your father?'

I nodded, pretending to be intent on drinking my tea.

'I'm so sorry. I shouldn't have blurted it out like that. I just didn't think . . . Did you come here looking for him?'

'Yes.'

She looked at me compassionately. 'I'm afraid I can't tell you much more than I already have. Although Keith Gunnell knew him fairly well, so I understand.'

'Keith Gunnell?' I said, lowering my teacup.

'Yes. Do you know him? He lives at the big house on the corner – the one with the willow tree. He's lived there for years apparently.'

That sounded like a lead of sorts.

'I'll check that out,' I said. 'Thank you.'

'Glad to have helped.'

I finished my tea in silence. And then I rose and went to the window to take one last look at the yews. So close to each other, their branches had become entangled, entwined, making it impossible to tell them apart, save for their solid red-brown trunks.

Nothing else in the landscaped garden was recognisable.

I turned back to Shirley. 'Thank you for your hospitality,' I said. 'But I'd better be making a move now.'

'Of course,' she said, nodding and seeing me out.

At the door, there was a moment when we held eye contact with one another. 'Family can be a real bugger, you know,' she said.

'Yes,' I said, forcing a smile. 'Well, thank you again for your kindness. It was most appreciated.'

'Good luck,' she called after me as I made my way down the steps. 'Hope you find what you're looking for.'

Her words seemed to echo in the wet morning air as I left my old home.

At the end of the driveway, I turned right on to Rose Lane and glanced back at the house. The door had closed.

I continued along the road, making my way towards the house with the weeping willow in its garden, my footsteps becoming slower, heavier.

I paused at the entrance to the property. The house straddled both streets – Rose Lane and the private road – and was grander than my old home. The iron gate was tall, with a keypad controlling entry.

I had to know when precisely my father had died. I couldn't leave Carlisle without this information; it was the whole point of my coming here.

Yet I didn't press the buzzer right away, took a moment to steady myself. The past felt horribly present. Even the air was old, familiar – the way that the cold bothered my skin and bones.

I turned away and leant with my back against the wall, concealed in the gloom of the willow tree, and closed my eyes, trying to pull myself together.

But it was no use. I could feel myself slipping backwards, down.

We're not going, Patrick, my mother said.

Yes, you are, my father said.

The silence stung. I was still holding the tickets. They were getting bent in my hands and clammy with my mounting heat.

If you don't go . . . my father said.

Then what? my mother asked. What will you do to me, Patrick? What will you do that you haven't done already?

I thought this bold of her. Sometimes she pushed her luck, but never quite as hard as she was doing now. I began to rock, whimpering softly so that they wouldn't hear me.

For crying out loud, Annie, my father said. Why do you have to make this so difficult?

He began to close the curtains in the lounge and then went to the kitchen to pull down the blind. It made a squeaky noise as it fell and I looked at my mother who was standing with her hands clasped together, composed, regal.

Go to your room, Suzy, she told me.

No, I said.

I wasn't leaving her. Whatever was about to happen, it was

worse than it had ever been before because my mother was disrespecting my father's company chairman and if there was one thing that my father insisted on above all else, it was that the chairman was not to be disrespected.

My father had come back into the room.

Do as your mother says, he said.

I threw the tickets on to the floor and looked up at him.

No, I said.

He stared at the tickets.

And then he erupted.

He lunged forward, but I was nimbler than him and swerved past him, running the length of the lounge towards the bookcase in the corner, the shelves of which looked very like steps to me. I scrabbled up the bookcase, which was several feet taller than me, jumped on top and down the other side, where I crouched, my heart racing.

My father stopped in front of the bookcase, banging on the top of it with his fists and kicking it. It was solid, heavy. Would he be able to move it?

He was shouting, cursing.

Come out of there, you spoilt little brat. Come out!

I clutched my knees to my chin, closed my eyes, begged.

Leave me alone. Leave me alone. Leave me alone.

I put my hands over my ears. It was horrible there, musty, dusty. I was sure there were cobwebs all over me, that a spider was creeping forward to touch my leg.

But then it went quiet.

I gazed up at the back of the bookcase, with its slippery smooth wood. I couldn't reach the top even if I stood up, jumped up.

I was trapped.

I had made things worse for my mother – had wound him up, aggravated him, and now I couldn't help her.

I moaned, pressing my hands to my face to stop my tears. I couldn't cry. I had to think. But even if I thought, I knew there was nothing I could do.

I stood up. The bookcase straddled two walls in the corner of the room, so the space behind it was triangular. I wasn't squashed, but I was stuck. I gritted my teeth, put one foot on the wall behind me, the other forward on the floor and pushed with all my might. But the bookcase didn't so much as wobble.

I jumped on the spot, biting my lip. I pinched my arms to punish myself. I banged on the back of the case with my fists until my hands hurt.

Mummy! Mummy! I shouted.

There was no reply. I couldn't hear a thing. Wherever they were, whatever was happening, it wasn't here.

I sank down on to the floor and sobbed, my hands covering my ears, my hair spread in the cobwebs.

What if no one came for me? What if I were stuck here for ever?

The only way forward, to move on, was to go through the gate.

I took a deep breath and pressed the button on the entry panel. After a few seconds, a man answered. 'Hello?'

'Mr Gunnell?' I said.

'Yes?'

'My name's Suzy Faire. I was wondering if I could have a few moments of your time.'

There was a slight hesitation. 'Faire, you say?'

'That's right.'

To my relief and apprehension, there was a beep and then the gate swung open.

I approached down the gravel path, gazing about me at the stone figurines and the fish pond, with the vague sensation of having done so before.

I halted on the porch and was about to reach for the knocker, when the door opened and there stood a portly man wearing a roll neck and chinos.

I didn't recognise him. But he seemed to know me – was chuckling at the mere sight of me.

'Well, well, well! Suzy Faire,' he said. 'I was wondering when you'd show up.'

I wasn't sure what that was supposed to mean. It didn't warm me to him very much.

If I had met him before, as a small child, I was certain that I wouldn't have liked him – would have coiled around my mother's legs the way Ruby did with me in front of strange men. He would have been too forward for my liking – rubbing my hair, tossing me coins, patronising me. All this I presumed in one glance.

An old Labrador appeared at the door, padding forward, nuzzling against his master's legs, sniffing the air. I wondered what the dog would have smelt about my person. Fear, in the main, I suspected.

'Well, you'd better come in,' Mr Gunnell said.

I followed him into the spacious lobby. The decor was minimalist, sparse-looking. There was a bronze bust of a man on a pedestal, and a glass bowl with perilously sharp edges. This was all I had time to take in.

'We'll go in here,' he said, shooing the dog off down the hallway and leading me into a room on our right. 'The wife's doing Pilates.'

I didn't know if that meant that she was here or not. I decided to take it that she was at home, not loving the idea of being alone here with an unknown man in a house that he controlled entry in and out of.

I tapped my phone in my pocket reassuringly, reminding myself that Mike was on speed dial if I needed him.

'Please,' Mr Gunnell said, motioning to the chair at the foot of his desk. 'Take a seat.' He sat down behind the desk and rolled up his sleeves methodically. Beyond him were dozens of obscure leather books in glass cases.

'So, Suzy,' he said, 'if I may call you that ... I gather you're here because of your father?'

'Yes.'

'Do you remember me at all?'

'No,' I said candidly.

He gazed at me. 'I see.'

Discreetly, I wiped my top lip. I was still wearing my coat; he hadn't taken it from me, perhaps not expecting my stay to be long enough to warrant his doing so.

'I was hoping you could give me some information about my father,' I said.

'What sort of information?'

'Well, anything really. I don't know much – hardly anything, in fact. I've been wondering about him ... '

'And why's that, may I ask?'

'Well, because it feels like a chunk of my life is missing,' I said. 'He was my father, after all. I'd just like some answers.'

He seemed to allow that as an explanation, nodded.

'Shirley, the lady living at our old house, mentioned that you knew him quite well. So how did you two know each other?' I asked. 'Because you were neighbours?'

'Golf,' he said bluntly, as though that were the answer to everything in the universe.

I seemed to remember something about that – my father's golf bag in the garage, the checked cap and trousers that he wore on weekends.

'Can you tell me what he was like?' I asked.

Mr Gunnell cleared his throat, then pushed back his chair and stood up, leaning one elbow against the bookcase. 'Well, he was a hard worker, for a start,' he said. 'Quick out of the blocks, you might say. Built a life for himself from scratch whilst young . . . something that few manage to achieve, especially in these parts and in those times.'

'Impressive,' I said, without a hint of sarcasm.

'He was a top salesman. Best one I've ever met anyway. You had to be sure when he was recommending something to you that he wasn't on commission on the sly.'

'And what was it that he sold?'

'You don't know?'

'No.'

He smiled. 'Patrick was a financial salesman. He preferred the term *advisor*, but he was basically a financial service sales agent. Had all the inside knowledge of the markets and advised people and organisations on how to invest wisely – that sort of thing. By the time he was managing director, he—'

'He was a director?' I said.

He nodded. 'Of course.'

'I didn't realise. So, was that when I was living with him?'

I thought of the doomed promotion that had unravelled our home – of the business trip to France that he had taken and the ugly toy monkey that he had brought back for me.

'It might have been,' he said. 'He was in his early thirties at the time, I believe . . . Does that fit?'

I would do the sums later. I already knew without working it out, however, that it would fit.

He examined his fingernail, picking at it. 'After you and your mother left, he threw himself into work harder than ever. Truth told, he wasn't the same again.'

I stared at him in confusion.

He threw himself into work *after* we had left?

I wiped my hands on my trousers, telling myself to stay calm. Mr Gunnell was looking at me intently, as though intrigued. I wondered whether I could ask him for a drink, to buy some time. But he was sitting back down, elbows on desk, hands together to form a temple. I had taken business classes too – knew the tricks, that he was projecting honesty.

'Your father was devastated when you disappeared,' he said.

A silence fell between us. I wondered what he wanted from me, what emotion or reaction he was trying to provoke in me: remorse? Guilt?

I tried then to feel sorry for Patrick Faire, even temporarily, but couldn't. If that made me inhuman and unfeeling, then I accepted the charge.

'He tried to find you,' he said. 'He never gave up looking, not until the day he died.'

I felt bad then, shifted position in my chair, uncrossing my legs, and in doing so caught sight of the chalk heart on my boot.

The thought of the children and of Mike gave me the courage to go ahead and ask for the information that I had come here for.

'When did he die, Mr Gunnell?'

It was such a bold question, I had no choice but to stare right at him, holding myself very still.

'Ten years ago,' he replied.

I tried not to look relieved, but I felt light-bodied, giddily so.

'How did he die?' I asked, clasping my hands together.

'Drink driving,' Mr Gunnell said. 'Drove into a concrete roundabout island and overturned his car.'

'Oh, God,' I said.

'Do you need a tissue or something?' he asked impassively. Whatever he had done for a living, it hadn't been in the care sector.

'No, thank you,' I said.

I wouldn't be crying here, was holding myself too tightly for tears.

'He hit the bottle after Annie left,' he said, reaching out to the paperweight on the desk and rotating it pensively. 'Over the years it became more of a problem. And in the end, it killed him.' He let go of the paperweight, set his gaze on me. 'No one loved their wife like Patrick loved Annie.'

Something about his choice of words, about the way he was looking at me – still looking for signs of remorse perhaps – enraged me.

'He used to knock her about,' I said.

His mouth formed a straight line. He looked angry. And I wondered why.

'Listen here, young lady,' he said, his voice low, terse, 'I don't know what went on behind closed doors, but that's quite an allegation. Patrick was—'

'He was what?' I said, trying not to raise my voice. 'Good at golf? A hard worker? A canny investor?' I stared at him, incensed. 'You say that you didn't know what was going on. Well, you should have. I was just a child. I didn't deserve that. And my mother sure as hell didn't.'

I broke off, waited for him to respond. When he didn't answer, began fiddling with the paperweight again, I knew that my work here was done.

I picked up my bag, stood and made for the door. 'Thank you for your time,' I said. 'I'll see myself out.'

I was halfway through the door when he called out to me. 'Wait.'

He got up from his chair stiffly and approached. When he drew level with me, he narrowed his eyes before speaking.

'You didn't come just for the money, did you,' he said.

This was the first time he had sounded kindly. I was thrown by that fact, rather than what he had actually said.

'Your father, for all his financial wizardry, died intestate. I don't think he knew who the heck to leave it to. Time and again I told him, as his solicitor, not to be a fool, to get it sorted. But he couldn't settle on a decision – always hoped Annie would return and resolve the matter ... And then he died suddenly, needlessly. And the first thing I thought was, *I told you so.*'

'Blimey,' I said, for want of something more intelligent to say.

He put his hand in his pocket, jangling the loose change within. 'I tried hard to find you. I think it's what he would have wanted. Personally, I can't stand it when the state swallows the lot.'

I couldn't quite follow what he was talking about, was watching his lips attentively.

'Better late than never, eh? You had twelve years to come forward and it's already been ten.'

'To come forward?'

'And claim the estate. It's worth just over 1.8 million, after tax.'

I stared at him in amazement.

'Where's your mother now?' he asked.

'She died,' I said. 'Recently.'

'Well, I'm very sorry to hear that,' he said. 'But given your mother's demise that makes you the sole inheritor.'

'What?'

'Congratulations, Suzy.' He snapped his front teeth together rhythmically, slightly ominously. 'You're a wealthy woman.'

PRELIMINARY MEETING

Monday 27 March, 2017

'Tell me why you are here today? What led you to call me?' He puts his pen down, dangles his arms over the back of his chair.

'Because I'm desperate for help and I didn't know where else to turn.'

'OK,' he says. 'So, we need to discuss how exactly I might be able to help you.'

He hasn't picked up on that word 'desperate' at all, doesn't seem at all put out by it. I rarely hear the word in my job, other than in the context of a joke: I'm desperate for caffeine. *But in Dan Cassidy's line of work, he must hear words like this all the time. I could say I was at the end of my tether, going insane, and he would pick up his pen as he is doing now and nod diplomatically.*

'Something that I'd like to do before we part ways today is to draw up an idea of what you want. We can work on this together in rough. Even if you don't know precisely how that might look, it'll still help.' He gazes at me. 'Does that sound like something that you might be able to do?'

I look at him.

Can I tell him what I want?

Of course, I can.

I've always known exactly what I want. That has never been a problem for me.

Yet somehow, I open my mouth to begin and no words come.

'Take your time,' he says. 'I know how incredibly difficult this is.'

13

'I don't want the money, Mr Gunnell,' I said.

'Please,' he said. 'Call me Keith.'

'Very well, Keith,' I said. 'Give it to the cats' and dogs' home.'

He laughed through his teeth. 'I can't. As it currently stands, the entire estate goes to the Crown. *You* could give it to the cats' and dogs' home though. But you'd have to take it first.'

'Then let the Crown have it,' I said. 'I don't want it. I mean it. I have plenty of my own money.'

'No one ever has plenty. Especially not a Faire.'

'And what's that supposed to mean?'

'You know very well what that means.' He tapped my arm. 'Come on. At least talk it over with me. Let's have a coffee ... Do you have time?'

I glanced at my watch. My train didn't leave for another three hours.

'If we're quick,' I said.

'Good.' And he led us past the bronze bust and through to the kitchen.

The kitchen was painted pastel blue, reminding me of one of Ruby's paper doll dresses. Sunshine was streaming through the patio doors and, to my surprise, there was a deer standing outside on the lawn.

Keith took no notice of the deer, told me to sit down on a stool at the central island, whilst he busied himself with the coffees. Then he turned to a cake stand, lifted the lid and cut a slice of Victoria sponge. 'Can I tempt you?' he said. 'My wife's a splendid cook.'

I needed the energy, felt depleted. 'Go on then,' I said.

He put a mug of coffee, a jug of cream and a sugar bowl before me, then handed me a plate of cake. 'There you go.'

He joined me and everything went quiet as we ate.

'This is delicious,' I said. 'I own a deli. This is good enough to sell there.'

'Really?' he said. And I knew from the way he was looking at me that it was the titbit of information about my deli that he was most interested in and not the idea of his wife as professional cake baker.

I picked up my coffee, wishing I hadn't said anything.

'If you run your own business, then a large injection of cash is always handy,' he said, pulling a handkerchief from his pocket and dabbing his mouth. 'Just think what you could do with—'

'I'm not taking the money,' I told him.

He frowned, put the handkerchief away. 'Do you have children, Suzy?'

'Yes,' I said.

I knew where he was going with this.

'How many, might I ask?'

'Two.'

He nodded. 'Don't you think the money would be beneficial for them, to safeguard their futures? It's getting tougher out there all the time.'

'I'm well aware how tough it is, because I've always made my own money,' I said. 'And I've done very well for myself, more than you probably realise.'

He gazed at me thoughtfully then. 'Well, in that case, you really are your father's child.'

'I doubt that,' I said quietly.

He shuffled on the stool, shifting position so that he was facing me. 'Tell me what went on,' he said. 'You said I should have known. So, tell me.'

'You honestly didn't know?' I said.

'Not an inkling.'

I took a deep breath, bracing myself. And then I exhaled, realising that I couldn't tell all – that I would always have to keep the worst bit to myself.

'There's not much to say, not any more. Other than the fact that he ruined my mother's life ... He was vicious, brutal. And things were getting worse. So, we ran away. I think if he had have found us, he would have killed us.'

Keith looked at me in shock.

'I had absolutely no idea. I can't quite believe it. Did anyone try to—?'

'Help?' I shook my head. 'Not that I know of.'

'Good Lord,' he said, hanging his head. Then he shook his head, smiled at me dolefully. 'He was always so charming. Bit of an egotist perhaps – liked to command the room, have an audience, that sort of thing. But I always used to put it down to his sales temperament, to bravado. I had no idea he had another side to him.' He looked at me thoughtfully then, pursing his lips. 'He used to put a lot of pressure on himself, mind you ... ever striving for the next big thing. Bigger car, bigger house ... more commission ... a fancier office.'

This struck a little note of familiarity with me. I thought of what my friends said about my constant need to do more, be more.

Over the years, I had removed myself so far from my father, it hadn't ever occurred to me that I might have shared some similarities with him.

'I think perhaps that it all got to him,' Keith said. 'Those were hard times, the eighties. A recession and all the pension mis-selling going on . . . '

'So, you're justifying wife-beating?' I said.

''Course not. But if you're ever going to forgive him then understanding how he was wired might help.'

'Forgive him?' I said. 'My mother's dead! I'll never forgive him. Holding on to my anger is my way of honouring her.'

'If that's what she would have wanted,' he said. 'Then yes. By all means, hold on to it.'

I gazed at him. It wasn't what my mother would have wanted at all.

He took a sip of coffee, then looked at me sympathetically. 'I'm very sorry, Suzy,' he said. 'I wished I could have helped you, that I'd known what was going on, or that someone else could have stepped in and sorted things out.'

'Well, they didn't,' I said. 'But it's OK. I mean, it's not OK obviously, but it's over now. He's gone. My mum's gone. And . . . '

I didn't know what else to say.

I looked at my empty plate and empty cup. Now seemed like a good time to leave.

I reached for my bag. 'I'd better be off,' I said. 'Thank you for the coffee and cake. Full compliments to your wife.'

'I'll pass that on,' he said and escorted me from the room.

On our way through the hallway, he reached into a trinket box on a dresser and pulled out a card. I lingered at the front door to say goodbye. The Labrador joined us, slumping on the floor at Keith's feet.

He handed me a business card. 'Here,' he said. 'Take this. Call me.'

I took the card, dropped it into my coat pocket. 'I won't be changing my mind.'

He squared his jaw resolvedly, his pupils shrinking to

businesslike dots. 'Take the money, Suzy. He owes you. Big corporations don't fork out compensation for nothing, you know. Money smooths the way. Use it to fix this.'

I shook my head. 'Nothing can fix it.'

'Do not reject this,' he said, pointing his finger at me. 'It'll change your life. And your children's.'

I nodded, thanked him again for his hospitality and turned away.

When I reached the front gate, it swung open automatically and I passed through, knowing that I would never do so again. As I turned the corner out of sight, I heard the front door shut with a sorry little click.

It was just over a mile to the station. I decided to walk so that I could think. Somehow, I knew the way.

Maybe I would always know the way, no matter how many years passed.

This was the way my mother and I had gone when we had fled.

Suzy!

I stopped crying, looked up.

My mother was peering down at me, over the top of the bookcase. She reached out her hand.

Quick. Climb up, she told me.

I hesitated. Where's—?

He's gone.

Gone?

To the folk group concert. Come on, *hurry*.

Hurry where?

She leaned further towards me. Take my hand. Climb up. Quickly!

I did as I was told and climbed up the back of the bookcase. When I was at the top, my mother lifted me down. She smelt funny – of washing up-liquid and perspiration. There was a large red mark on her cheekbone.

Does that hurt, Mummy?

We don't have time for that, she said, leading me from the lounge. Come on.

And that's when I saw the suitcase by the front door.

We're leaving, my mother said. We have to hurry. I've packed for you, but is there anything you want to take? We don't have much space, so it would have to be small. But if there's anything you need then you have one minute to grab it now. We won't be coming back.

We won't be coming back.

I thought about that.

Now! she said, her voice shrill.

My sock, I said, and darted upstairs to my bedside drawer to retrieve my treasured sock that contained marbles, Fruit Salad chews and one of my baby teeth.

I was racing back across the landing, about to go downstairs, when I heard the front door slam.

Annie? My father was calling. Annie, I was halfway to the concert when I realised I didn't want to go without—

He stopped. What's this? he said.

My mother stepped forward. She was wearing her coat.

We're leaving, Patrick, she said.

What? Why?

You know why.

She reached for her hat and scarf.

But where are you going? he said. He looked absolutely astounded.

I put my sock in my pocket, crouched down and watched them between the banisters. He didn't know I was there, hiding in the shadows. It felt like the only advantage.

What about Suzy? he said. She needs me.

No, she doesn't, she said. Not like this. Not someone like you.

She lowered her voice. You're sick. You need help. We can't raise a child like this. It's not fair on anyone, least of all Suzy.

To my dismay, he began to cry then, hat in hand.

Don't leave me, Annie, he said. I'm begging you.

I've made up my mind, she said. We're going. Please don't follow us. Good luck in life. I hope you find peace.

He was really sobbing now. No. Don't say that, Annie. Don't say that.

The thing was, the way I saw it from above, my mother was saying that she was going to leave and my father was telling her, no, she wasn't. The suitcase was by the door, I was up here and my mother was in the hallway. And to get both me and the case and reach the front door, we all had to get past my father.

There was no way that we were getting out of here.

My father was moving towards my mother, slowly, his arm outstretched as though approaching a lion that had escaped from the zoo.

You're not leaving, Annie, he was saying. If you leave, you know I'll find you. I'll never stop looking for you. There's no point running.

Think of Suzy, my mother said. This isn't what you want for her, surely? What will become of her if she stays here? Let her go, Patrick. I beg of you. Set her free.

It was the most impassioned speech I ever heard my mother make. I had never heard her speak like that before and never did again. It threw all of us for a moment, even my father. He paused. I'd like to say that it was because he was considering her plea – the moral dilemma that it presented – but to my horror he was doing something else entirely.

He was unbuckling his belt, pulling it off his waistband in a silent snaking of leather.

Would he hit her with it? Strangle her? He was holding it tautly in his hands and my mother had stopped still as though movement might betray her presence.

She did one little thing.

He didn't even notice, didn't appear to at least.

She lifted her eyes and looked at me. It was only fleeting, over in a flash.

I let go of the banisters and sank back into the shadows, looking about for my weapon.

It took me two seconds.

14

I went back along the private road from Keith Gunnell's to the main road, my hands deep inside my coat pockets, my face pressed into my scarf, my footsteps seeming louder for the lack of noise around me. I wanted to think about the money, about what had been happening at home in Bath that had led me to this point, but instead my thoughts kept being pulled backwards.

As I crossed the bridge over the river and passed by the park, I barely noticed my whereabouts and the landscape around me. All I knew was that I didn't feel alone – had my mother beside me, urging me to hurry. *Hurry.*

Crouching in the dark at the top of the stairs, not daring to make a sound, I reached out to the table by the wall and tried to pick up the ashtray.

I couldn't lift it with one hand. It was too heavy. I stood quietly and picked it up with both hands.

I didn't like it much. It belonged to my father and I didn't know that it was an ashtray at the time, but thought it was an empty fruit bowl. It was made from green glass and had circular segments like a flower. Turned upside down, it would have looked like the moulded lime jelly we had eaten for tea.

In my hands, it felt huge – the size of a small dinner plate.

Please, Patrick, my mother was saying. Don't.

I positioned myself above him.

Why do you make it so difficult, Annie? he said. Why can't I—

I let go.

There was a horrible thud, a moment of silence and then another thud as my father hit the floor.

I thought that the ashtray would smash, but it was solid and our carpets were thick, and my father's skull had broken its fall.

I stared at the blood seeping onto the carpet. My mother was holding her hands to her face. Then she looked up at me in dread.

Suzy! What have you done?

I began to cry. I don't know what I was expecting to happen if I dropped a heavy weight on his head, but it wasn't this.

Quick! My mother was shouting at me. Come downstairs. Now!

I was howling. My mother took me firmly by the arms and shook me. Stop it, Suzy. Stop it! I can't think!

I stopped crying. My mother stood there, staring at my father. He was lying face down in a growing patch of dark crimson blood.

Should we call an ambulance? I said.

No. We have to go, she said. Get your coat. Now!

I did as I was told, pulled my coat down from its peg.

My mother made for the door.

Mummy! I said. Your shoes!

She looked down, saw that she was in her slippers. And that's when she began to laugh and I thought it such a strange thing to do that for a moment I wondered if I had driven her to insanity.

I ran to get her shoes for her. We were in such a flummox that we almost forgot the suitcase. I grabbed that too.

And then my mother hurried me out of the front door and we both stood there for an instant, looking back in, our breath visible in the night air, before she slammed the door shut and we left.

Outside, it was freezing cold, was snowing. My mother wasn't laughing now, but whimpering. It was a funny sound. I listened to her strange noises and held her hand and realised that I didn't have a clue where we were going – that I was still wearing my birthday dungarees and had special ribbons in my hair. I remembered my sock then and felt inside my pocket to see if it was still there. But thinking of the Fruit Salad sweets inside the sock made me cry. My father had bought them for me. I had killed the man who bought me sweets. I had killed my own father.

I thought of standing up in court with men wearing wigs, and officers of the law taking me away, and my going to prison, which would be wet, dark, smelly – worse than being trapped behind the bookcase in our lounge. I felt guilt burning my insides and was wretched with the fear that this would be how I would feel now for all eternity.

The train station was before me. As I approached the imposing building with its clock tower, a sudden gust of wind blew debris – a crisp packet, twigs, leaves – rustling past me. I checked my watch, then pulled my ticket from my bag. My train wasn't leaving for nearly two hours. I didn't want to linger in Carlisle, would speak to someone about the possibility of catching an earlier train to Glasgow and wait there instead. Then I would ring Mike.

As I glanced up at the clock tower, I could see not February rain in the air but November snow.

My mother was tugging on my hand, urging me to go faster. I was holding my other hand to my hood as my ears were throbbing with the cold. My mother's hair was scraggly, wet with snow. I could see the bruise on her face underneath the station's lights.

I looked up at the clock tower, wondering if I would ever see it again, but my mother was telling me to hurry, that our train was leaving in two minutes.

We didn't have tickets. My mother said we would pay on the train. She tugged my hand and we ran down the platform, knocking into people, who cursed at us as we ran on. My mum pulled on the train handle just as the whistle blew and a man in a hat told us it was too late to get on, but my mum already had the door open and one leg on, so she jumped inside and pulled me after her.

The man at the turnstile examined my ticket, said there was no problem with my taking an earlier train to Glasgow.

I thanked him and made my way to the platform, glancing at a poster on the wall that said that Carlisle was Britain's most haunted station. I paused, read the text. The station was a Grade II listed building with an underground labyrinth of tunnels, built on an old slum site known as the Fever Pit.

I carried on through to the platform. It was very quiet. I could hear the snack machine buzzing beside me. I sat down on a bench, watched a rat scurrying along the train track, tried not to think about the tunnels below.

I would ring Mike from the train, I decided. I wouldn't tell him about the money over the phone though, would wait until I got home.

I glanced about the platform. There was an old lady on the next bench along from me wearing green tights that were absurdly baggy on her thin ankles. She was singing to herself.

I felt relief then – finally allowed myself to feel it.

I had spent my life bearing the guilt of something I had not done.

My mother needn't have hidden, not for the past ten years since my father's death, at least. She could have lived that decade to the full. I would always regret that she hadn't had the chance to do so.

He hadn't died the night we had left him. He had died in a car crash twenty-five years later than that.

And *that* was the truth.

'What a relief,' I said into my scarf. ' . . . After all these years.' I looked about me again, checking that there was no one around. But there was still no one there – just me, the old lady, the rat and the lost souls floating in the Fever Pit below.

'It wasn't me, Mum. I didn't kill him.'

We made our way through to the carriage, where it was deathly quiet. My mother was panting for breath, trying not to do so too loudly, as was I. She led me all the way to the end of the carriage where there was no one around. We chose a pair of seats that were poorly lit and without a table, so that no one would trouble us.

She took our coats off and folded them up, placing them and the suitcase above us. And then she sat down, smoothed her hair, picked up my hand, placed it on her lap and gazed past me, out of the window.

I had to ask.

Am I going to prison, Mummy?

No, she said, shaking her head. You're going to Bath.

Bath? I said. Where's Bath?

Shush! She glanced around us. Keep your voice down, Suzy.

But where's Bath? I whispered.

She reached into her pocket and pulled out a clean tissue, unfolded it and then pulled a lipstick from her other pocket and used it as a pen.

This is us now, she said, drawing a circle at the top of the tissue. We're right at the top of the country.

Then she drew another circle, further down the tissue, a bit to the left.

And this is where we need to go, she said.

I gazed at those circles in wonder. Maybe there was a chance that I wouldn't go to prison or to hell. Maybe this new place, Bath, would be fantastic.

I looked out of the window. It was dark. I couldn't see anything now, other than our reflections. After a short while, I could see that my mother was crying.

I'm sorry, Mummy, I told her. And I'm sorry about your face. It looks sore.

It is sore, she said. But it's the last one.

I had one more question.

Is he dead?

She sniffed, used the tissue to wipe her eyes. I don't know, she said.

I felt the guilt burn again. I wriggled in my seat.

She set her eyes on me. You mustn't torture yourself, Suzy. This isn't your fault. You understand? It's not your fault.

It was because you told me to do it, I said.

She looked shocked. I told you to do it?

Yes, I said. You looked at me for help.

She paused in recollection. Yes, I did, she said.

She took my hand again, held it.

It's going to be all right, Suzy. It's going to work out. We've got each other.

She turned in her seat to look at me, her expression very serious.

It's going to be obvious that it was us. So, we're going to have to hide. And we mustn't speak of it again – not to anyone. You understand?

OK, I said, nodding.

It sounded like a tall order, but I wasn't in a position to argue.

We'll never know when this is going to catch up with us, Suzy. We'll have to stay on our toes.

OK, I said again.

She looked ahead then, at the back of the seat in front of her.

There's a YMCA in the city centre that we'll stay in until we get ourselves straight. We'll need to change our names.

Change our names? I said in awe.

Of everything we were doing, that sounded the most extreme – not leaving someone for dead or taking off on a train to traverse the length of the country.

What will we call ourselves? I asked.

She smiled sadly.

Stone, she said.

PRELIMINARY MEETING

Monday 27 March, 2017

'Well, I think we've covered everything for now,' Dan says, putting his pen back in his shirt pocket and closing his file. 'We did a pretty good job, don't you think?' He smiles at me.

I return the smile, even though it's the last thing I feel like doing.

I reach to the floor for my bag and then stand up, my limbs stiff and achy where I have been holding myself so rigid.

'The important thing,' he says, standing up and moving towards the door, 'is that we've made a start. You were brave. You got the ball rolling.'

I don't feel brave.

'What happens now?' I ask, following him out to the corridor. We are moving along the narrow corridor again, floorboards creaking. From behind a closed door, someone laughs abrasively, startling me.

Dan is holding the white door open. 'I'll give you a call later this afternoon once I've checked my schedule and we'll go from there.'

I nod. He reaches for my hand. 'Thank you for coming in, Suzy,' he says.

And then the white door closes and I am left standing in the reception.

Momentarily, I feel lost, panicky.

I'm no longer in that confidential room with Dan Cassidy, nor am I out on the street of normal life with the shoppers and tourists.

I'm in limbo.

15

I pulled up outside our house, turned off the car engine, sat still, thinking.

I was exhausted, felt as though I had lived a lifetime in one day. The dashboard clock said that it was five o'clock.

I had made it home in time for tea.

I wanted to cry and laugh at that, had so many different emotions. I wanted to run in and see my family and tell them that I was free, *free!*

But I didn't move. Instead, I watched the rain falling softly underneath the street light.

Who would have believed it: my father had left me a fortune?

Except that he hadn't bestowed it on me. I hadn't been in his life, had walked out of it most conclusively. The inheritance wasn't mine. I didn't want it.

Yet would Mike feel the same way? Was Keith Gunnell right in saying that the money was compensation?

I gazed at my home, so tranquil and attractive at this time of night. I would go in now and see my beautiful family.

Inside the house, it was blissfully quiet. I kicked off my shoes and looked in the mirror, putting on a dab of lip gloss and blusher before seeing Mike.

As I approached the kitchen, I could hear the children's high-pitched voices and Mike's rumbling replies.

Ruby spotted me as soon as I descended the stairs. 'Mummy!' she shouted, scraping back her chair and hurtling towards me, arms outstretched. 'You're back!' She hugged my legs.

Jake, who was colouring in at the table, tossed his pen aside and followed in his sister's wake. 'Hi, Mummy!' he said, smiling broadly at me.

I tussled his hair. 'Hello, my gorgeous boy.'

Mike, chopping onions, wiped his eyes on his sleeve. 'Welcome home,' he said. 'Everything all right?' He looked at me enquiringly, scanning my face.

'Yes,' I said. 'And I've got something incredible to tell you.'

'Eh? You didn't mention that on the train.'

'No,' I said, reaching to the table for a carrot stick and biting on it with a loud crunch. I realised that I was starving, hadn't eaten since the cake at Mr Gunnell's that morning.

I hadn't planned any of this – how to say it, when to say it. If anything, I had anticipated a glass of wine with Mike once the children were in bed, over which I would tell him the bizarre news.

But suddenly I didn't want to wait any longer.

'We're rich,' I said.

Mike stared at me.

'From selling quiche?' Jake said. 'I thought you said we—'

'No,' I said. 'My father – your grandfather – died ten years ago. And I only just found out today. That's where I've been, in my old hometown . . . ' I turned to Mike. 'He left 1.8 million.'

'Pounds?' Jake asked.

Children liked to ask the obvious. It was one of their most endearing traits.

'Yes, Jake,' I said.

There was a silence. Mike dropped his chopping knife on the floor, didn't seem to notice. 'Ten years ago?' he said, frowning.

'Yes,' I said.

'So, you . . . ?' He didn't finish the sentence.

I moved towards him. 'No,' I said. 'I didn't.'

'Didn't what, Mummy?' Jake asked.

All this time, Ruby had been gazing up at us. Suddenly, she burst into tears. I looked at her in surprise. 'What is it, Rubes? Why are you crying?'

'I don't want to move,' she said, screwing up her nose, sniffing. 'I like our home.'

'And we do too,' I said. 'What makes you think we'll move?'

'Because we'll have to go and live in a palace now.'

I laughed. 'No, we won't. We'll stay right here.' And I drew her into my arms, kissing her on the tip of her nose.

Mike stooped, picked the knife up from the floor and returned to the counter. I joined him and stood watching his hands rhythmically, mechanically chopping onion.

'I have so much to tell you,' I said. 'It's been a really strange day. But it's all good, I think.' I placed my hand into the back pocket of his jeans, kept it there.

Suddenly, Mike tossed the knife aside. 'Stuff this,' he said. 'We've just inherited 1.8 million. We're eating out!'

Everyone began to talk at once. Ruby wanted fish and chips; Jake wanted pizza. Mike was protesting, saying that it was more of a gourmet burger night.

They were already up the stairs, getting their coats, grabbing shoes and hats. 'Wrap up warm,' Mike was saying. 'It's chilly out, right, Mummy?'

'Yes, it is,' I said, following them.

Halfway up the stairs, I thought I heard a noise behind me.

I stopped, listened. Mike and the children were already on the next level, their voices distant, echoing.

I looked at the back door and the window beside it. There was a glass panel in the top of the door. I could see the bottom half of my reflection in the glass, elevated as I was.

I could have sworn that something had passed by the glass panel.

Perhaps it was my own reflection.

'Mummy?' Mike was shouting. 'Where are you?'

'Coming!' I shouted back.

And turned out the light.

The next day, Mike and I ate lunch together, meeting in the deli kitchen for a plate of cold meats and salad. Mike had just been to the gym, was wearing a black beanie hat that framed his brown eyes nicely.

'So, are you sure about this?' he said.

'I think so,' I said, pronging a salad leaf with my fork. 'It seems like the right thing to do for the kids. And for you.'

'Leave me out of it,' he said. 'Seriously. This is your money, your family – your decision.'

'No, it's not. It affects all of us.'

'But I want you to take it for the right reasons.'

'Which are?'

'To secure the kids' futures . . . And our retirement, perhaps.'

'And I couldn't agree more,' I said.

'But you don't have to do it for me. I mean, of course the money would be great and all that. But you don't need to use it to smooth the way.' He looked at me earnestly. 'I'm OK with everything you've told me. All right?'

'Thank you,' I said, placing my hand on his knee.

We ate without talking for a few minutes, with the noise from the shop floor interrupting our thoughts – plates clattering, chairs scraping, the phone ringing.

'I'd better not be too long,' I said.

'No. Sounds busy out there,' he said, pushing his empty plate away and picking up his beanie hat. 'Can I do anything to lighten the load – call the solicitor, get the paperwork trail going? These things can be a real nightmare.'

I considered the offer.

'No,' I said. 'I'll be all right ... I'd like to do it myself – to earn it, if that makes sense. I'll call Keith Gunnell tonight. And if it gets too much, I can always ask him to act on our behalf where possible.'

'Sounds sensible,' Mike said, standing up. 'Parents' evening tonight, don't forget.' He kissed me on the forehead. 'Meet you here at three.'

'Yes,' I said, smiling. 'See you at three.'

I had completely forgotten.

My friends met me after-hours two days later. I had summoned them with the promise of news, so when they arrived they made even more noise entering the deli than usual.

Leo had already gone home. I had switched the fairy lights on in the book corner and along the front of the counter, dimming the main lights. The deli had the pre-loved look that it acquired after a busy day.

I watched my friends as they chatted on the sofa by the book corner, whilst I made the drinks. Nicole was looking especially beautiful in a midnight-blue dress. Donna was yawning repeatedly; her husband was away in Dubai.

'Try doing it *all* the time on your own,' Nicole said.

'I do,' Donna said, yawning again. 'Just because I've got a husband, doesn't mean he's any use.'

'Not everyone can have a Mike,' Helen said. 'Or maybe we can ... Can we rent him, Suzes? What's he like at ironing?'

'I wouldn't know. I do it ... I don't just swan around the deli, serving lattes, you know,' I said, whilst handing the lattes round.

'So, what's this news?' Nicole said.

'Well . . . ' I said, sitting down and picking up my coffee mug.

'Don't tell me.' Nicole held up her hand. 'You're a direct bloodline to the Royal Family. No. Wait. Jake's been scouted for Southampton FC and you're moving there to become a WAG.'

Donna tutted. 'For goodness' sake, let the woman speak.'

Everyone looked at me.

I sipped my latte. 'You're not going to believe me.'

'Try us,' Donna said.

'I just found out that my dad died,' I said.

'Oh,' said Helen, crestfallen. 'I'm sorry. And there we were, mucking around.'

'It's OK,' I said, glancing at them in turn. 'I mean, it wasn't recent or anything.'

'So how did you find out?' Helen asked. 'I didn't think anyone was in touch with him. Didn't he walk out on you, years ago?'

'Yes,' I said. 'He did.'

Then I rethought this automatic, well-worn response.

'Actually,' I said, 'that's not quite what happened . . . '

And I told them the truth.

When I stopped talking, there was a long silence.

'I still don't understand why you went to Carlisle on Sunday,' said Donna.

I gazed ahead of me at the shop window, watching people pass by, heads bent against the chill. 'Because after Mum's funeral, strange things started happening.'

'Like what?' said Helen.

'Little things that made me think of my father. I think now that it was my subconscious telling me to find out what happened to him. So, I did. And now I know.'

Nicole, opposite, had her mouth open, her coffee cup held mid-air. 'Wow – 1.8 million,' she said.

'Really?' said Helen, turning to look at her. 'Out of all this, *that's* what you're homing in on?'

'Well, it's a lot of money,' she said.

'Are you going to take it?' Helen asked.

''Course she is,' Nicole said. 'Why wouldn't she?'

'Because it's blood money?' Donna said.

I looked at her.

'Perhaps you could find a nicer term,' Helen suggested.

Donna shrugged. 'Just calling it what it is.'

Helen sighed.

My friends stayed with me for another hour. Afterwards, Nicole gave me a lift home. She was noticeably quiet. When we pulled up outside my house, she turned off the engine, looked at me.

'You should have told me about your dad, about what happened when you were little,' she said.

'I know,' I said. 'Mike too.'

She gazed past me, at the house. 'He didn't know?'

'No.'

She patted my hand. 'You'll get through this. Mike loves you. This is all going to work out.'

I undid my seat belt. She started the car engine.

'Nic?' I said.

'Yep?'

'I'm sorry.'

'Don't be. It's all right. Just look after yourself. And give me a shout if you need me.'

'Will do.'

As I walked away, the car window whirred down and Nicole called after me. 'Do you know what I'd do in your situation, hun? I'd take the money and run.'

I nodded, waved goodbye, went up the path to home.

Inside the hallway, I pulled my phone from my pocket,

picked up the business card from the side table and dialled Keith Gunnell's number. It was dark in the hallway. The only light was coming in from the glass panel above the door.

Keith answered after several rings.

'It's Suzy,' I said. 'I just wanted to ask you – how long do I have to decide?'

'Technically, two years,' he replied. 'Then the state will snap it up . . . If I were you – if I wanted those cats and dogs to have it – then I would get the ball rolling now.'

I hesitated.

He exhaled into the phone. The line crackled. 'Give the whole lot to charity if you like, Suzy,' he said. 'Give it to a shelter for battered wives or to the homeless. Or keep it for yourself. But just take it, for heaven's sake. And decide what to do with it later.'

The door of the drawing room opened and Mike appeared in a pool of light wearing his glasses, Ruby's reading record in his hand. 'Everything all right?' he whispered.

I nodded in response.

'OK,' I said into the phone.

'OK what?' Keith said.

'Get the ball rolling.'

'Very well,' he said. 'For what it's worth, I think you're doing the right thing.'

'I'm not so sure about that,' I said. 'But it's a decision and it is positive action, and that's what I need right now.'

'Quite right too,' he said spiritedly. And we ended the call.

16

At the end of that week, late on Friday afternoon, Tim came in to see me at the deli. My saying that he was there to see me was purely self-flattery.

We had just had our most profitable week to date. Leo had cranked up the music; the sun was out; my staff were happy, full of banter. Leo was gearing himself up for a date later with a woman whose online profile said she was a Wet Leisure Assistant, which we had worked out meant a lifeguard, much to our amusement.

Tim was listening to the conversation about wet leisure with one eyebrow raised, a look which he had mastered to some effect several decades before.

'Is everything good with you?' he asked me, drumming his fingers on the top of the counter.

'Yep. All good,' I said. 'So, what can I get you? I'm surprised to see you back so soon, I must say.'

He put his briefcase on a nearby empty table and loosened his tie, before turning back to me. He was wearing a dark blue suit with a raspberry-coloured shirt. It was very dapper, the sort of thing that Mike would never have worn.

'Yeah, well, I'm sorry about that,' he said, his dimples appearing. 'But I'm afraid you're going to be stuck with me for a while.'

'How so?' I said.

Beside me, Leo smirked to himself, whilst rearranging the pies.

Tim put his hands on his hips, his suit jacket swinging open, his flat stomach on display. I averted my gaze. 'An architectural firm are moving into the property two doors down. The owner's a friend of mine. I'm overseeing the installation of the IT software.'

'Oh,' I said. 'You are?' It took me a moment to work out where he meant. 'That's where my deli used to be.' I smiled a little awkwardly. Feeling daft, I turned away, busied myself with stacking plates. 'Are you staying to eat?' I asked over my shoulder.

'No. Just a cappuccino to go, please.'

I loved Mike; yet I also registered the disappointment that I felt on hearing this. 'Absolutely,' I said, reaching for a takeaway cup.

At moments, in Tim's presence, it was as though time had reversed and I was back working with him at JB Alliance. I wouldn't have traded my new life for anything, but still . . . nostalgia made the heart fickle and prone to fantasy.

Tim paid and left then, giving me a courteous nod as he departed.

As he passed the window outside, he pulled out his phone, began to talk. I wondered what he was saying, whom he was talking to. Probably colleagues, clients – his girlfriend or wife. I hadn't noticed a wedding ring though, to my satisfaction.

But this was all useless internal dialogue because he was already off into another world, not interested in me beyond obtaining a good coffee. His brown hair was lit by the sun; his suit glowed on its edges.

He was gone, yet the vision of him lingered. For the remainder of the working day, I saw navy blue and raspberry wherever I looked.

*

I let Leo and my other staff go home earlier than usual that evening, telling Leo to enjoy his wet leisure date. He threw a bread roll at me in response.

Mike and the children would be at football training, so I lingered in the deli's kitchen with a peppermint tea and a pile of paperwork.

When I looked up, to my surprise it was seven o'clock.

I yawned, gathered the paperwork and tipped it into my holdall along with several containers of food for supper, and then locked up the deli.

As I walked along the high street, I realised that I hadn't called Mike to tell him I was running late, so I stopped to pull my phone from my bag. I was adjacent to an old public toilet, a disused building that had fallen derelict. The site tended to attract rubbish and the occasional sleeping bag of a homeless soul seeking shelter.

Setting off again, I glanced into the darkness of the building's former entrance. It would be impossible to spot anyone standing there, yet I looked nonetheless.

It was very cold out, considering that it was March. I drew my coat about me and was about to tap the screen to connect the call to Mike, when I heard a noise behind me.

I looked over my shoulder, but there was nothing there. I quickened my pace, dialling Mike.

I was now on the corner of the high street, about to turn the corner on to the hill. Before doing so, I glanced back again and this time I glimpsed a dark shape coming out of the derelict building towards me.

I gasped, dropping my phone. It landed on the pavement with a smack.

'No!' I said, reaching down to grab it. The screen was cracked, dark – no longer ringing Mike.

I tossed the phone into my bag and ran as fast as I could

around the corner of the street, on to the hill. The holdall was so heavy. I considered tossing it into a garden, but there were important invoices inside. I firmed my grip, mounted the hill.

I looked back only once, at the point where our house came into view. I had to stop because I was feeling sick, had a stitch.

He was at the foot of the hill, approaching steadily. He was wearing a dark long jacket and a hat with flaps that obscured his face. Was it a deerstalker hat? At this distance, he was just an outline.

There were figures up ahead, coming towards me. It was a group of army cadets, the same lads that I often saw on my way home. The man wouldn't be able to do anything in their presence, underneath the street lights.

I was on the flat section of the road now. A neighbour was putting out her bins. I slowed down in order to avoid being sick, just as I passed the area of the railings where I had first seen the toy monkey.

The cadets passed me, jostling, talking loudly. I hurried up the path to home, concerned that it looked dark inside. I hadn't expected to return to an empty house.

I grappled for my keys, pushing the door open and slamming it shut behind me.

I stared ahead of me into the darkness. 'Mike?'

I glanced at the coat rack. The coats were gone, as were Mike's boots.

Why weren't they back yet?

Quickly, I turned the hallway light on, then went into the drawing room and turned the light on there. Then I ran upstairs to put the hallway and bedroom lights on. To someone outside, it would look as though the house was fully occupied.

I returned downstairs and was sitting at the bottom of the

stairs, wondering what to do next, when I heard footsteps and voices outside.

It was Mike and the children. I could hear Ruby chattering. I stood up, waited for them.

Mike came in first, shaking off his boots. 'Where have you been?' I said.

He looked at me in surprise. 'Getting groceries, like you asked. Why?'

I stared at him, having forgotten that I had rung him earlier to ask him to pick up some supplies after training.

And it was then that I burst into tears.

Jake and Ruby looked at me in dismay. 'What's wrong, Mummy?' Jake asked.

'Did you drop the milk again?' asked Ruby.

'Are you sure that it's the same bloke?' Mike said, perched on the arm of his chair. I was sitting in the opposite armchair. We were in the sitting room. The curtains were still open, the city's lights winking at us.

'No,' I said. 'I'm not sure at all. I thought that going to Carlisle would clear this up, but if anything, it's getting worse. Going there changed nothing.'

I frowned, glanced at the clock. The children were in bed, reading. I would have to go upstairs shortly to put their light out.

'Maybe I'm going insane,' I said.

''Course you're not,' Mike said.

Then I thought of something. 'You must have passed him in the street when you drove by. Didn't you see him?'

Mike shook his head. 'Not that I noticed.'

'Then I *am* going insane.'

He stood up, approached, stopping before me. 'Look, Suzy,' he said, 'don't be so hard on yourself. Jumping to the conclusion that you're crazy isn't going to help anyone, least of all you.'

'I was sort of joking,' I said. 'At least, I think I was.'

'Just give yourself a little time and some breathing space. You haven't stopped. It's only been a few weeks since your mum died, remember?'

I gazed up at him, grateful for this reminder – clutching at it. My mother hadn't been dead very long and somehow, I hadn't factored this in.

It made me feel better. And then worse. Because if there wasn't someone following me, then it was all in my mind.

But why? I didn't believe that grief in itself was enough to do this to me. There had to be more to it.

Mike was continuing to speak, stooping to place his hand on my shoulder. 'I can help out more. Just say what needs doing. And get Leo to do more at the deli too.' He squeezed my shoulder. 'Delegate, my love.'

I stared at him. 'Delegating isn't going to stop me from seeing things!'

'How do you know you're seeing things?' He moved behind me then, massaging my shoulders as he spoke. 'You're not running from the bogeyman, Suzy. This is obviously something.'

'But I don't know what it is. I mean, it could have been someone following me. Or it could have been . . . '

'What?'

'Well, it could have just been someone walking home.'

'You couldn't tell the difference?'

'No,' I said. 'I was too busy running away. I wasn't going to wait around to see whether he was going to clarify his intentions.'

'Fair enough,' Mike said. 'But that's exactly what we need: clarification. We need to know whether this bloke's real, and if so, what he wants. So, until he does something to prove his existence, all we can do is watch and wait – which is what we've already agreed to do. And in the meantime, you have to try to help yourself a bit.'

'Meaning?'

'Taking every chance that you get to relax . . . Starting now.' He picked up the remote control and dropped it on my lap, a grand gesture; he never parted with the remote. 'Find something for us to watch on telly. And I'll go get the wine.'

Whilst he was gone, I flicked through the TV channels restlessly.

We had to watch and wait, Mike had said. But I liked to do things, to make things happen.

I hated watching and waiting.

That night, I couldn't get to sleep. I rolled around the bed fitfully, beyond tired, words and pictures swirling in my mind.

In my frustration, I made the mistake of reaching for my phone to check the time – three o'clock in the morning – and found myself surfing the internet.

I typed in: *seeing things.*

The first item took me to a webpage entitled *Experiences of psychosis.* I didn't want to read about the symptoms. I wanted to know what caused hallucinations. I scrolled down.

Drugs; dementia; brain tumours; mental illness; intense stress.

I stopped there, read the paragraph about stress, pausing on one line in particular.

Strong emotions such as grief can cause people to imagine that they see loved ones after their recent death, for example.

Mike shifted position in bed beside me. I put my phone away, lay down again.

I hadn't just lost my mother, but my father too. Given what had taken place in the past, I would be foolish not to factor grief into this – the impact of their deaths on my mental state.

Was the man who was following me something to do with my parents – a manifestation of grief, guilt?

I closed my eyes, tried once more to sleep.

It seemed to me that the best possible outcome of this was that the man would prove himself to be real, meaning that I wasn't delusional.

And yet surely that would also be the worst.

PRELIMINARY MEETING

Monday 27 March, 2017

As I pass the receptionist, she stops typing. 'Is there anything else we can do for you today?' she asks.

'No, thank you,' I say.

I note that a couple of the chairs are occupied. It's impossible to tell in a glance whether the two people know each other. The man – very young – is jigging his leg so vigorously that I want to place my hand on his knee and tell him to stay calm.

No one should have to come here alone. Yet they do. Day in, day out, people arrive and leave.

'Bye for now,' the receptionist calls after me.

I don't reply. I am too busy concentrating on keeping my emotions in check.

I now know why that man looked so distraught leaving here earlier. You hold yourself together so much in that little room, beyond that white door, that when you get outside it's all you can do not to choke on your tears.

As the cold air meets me and a group of little schoolchildren in winter hats files past on the pavement below, I find myself overcome with sadness.

I have crossed a line coming here. I have set something in motion that cannot be undone.

At the foot of the steps, a woman is hovering, looking up at me fearfully, just as I was before.

I want to smile at her reassuringly, but I am too upset. Instead, I blow my nose, turn my collar up and hurry off.

17

The next night, Saturday, Ruby had a ballet recital at the top of town. As I was working during the afternoon, getting her ready was a hectic affair. I didn't have time to eat, concentrated instead on fixing Ruby's hair into a perfect bun. She trotted diva-like out to the car, spreading her tutu out around her on the back seat, which Jake said was annoying as the gauze prickled his legs.

'Don't sit so closey then,' Ruby said, thumping him.

'Hey!' I said.

I was driving; Mike was in the passenger seat. 'Cut it out now,' Mike said. 'Mummy can't concentrate if you're fighting . . . It's dangerous.'

We crossed the city quickly. At just after six o'clock, there was little traffic. It was all going fine, until we met the steep hill on the other side of Bath, together with a sheet of thick rain. The windscreen wipers were on full; the windows had steamed up; the hill was such a harsh incline it felt as though we were about to aquaplane backwards.

'I can't see a damned thing,' I said, squinting.

Mike drew the windows down an inch either side of us and adjusted the fan on the dashboard. They were blowing so loudly I could barely hear him speak. 'Take it nice and easy. There's no rush. We've plenty of time.'

That wasn't quite true, but I didn't want to argue.

I didn't like night-driving, but Mike had had a beer whilst watching the rugby earlier, so I was the designated driver. My head was throbbing with the start of a headache. I gripped the wheel tensely, hoping to make it up the hill in one piece.

To my relief, I spotted the sign for the school where the recital was taking place and turned into the entrance gate and on to the flat, where I felt infinitely safer.

Inside the school, it was sweltering. Families were peeling off wet coats, shaking umbrellas. There was little space between the rows of chairs; we were all crammed together.

Ruby and her classmates danced to the 'Sugar Plum Fairy' and 'The Entertainer' as best as they could at their tender age; and then she was done.

During the interval, we shamefully contemplated leaving. But Ruby begged us to stay for the second half. Mike was talking to a father about the rugby; Jake was locking heads with another boy, staring at a phone. And I found myself by the drinks table, picking up a complimentary white wine.

It was so soothing, so welcome, I gulped it too quickly, swivelling around on my heel, looking for parents to chat to. But everyone seemed occupied and so I stood alone, with my thoughts, enjoying the wine.

It was only in the second half when the lights dimmed that I realised my error.

'I'm sorry,' I whispered to Mike. 'I completely forgot. I had a drink.'

Mike went to reply, but the music was booming from the loud speakers.

During a quiet moment, he whispered into my ear. 'I can drive. I only had one beer.'

'Oh,' I whispered back. 'Thank you.'

He touched my knee, kept his hand there.

But I couldn't concentrate on the stage, on the children dancing. I was wondering instead how I had managed to drink a large glass of wine on an empty stomach with no recollection of the fact that I was supposed to be driving.

After the recital, Mike drove us home. The rain had stopped, the streets were shiny. I listened to the sound of the tyres whispering along through the puddles.

'You all right?' Mike said, glancing at me.

'Yep,' I said.

'You seem quiet.'

'I'm just thinking.'

'About?'

'About how I managed to forget I was driving.' I looked behind me at the children. They were talking animatedly, Jake telling Ruby about the game he had played on the boy's phone. I faced forward again. 'I seem to be forgetting a lot lately.'

'Well, like I said last night: you're tired and stressed. And until we know for sure who or what you've been seeing then we need to—'

'I don't think it's just that, Mike ... I think ... well, maybe there's something wrong with me.'

'Like what?'

'I don't know. You tell me. I'm not sleeping. I'm on edge. I can't concentrate. And then there's' – I looked at the children again; they were still talking, not listening to us – 'that man following me, who may or may not be real ...' I trailed off, gazed at Mike. He was staring at the road ahead. 'What does it sound like to you?'

I thought of the list of possible diagnoses that I had read on my phone last night: *dementia; brain tumours; mental illness; intense stress.*

Mike had stopped at a pelican crossing, was waiting for a

mother and three children to cross. It was several minutes before he replied.

'Have you considered that it might be PTSD?'

'PT whatty?' I said.

'Post-traumatic stress disorder. I know a little bit about some of the symptoms. One of the lads in my unit suffered from it. Sounds similar to what you're describing.'

I looked at him. 'Are you serious? Why would it be that?'

'I'm not saying that it is.'

'Then what are you saying?'

'Just that you experienced a trauma in the past, which was suppressed for many years. And now, possibly because of your mum's death and the news about your father, you're imagining him in the present, reliving some of the trauma, experiencing some symptoms.'

'Like what?'

'Suzy,' he said gently. 'Did you or did you not start this conversation saying that you thought there was something wrong with you? It feels as though you're trying to catch me out. But I'm just trying to help. I'm on your side.'

I wasn't aware that I was sounding antagonistic. I tried to soften my tone. 'So, you think that my symptoms match?'

He scratched his head, ruffled his fringe. 'Some of them, yes. With PTSD you can experience flashbacks, nightmares, repetitive mental images, feelings of guilt. There can also be emotional numbing, which is basically where you don't talk about the trauma or deal with it. There's also hyper-arousal, which is feeling on edge, and problems sleeping and concentrating . . . ' He glanced at me. 'Any of that fit?'

I swallowed hard, looked ahead of me. 'So, what, I have a serious problem?' It was raining again. The windscreen wipers began to move melancholically, scraping the glass.

Mike took my hand. 'You had a difficult start in life and it's finally caught up with you, that's all. Even if it's nothing to do with what you've been experiencing lately, the fact remains that you're having to deal with some tricky stuff.'

'So, what do I do?'

He paused. 'Well, you could always talk it through with someone?'

'Like who?' I said. 'A therapist?'

'If that's what it takes, then yes. Maybe consider it.'

I shook my head. 'No. I mean, I'm sure it's the recommended route, but I really feel that I'm OK with the past – now more than ever. I don't see how dwelling on it is going to help.'

'It's not dwelling on it, Suzy. It's dealing with it. There's a difference.'

'No,' I said. 'I'm not doing it. I want to get on with my life, not keep looking backwards.'

'All right,' he said. 'Then what about seeing the GP?'

'What for?'

'To get something to help you sleep and to relax, for starters – something to get you through this in the short term.'

'You mean medication?' I asked.

'Maybe, yes. You don't need to talk about the past or get into specifics. You can just say you're stressed and need something to help you relax. She'll understand. It's common enough.'

I didn't speak again until we pulled up outside the house. The children unbuckled and jumped out of the car, running up the path and around the concrete forecourt, darting in and around the potted plants, Ruby still in her tutu.

'OK,' I told Mike, as I got out of the car. 'I'll see the doctor.'

'Good,' he said. 'Do you want me to come with you? It might help.'

The last time someone had gone to the doctor's with me

was when my mum had taken me during my teens about period cramps.

'No. I'll be fine,' I said. 'But thanks for the offer.'

'What sort of hallucinations?' said Doctor Hill.

'Well, I wouldn't use that word, exactly,' I replied.

I hadn't intended to discuss anything in detail. However, within moments of sitting down in the consulting room that Tuesday morning, I had told the GP that I'd been having some strange experiences of late.

I think it was because she had grey hair in a bun and a reserved demeanour, both of which reminded me of my mum. Whatever it was, I wanted her to take care of me and knew that in order for her to do so, I would have to give her something more than *I'm a bit stressed*.

'What word would you use then?' the doctor asked, her fingers poised on the keyboard.

'I can't say for sure. Which is why I'm here, in the hope that you can help me and tell me what's wrong.'

I closed my mouth, fell quiet.

Maybe I had said too much and she would definitely suggest a shrink now and I would have to go back over the Carlisle mess, just as I was starting to feel free of it.

'Look,' she said, spinning round in her chair to face me, taking her glasses off and letting them dangle on their chain. 'I think, personally, from everything you've told me, that there's nothing wrong with you. You're tired, grieving, working, parenting . . .' she paused, before getting to the final point '. . . anxious.' She put her glasses back on, turned back to the keyboard. 'Anxiety is the only thing I'd diagnose at this stage – mild anxiety at that.'

She continued to talk whilst typing. 'I'm going to prescribe temazepam. It's best used as a short-term solution. It'll help you sleep and keep you calm.' She hit a key vigorously and the printer chugged to life behind her. 'Take two before bed for two days, then one for three days. Then come back and see me.' She handed me the prescription. 'Don't drive if you're feeling sleepy. And don't drink alcohol during the course of medication.'

'Are there any side effects?' I asked.

She smiled faintly. 'Yes. You may feel light-headed, confused, aggressive, forgetful. You may also get blurred vision or headaches. Come and see me if you have any problems.'

I folded the prescription up, put it in my pocket. 'I don't see the point of making me more forgetful than I already am,' I said. 'Is that wise?'

'Like I said, it's a short-term solution to get you back to where you normally are.'

'OK,' I said, nodding. 'Then I guess I'll give it a go.'

'Good,' she said.

I stood up, feeling heavy and sad all of a sudden.

As I reached for the door handle, she spoke again. 'Don't sell yourself short.'

I turned on my heel. 'Sorry?'

She lifted her shoulders, sighed. 'I've been doing this job for over thirty years,' she said. 'There's not much that I haven't seen or heard. And if there's one thing I can spot a mile off, it's a mother being hard on herself.' She sighed again. 'I raised four children, you know.'

'Really?' I said, before realising that I sounded surprised, judgementally so.

'Yes. And over the years I took criticism from all sorts of people – neighbours, colleagues, relatives, complete strangers.'

'Oh?' I said.

She nodded. 'A mother working full-time was practically unheard of back then. I had a nanny, and people were forever telling me that she was raising my children, not me. But so far as I could see, the nanny hadn't given birth to them, didn't have stretch marks or varicose veins, wasn't there holding them at night when they were poorly. And she just walked away when the contract ended, like no mother ever could. So ... you see,' she said, 'you need to take care of yourself. And don't sell yourself short. Don't come in here hinting that you're failing or neurotic. You're fine.'

I was touched by her speech, was welling up.

But she had already turned away and was typing again. So, I just let myself out.

18

Temazepam changed my life; at least, it did for the five days that I was taking it.

I must have been exactly the type of person that it was designed for. Others might not have benefited from it the way I did. You had to be really tense to begin with, to appreciate the way it smoothed out the knots in the body.

I had always carried myself tightly. Even at school, I was the girl with the socks pulled up straight to the knee. It was rare to catch me nowadays with a crease or stain, even in my job behind a food counter.

Whenever I went for a massage with my friends, the masseur would set to work determinedly on my shoulders, pummelling them, grinding my muscles. She could grind them all she liked; she never managed to set me loose. My shoulders were like an enchanted forest of knotted vines that grew back the moment they were cut.

On temazepam, I could almost feel the vines unravelling, hear the crack and hiss of bark and leaves creeping forward, uncoiling, unknotting.

I went straight to sleep after taking the first two temazepam of the course, thinking to myself that it was just as well that it was addictive so I wouldn't be able to make it a permanent way of life.

What a pity.

Crack. Hiss. Forest. Vines. Knots.

And then I was asleep.

'Suzy.'

I moaned, licked my lips. I was so thirsty.

'Suzy!'

Mike was shaking my shoulder. I batted him away, pulling the duvet over my head.

There was a scraping sound as he opened the curtains. I rolled on to my other side, away from the light.

He returned, stood over me. 'It's eight o'clock,' he said. 'I've let you lie in as long as possible, but you need to—'

'Go away,' I said.

'Suzy,' he said, tugging the duvet from my grip. 'You need to get up. Come on. Let me help.'

He began to pull me up. And that's when I snapped.

I knelt up, clutching the duvet. 'Leave me alone!' I said. '*Let me sleep!*'

He stared at me in astonishment.

I bunched myself underneath the duvet again and lay back down, but I didn't feel so good now. I was dizzy and for a moment I couldn't think where I was.

'Maybe we should call the doctor,' he said.

'No,' I said, sitting up again, too quickly. I rested my head against the wall. I had pins and needles in my legs; my eyes felt grainy, heavy-lidded.

He sat down on the bed, cupping his hand to my forehead. 'What are your symptoms? How are you feeling?'

'Fine,' I murmured to my knees.

'What did the doctor say about side effects?'

'Have a read.' I pointed to the bottle of pills on the bedside table.

He unfolded the sheet of paper containing the medical information. There was a silence as he read. I didn't want to look at him, didn't want to hear that my new friend was bad for me.

'Looks like your body just needs to adjust to it,' he said, folding the piece of paper up again. 'The point is that you slept well, right? So, it has served its purpose.' He stood up. 'But you still have to go to work.'

''Course,' I said.

He frowned at me. 'Starting by getting up,' he said.

'OK, OK,' I said and was showing signs of moving, when I heard Ruby running up the stairs, shouting.

'Mummy! Jake put jam on Teddy's face! Mum*mee*!'

'I'll see to her,' Mike said, going towards the door. 'Do you want me to call the deli and say that—'

'I'll be fine,' I said. 'I'm getting up now.' I tried to smile, but my facial muscles weren't up to it and my mouth spasmed.

I waited for Mike to leave the room, for the house to fall silent, before lowering my feet on to the carpet. I stepped into my slippers, padded my way to the wardrobe and opened it.

I stood swaying, looking at my clothes, tugging on the sleeves of tops that I might or might not wear that day. In the end, I chose a plain black dress. Wearing it would be sobering, I felt.

As I struggled into the dress and brushed my hair, I began to laugh to myself. Temazepam was amazing. I couldn't wait to tell my friends about it. I was pretty sure that they had no personal experience of it. I would be their messenger.

To think that there were people out there running around at pace, taking on too much, unable to cope ... and all along there was temazepam. I could think of so many women who might benefit from it.

I put on my make-up, still smirking, before making my way downstairs.

In the kitchen, the children had finished breakfast. Jake was reading at the table, his school sweater wrapped around his head like a ninja.

When Ruby saw me, she threw her doll down and ran to me, pressing her head into my legs. 'Mummy! You're awake!'

'I haven't been in bed that long,' I said, going to the fridge in search of water.

'But you're always up before me. This is the first time that I got up first, isn't it? Normally it's you first and then it's Daddy.'

'Mmm,' I said, pulling a chair out from under the table and sitting down, sipping the glass of water.

'Sometimes Jakey is first if he has a bad cough. And sometimes it's Daddy, if you are tired. But normally it's you first and then Daddy and then me and then Jakey.'

Suddenly this didn't feel so hilarious any more. If this was what laid-back felt like then I wasn't sure that I liked it after all.

'Is my kit ready, Mummy?' Jake said, peering at me from over his book.

'Your kit?'

'For hockey,' Mike said, handing me a plate of toast, cut into triangles, coated in jam. 'I've seen to the kit. Don't worry.'

'Normally I get up about seveny. Is that right, Mummy? Yes, seveny. And then Jake ... he gets up just after me nor-mall-ee ... '

I took a mouthful of toast, chewed dispassionately.

'And there's a parents' morning where you get to come in and see my presentation. The one about Narnia?' Jake said.

Narnia. Presentation. Parents' morning.

'When, Jake?' I said.

'Today, I think, maybe. Or tomorrow.'

I looked at Mike. 'Leave it with me,' he said. And then he glanced at his watch. 'Let's all walk down together.' He forced a smile at me. Had he not done so, I would have taken his words at face value. As it was, it seemed as though he were really saying that I couldn't be trusted to make my own way down the hill.

'Super!' Ruby said, clapping her hands. She held out her hand to me. 'Let's go.'

'Oh,' I said, realising that she meant right now. I grabbed a piece of toast, gulped the last drop of water, and we went upstairs to assemble coats, bags.

Were it not for Ruby's sharp eye for accessories, I would have made my way down the hill in mismatched shoes.

If I had pictured myself floating around the deli on meds, easy breezy, it didn't turn out that way at all.

Being chilled out wasn't what I had thought it would be. I had always admired the Doc Marten mums that came into the deli with their bare faces and greying hair. Not bothering to put on a mask or to constantly tweak and groom themselves, they exuded self-acceptance. Serving them, with my glossy smile and L'Oréal hair colourant, I felt insecure by comparison – fake.

Some people were born confident; others had to fight for their place in the world, building themselves molecule by molecule. I was the latter.

That day at the deli there was a group of Doc Marten mums taking up almost the entire main room with prams and changing bags. I didn't mind, not even when Mr Hum couldn't get past them to settle his bill. In fact, I couldn't have cared less. And that was why that day was so difficult for me.

I had forgotten my holdall, so I didn't have my diary – didn't know what was going on, hoped that nothing was.

I ran out of croissants. Leo kept prodding me when I was spacing out; and when Helen called by that morning, she led me immediately to the kitchen.

'You've only got make-up on one eye,' she said delicately.

I blanched at this, putting my hand to my face. 'What?'

Why hadn't anyone told me? Maybe my staff were too polite, Leo aside.

Luckily, Helen had her make-up bag with her, so sorted my naked eye out there and then.

'There you go,' she said, drawing back to assess me. 'Perfect.'

'Thanks, H.,' I said. 'What are you doing here anyway?'

'I had a spare couple of hours and was just passing by . . . '

'Were you really?' I said. 'Or were you checking up on me?'

She smiled. 'Guilty as charged. But after what you told us the other day, I just wanted to see if you're OK . . . ' Then she frowned, glanced down at my body. 'You're getting a bit . . . skinny, my lovely. Have you lost weight?'

'Maybe,' I said. 'But there's been a lot going on. I wouldn't be surprised.'

'Then why don't you let me help out? I could do a few hours here to cover you, or take the kids out for the day to give you a break?' She stooped slightly to look in my eyes. She was tall, Helen – tall and kind.

'It's sweet of you to offer. But I'm fine. I like being busy. It helps.'

'With what?'

I shrugged. 'Everything.'

I would have told her about the temazepam then, but the doorbell had been ringing non-stop. I had to get back to work.

She packed up her make-up with a sigh, kissed me goodbye and departed.

Before returning to the shop floor, I phoned the doctor. I wanted to know whether it was normal to be so out of it. But Doctor Hill wasn't available. So, I just got on with the rest of the day, trying to do as little damage to myself and to the deli as possible.

Doctor Hill returned my call later, as I was locking up.

'Everyone reacts differently,' she told me.

'But does this sound right? I barely know what I'm doing.'

'Well, if it's bothering you then stop taking it. And we'll review it. Just book an appointment.'

'No, it's OK,' I said. 'I'll see how I get on tonight.'

'As you wish,' she replied. 'But call me tomorrow if you're still concerned.'

I hung up, set off for home, my arms flopping uselessly at my sides, lost without my diary and holdall.

My mouth was dry with a thirst that couldn't be quenched; I couldn't have drunk any more water than I already had. My head had been hurting all day and my vision was blurry. I couldn't think straight, was torn between laughing and sobbing. Yet despite this – or perhaps because of it – I was looking forward to bed and to another deep sleep.

Once again, I took two tablets as instructed, before slipping eagerly underneath the bed sheets.

Beside me, Mike was reading, glasses on, his fringe dangling on to the frames, his mouth pouting in concentration. I would have reached out and pushed his hair away from his eyes or kissed his lips, if it weren't for the fact that my limbs felt so heavy. So, I left him alone and within moments was asleep.

My mum came to me almost immediately, so it felt.

Hello, Suzy, she said warmly, as though she weren't dead or even living away from me. With her finger, she drew a pattern in the velveteen surface of the fleece blanket. *This is you here*, she was saying. She drew a circle on the blanket. *And this is me.* Two circles next to each other. *And we need to get here.* She reached as far across the blanket as her arm would reach.

I had a feeling I had heard this somewhere before.

I flicked my foot. It felt tickly. I was so thirsty.

Something was happening to my foot, I realised then; it was being touched.

I opened my eyes, but my mind was slow to follow, wanted to remain with my mum. If I woke up, she would be gone and I might not ever see her again.

But I had to wake. Something was wrong.

A warning signal was circulating languidly around my body. Flight or fight wasn't supposed to work that way. Temazepam was no friend to my natural defence system, was working against me now.

I was facing the windows, my back to Mike. A chink of light was spilling underneath the curtains, but it wasn't enough to see by. It was the darkest of nights. Yet I could see something out of the corner of my eye, at the foot of our bed.

Worse, I could feel it. It was touching me.

I wouldn't be able to jump up quickly enough – would be sluggish, cumbersome. So, I called for help.

'Mike,' I said, but my voice was croaky. I tried again. '*Mike*.'

I wrenched my foot away. There was a rushing sound then as someone ran towards the door.

I tried to get up, but toppled forwards, catching my leg in the duvet. I didn't know if it was the medication or panic, but it felt as though my blood were bulging inside me, too big for my veins.

I sat up with my head in my hands, feeling faint, fighting to stay conscious.

Mike was up now, grappling for the light. 'Stay there, Suzy!' he shouted as he hurried to the door. 'Don't move!'

Where was he going? After the man? Was the man real? Was I even awake?

I stood up, went to the wardrobe, opened the door and consulted the mirror within, swaying unsteadily. I looked ghastly. I had lost all colour from my cheeks. My eyes were sunken. I was coated in perspiration.

I put my hands to my face and was wiping myself dry, when I realised that I couldn't stay here as instructed. I had to help Mike.

I left the room, my legs wobbling as I made my way downstairs.

Mike had put the lights on as he had passed them. He wasn't that far ahead of me; I could hear him. I tried to speed up. 'Mike?' I called in a whisper. 'Mike?'

When I got to the ground-floor hallway, Mike was coming towards me, away from the front door.

'How the heck did he get in?' he said, more to himself than to me. And then he frowned at me disapprovingly. 'I thought I told you to wait upstairs?'

'I didn't want to,' I said.

He turned away, heading towards the next flight of stairs. I followed after him, willing my legs not to give out beneath me.

Downstairs in the kitchen, all was quiet, untouched, just as we had left it.

I looked about me in a stupor. But Mike wasn't stopping, had gone through to the lower hallway, which ran between the storeroom and the utility room.

He was making for the tradesman's entrance. We rarely used this passageway, only when we wanted to bring bicycles in and out of the house. It wasn't an easy place to navigate, narrow, with bikes and the children's scooters leaning against the walls.

The light was poor here – a single wall lantern halfway down the passageway, inadequately casting light upwards. Mike had stopped, so I stopped too. He was using the torch on his phone, casting the beam around him.

I held my breath, watched him. I was standing next to Ruby's bike, the pink and silver handlebar tassels fluttering noiselessly in the breeze.

The breeze?

I saw it the moment that Mike lifted his phone to illuminate it: the ugly gash in the door where the window had been smashed.

'Oh, no,' I said, putting my hand to my mouth.

'Those things that you've been seeing?' Mike said, turning to look at me, his expression grim. 'Looks like they've just turned real.'

My stomach shifted fearfully. I placed my hand against Ruby's bike for support, watching Mike's torch as it made its way along the floor, tracing the trail of glass.

'What's happening, Mike?' I said.

'I don't know,' he said. 'But we're going to find out.'

He keyed a number into his phone, the screen illuminating his face, casting ghastly blue shadows.

'Ed?' he said into his phone, then laughed very briefly. 'Yeah, long time, mate.' His face grew serious again. 'Don't suppose you can swing by tonight, can you? I've got something I need you to look at as soon as possible.'

Something caught my eye then. There was a long shard of glass lying right by my bare foot, like an arrow pointing to me.

He hung up. 'They're on their way,' he said.

THE INFORMATION AND ASSESSMENT MEETING

Wednesday 29 March, 2017

I am back here already, sooner than I had expected.

I don't feel braver for knowing what lies beyond. I feel sick, afraid. I think I will feel that way no matter how many times I walk up these steps.

It's the same receptionist as before. 'How can I help you?' she says.

'I'm Suzy Taylor. I have an eleven o'clock.'

'Take a seat,' she says. 'Mr Cassidy will be right with you.'

To my surprise, I'm the only one here. Am I early? I look at my watch. No, I'm right on time.

I pick up a magazine, scan the pages.

The front door opens then and I set my face to amicable, welcoming, but it's a very thin woman in a too-thin coat. She looks pale, cold.

'I'd like to see Mr Cassidy,' she tells the receptionist.

'I'm afraid that's going to be tricky,' the receptionist says.

'Oh,' the woman says, glancing about her, her mouth wobbling. I look away, down at my magazine. 'Could I wait for him?'

'It'll be a long wait. He has a full diary. Perhaps if—'

But the white door has opened and Dan Cassidy is standing there, a veritable knight in shining eyewear.

I can't tell if he is looking at me, since his thick glasses are catching the light. The woman is edging towards him. 'I need to see you,' she says. 'I'm really sorry to burst in like this. But I'm . . . ' She lowers her voice; I hear her anyway. '. . . going out of my mind.'

I remain seated, watching them nervously, my stomach churning.

I wonder how far along this woman is, whether she is at the beginning or the end?

And of what?

I have no idea what I have signed up for, no idea what really lies at the end of that corridor, beyond that innocent-looking white door.

19

Mike didn't go back upstairs to wait for the police but went outside instead.

I followed him. 'Where are you going?' I asked.

'To take a look around,' he said.

I didn't know what to do, was freezing cold, but didn't want to go back indoors. Then I recalled that the children were inside. Should I have gone upstairs before now to check on them? I looked at Mike for guidance, but he was crouched down examining the flagstones.

He was heading back indoors now, picking a safe passage across the glass. 'Come this way,' he said, pointing to the left side. 'Bloody daft that we're doing this in bare feet. But still . . .'

We were going into the utility room. I was trailing behind, numb, bewildered. Then into the storeroom. Mike was out of breath with the effort of walking on his bad leg at this time of night. At the threshold of each room, he reached for the light, pushing the door open with his back against the wall, one arm outstretched towards me protectively.

'What are we doing?' I said, as we made our way up to the ground floor.

He halted outside the drawing room. 'There could be someone still here,' he whispered.

I hadn't thought of that.

'Could even be two of them. Maybe more. We need to make sure no one's inside the house.'

I nodded meekly, clamped my mouth shut.

We went to every room, Mike opening each door in the same manner. Upstairs, we went to the children's room first, saw that they were sleeping soundly. All appeared to be normal, undisturbed.

We returned downstairs to the kitchen to make tea and wait for the police. 'They could be some time,' Mike said. 'Depends what sort of night it is.'

We sat down at the table, opposite each other. I glanced at the kitchen clock. It was half past midnight. Mike looked his fifty years – hair ruffled, eyes red and tired.

'You were right,' he said. 'This was real. I should have been better prepared.'

'It's not your fault,' I said. 'I didn't know any more than you did whether this was real. Neither of us knew what we were dealing with. We still don't know.'

He ran his fingers through his hair, rubbed his face. 'But I should have taken you more seriously and put some precautions in place.'

'Don't beat yourself up. You made me see the doctor, remember? Sounds to me as though you were taking it seriously.'

He nodded but looked unconvinced.

I knew the bit that he didn't say: that he wouldn't have suggested my seeing the doctor had he really thought that any of this were real.

I reached for my mug of tea. 'Mike,' I said. 'What do you think is going on?'

'I don't know,' he said. 'Really, we need to—'

There was a rapping upstairs on the door then and we both looked at each other for a moment. I didn't want the police to disturb the children, so hurried upstairs ahead of Mike to greet them.

They came in quietly, gathering in the entrance hall, their radios crackling. Everything was subdued, formal, until Mike arrived. He reached his hand out to the first officer, who had grey hair and a rotund stomach. 'Evening, lads,' he said. 'Thanks for coming.'

'I think *lads* is stretching it a bit, mate,' the officer said, shaking Mike's hand vigorously.

'Nah, you don't look a day older than twenty-one, Ed,' Mike said.

The second officer, a fair-haired man with red cheeks, slapped Mike on the back.

'How you doing, Brian?'

'Not so bad, mate. Not so bad.'

I stood blinking at this display of camaraderie, wondering if they had forgotten about the smashed glass downstairs.

'Suzy, you remember Ed,' Mike said, turning to me.

I couldn't remember this man at all.

'He was at our wedding – at the evening do.'

He was?

I shook Ed's hand. 'Of course,' I said. 'Lovely to see you again.'

'Come on,' Mike said. 'Let's go through here.'

Mike led the men through to the sitting room, where they made a few jokes and comments about old times, about people I didn't know.

I listened to them, smiling politely.

And then Mike began to tell them about the break-in, the Rizlas, the other sightings of the man.

'So, Suzy . . . ' Ed said, pulling a notepad from his breast pocket. 'There's been a few strange things going on, prior to the break-in. Can you describe exactly what happened tonight?'

'Well, I woke up at . . . ' I hesitated.

'Just before midnight, I'd estimate,' Mike said.

'OK,' Ed said, notebook open on his lap. 'And what happened?'

I clasped my hands together apprehensively. 'There was someone stood at the foot of the bed.'

'And what did they do?'

'They touched my foot. At least, I think that's what woke me. But when I screamed, they disappeared, just like before.'

'Oh,' said Ed, his mouth forming an 'o' for longer than necessary – the same way Mike did when Ruby told him to be careful when hoovering so as not to suck up the fairies underneath her bed.

'And would you say you've been under stress lately?' Brian asked.

'I'm not quite sure what that's got to do with it,' I said, glancing at Mike. He nodded at me as if to say, *Just answer their questions, love.*

This seemed to be the general consensus, judging by the silence. So, I complied.

'Well, my business just upsized. And ... my mum passed away a few weeks ago.'

'I'm very sorry to hear that,' said Brian. 'It sounds as though you've had more on your plate than usual then. Is that a fair comment?'

I felt my cheeks colour. 'So, you're saying ... ?'

Brian opened his mouth to reply but didn't.

'Standard questions,' Ed cut in. 'No offence intended ... So, can you describe the intruder to me?'

I thought for a moment. 'He smelt of smoke. Every time I see him, he has a cigarette lit or smells of smoke. And of course, I found the Rizla wrapper and smelt smoke in—'

Ed cut me off. 'You think it's a he?'

'Yes,' I said. 'I'm sure.'

'Can you describe his build, his features?'

'No. I'm sorry. I can't.'

'Yet you're certain he was male?'

'Yes. He was broad.'

'Broad,' Ed said, writing on his pad. 'Anything else? Even if it sounds trivial?'

'No,' I said. 'I don't think—'

'He has a beard,' Mike said. 'Didn't you say that, Suzy?'

'Yes. Sorry, yes. I think I saw a beard.'

Damn it. I couldn't believe I had left that bit out.

I really didn't want to come across as vague, ditsy. It was just so difficult to think clearly, being put on the spot, on temazepam, in the middle of the night, in a state of shock.

Ed frowned, tapped his pencil on his knee. 'No sign of theft?' he asked Mike.

Mike shook his head. 'Not that we know of.'

'Hmm.' He gazed at Mike for a few moments. 'OK, mate,' he said.

Brian stood up. 'Well, we'll need to examine downstairs and poke about a bit, if that's all right with you.'

''Course,' I said.

'How many entrances does your property have?' Ed was asking as the men left the room.

We had four entrances: the front door, the tradesman's entrance, a back door to the garden on the lower ground, and a back door from the playroom to the garden even lower down.

Our house, perfect only an hour before, suddenly felt gappy, insecure.

I drew my knees to my chest. It was chilly in the sitting room. I gazed at the log burner, willing it to light itself.

I groaned, pressed my head against my knees, thinking of the children lying upstairs in their beds. Snuggled underneath blankets, they were oblivious to what was going on down here. The thought made me feel inexplicably guilty, as though I were somehow inflicting this on them.

I realised then that I was still thirsty, that I had abandoned my tea in the kitchen. So, I went downstairs to make a fresh cup.

The men returned after a short while, gathering around me at the table. Only Mike sat down, stretching his leg out. I offered to make everyone tea, but they declined.

'Do you have any idea who might be doing this, Suzy?' Ed asked.

'No,' I said. 'No idea. I don't understand what's happening at all.'

The kitchen fell silent. I could hear the clock ticking, the fridge humming.

'Got any enemies?' Ed pulled his notepad from his chest pocket again, wet his finger, flicked through the pages. 'Anyone that might want to dick about with you? Come on . . . Have a little think. You're somewhat in the public eye in your job. There must be someone you've hacked off over the years?'

I thought of Mr Hum and, despite the situation, smiled nervously.

'It's a deli,' I said. 'People eat quiche. I can't think of one person who would want to do this.'

'What about outside of work?' Brian asked. 'Someone in the school community, perhaps? Have you argued with anyone, now or in the past? What about men who might fancy you? Any admirers? A disgruntled ex, maybe?'

I was about to scoff at the thought of my having an admirer – the likelihood of it – but then I remembered Tim. If the sudden revelation showed on my face, I tried not to let it. I picked up my mug, sipped my tea decorously.

I wouldn't set the police on Tim, prowling around his workplace, casting aspersions. I couldn't do that to him just because he'd had the bad timing to resurface in my life now.

'Like I already said, I can't think of anyone. I haven't got any admirers that I know of, nor have I angered anyone. I'm not that sort of person. I try to get on with people, try to be on good terms with everyone.'

'Fair enough,' Brian said. 'So, is there anything else you can tell us that might be helpful?'

'No,' I said.

'I see . . . ' Ed said, looking at me sceptically. Perhaps he had caught that look on my face after all.

Either way, he was making me feel ashamed. Maybe this was what the police did when they suspected time-wasting, truth-bending, information-withholding. I couldn't think what else he suspected me of, but it felt at that moment as though the list were longer.

'Well, for what it's worth,' Ed said, 'I think this is personal. Someone's targeting you. They've not stolen anything by the looks of things and the approaches are varied and probably will become more so. But it's basically stalking.'

Stalking.

I felt my skin tighten with anxiety.

Stalkers. Prowlers. Men that crept about in the dark.

Mike had said that this wasn't the bogeyman, yet it was beginning to sound that way.

I shivered; I was only wearing my plaid pyjamas, hadn't had time to get my dressing gown. My lips would be blue by now, morbidly so.

'To be honest,' Ed said, pulling his trousers up and over his belly, 'stalking's a bit of a grey area. It was made a criminal offence in 2012, but the nature of the offence makes it hard for us to deal with. We can investigate property damage and if we find the culprit, we can issue him a harassment warning. But that's about it, I'm afraid.'

'They don't get a lot of training on it,' Mike added, looking at me.

'Because it mostly affects women?' I murmured.

'Because what, love?' Ed said, cocking his head.

I shouldn't have said that. I was tired, emotional, out of line.

Ed drew himself to his full height. 'Do you get much local press?' he asked me.

I looked at him. 'Why?'

'Can you please just answer the question, Suzy.'

The atmosphere had suddenly become rather awkward.

'Not much,' I said.

'So, you didn't court the media when your business upsized recently?'

'I wouldn't say *court*. But there was a small piece in the paper, yes.'

'With the kids?'

I shook my head. 'No. I've always been careful not to feature them in the press or on any of my social media channels. Nor on the deli's website.'

'OK,' Ed said, nodding. But he was continuing to look at me, as though slowly digesting that list of possible portals into my exorbitant, overachieving world.

'Well, I don't think we're going to get any further tonight,' he said, hitching up his trousers again. 'It's late. We'll leave you to get some kip. But give us a ring if you need anything.' He patted Mike on the arm. 'Take care, mate.' To me, he nodded.

Mike stood. 'Thanks, Ed, Brian. We appreciate you coming here this late at night and so promptly.' And we all went upstairs to see them out.

As Mike stood outside the front door talking to the officers, I remained in the hallway, sitting at the bottom of the stairs. My gaze fell on Ruby's paper doll book which was lying in its usual place on the floor by the door. A rose-pink dress had been soiled by one of the men's footprints.

I picked the dress up, trying to clean it with a little saliva and finger-rubbing, but the mud wouldn't lift.

Mike closed the front door, pulled the latch chain across.

'Well, hopefully they'll come up with something,' he said. 'Are you all right?'

'Yes,' I said. 'I think so.'

'Come here.' He pulled me up and into his arms, kissing me lightly. His lips were cold from being outdoors. He tasted of winter air. 'Everything's going to be all right. I love you.'

'Love you too,' I said, pulling away from him.

'I'll turn the lights out,' he said. 'You go on up.'

I climbed the stairs, slowly. I was thinking about what Ed had said about stalking being a grey area.

Why was that?

Not long ago, I had read an article in the paper about a female celebrity in London who had been stalked for seven years before the offender was finally charged with burglary.

The article had quoted some bleak statistics that had stuck in my mind: half of cases where the woman had known the stalker beforehand had resulted in physical attacks; most domestic violence included stalking; on average, the victim experienced over one hundred episodes of stalking before she even told the police.

In the bathroom, I began to clean my teeth on autopilot, still thinking about the newspaper article.

Mike came in just as I was about to leave the room. I hovered, perching on the edge of the bath to talk to him.

'Why would a stalker be charged with burglary and not with stalking?' I asked. 'I mean, why did Ed talk about property damage, rather than the act of stalking itself?'

He yawned, picked up his toothbrush, ran the tap wearily. 'Because, as he told you, it's a grey area. Burglary's more tangible. It's hard to measure fear.'

'Is it?' I said. 'Or *is* it because it affects women, because men still make the rules? I read once that more research would be done into breast cancer if it affected the male scientists who—'

'Don't be daft, Suzy,' Mike said gruffly. 'Someone broke into our house and came up to our room tonight. We don't know what he wants. He could be armed and dangerous. Don't you think we've got more important things to worry about than sexism in current legislation?'

I opened my mouth to reply, yet suddenly felt overcome with fatigue.

He seemed to reach the same point at the same time. He looked depleted, in pain.

'Sorry to snap,' he said. 'It's just that this thing is getting to me ... There was a time when I could just sound the alarm on the top of my car and go out and nail the bastard. But now I can't do anything except limp about and ask other people to help ... And we need some bloody sleep. We can't begin to do anything about this if we're staggering around, knackered.'

I looked at the bathroom clock. It was half past one.

'I'm sorry,' I said.

He turned to look at me in surprise. 'What for?'

'For this. It feels like it's my fault.'

'I didn't mean you, love. I'm not angry with you,' he said. 'I'm angry with the moron out there who's trying to scare you. That's exactly the way he wants you to feel – apologetic, victimised. So, don't let him. You have to stand firm.'

I loved Mike so much at that moment that I would have hugged him if it weren't for the foamy paste all over his hands from teeth-brushing. So, I smiled instead.

But as I crossed the landing, my smile vanished.

I wanted to stand firm – for Mike, for the children, for me. Yet I had been here before, many times over.

There was only so much fear I could handle.

What if I was reaching saturation point? What would that look like? Was I there already?

20

Breakfast was subdued; Mike and I were exhausted, tight-lipped.

'When are you going to sleep in my bed again, Mummy?' Jake asked as I poured milk on to his Weetabix.

Sometimes, as a treat or if one of the children were poorly, I slept on the top bunk of Jake's bed. He had mentioned it several times lately and it crossed my mind now that he might be feeling unsettled, clingy. For even if Mike and I were good at pretending that everything was fine, there was an undeniable air of tension in our home.

'I'm not sure, my love,' I said. I glanced at Mike, but he was intent on packing the lunch boxes, tutting because nothing seemed to fit, jiggling water bottles, taking foil parcels in and out.

'Why do you sleep in Jake's bed?' Ruby asked, wrinkling her nose at the whiff of favouritism. 'That's not fair.' Then she smiled at me, in the instant way that children switched emotions. 'You can sleep in my bed, Mummy. There's plenty of woom.'

'Thanks, Rubes. That's a kind offer. But I would probably squash Teddy.' I crouched down to Jake's level, put my hand on his lap. 'Sweetheart, I promise I'll sleep in with you soon.'

'OK,' he said, nodding glumly, spooning cereal into his mouth.

At the front door, Mike waited for the children to start their usual kerfuffle as they put on their coats and shoes, before he turned to me. 'I think we should all walk down together,' he said.

'Oh,' I said, glancing at my watch. 'I suppose I can wait a minute . . . '

'Good. Because I don't want you going anywhere on your own right now. Especially not in the dark. We can walk with you to work each morning and we'll pick you up.'

'Oh,' I said again. 'Are you sure? That sounds like an awful lot of—'

'I'm sure,' he said. 'It's just for now. Until things are resolved.'

I shrugged in agreement and helped Ruby on with her shoes and buttoned up her coat.

'Why can't you go anywhere on your own, speshurly not in the dark?' she asked, touching my lips and examining the patch of gloss that it left on her finger.

'Because it's always best to be cautious, Ruby,' Mike said, answering for me, putting on his coat. 'It's still winter. It gets dark early. You don't know who's out there.'

Ruby gazed at the front door, her eyes widening.

She would forget about it as soon as she stepped outside and became distracted by a falling leaf or a whistling bird. But it was Jake who was troubling me. He was standing very still, watching me with his dark, solemn eyes.

'It's OK,' I told him, reaching for his hand. 'There's nothing to worry about.'

He nodded. I kissed him on the tip of his nose.

And then we were off on our way to school and work.

Mike and I held hands; Jake and Ruby walked ahead of us, chattering. Jake's mood had lightened. He was telling Ruby why she would never be any good at football. Ruby was responding by trying to kick him between the legs.

Outside the deli, I kissed the children goodbye and tightened Ruby's ponytail.

'Look after yourself,' Mike said. 'And stay vigilant. If you see anything that worries you at all – anything whatsoever – then call me right away. OK?'

I swelled with love for him, just as I had in the bathroom the night before, but there was a fair amount of gratitude mixed in there too.

'Will do,' I said.

'Bye, Mummy!' Ruby said as she skipped off, trying to catch hold of Jake's hand.

I watched my family as they walked away. Jake was knocking Ruby's hand from him, but she persisted. And then just before they rounded the corner and went out of sight, Jake gave way and the two of them were holding hands.

I smiled. Mike turned and gave me two thumbs-up before disappearing – his way of saying, *Hang on in there*, the sight of which made me well up.

I told myself not to be so emotional and got on with opening up the deli.

The sensation of being watched, stalked, was ultimately debilitating. There surely was no other crime out there that was so effective, so well designed to achieve its goal and go undetected. All the perpetrator had to do was creep around, unseen. The less visible, the better. The less you could prove his existence, the better. The less plausible, tangible, the better. It was a win-win for nearly all concerned. The police could say unequivocally that it was a grey area; the culprit could continue to prowl. And the woman, for it was almost always going to be a woman, I felt, would slowly go under.

Being stalked wasn't like having a shadow. It was like having a second defective skin that rather than acting as a barrier to protect the body from harm, attracted decay and deterioration instead. You couldn't shake it off, just as you couldn't shake your first skin off. You had to somehow live with it.

I didn't know how long I would have to live with it for. A week? Seven years? Everything about it was uncertain, which was one of its key strengths.

I had said only a few weeks before, after my mother's death, that I hadn't believed in ghosts. Yet now I was inarguably haunted.

Nicole noticed the change in me right away.

'What's wrong?' she said, entering the deli mid-morning and coming around to my side of the counter, even though I was always telling her not to do so.

'Health and safety?' I said, alluding to the steaming pot of coffee behind us.

'It's fine,' she said, flapping her hand. She was wearing a fluffy jumper, and as she moved, wisps of mohair drifted into the air, probably into the salads. 'So, what's going on?'

'Move,' I said, tapping her legs. 'You can't stay there. There's not enough room.'

'Please ask your friend to leave,' Leo said.

'I can't,' I said. 'She's like Velcro.'

'Velcro?' he said, frowning. Every now and then, a word needed translating. But a customer had approached, so Leo turned away to serve them.

'Come on,' I said to Nicole. The pains au chocolat needed replenishing so I picked up the basket. 'We can walk and talk.'

In the kitchen, I began to lift pastries from catering boxes into the basket.

'So much for talking,' Nicole said, placing her hand on my

arm. 'I know something's up, hun. That's why I'm here. Helen said that you didn't seem your usual self yesterday.' She prodded me gently in the tummy. 'And you've lost weight … So, what's up?'

'Nothing,' I said, sounding unconvincing even to myself.

'Suzy … ' she said, prising the tongs from my grasp. 'Come on. Talk to me.'

I leant back against the kitchen table, fiddling with the pocket on my apron. There was a stack of washing-up to be done. Over in the corner on the table beside the fridge was a large pile of invoices to file. I had so much to do.

'Suzy … ' Nicole said again.

I looked at her, feeling my shoulders sink in resignation.

'OK … Look, you know I told you about those strange things that started happening after Mum died? Basically, I thought that someone was following me … Remember the night at the deli when I thought I saw someone outside?'

'Yes, I think—'

'Well, it was real. Someone's stalking me.'

She stared at me.

'Last night he broke into the house and came up to our room. There was smashed glass everywhere. We called the police.'

'Oh my God, Suzy!' Nicole said. 'You must have been petrified! Were the kids all right?'

'They were fine,' I said. 'They don't know anything about it. They were tucked up in bed.'

She scowled. 'So, who the hell is this moron? What does he want? Did he steal anything?'

'Not that we know of. To be honest, we don't know very much at all.'

'It sounds like a bloody nightmare,' Nicole said. 'But why didn't you tell me before now that you thought someone was following you?'

'I don't know,' I said. 'I was embarrassed, I suppose.'

She reached for my arm, rubbed it. 'Embarrassed? What about?'

'I dunno,' I said. 'Maybe because I didn't know if it was real. Until last night, I thought I might even be hallucinating.'

'Oh,' she said, gently.

I moved away then to get Nicole to drop her hand from my arm. I couldn't wholly explain it, but I didn't want to be touched.

It was because of the second skin perhaps. It didn't welcome friendly contact, was only there to drag me under.

'Do you think you know him?' she asked. 'Do you have any kind of sixth sense about it?'

'No. At least, I can't imagine who it might be. But the police think that it's personal, that he's targeting me ... It feels as though he's slowly taking more risks, getting closer.'

'To what?' she said.

'To me, Nic. Closer to me.'

I turned back to the pastries, began to lift them into the basket again, but my hand was shaking and any poise that I had achieved earlier was gone.

'I just can't believe it,' Nicole said. 'It's so hard to take in ... What's Mike doing about it?'

'Everything he can. We called friends of his in the police. But they said they can't do very much about stalking.'

'Can't do very much?' she said. 'You're not going to stand for that crap, are you?' She tossed her hair over her shoulders, folded her arms. 'Are they going to investigate or not?'

'Yes,' I said. 'But they don't have a lot to go on. Whoever he is, he's being really careful. All I can do is try to work out who he is. And be vigilant and ready for when he returns.'

Nicole looked appalled at this. 'So, you just have to sit around and wait for him to strike?'

'Well, it's not quite like that ... But what else can I do? I have to stay calm. Cracking up is probably what he wants me to do. So, I'm going to do my very best not to.'

I was cradling the square basket in my arms, the wicker creaking as I squeezed the handles anxiously.

'You're so brave,' Nicole said. 'If it were me, I'd be in a coma or something.'

'You wouldn't,' I told her. 'You're tougher than you think.'

She gazed at me dubiously for a moment. 'So perhaps I should tell Helen and Donna so that they can help?'

'Fine,' I said. 'Not that they can do anything. But please be discreet. We need to be cautious. Until we know what this—'

There was a noise behind us then and Leo poked his head around the door. 'Sorry to interrupt, ladies,' he said. 'But there's a bit of a queue ...'

'Thanks, Leo,' I said. 'I'll be right there.'

We returned to the shop floor. 'I'll ring you tonight,' Nicole said as she left, looking at me meaningfully.

There was a brief commotion at the door as she bumped into someone – laughter, an exchange of words – then the door closed and in her place was Tim.

I watched Nicole as she passed the shop window, looking in at me, her hands outstretched in a gesture that said, *How was I to know he was actually going to call in?* But then her face changed, clouded and, in that second, I knew what she was thinking.

It's not Tim, my expression said back.

His resurrection was a huge coincidence, granted. But it wasn't him.

When Mike and the children came to collect me and we walked home up the hill, talking about our days, I sensed that Mike had become my unofficial bodyguard. He wouldn't let go of my hand and held my back protectively when a young lad came up behind us suddenly on foot.

Ruby was skipping alongside us, lunch box cutlery rattling in her backpack. She was telling us about a dead wasp that she had found on the picnic bench outside her classroom. She hadn't seen one before, hadn't known that wasps could still sting even when dead, so the dinner lady had told her.

'Imagine stinging, even when you are *deady*,' she said.

Jake, bouncing a tennis ball as he walked along, tutted loudly.

'Can we do things if we are deady?' Ruby asked me.

'Huh?' I said.

'Us, when we are deady.'

'I don't know, poppet,' I said. 'Probably not.'

'I hope I can do things when I am deady,' she said happily, skipping ahead.

'Talk about having aspirations,' I said to Mike. 'So, did you get done what you wanted to do today?'

'Yep. I fixed the broken window,' he said. 'And I checked out a decent security system. The only trouble is, they can't install it for two weeks.'

'Oh,' I said, looking up at him apprehensively. 'Is that going to be all right?'

'It'll have to be.' He squeezed my hand. 'In the meantime, I've improved the locks on the tradesman's entrance and on the back doors.'

Ruby appeared to have overheard this, was hanging back to speak to us. 'Why did you do that, Daddy?'

Jake tutted again. 'To keep us safe, of course, Dumbo.'

It was a logical enough response. But an older child than Jake would have asked: *Safe from what?*

'Well, that's a good start, at least,' I said to Mike, as the children ran on ahead up the hill.

'It's the best I can do for now,' he said.

I watched Ruby as she climbed on to a low wall and snatched twigs from the hedge, firing them at Jake. He ran away from the air strike and stood, hands on hips, waiting for her to catch up with him. When she did, he put his arm on her shoulder and they walked the last few yards up the hill together.

'Do you think they're safe?' I said.

Mike gazed in the direction of the children. They had disappeared momentarily, having crossed the brow of the hill.

'I don't know,' he said. 'But we're doing all we can ... I'm well placed to tackle this. And the police are involved now.' He squeezed my hand again. 'We have to trust the system, Suzy.'

We could see the children now. They were waiting on the front doorstep, wrestling with each other.

As I waited for Mike to unlock the door, I looked at the ash trees on the other side of the road and thought of the yews in the gloomy corner beyond my mother's grave.

I had thought I had seen something that day too, at the funeral, I remembered then.

It could have been my imagination.

Or it could have been the shadow, the one that had been with me all my life.

Securely installed inside our house, I cooked supper, helped Jake with his maths homework and read *The Princess and the Pea* to Ruby, during all of which I felt very alone.

As I gazed with disinterest at the TV – Mike was watching a documentary about the Great Barrier Reef – I turned instead to the book on my lap but found that I was unable to concentrate on reading.

Mike was pursing his lips, fully absorbed in the programme. I rose listlessly and went to the window, pulling back the curtains to look out.

It was such a still night, a clear sky. The sight of the stars brought tears to my eyes.

I wished so much that my mum was with me.

She had always been there for me – a tour de force, in her gentle way. And now, for the first time in my life, I couldn't ask her for help.

I sniffed, blinked away the tears. I couldn't waste energy on feeling sorry for myself. Were my mother still alive, I was certain that she would have told me to reserve my strength and focus on not letting this man drag me under – that I wasn't to let anyone ever do that to me.

I thought again of her funeral, of the figure lurking by the yew trees. That had possibly been the first sighting of the stalker, the moment that had started this off.

Was that significant? I didn't know.

I turned away from the window, sat back down in front of the TV. 'Is it good?' I asked Mike.

'Yeah, really good,' he said, sipping a mug of tea. 'You should watch it. Take your mind off things.'

'I can't settle.'

He glanced at me. 'Try to.'

'But what if . . . ?'

He picked up the remote control, paused the programme. 'He's not coming back tonight, Suzy. He wouldn't be that stupid. You heard what Ed said – he'll vary his approaches.'

'And that's supposed to reassure me?'

'It should do,' he said. 'It means that it's more than likely that he'll never come here again.'

'Which means that he'll approach me, where, at work? In the street?'

'Possibly,' Mike said. 'But it'll be broad daylight, because you won't be going anywhere on your own in the dark. You might never even see him again for all we know. He might have got what he came here for. We'll just never know what that was.'

Again, that didn't reassure me – the idea that a strange

man had been creeping around our house in the dark on an unknown mission. But I didn't say as much.

Mike was just trying to help. He pressed play on the remote control and the programme came to life again. As he picked up his mug and dunked a biscuit into his tea, eyes firmly on the screen, I felt sorry for him – sorry that I had brought this on us, whatever it was.

I made a pretence of watching the documentary, but afterwards I couldn't have answered a single question about it.

Fear was pumping through my body as quietly and naturally as my blood; there wasn't a single fragment of my being that wasn't permeated with it. It was part of me now.

Mike could try to reassure me – would continue to do so, as that was his job. But I knew that I would be seeing that broad shape again: the cigarette light, the deerstalker hat. It was just a case of when.

THE INFORMATION AND ASSESSMENT MEETING

Wednesday 29 March, 2017

Dan glances at me and then steers the thin woman so that she has her back to me. He addresses her, his voice low. I can only hear the odd word.

'. . . official appointment . . .'

'I don't think I can wait,' the woman says, pulling a tissue from her pocket and blowing her nose.

Dan says something else quietly.

'Oh, thank you,' she says. 'Thank you so much.' Then she turns away, taking a seat in the chair furthest away from me.

Whatever we have all got, it could be catching. No one huddles here, despite the need to.

Dan is approaching me. I wipe my damp hands quickly on my coat, stand up.

'Good morning, Suzy,' he says. Then he glances around the reception, raises his eyebrows at me, consulting his watch.

I'm watching him dumbly, unable to find words.

'Well, I guess there's no point us standing here,' he says. 'May as well go on through . . . Excuse me, just for one moment.'

He goes behind the desk, murmurs something to the receptionist.

Now he's holding the white door open for me and we are

leaving the room under the watchful eye of the thin woman who must wait her turn.

We are going along the creaking corridor.

When we reach the little room, he glances at his watch again. And then we go in.

21

Two days later, on the Saturday morning, my friends and I arranged to meet at the park in the city centre. It was partly so that Helen and Donna could see me in light of the stalker news from Nicole, and partly a way to get me out of the house for something distracting, normal. I welcomed normal wholeheartedly.

At the appointed hour, Jake, Ruby and I were standing outside our house, experiencing the freedom of our first outing that year without woollen accessories. It felt liberating, invigorating – the breeze in my hair, sunshine on my skin. With my body temporarily hijacked by fear, every ounce of sunshine seemed to be helping my cells to fight back and restore me.

Beside me, Jake was kneeing a football, his legs glaringly pale in football shorts. Ruby was glaring also: she had insisted on wearing her bright yellow *Beauty and the Beast* Belle dress. There was a time when I might have argued otherwise. But after the shock of the break-in, I was feeling as though I would give my children the world on a plate were I able to do so.

Nicole pulled up promptly, with her son, Zack in the back of the car. 'Is that what you're wearing?' he said to Ruby.

We all got in and Nicole took off, telling me on the way

about her argumentative boss, the boys chattering all the while about football.

'Boring, boring,' Ruby kept muttering, kicking the back of my seat.

I listened to Nicole, my face turned towards the sun, feeling its warmth on the window. I think I would have fallen asleep, given the chance.

At the park, we headed for the outside area of the café to meet the others. Helen and Donna were already there, had commandeered the largest table, spreading their bags and coats out.

The children dumped their coats down and ran off to play, heading for a rope climbing frame. We would be able to see them clearly from here, set at the top of the park as we were, on a bank looking down. There weren't many people here yet. Ruby stood out in yellow, as did Jake in orange.

I sat down, glanced around the table, wondering who was going to be first to mention the stalker. Helen was watching me warily. Nicole was looking at her phone. Donna – who would have tackled the issue head on – was inside the café getting the drinks.

I put my sunglasses on and pulled my diary from my bag. I was working in a few hours' time and wanted to check what was scheduled in.

'Did you have to bring that with you?' Nicole asked.

'Well, you've got your phone,' I replied.

She shrugged, dropped her phone into her cardigan pocket. 'There,' she said. 'Gone.'

I was meeting with a chef at three o'clock about salt-free soup. I circled the appointment in red ink. Then I closed the diary and put it away.

I watched the children. They had moved from the climbing frame to a long tunnel. I didn't like not being able to see them, waited for them to appear at the other end. When Ruby popped up and waved at me, I waved back.

Donna was returning with the drinks. 'Thanks, love,' I said. 'How much do we owe you?'

'Nothing but your company.'

'My treat next time,' said Helen. Then she rubbed her arms. 'Anyone else chilly? I think it's chilly.'

As she spoke, the wind rattled the branches of the tree above us. 'It's snowing,' said Nicole, holding her hands out. Cherry blossom petals were floating down, landing around us.

I picked one up, held it on my palm. I thought of the cherry blossom trees on my old street, Rose Lane – of how they would also be in blossom now.

And then I let the blossom go, picked up my coffee cup.

'So, about this stalker . . . ' said Donna, setting her eyes on me. 'What's going on?'

'I don't know,' I said. 'I can't tell you anything more than I already told Nicole. Nothing else has happened since the break-in.'

'Well, I'm sorry to sound alarmist,' Helen said, 'but I don't know how you're managing to be so calm about this.'

'That's exactly what I said,' Nicole said.

I looked at them in turn. 'What do you expect me to do? Scream? Go hysterical? Mike used to be a police inspector, remember? I know what these things are like. And he's used to handling situations such as this. I can't fall apart. I have to be strong – for my family.'

I glanced at the play area again, saw that the children had been joined by Donna and Helen's teenage daughters, who were pushing them on the swings whilst chatting to each other.

'If I go to pieces, then I'm giving the stalker exactly what he wants,' I said.

'That's a fair point,' said Donna.

'And besides,' I said, 'I've got some help.'

‘What sort of help?’ Nicole asked.

I raised an eyebrow.

‘Meds,’ said Donna, tapping the table top with her hand. ‘Knew it.’

‘Oh, you did not!’ Helen said.

‘Yes, I did. My sister was on tranks last year. *Actually*.’

Helen rolled her eyes, turned to me. ‘How long have you been taking them?’

‘Just since Tuesday. My GP prescribed them to help me sleep and to keep me calm. It’s my last one tonight and then I’m done.’

‘Good,’ said Helen.

‘You don’t approve?’ Nicole asked.

‘It’s not that ... ’ Helen said, glancing at the others.

‘Then what?’ I said.

‘Well, I just wondered whether it might make you groggy – whether you’d be better off being more alert given what’s going on.’

‘I know what you mean,’ I said. ‘But I think the fact that the pills help me to relax puts me in a better position than if I wasn’t taking them, if that makes sense?’

‘I suppose so,’ said Helen.

I heard the sound of a ball being booted then and turned to look. The children had left the play area and were on the grass behind us, playing football. Ruby was in goal, between two trees; in the opposite goal, Donna’s daughter was leaning against a tree, texting. Jake, Zack and Helen’s daughter were charging up and down the grass with the ball. Ruby wasn’t even watching them, was twirling around in her dress, looking up at the sky.

‘I didn’t mean to upset you, or to be judgy,’ Helen said, touching my arm.

I turned back to her. ‘You could never upset me, H.’ I smiled to reassure her. ‘I know you’re just looking out for me.’

I watched the children again. They were making such a nice montage with the vibrant daffodils in bloom around them, I pulled my phone from my pocket and filmed them in action for a few moments.

'How's Mike coping with it?' Helen asked.

'Exactly as you'd expect. He's doing everything he can and a bit more.'

'He must know lots of people who can help?'

'Yes,' I said. 'He does. But you'd be surprised how little the police can do. There isn't any evidence, for a start. All we've got is smashed glass and lots of creepy little incidents that only I can attest to.'

She grimaced. 'It's really horrible, Suzes. I don't think I've heard of anyone being stalked before, not in my sad circle of—'

'Who you calling sad?' Nicole said.

'I don't mean you lot,' Helen said. 'I mean the mums at school and work. It just seems so celebrity-ish, having a stalker.'

'Our Suzy is a celebrity, locally,' Nicole said. 'Everyone's heard of her deli. And besides, it could happen to anyone. There was a woman at work who got stalked. In the end, she moved to Swansea. Not saying you have to do that, mind . . . '

'Well, don't worry,' Donna said, sipping her cappuccino. 'They'll get the bastard in the end. They always do.'

I turned to look at the children then, expecting to see Ruby still in goal. But she wasn't there.

'Where's Ruby?' I said.

There was a pause as everyone looked.

'There,' Nicole said, pointing to the tree. From behind the trunk, there was Ruby's yellow dress sticking out.

'Oh, thank goodness,' I said.

We exhaled collectively.

Helen hesitated, before speaking. 'Are you worried about them?' she said.

'Yes,' I said. 'I am.'

The wind blew the branches above us again then, the blossom twirling, falling.

'Bound to be,' said Donna. 'There's no reason to believe that they'll be involved in this though, is there?'

'No,' I said. 'But I would find that easier to believe if I knew exactly what this was in the first place.'

'Of course,' she said. Then she shuffled her feet and stood up, clapping her hands together. 'What we need is sugar. I'll go get some snacks.' And she headed into the café.

Jake's name was being called. It was Helen's daughter, waving at him to pass her the ball. But he was ignoring her, was setting himself up to take a free kick.

I watched him as he took slow purposeful steps backwards before charging towards the ball. Zack was watching, hands on hips, chewing a blade of grass. Ruby was giggling, jumping up and down. The ball was heading towards her. But it sailed right over her head and landed with a plop in the middle of the duck pond.

'*Jake!*' everyone shouted in unappreciation.

I laughed as the children sped over to the pond and began pulling sticks from shrubbery to retrieve the ball with. 'Look at them,' I said.

'Bunch of muppets,' said Nicole.

I laughed again and was about to point out that Helen's daughter was going to fall in if she reached any further over the water, when I caught sight of something.

There was a row of benches alongside the pond. Sat in the middle of the row was a lone man.

I might not have thought anything of it if it weren't for the hat. And the beard.

'Oh God,' I said.

'What?' said Nicole, frowning at me.

Helen's daughter had managed to reach the ball. She threw it to Zack who missed the catch.

The ball rolled towards the man, who trapped it under his foot.

'Oh, God, no,' I said.

'Suzy,' said Helen, tugging my arm. 'What is it? What's happening?'

I was trying to assess the situation – to weigh it up in a matter of seconds, reviewing what I knew to be true.

The deerstalker hat, the beard. That was all I had.

But now the children were running over to the man to retrieve their ball and Ruby was leading the way, her dress ballooning as she ran.

The man was rooting through his pockets for something. I saw it as soon as it met daylight: the red Rizla packet.

I stood up, my chair toppling over.

'Suzy! Wait!' Helen and Nicole called after me. But I was already gone, running down the bank.

'Ruby!' I shouted. 'Ruby! Stop! Wait!'

She was standing in front of the man. I couldn't see him. And now I couldn't see Ruby. The rest of the children were bunching around her.

I ran faster, was with the children in moments, grabbing their arms, pulling them away. 'We need to go,' I said. 'Right now.'

'Go?' said Zack. 'Go where?'

I purposely didn't look at the man on the bench. I led the children away, across the grass. I could barely breathe. My heart was hammering. 'Just up to the café,' I said. 'Your mum wants to see you.'

'She does?' said Zack.

I took Ruby's hand. 'We're going to take a break,' I said. 'Donna's getting snacks.'

Zack was dribbling the ball as he walked. 'Pass to me,' Jake was shouting. 'Pass the ball, Zack! Zack! Zack! Pass!'

I intercepted the ball, tucked it under my arm. 'That's enough, boys,' I said.

They both looked at me as though wounded.

We arrived back at the table, just as Donna arrived with a plate full of cookies and flapjacks.

'Flapchats!' Ruby said, clapping her hands incessantly.

I turned my back to the group, watched the man on the bench. He was still sat there, seemingly oblivious to what had just happened, licking the edge of his roll-up cigarette to seal it.

Helen joined me. 'Is that who I think it is?' she said.

I glanced at her. Her eyes were wide, fearful. Behind us, the children were attacking the plate of food noisily, accusing each other of overeating, all grabbing handfuls.

'Stay here,' I said. 'And watch the children.'

'Where are you going?' Helen said.

Nicole joined us. 'What's going on?' she said. 'Can someone please . . . '

I was on my way, sliding back down the grass bank, my mind blank.

I didn't know what I was going to say or do. I was just heading towards him, my arms wrapped around me protectively.

As I drew nearer, I began to doubt myself, my steps slowing.

I came to a stop in front of two heavy-duty boots. It was a moment or so before I could bring myself to look at their owner.

He was still licking the roll-up. His hands looked dirty, his nails stubby, red-rimmed where they had been bitten precariously low. The deerstalker hat hid most of his face, as it was designed to do. His beard was bushy and almost all grey, with the occasional black hair.

The sight of him sickened me, repulsed me.

To him, I would appear weak, vulnerable. I would have to try to prove otherwise.

'What is it that you want?' I said.

I glanced back at the children. Whatever happened, I didn't want them to be a part of this – wanted them at a safe distance. They were still gathered around the table, eating. Helen was standing with her hand to her eyes watching me, stoic, still, like a woman waiting for her loved one to return from sea.

He replied with a low chuckle.

I stared at him in abhorrence.'This is funny?' I said.

He continued to chuckle.

It crossed my mind then that maybe I had the wrong person. He didn't seem homeless exactly, but maybe this was a harmless old man – mentally ill, unkempt.

'Do you know who I am?' I said, folding my arms, stiffening my knees resolutely.

He stopped laughing, pulled a Zippo lighter from his pocket, lit the roll-up that was hanging from his lips. I could smell the gas from the lighter, saw the yellow nicotine stain in his beard below his mouth.

He said something then. It sounded like my name, but I couldn't be certain. An ambulance was passing by on the road behind and he hadn't spoken very loudly. He was drawing contentedly on his cigarette, gazing into space, as though I weren't there.

I glanced back at the children once more, saw that Helen was just starting down the bank, coming after me.

'The police know about you,' I said hurriedly. 'I'm going to get a restraining order against you. So, stop this right now and leave me alone.'

Suddenly, he looked me in the eye. 'What the hell are you talking about?' he said. 'I've never seen you before in my life. What are you, some sort of nutter?'

This threw me.

I looked about me, wondering if I had made a terrible mistake.

There was a noise behind me and I looked over my shoulder to see Helen drawing closer. The look on her face – the fear – was heartbreaking.

My voice wavered when I spoke again. 'If you ever go near my children again, I'll . . .'

I didn't know what I would do, how far I would go. But it felt quite far at that moment.

Helen tapped my arm to tell me she was there. I couldn't – wouldn't – drag her into this. I turned abruptly on my heel, heading back to the café at a pace.

'What happened, Suzy?' she said, following after me. 'What did he say?'

I didn't reply.

Nicole was coming towards us. She met us halfway. 'What's going on?' she said. 'I didn't know whether to stay with the kids or not. Did I do the right thing?'

'Who knows?' I snapped. 'Who knows anything? I can't tell you what's happening because I don't know what the hell's going on. I could be going insane for all I know!'

I was shouting. I glanced around the café. I had walked further than I had realised. Everyone was looking at me, my children and half the café's customers included.

It was Jake's expression that got to me the most. He knew now that I had been lying – that there was something to worry about after all, something big.

'Suzy, would you like me to—?'

I didn't let Helen finish. 'No. I don't want anything,' I said. I picked up my bag, my hands shaking. 'Come on, Jake, Ruby. We need to go.'

'Don't go, Suzy,' Helen exclaimed. Then she lowered her

voice. 'Not like this.' She was looking at Nicole and Donna for backup, but no one spoke.

'I have to go to work,' I said.

Nicole was looking tearful, her head bowed. I shouldn't have shouted at her like that, hadn't ever done so before.

Jake and Ruby were motionless, watching me. 'I mean it, kids. Come on. Now!'

Jake stood up. 'You can take your flapjacks with you,' Donna said, trying to placate them.

Ruby got down slowly from her seat. My voice was stilted when I spoke. 'Bye, everyone. See you soon.'

As we walked away, Ruby tugged on my sleeve. 'Why did we have to leave?' she asked.

Jake didn't say a word. I wanted him to speak. It seemed worse that he wasn't saying anything.

'Because we had to,' I said, rooting through my bag for my car keys and my phone.

As the children walked ahead, I called Mike, looking about the park, scanning the horizon, but the man was nowhere to be seen.

'I saw him again,' I said, when Mike answered. 'He was at the park, with the children ... He spoke to them. He's not going to leave them out of this, Mike. He's going to drag them into it to get at me.'

A family was passing by, looking at me inquisitively. I turned away and watched Jake and Ruby, who were waiting for me by the park railings.

'Suzy, you—'

'I can't do this. I can't cope with this. Not if he's going to mess with—'

'Suzy. *Listen* to me,' Mike said.

I broke off.

'Take a couple of deep breaths. Then drive home nice and steadily. That's all you have to do. OK?'

'OK,' I said. I hung up, walked towards the children.

Something was nagging me, trying to grab my attention.

'Mummy . . . ?' Jake was saying, a puzzled look on his face.

'Suzy! Wait up!' Nicole was calling to me, hurrying towards us. My phone was ringing. I looked at the screen, saw that it was Mike.

We all remembered at the same time.

I turned to Nicole. '*You* drove,' I said.

'*I* drove,' she said simultaneously.

And then we hugged, the fur from Nicole's hood tickling my cheek, her perfume sweet, comforting.

All I could think was how relieved I was not to have to drive home.

'I'm sorry for snapping at you,' I said.

'Don't be daft. It's OK, hun.'

The children edged towards us. 'Is everything all right, Mummy?' Ruby said anxiously.

I held out my hand to her. 'Yes, it's fine.'

'I'll grab Zack and then I'll take you home,' Nicole said. And she was off, running back to the café.

I watched the back of her hair bouncing up and down, her slender form as she ran. She had always been terrible at PE at school, ran as though on ice. But the sight of her doing so – for me – made me well up.

I sniffed, pressed my hands deep into my pockets and kicked at the sandy path, staring down at my feet – anywhere but at my son, who didn't appear to have taken his eyes off me.

22

At home, I ran upstairs to change. I was damp with nerves. I peeled off my clothes, stepped into the shower and stood underneath the spray, facing upwards. I could have stayed there like that, not leaving the cubicle, not going back outside that day.

When I returned to the bedroom, Mike was sitting on the edge of the bed, waiting for me.

'Where are the kids?' I said.

'Watching TV so we can talk.'

'Oh.' I began to look through the wardrobe for something to wear to work, something baggy to hide in.

'Tell me what happened,' he said.

'I already told you,' I said. 'He spoke to the kids for a moment.'

'What did he say?'

'Nothing coherent. Apparently, he only muttered something, according to Jake.'

'And what next?'

'Well, I pulled them away from him. Then I went back, had a go at him and—'

'What did you say exactly?'

I turned to look at Mike. 'That I wanted him to leave me alone, that I had told the police and was going to get a restraining order against him.'

He gazed at me expressionlessly. 'What else?'

'Nothing,' I said. 'Helen came along then, so I left. I didn't want her involved. It's bad enough as it is.'

I picked up a tub of moisturiser and sat down on the bed, smoothing cream on to my legs.

'I don't think that was the best way to proceed,' Mike said. 'You should have consulted me first.'

I stared at him with what felt like anger, had I the strength to muster it. 'Best way to proceed? Consulted you? Are you kidding? He was in the park, Mike – with our kids! I wasn't thinking about procedure. I was trying to scare him off, to tell him to back off.'

'I'm aware of that,' he said. 'But until we know who this man is and what he wants, it's best not to provoke him.'

'Maybe so. But he'll think twice about coming anywhere near me, now that I've threatened him with a restraining order,' I said, standing up.

'You can't do that,' Mike said. 'He needs to be convicted or acquitted of a criminal offence before being made the subject of a restraining order.'

'Well, how was I supposed to know that?' I said. I was back at the wardrobe, pulling irritably on the sleeves of dresses and blouses.

'By asking me,' he said. 'You can't take the law into your own hands and go off on one at this man. You had the kids with you. He could have been armed.'

I felt my bare skin goosebump at that.

'If it happens again, you must get to a safe place with the kids immediately and call me so I can talk you through it. It's just common sense.'

'Sorry,' I said, my voice low. 'It was a bit rash. But I just saw red . . . I wanted to do something, anything to stop him.'

Mike stood up, approached, curling his hand around the

wardrobe door. There was a mirror on my side; I watched my reflection wobble as the door moved. 'This isn't the same as what happened to you as a child,' he said.

I gazed up at him, feeling just like that child.

What was the difference, after all? Fear was fear, north or south, young or old.

'I know it's hard, but you must try not to project the past on to this,' he said. 'It'll make it ten times worse. This isn't about your father. He's not here any more. This is different. OK?'

I gazed unhappily at the row of clothes before me, my eye stopping at a lumpy cardigan. My mother had bought it for me some twenty years ago. It was misshapen, fawn-coloured, bland, perfect for today.

'We need to focus on providing strong evidence of a crime,' Mike said. 'We don't even know if you had the right bloke.'

I thought of the moment at the park where the man had looked up at me indignantly.

What are you, some sort of nutter?

'He could have been an old man on a park bench, smoking a fag, minding his own business. We can't prove otherwise. There's nothing linking him to the break-in or to the other sightings of the stalker.'

'Aside from the Rizla wrappers.'

He nodded, smiled faintly. 'Aside from those.'

I turned back to the wardrobe, holding the cardigan in my arms.

He shifted position then, moving the wardrobe door, my reflection wobbling again. 'I'd best get lunch started,' he said. 'No need for the whole day to go to pot . . . I'll ring Ed later and fill him in.'

I pulled a pair of boyfriend jeans out of the wardrobe, began to get dressed.

As Mike walked towards the door, he paused, turned to look at me. 'We have to abide by the rules, Suzy. I know it might seem as though we're not doing anything, but that's not the case. We're following the rules because they keep us safe.'

I nodded and sat down to do my make-up. The foundation came out in dollops; the mascara was clumpy. I noted the scarlet veins in my eyes.

What are you?

I looked like exactly what I was: someone who was no longer sleeping without the help of medication – someone who was barely keeping it all together.

Lunch preparations – normally animated in our house because we never knew what leftover morsels the deli would offer up – were moody today. I was due at work in half an hour and it turned out that Jake was going out too.

'Where's Jake off to?' I asked Mike, but he was on his way through to the storeroom and didn't hear me.

'Do we have any smowzers, Mummy?' Ruby asked.

'I'm not sure,' I said, peering into the fridge. 'I don't think so.'

'*Samosas*,' Jake said. 'I hate them.'

'Do you? I thought you liked them,' I said.

'No. They have peas in.'

I carried several deli food cartons from the fridge to the table, placing them next to Ruby who was colouring in. Jake, opposite, was drawing an intricate maze, frowning in concentration. 'Football tournament,' he said.

'Hey?' I said.

'You asked where I'm going.'

'Yes . . . So how come I didn't know about it?'

Mike returned, carrying Jake's studded boots. 'You did know,' Mike said, his voice muffled as he reached into the cupboard for a carrier bag. 'I told you this morning.'

'You did?' I said.

'Yep. At breakfast.'

Everyone looked up then. Ruby had a habit of continuing to colour in whilst gazing around the room, watching what was going on. She did so now, her pen hissing on the paper.

'Really?' I said, trying to think back to that morning.

'It's not a big deal,' Mike said. 'You can't do everything.'

I wasn't trying to do everything. I was just trying to remember things – important things.

I unfastened the carton lids, moving more hurriedly now. Nothing made my wheels spin faster than a diary malfunction.

'We'll give you a lift down to work,' Mike said, setting the table. 'And we'll pick you up later.'

'Only if the timing—'

'We're picking you up,' he said firmly, his eyes meeting mine for a moment.

'Can I come with you, Mummy, and play in the deli?' Ruby asked, pushing her pens to one side and climbing on to my lap. 'I still haven't read the book about the jam cat.'

'It's marmalade – a marmalade cat,' Jake said. 'Not jam. *Duh.*'

Ruby ignored her brother. 'I don't want to go to football, Mummy,'

'Sorry, poppet,' I said. 'But I've got a meeting this afternoon. You'll have to go to football, I'm afraid.'

Mike stopped, holding a glass of milk mid-air, looking at me. 'She's going to Tilly's,' he said.

I started in realisation, then tried to make a show of nonchalance. 'Oh, that's right,' I said.

Of course, she was going to Tilly's. I had set the play date up myself, earlier in the week.

'OK,' Mike said, clapping his hands. 'Let's get this stuff cleared up for lunch, shall we?'

As the children scooped up handfuls of pens, I took the opportunity to slip from the room, heading for the solace of the breakfast room across the landing.

I couldn't understand how I had forgotten about both the tournament and the play date. Why hadn't I written the appointments down in my diary the moment I had made them? It was so disconcerting, even given all the turmoil of late. It made me doubt myself, and I hated doing so.

I took a deep breath as I entered the breakfast room and headed to the window where I gazed at the view. It was a beautiful day. The buds on the trees were ready to burst. Seagulls were circling the air, enviably high. A neon line of tourists was caterpillaring across the field on the horizon, walking the Bath Skyline trail.

I heard footsteps behind me. Mike was approaching, a contrite look on his face. 'Sorry if I sounded like an ass just now,' he said, 'lecturing you on procedure.'

'You didn't,' I said.

'It's just that I can't help but see this as a series of steps that we have to take in order to bring about the desired result. I was trained that way. And I was good at it,' he added.

'I know,' I said.

He placed his hand lightly on my waist. 'I just want to keep you and the kids safe.'

'I know,' I said again.

He sighed. 'I feel bloody useless with this leg . . . It's all I've got – that bit of training. And if I don't have that, if you don't let me help with this and advise you . . . well, then . . . I've got no role.'

'Mike,' I said, interlinking my fingers with his. 'You always have a role. You're our handsome hero.' I went on tiptoes to kiss him. 'I promise I'm going to listen to you from now on. No more going rogue.'

He smiled, yet still didn't look satisfied. How could he, given what was going on?

Yet we returned to the kitchen, where we enjoyed lunch

with our children as though it were any other Saturday. We talked about the day ahead – about what position Jake was likely to play in, what Ruby wanted to take to Tilly's, about whether Leo could be persuaded to make another Italian cake since it would be very welcome for our tea.

I was sure I had put the inhaler in.

Before we left, I packed a bag for Ruby, plus Jake's rucksack for football: a sweater, sports bottle and his inhaler with its spacer attachment. Although it was sunny out, he would be running around on a pitch that was high above the city and famed for its bitter winds. Damp freezing weather was an asthma trigger for Jake.

And that was the last I thought of it.

It was possible that I only premeditated putting the inhaler in his bag, only intended doing so and didn't actually carry out the deed.

These were my thoughts when I saw my son later, when I realised the error I had made.

I was waiting outside the deli, my hands clenched inside my coat pockets to keep warm. Earlier, Mike had told me to wait inside the deli for them to arrive. But he had rung minutes ago, telling me to go ahead and lock up – they were on their way. He had sounded flustered, couldn't speak for long since he was driving, shouting his message on speaker phone.

I buttoned up my coat and set my eyes on the section of the road where Mike would appear. For a Saturday evening, it was quiet on the high street. It was the crossover period: shoppers had gone home; party-goers were at home getting ready to go out. I didn't like standing here like this, in the dark, alone – wondered at Mike having asked me to.

But then he appeared and I could tell by his expression and the children's taut faces that something was amiss.

'What's going on?' I asked him as soon as I got into the car. He was driving faster than normal. After a few yards, he did a jerky three-point turn, before tearing back down the road towards home. I glanced into the back seat. Ruby was behind Mike, clutching her bag fretfully. Behind me, Jake was quiet. I had to swivel in my chair to look at him.

'He's wheezy,' Mike said.

Jake looked grey-pale with red blotches on his cheeks. His breathing was erratic, whistly; his bare knees were bony in his football shorts and socks. He seemed much smaller than when I had last seen him.

I reached out to hold his hand. It was cold, clammy. 'Where's his inhaler?' I said.

Mike didn't reply. We were steaming up the hill, the overhanging trees a blur above us.

We pulled up outside our house and ran indoors, Jake following reticently. I hurried downstairs to the kitchen, my back juddering.

The inhaler was in the fruit bowl on the kitchen table, not in Jake's bag, not where he had needed it to be.

I hastened back up the stairs, attaching the spacer to the inhaler and shaking it as I went.

Jake was leaning against the wall, his eyes turned upwards. He grabbed the inhaler from me, puffed, held his breath for five seconds.

Mike was watching attentively, phone in hand.

Something moved out of the corner of my eye. I turned to look. Ruby was clutching her pants, a damp patch staining her dress, a puddle of liquid at her feet.

I looked back at Jake.

'All right, son?' Mike was saying, his arm on Jake's shoulder.

Jake took another puff. Then he nodded, breathed easy.

'Thank goodness,' I said, relaxing my shoulders and stepping towards him. 'Oh, sweetheart, you had me worried there for a second.'

I went to pull him into my arms, but he did something that he had never done before: he pushed me away.

He went through to the drawing room, leaving the door open.

'Sit down and rest,' Mike called after him. Then he turned to me. 'I think we should phone 111 for advice.'

'Here,' I said, taking the phone from him. 'You go and sit with him. I'll do it.'

I had to do something. This was my mistake.

The lady who took my call asked me a series of questions, at the end of which she deduced that Jake wasn't in immediate danger, that it was an asthmatic episode induced by strenuous exercise in cold weather.

I hung up and went through to the drawing room. Jake was sitting on the sofa, his pallor back to normal. 'You're all right,' I said. 'We need to follow up with our doctor next week.' I held my hand out to him. 'Come on. Let's run you a bath.'

He didn't move.

I knelt down before him. 'Please, Jake. I'm sorry ... I brought cream cake home for tea ... ' My voice rose at the end in appeal.

He looked at me, tears appearing in his eyes.

Mike tapped Jake's knee. 'Come on,' he said. 'Do as your mum says. Let's get you in the bath. The steam will help your chest.'

Jake stood up droopily then, left the room, leaving a trail of mud on the carpet. He was still wearing his studded boots, but I could scarcely tell him off for doing so.

Mike followed after him, bending to pick up clumps of grass.

'I'm really sorry,' I said.

He turned to look at me, his palm cupped to hold the mud. 'It's all right,' he said.

'It isn't. What if it had been worse?'

He stood up straight. 'He's fine. It's never happened before and it's not likely to again. To be honest—' he lowered his voice, glancing at the door '—I thought he might be putting it on a bit.'

'Putting it on?' I said. That wouldn't have occurred to me. 'Why would he do that?'

'To get your attention? It's understandable, isn't it, what with everything that's going on. You're not superwoman, Suzy.'

He was stating this matter-of-factly, without a note of accusation. Yet I still found it unbelievable. 'So, he faked an asthma attack?'

He went towards the door. 'No, I'm not saying that. He was definitely wheezy. I just wondered if he played on it a bit. He knew it was your mistake and that he could punish you for it.'

'Why would he want to punish me?' I said. 'I'm his mum.'

He shrugged. 'Boys can be funny about their mums. They can expect a lot and be unforgiving if you cock up.'

The more that Mike said, the more I was beginning to recall all the times that Jake had looked at me hesitantly, watchfully during that past week.

'I'm not saying that's what he definitely did,' Mike said. 'Just thought it was worth bearing in mind.'

He left the room. I stood staring after him.

Was Jake doubting me, questioning whether I was a good mum?

My eye turned to the picture on the wall. I gazed at the spikes of paint depicting a mother and child on a swing. I had bought the painting when I was expecting Jake, swollen with notions of becoming a perfect parent.

But I saw now that the image represented nothing of the sort. It wasn't a projection of my future; it wasn't Jake and me on that swing, for it was a mother and daughter. It wasn't even Ruby and me.

It was my mother and me. All along, it had been about us.

That was why I couldn't get away from that six-year-old child. She had been right before me in the heart of my home the whole time, without my even knowing.

I suddenly remembered Ruby stood out in the corridor in her wet dress and hurried from the room to see to her. But she wasn't there.

I could hear the bath water running and the sound of the children's voices echoing around the high-ceilinged bathroom.

I ran upstairs, where I relieved Mike of his duties, took charge of Ruby, gathered the trail of football kit that Jake had left down the hallway, and poured bubble bath under the running tap.

Jake entered the bathroom, his eyes clouding when he saw me.

I knew then that there was a fraction of truth in Mike's words. I just didn't know what the fraction was – how bad things were, how sizeable the grievance.

But I did know that children bounced back, moved on, didn't bear grudges.

It was a case of starting as I meant to go on. A few shared jokes, a slice of Leo's cake, a book at bedtime and the inhaler episode would be forgotten.

I pulled him towards me. His skin was mottled with the cold, his shoulder blades sharp as I hugged him. I felt him give way though, felt his body relax in my arms. And that little bit of information was all I needed to know.

'I'll never let you down again, Jake. I promise.'

He nodded, stepped into the bath with an exclamation at the heat of the water.

But I broke my promise, almost immediately.

THE INFORMATION AND ASSESSMENT MEETING

Wednesday 29 March, 2017

I swear that it's freezing in this room today, no longer stuffy. I wrap my arms around me, wishing I had worn more layers. I'm wearing a black dress, the same dress that I wore for the funeral. I didn't purposely choose it because I wanted something sombre. Rather, it felt like the most fortifying thing that I could wear. It witnessed my mother's burial. If it can go through that, it can go through anything.

Dan Cassidy seems warm enough, is flushed in the face. He doesn't appear to be wearing a vest. I can see a shadow of chest hair beneath his white shirt.

There's a quiet knock and the receptionist appears, poking her head around the door. 'Sorry to interrupt,' she says, holding the door fully open. 'Got room for one more?'

I appreciate the light touch. I am feeling ill with nerves. I set my eye on the wall clock, watching the second hand quivering its way around the face. I am like that hand. I need to keep on going, no matter how jittery.

I don't want to watch everyone shaking hands, sitting down, settling. I want to pretend that I'm still here on my own with Dan, that the third chair between us isn't occupied. It's easier that way. I am concerned that if I look, if I absorb too much, I will fall apart.

My mouth is trembling. I press my lips together, clamp my jaw.

Perhaps no one will mind if I put my coat on. If I don't, I will freeze to death.

I pull my coat from the back of my chair and slip it on, doing up the buttons with fumbling hands. Then I sit back, settling deep into the soft wool of the coat. It smells of my perfume, of home.

Dan is smiling compassionately at me. 'OK, Suzy?' he says.

23

Whilst I was normally an early riser and first up in our household, there wasn't much incentive to get up the next morning. The bedroom air felt inhospitably cold on my face. Rain was lashing against the windows. I sank a little deeper underneath the duvet, weary in the extreme.

But then Jake burst into the room to remind me that he was going to a birthday party in an adventure woodland that was based ten miles out of town, which Daddy could take him to if I wanted to lounge in bed some more.

That got me up.

I told him that I would drive him so that we could spend some time together. Everyone seemed happy with this. Ruby wanted to stay home and rearrange her toys; Mike's leg was playing him up; Jake was keen to tell me all about the new system at school break-time for picking football teams fairly. I would listen, ardently.

We were putting on our shoes when my phone rang.

I answered it, pointing to Jake to grab his anorak. The invitation said that the children needed waterproofs, boots and hats.

The rain sounded hard, solid against the front door. Jake pulled the door open and held his hand out, hailstones bouncing on his palm, like jumping beans. 'Wow!' he said. 'Look, Mummy!'

'Sorry?' I said into my phone. I couldn't hear what the voice at the end of the line was saying. It was very muffled.

'... Wondering whether you could come by and get Ethan ...'

There was an Ethan in Jake's class, but we didn't know him or his parents very well. The mother was always tanned, with a penchant for skinny jeans. She hung out with the other mothers of a certain calibre, which I fell short of as a working parent, in a deli to boot.

She was practically yawning down the phone. 'Hopefully it's not too far out of your way. I'd take him myself, but our BMW's in for a MOT, and Geoff's in HK ...'

Why was she speaking in letters? It took me a moment to work out that HK was Hong Kong.

I wanted to ask her why she had left it so late to call me. How would the child have got to the party if I hadn't answered my phone?

I wished I hadn't answered.

'That's fine,' I found myself saying. 'I'll be with you in ten minutes.'

Ethan didn't have his coat or boots ready. He wasn't even waiting by the door. His mother answered the door wearing Ugg boots, her fingers wrapped around a steaming mug, and I thought how nice it must be to drift around the house on a Sunday morning with one's jumper hanging off one's shoulder.

Temazepam, I thought.

Once Ethan had come downstairs and had located his boots and his coat and his hat, we set off. I didn't like to mention that the kid didn't appear to have a birthday present with him.

My mood was unpleasant by this point. I drove with tense

shoulders, irked that we had been delayed by twenty minutes, that we would be late ourselves to the party now and that I had been robbed of valuable alone time with my son. After yesterday, I had wanted so badly to show Jake how much I was there for him.

Instead, I had to listen to Ethan's opinion on everything from *Star Wars* to Jon Cena, whoever that was.

After I dropped the boys off, I drove a mile further along the main road before turning down a bumpy country lane. There was a café in a converted cowshed down this way that I sometimes met a supplier in.

The car park was busy. I was intending to complete some paperwork inside the café whilst waiting for Jake. But I suddenly felt weary again, my energy surge having been short-lived.

I pushed my seat back, nudged the window down an inch and closed my eyes. It was quiet, wondrously so.

I would have fallen asleep if it weren't for the sound of a child laughing. I opened my eyes to see a little girl being led by her father to the car next to mine. The girl was talking, and the dad – I assumed it was her dad – was listening attentively.

I would always find this painful, the sight of a father and daughter, no matter how old I grew.

I decided not to watch them, but to go into the café instead, where I ordered a coffee, found an empty corner table and lost myself in work.

I didn't have as much time as I had thought. I had barely finished my drink, completed my paperwork, before I had to go.

As I drove, my mind was full of Jake, of how much I loved him.

When I saw him stood there in the woodland car park, he looked so happy to see me, his face smeared with mud, a wooden whistle in his mouth, waving a party bag at me, that I felt myself lift up to the clouds with joy.

I thanked the hosts for having Jake. And then I put my arm around him and he began to tell me about the den he had made using moss and branches, and I led him to the car, told him to sit next to me up front so that we could chat. And I drove away from the woodland and went back to Bath, without Ethan.

24

'Mummy?' Jake said, as he lowered his window. The sun had come out, hitting the wet road ahead with blinding splashes of white light.

'Hmm?' I pulled the sunshield down, reached for my sunglasses. We were about a mile from home. It had been a pleasant drive.

'Mummy?' Jake said again. He was dangling his arm out of the window, riding the airwaves with his hand.

'Don't do that,' I said. 'We're passing hedgerows. It's dangerous.'

He obeyed, pulled his arm in, looked at me. 'Were we supposed to bring Ethan home with us?'

I kept my eyes on the road, my heart growing so light and still that it didn't seem to be beating.

'I'm not sure,' I said.

I couldn't bring myself to tell him the truth: that I had forgotten the child.

I made a show of sounding unconcerned. 'I'll pull over when I can stop and we can check my phone to see if Ethan's mum's rung. Maybe he went home with someone else.'

Like most eight-year-old boys, Jake wasn't looking for problems or details. He reached forward and put the radio on, searching for a song that he knew and liked.

There was nowhere for me to stop. We were doing sixty miles an hour along a country road on the outskirts of the city and there was a large black SUV behind us that kept swarming close and falling back again, like a gigantic house fly. The vehicle was menacingly erratic, as was the sunshine which was flashing through the trees. I could feel perspiration breaking out on my top lip and underneath my hair at the back of my neck as I bit my lip, told myself not to panic, to stay calm.

We were approaching a turning on the left. The black SUV was on top of us again. I couldn't think quickly enough. Turn or not turn?

I indicated at the last minute and swerved around the corner.

I saw the pram, the woman with her ginger hair and sky-blue cardigan just in time, slamming my foot on the brakes, Jake lurching forward and then back again.

I was motionless for a moment, hands on lap, the engine stalling.

'*Mummy*,' Jake said faintly.

The woman, paused right in front of our car, continued to the other side of the road, pushing her pram. As she went, she turned her furious face towards us.

'You could have killed us!' she shouted. 'You stupid bitch!'

I murmured an apology, started the car and eased forward, wiping my top lip. It wasn't a residential area, was a country lane, but there was a driveway of some description ahead. I did a three-point turn there, came back down the road. The woman was still standing there, waiting for us. I felt nauseous.

Jake's window was open. The woman was on his side of the car. 'Do your window up,' I told him. 'Quickly.'

He pressed the button and the window rose, closed.

I should have gone slowly in respect, but I was fearful for Jake, for what he might see or hear. So, I accelerated past her, back to the road.

Jake was looking at her fretfully. 'She's swearing at us, Mummy,' he said.

I glanced in my rear-view mirror as I waited for the traffic on the main road to clear. She was still shouting, her teeth bared in ferocity. I couldn't hear her through the windows, over the traffic. It was just as well.

I pulled away, opened the car windows again, exhaled.

'Is she going to tell the police?' Jake asked.

'No,' I said, glancing at him. 'Why would she do that?'

He was jigging his leg up and down. 'Because we nearly knocked her over.'

I felt very hot, nudged the window further down on my side of the car so that the air lifted my hair.

'We didn't do anything wrong, Jake,' I said. 'I was within the speed limit. She shouldn't have been crossing so close to the edge of the road on a blind bend. Bloody idiot.'

I shook my head indignantly. I might have taken the turning a tad too quickly because of the car right up behind me, but it was a country lane and she had been crossing stupidly, irresponsibly on a blind corner.

My sense of outrage, muddled by fear and panic, was so strong that I was tempted to go back and tell her so – that she was wrong to shift the blame on to me so thoroughly. But then I considered that she was the least of my worries, that I had a bigger problem waiting for me back at the adventure woodland.

I put my foot down and sped off, Jake not saying another word the whole way.

The adventure woodland was desolate.

I got out of the car, walked towards the booth where the party organisers were based earlier with clipboards and drink bottles. There was nothing there now, except a crushed empty carton of juice.

Not having slept well and the after-effects of temazepam were catching up with me. I couldn't feel my heart beating. My chest felt empty. I was sweating far too much – the back of my hair was damp; my jumper was sticking to me.

Should I even be driving? I tried to remember what Doctor Hill had said about that. I had completely forgotten about the medication so far as driving was concerned.

How dangerous was I exactly? I thought in alarm.

You could have killed us. You stupid bitch.

I had to drive us home though, had to get us out of this pickle. I would go at a moderate pace. And I wouldn't drive again on medication.

Jake got out of the car and joined me, squinting. 'Where is everyone?' he said.

I looked at my watch. 'They must have gone home.'

'So, what do we do now?' he said.

I didn't know.

I didn't have Ethan's mother's number. This whole thing had come about because someone who didn't know me very well had asked me to take charge of their child and at the last minute. This was what happened when parents were sloppy, substandard – both she and I.

I gazed about me. We were in the middle of nowhere, fir trees all around as far as we could see. Behind us was the dusty track leading back to the main road. Everything felt unreal, disconnected from me – the colours too sharp, my purpose here unclear.

I needed to sit down. 'Let's go,' I said.

In the car, I flicked through my phone, my chest now tight. 'Who's Ethan friendly with?' I said. 'Who else might he have gone home with?'

'Not sure,' Jake said.

'Please think,' I said, frowning at him.

He frowned back. 'Maybe Matty. Or Archie. Or Sam.'

'Matty, Archie, Sam,' I said, scrolling through the numbers on my phone. 'I have Archie's mum's number.'

I pressed the number, waited, trying to collect myself.

She answered. 'Hello?'

'Hi, it's Jake's mum, Suzy . . . Did you take Ethan home from the party?'

'Ethan? No.'

'Did you see him at the end of the party? Did he leave with anyone?'

She paused. 'No. I don't think so . . . What's up?'

I closed my eyes briefly. 'I don't know where he is. I was supposed to take him home.'

'Well, don't panic. I'm sure there's a simple explanation. I'll make a few calls and if I find out anything, I'll call you right back.'

'Thank you,' I said.

I hadn't spoken to her much before. She sounded nice. I was grateful.

I hung up.

'What now, Mummy?' Jake said.

'We go to Ethan's house,' I said. 'And we pray that he's there.'

The air thickened between us.

I shouldn't have said that. Jake looked pale with worry.

It had always been my mission to shield him from this sort of adult messiness. And now I had tossed him right into the mire.

'It's all right, Jake,' I said, putting the windows up as we went back down the dusty track. I reached for his hand as we rocked about on the rubble. 'He'll be there. I'm sure of it. These things always work out.'

But that was a lie. These things didn't always work out. People made stupid mistakes all the time that cost them dearly.

'Wait a minute,' Jake said, pulling his hand away from me

and holding his index finger up in declaration. 'Didn't Ethan's mum call you this morning?'

'Yes,' I said.

'Then you do have her number! It'll be on your phone.'

I stopped the car, looked at him. 'Gosh, I'm a fool. You're right.'

This wouldn't have happened before. I would have worked this out instantly.

I looked through my phone, found the number and dialled it, holding crossed fingers out to Jake.

He smiled at me – a smile that was full of childish optimism.

It went straight to voicemail.

'Try again,' Jake said.

I did; voicemail again.

'Well, there's nothing for it but to go over there,' I said, driving away, the dust rising around us.

Ethan's house looked the same as before: as though no one was home. When we pulled up, our tyres crunched on the tarmac, the sound crackling in my ears. Everything felt intensified – the sounds, smells, colours. I pulled the sun flap down and looked in the mirror, wiping the shine from my forehead, specks of make-up from my eyes.

'Stay there,' I told Jake as I got out of the car and walked the few steps to the door. I rang the bell and waited, glancing back at Jake. His face looked very small and white beyond the windscreen.

The door opened and the mother looked glassily at me. She didn't speak, folded her arms.

'Is Ethan here?' I asked.

She paused before replying, allowing me to dangle a little longer.

Behind her, I could hear a child talking. I glanced past her and saw Ethan stood in the hallway with a younger boy – a sibling, I presumed.

'Oh, thank goodness,' I said, putting my hand to my chest. 'I'm so relieved.'

'I bet you are,' she said. 'Luckily for Ethan, Venezia brought him home.'

I didn't know who that was.

'Well, I'm not sure how that happened. I was—'

'You were supposed to bring him, yes,' she said. 'But when you forgot him, Venezia drove him instead.' She gazed at me, her face a maze of frown lines.

'That was nice of her,' I said, trying to sound amicable. 'And I'm sorry for any misunderstanding. I'm just glad Ethan's OK.' I began to back away, taking my sunglasses from my hair and putting them on. 'See you soon.'

She didn't move. Even as I walked away, my back to her, I could tell that she was still standing there.

'That's it?' she said.

I stopped.

'No apology?'

I didn't like her tone. It was loaded with contempt.

I was facing Jake. He was watching with anxious eyes. I took a deep breath and continued walking. 'I said sorry,' I called out, as I opened the car door.

'Didn't sound like it to me.'

I hesitated, my breathing tight. Jake was looking up at me, his face still smudged with mud from his woodland adventure, the party bag of cake melting in the sun on the dashboard.

I turned to look at her, my voice calm. 'I drove your son to a party, even though I barely know you and it made us late and you gave us very little notice. I then forgot him because the arrangement was so loose and because, believe it or not, my life doesn't revolve around you. You could at least have called to tell me what had happened, instead of having me driving around in a panic for the last half an hour.'

I got into the car, reached for Jake's hand. 'Come on, sweetheart,' I said. 'Let's go.'

She was coming towards us now in her skinny jeans, her cloud-grey jumper hanging off her shoulders. I pushed the windows up on both sides and started the engine. But I still heard her when she spoke.

It was so clear, distinct, vitriolic.

'It's Jake that I feel sorry for,' she said.

We left, reversing down the driveway, not looking back at her.

As we drove off the estate, towards home, Jake was tense beside me, barely moving.

'I'm sorry,' I said. 'Things have been difficult for me lately, since Granny Annie died. But it'll get better, I promise. Things will settle again. Just . . .' I steadied my voice before continuing. 'Just promise me that you'll bear with me, that you'll let a few things slip if I mess up. OK?'

He didn't answer.

I looked at him. 'Because I'm normally on the ball, you have to admit.'

He looked at me then, half smiled. 'Yep,' he said.

'Yep,' I echoed. 'That's me. So, if I'm a bit scatty for a while whilst I sort myself out, don't worry or be too cross with me. Does that sound OK?'

He was thinking about it, picking at a scab on his arm. 'Do you have any Skittles?' he said.

I chuckled, my laughter spluttery, like out-of-date milk. 'In the glove compartment,' I said.

Jake leaned forward to the compartment, pulled out a packet of Skittles. I always kept a few packets there for emergencies.

He reclined happily, tearing into the sweets. I had appeased him for now, but I was drained.

When we arrived home, Jake went on into the house to find his daddy and tell him all about the catastrophe. I paused inside the car, wondering how that conversation would go down.

Mummy forgot Ethan. And then she nearly killed someone.

I watched a sparrow pecking the gravel in our forecourt. The pavements were wet. The sun was high, fierce. I was still seeing things in technicolour, hearing high-pitched noises, like a dog.

I didn't know whether I was better with or without temazepam.

I didn't know whether to go inside the house or sit here.

Mike appeared on the doorstep. I didn't look at him as he approached. He knocked on the window for me to lower it, then put his hands on the roof top, leaning in. 'What the heck happened?' he said. 'I thought you said no more going rogue.'

I shook my head. I didn't have any explanations for him.

'Jake said you nearly ran someone over. Is that true?'

'Not really,' I said.

'Well, is it, or isn't it?'

It was the first time that I had ever heard him take that tone with me – as though I were to be mistrusted, as though I were one of his old suspects.

'I . . . ' I cleared my throat to speak, but I had no words.

'Suzy, we can't carry on like this,' he said. 'Didn't any of what I said yesterday hit home?'

I gazed at him, dumbly.

He sighed. 'What if you spoke to someone . . . ? Maybe I was right about the PTSD? What if I made a few calls, found out who—'

'No,' I interrupted, finding my voice. 'It's not PTSD. Are you forgetting that I'm being targeted by someone? I was fine before all this began. Even the most stable person would be unhinged by this.'

'Which is why we have to focus on keeping you safe. He's tipping you over the edge. Can't you see that?'

'So, I'll figure it out. I'll figure out who's doing this. And then it'll be over.'

'But what if by the time you've worked it out, it's too late?' He glanced about him, lowered his voice. 'What if you'd actually run someone over today?'

I pulled the keys out of the ignition, got out of the car. 'What do you want me to do? Because the police don't seem to be doing anything. I'm not waiting seven years, Mike, like that celebrity. Don't expect me to—'

'What celebrity?' he said, frowning.

We were level with each other now, staring at each other, whilst trying not to be overtly argumentative in view of the neighbours. One of the doors along from ours had opened and a young woman was coming out in a Burberry trench coat to take her pug for a walk. I smiled at her.

'What I want,' he said, 'is for you to stop running around like a live wire and get a grip on yourself before someone gets hurt.'

I turned away from him, went up the garden path. 'Well, maybe if the police got a grip on the situation then that would be easier,' I said. 'I mean, why should I trust the system? No one ever helped my mum. She could have been beaten to death and no one would have done a thing.'

Mike pulled on my arm, got me to stop. He was never rough with me, was always gentle, but I felt his strength in that small movement.

'*That's* what I'm talking about,' he said, wagging his finger at me. 'That right there.' He glanced about him, checking no one was in earshot. 'This isn't about the past. This is about us – about here and now. It's about protecting our family and dealing with a potentially dangerous situation. And all you're doing is making it worse . . . What about the kids? Where are they in all this? Are you thinking about them at all?'

I looked at him without blinking, but then my eyes stung and I looked away.

'Please, Suzy. See reason. The police are doing everything they can. All you have to do is stay calm and alert. Think of Jake and Ruby. And for their sake, dial it down a notch.'

'And what does that mean exactly?' I said crossly.

'Well, maybe you shouldn't drive until this is resolved.'

'Fine,' I said, folding my arms.

'And maybe you should think about going back to see the GP.'

'Fine,' I said again. 'I've got to see her this week anyway because I've finished the course.'

'Good,' he said, his face brightening in relief. He wiped his forehead and I saw that it was wet with sweat, even though it was cold outside with hailstones lining lawns and windowsills.

I felt remorseful then – ashamed for everything that had taken place that morning. My bottom lip wobbled.

'I'm sorry,' Mike said, taking my hand. 'I know this is difficult. But we can't let it drag us under. Do you understand?'

I didn't reply, bowed my head.

'How about I give Ed a call and see if he can come over and give us some guidance on procedure. I agree – it doesn't help that everything's unclear in that respect. Would that help?'

'S'pose,' I said.

He touched my chin. 'Come on. Smile for me.'

I had never forced a smile so much and to so little effect.

'Let's go in and put the kettle on,' he said. 'You don't have much to do today, do you?'

I couldn't remember, couldn't picture what I had read in the diary that morning at the cowshed café.

'No,' I said and followed him inside.

THE INFORMATION AND ASSESSMENT MEETING

Wednesday 29 March, 2017

'Thank you for coming in today,' Dan says, sitting forward in his chair, elbows resting on his legs. 'First off, I'd like to tell you a bit about the process to make sure that everyone knows what we're doing and what we're hoping to achieve. It's important to remind you that everything you say here is confidential. I take notes for my own reference, but nothing that you say will leave this room.'

He picks up his leather file and his silver pen, writes the date at the top of his page, underlines it. I like the familiarity of this. By the time I leave, I will know every freckle on his hands, every crease on his bald head, such is my focus on him.

'If you have anything worrying you, then I advise you to go ahead and talk about it. If you feel uncomfortable about this, you can always step outside with me. It can really help. So, don't feel awkward about requesting to do so. It's all perfectly normal.'

He removes his glasses, rubs the bridge of his nose. Without the thick lenses, his eyes are smaller, kindly looking. He smiles, takes a polite pause, allowing his words to settle.

I can imagine how people might become attached to him, to the safety of this process. Some might be reluctant to leave at the end, unwilling to walk out of here and go about their day unaided.

I'll admit that I'm one of them.
'Any questions?' he says.
I'm too frightened for questions.
I shake my head, continue to stare at him.

25

When I got dressed that Monday morning, I noticed that my bra was gaping – that I could have fitted a doughnut inside the cup, had I wished to. The skirt that I chose to wear, one of my favourites, was too big. I had to secure it with a safety pin. Once more, I hadn't slept well the night before.

It was exactly one month today that the new deli had opened. That felt like a different world now, a naive one in which I had created a cosy book corner for Jake and Ruby in the misguided belief that I was going to spend more time with them.

And now I was sitting with my children at the breakfast table, feeling as though there were hundreds of miles between us.

Was this because I really was becoming distant from them, and them from me, or was it all in my own mind – of my own making?

My mind was crammed with voices from the weekend. They were all talking at once yet seemed to be saying the same thing.

What about the kids? . . . Are you thinking about them at all?

You could have killed us. You stupid bitch.

What are you, some sort of nutter?

It's Jake that I feel sorry for.

Mike kept stressing that this wasn't about Carlisle, and it wasn't; even I could see that. Yet at the same time he was suggesting that the dormant trauma from that period of my life was affecting me.

It was bound to be. I had spent almost my entire life thinking I had killed my father.

I cringed as I spooned porridge into my mouth. It was so hard to find the appetite to eat, but I had to.

'Are you all right, Mummy?' Ruby asked.

'I'm fine, Ruby, thank you. Just a bit tired.'

'So's Teddy,' she said solemnly.

I vowed then to sort myself out. Yesterday couldn't happen again. I would read to Jake tonight, taking extra time to cuddle him. I had read once in a baby manual that boys were cuddlier than girls, needed more hugs from their mums. I would hug Jake so tightly tonight, he wouldn't be in any doubt about my love for him.

I would talk it through with Doctor Hill too. She would be able to help me.

When I got to the deli, I walked the phone out to the privacy of the kitchen to make my call to the doctor. As usual, she wasn't available to talk until after evening surgery, if I could hang on that long, the receptionist said.

Could I?

I managed to hang on. When Doctor Hill called me at five o'clock, I was on my own in the deli, wiping tables down, waiting for Mike and the children to pick me up.

'I think that I might need some more temazepam,' I told her.

'You do realise that they're highly addictive?'

'Yes,' I said. 'But I think that's the lesser of the two evils. I'm so on edge and I'm becoming more forgetful. I have to settle my nerves somehow.'

'Well, in that case,' she said, 'I need to see you.' And she put me through to the receptionist so that she could organise an appointment for me.

'So how have you been?' Doctor Hill asked.

I leant one arm on the desk. 'Not too good, actually,' I said.

The clock was ticking louder than usual. I hadn't ever heard it tick like that before. I could barely hear my own thoughts.

'Even with the temazepam?'

'I'm not sure about that because I finished the course on Saturday.' Today was Wednesday. 'But I think I'm getting worse without it.'

'I see,' she said. 'Well, no pill is ever the solution in itself. We need to look at the problem and its underlying cause. What, in your view, *is* the problem, precisely?'

I looked at my holdall, at the paperwork and diary within, my throat constricting with emotion.

'I think . . . well, it feels like I'm losing control,' I said.

'Of what?'

'Everything.'

'And that bothers you?' she asked.

'Of course. Wouldn't it bother you?'

'Yes,' she said. 'But it's a bigger issue for some than others.'

'So, I'm, what . . . controlling, obsessive . . . ?'

She smiled. 'No,' she said. 'You're punishing yourself.'

'Oh,' I said.

'If only we knew what for,' she said, tapping her pen on the desk, gazing at me thoughtfully. 'Maybe you'd be better off talking to a—'

'Don't say a therapist,' I said.

She smiled again. 'I wasn't going to. I was going to suggest a counsellor. You're still grieving. Temazepam isn't generally advisable under those circumstances. It can mask your feelings, distort them even. You might be better off talking to someone.'

I shook my head. 'I really don't want to. I mean, therapy's not for everyone, is it?'

'Hmm,' she said in semi-concession.

There was a brief silence whilst she thought. 'What are your main symptoms, would you say?'

'Forgetfulness,' I said. 'And feeling on edge.'

'OK,' she said, 'both of which could be attributed to something simple, such as skipping meals, which can cause a dip in blood sugar levels, for example.'

'With all due respect, this isn't about my blood sugar levels,' I said. 'It's . . . '

'It's what?'

'It's more complicated than that.'

'So, it's emotional? Circumstantial?'

'I, uh . . . ' I was dithering, trying to find the right words.

She turned to her screen, put on her reading glasses, tapped several keys. 'When you were last here, you said you'd been seeing things.' She lowered her glasses to look at me. 'Is that still the case?'

'No,' I said. 'It's changed.'

'How?'

'Because after I saw you, it turned out to be . . . '

I was going to say *real.* Yet nothing felt real about any of this.

'If you don't give me all the facts,' she said, 'I can't offer you an accurate diagnosis.'

She was right, naturally.

'I'm being stalked,' I said.

She didn't attempt to hide her surprise. 'Do you know the offender?'

'No,' I said. 'At least, I might do, but I don't know who it is that's stalking me, no.'

'Have you told the police?'

'Yes.'

'And they're helping?'

'As best they can.'

She nodded, was looking at me with curiosity and pity.

I felt like crying then and tried not to, but tears were coming. I just wanted to get back to normal, to be a good mum and fulfil the honest intentions I'd had on opening The Big Little Deli. Because without my high-level functionality, I was beginning to feel like the old Suzy Faire, the helpless soul whom I had worked so hard not to be stuck with.

Doctor Hill pressed a button on her phone, spoke into the speaker. 'Sara, please hold off for ten minutes. Thanks.'

I wiped my eyes. 'If you have other patients . . . '

'It's fine,' she said. 'You're the last one this morning.'

She smiled kindly then and, once more, she put me in mind of my mum.

I sniffed, sat up straight, decided to ask for what it was that I had come here for. 'Nothing much can be done about the stalker at the moment,' I said. 'But please could I have another course of temazepam?'

The doctor stared at me for what felt like a very long time. And then she turned to her keyboard and began to type, the printer chugging next to her.

'I'm not convinced that this is what you need, especially given what you've just told me. I still feel that you'd be better off talking to someone. However,' she said, handing me the prescription, 'given what you're experiencing, I'll give you what you want. But don't bank on it happening next time. Temazepam is intended for the shortest possible duration.'

I saw what she was saying, nodded, gathered up my belongings.

As I left the room, she called after me, just as she had before.

'I wish you luck,' she said. 'Whoever this man is, whatever he wants, I hope it ends soon.'

I stopped, turned to look at her. 'Me too.'

'Until then,' she said, 'you must look after yourself. And you must prioritise.'

'Prioritise? I'm quite the list-maker already,' I said, patting my holdall.

'I don't doubt,' she said. 'But I'm not talking about a to-do list. I'm talking about what is most important to you – your number one priority.' She raised her eyebrows to indicate that she was expecting a response.

'My children,' I said.

She nodded. 'Then start there. Take care of them, and yourself, of course. And let everything else take second place, or even last.' She swivelled around in her chair and faced her computer again.

'Thank you for this,' I said, flapping the prescription.

'See how you get on with it,' she said. 'I'd like to see you when you've finished the course in six days' time, so make an appointment on your way out, please.'

'OK,' I said.

And I left, walking straight past the receptionist and back to work.

I'm not sure if this was because I'd already forgotten to do as she said, or whether it was because I didn't even know where I would be in six days' time.

Either way, I didn't go back.

26

Ed and Brian came around that evening much later than planned. I was restless before they arrived, had been upstairs several times to check on the children, unable to sit still. When ten o'clock came, I got into my pyjamas and tried to concentrate on reading a book in bed, losing hope of the police arriving. Mike had more faith than me, waited up.

It was gone eleven when I heard the crunch of tyres on tarmac. I peeked between the curtains, saw the police car – Ed getting out, pulling up his trousers, saying something into his radio, glancing up at the house.

I drew back, got my dressing gown, went downstairs. I hadn't yet taken my bedtime temazepam – was glad of that fact when I saw the two officers in the hallway.

Ed and Brian were apologising for their tardiness. 'One of those nights, eh?' Mike said wistfully.

I drew my dressing gown belt more tightly around me as I approached, extending my hand in greeting.

'Let's go in here,' Mike said, pushing the drawing-room door open. 'Either of you like a cuppa?'

'No, ta,' Ed and Brian said in unison.

The officers stood legs astride in front of the window as though manning an event. I perched on the arm of the sofa, not sure if it was a sitting down sort of occasion. Mike was standing also, arms folded, in front of the fireplace.

'Thanks for coming,' he said. 'I was hoping this would die a death, but sadly that's not happened ... And at this stage, Suzy feels – as do I – that it's unclear as to what she's supposed to do in the event of seeing the offender. I know there'll have been some new developments to procedure that I don't know about. So, basically, is there anything that we can do to stop this from escalating?'

''Course,' Ed said, pursing his lips. 'I understand.' He turned to me. 'Have you seen him since Saturday?'

'No,' I said. 'Do you think I scared him off?'

'Sadly, no. I think it might have aggravated the situation.' He clasped his hands behind his back, his stomach prominent. 'Like I said before, it's a grey area. But there is some general advice procedurally. One of the main points, which sounds obvious but can't be stressed enough, is not to have any contact.'

'What if he contacts Suzy?' Mike asked.

'Then she's to get herself to a safe place as quickly as possible and notify us right away.' He looked at me. 'And don't show any fear. Easier said than done, I'm sure. But don't give him any sign that what he's doing is getting any pay-off.'

I nodded.

'You also need to spread the word amongst friends, family, neighbours,' Brian said, 'so they can support you, as well as supply evidence should the case go to court. But, more importantly, it's so they don't give away vital information about you without realising. If their guard's not up and no one knows who this bloke is, then no one knows when they're talking to him, eh?'

I lowered my face so that my chin was nestling into the towelling of my dressing gown. It smelt of my lavender bubble bath.

'We've got a home security system ordered,' Mike said. 'Plus,

Suzy's now got a smart personal alarm that takes a photo of the assailant. Bought it today,' he added, looking at me and then back at the officers. 'Should have got one sooner. But, to be honest, I thought this was going to blow over.'

'Don't worry, mate,' Ed said. 'The biggest problem with these cases seems to be that no one quite takes them seriously, for a whole host of reasons.' He glanced at me. 'And not because it affects women, but because it's a softly-softly sort of crime. Lots of sneaking around without trace. Impossible to say for sure what the hell's going on. Right?'

'Yes,' I said. 'That's exactly how it is.' I flickered an appreciative smile at Ed and, to my surprise, he reciprocated. It was the first time I could remember him smiling at me.

'You'll already know this Mike,' Ed said, 'but collecting evidence is vital in these cases, else we've got bugger all to go on.'

'Try to keep a diary with the key details logged,' added Brian. 'Save everything – voice messages, emails, texts. And if you do find any physical evidence, handle it with tweezers and bag it.'

''Course,' said Mike.

'We'll do everything we can,' Ed said. 'But ultimately you're responsible for your own safety.'

There was a silence.

Brian cleared his throat. 'You've got our phone numbers, haven't you, Suzy?' he said.

'Yes,' I said. 'I have.'

'Well, we'll leave you in peace,' Ed said, moving away from the window towards the door, Brian following. 'Keep us abreast of any developments.'

'Will do,' Mike replied, before seeing the officers out.

He returned to the drawing room, rubbing his hands together. 'Well, at least we can be assured that we're doing all we can for now.'

'Yes,' I agreed. I turned out the lights and made my way back upstairs. Before turning into our room, I decided to go up to the children's room to check on them again.

I sat on the edge of Ruby's bed, watching her chest shifting up and down. Her face was flushed. I inched the duvet away from her chin, brushed her hair from her eyes. She stirred, ground her teeth, moving her head brusquely from side to side, before falling still again.

I rose, went to see Jake, kneeling down beside him.

I watched him sleeping for several minutes, before going to the window where I stood looking out. It was raining lightly. Opposite our house were three ash trees, tall and still. They were laden with clumps of winter buds, black and motionless, like bats hanging there.

Who are you? I thought.

Who was doing this to me?

He was somewhere out there, maybe not so far away. Maybe he was watching me now from an adjacent window, or from a dark corner.

Ruby was saying something in her sleep. I turned away from the window to look at her, but she had stopped talking and was silent again.

I faced the window again, feeling its chill, a draught touching my temples. The street lights had been replaced recently by energy efficient bulbs that cast a fiercer beam over a smaller area. The effect was ghostly, ethereal, with pockets of bright light and deep shade, and nothing in between.

'Whoever you are,' I said quietly, 'wherever you're hiding, you can't hide for ever. Eventually, you'll make a mistake. And that's when I'll get you.'

The wind whistled then and the string of solar lights in our neighbour's garden shook vigorously.

I withdrew from the window and slipped noiselessly from the room.

THE INFORMATION AND ASSESSMENT MEETING

Wednesday 29 March, 2017

I can't sit here like this, slouching into my coat. I have to do something, say something.

'May I?' I say, rising, going to the water cooler.

'Be my guest,' he says. I press the nozzle, the water glugging, bubbles rising as the plastic cup crackles and swells, growing cold in my hand.

I return to my seat, sip the water, realising that there is nowhere to rest the cup. I set it on the floor to the side of my chair, making a mental note to remember that it's there.

'So, these meetings work best,' Dan says, 'and really only work at all, when we try to maintain an open and honest atmosphere. The well-being of . . . '

He glances down at his notes but cannot find what he is looking for. He sucks the end of his pen, flicks over to another page.

He looks up, continues. 'The well-being of Jake and Ruby is our primary concern.'

'Yes,' I say, bending down to pick up my cup again.

Yes *isn't a lot, but it's a start. It's all I've said so far, other than* May I?

'As you know, everything's confidential. But if there's something that touches on child protection then I'm legally obliged to pass it on to the appropriate parties.'

I nod, sip the water, feeling it trickle down through my body.

I want the children protected. Naturally I do. Yet I wish that there were someone protecting me, that I were a primary concern also.

From the moment you cross the line into adulthood, you have to look out for yourself.

That's just the way it goes.

27

The procedural advice on what to do if being stalked seemed full of mixed messages. On the one hand, the victim wasn't to have any contact with the stalker, or to show any fear; on the other hand, she was to take full responsibility for her own safety. It felt passive and impassive, assertive and unassertive. And it was – I couldn't help but think – precisely the way my mother had come to be under my father's brutal hand. If she had often seemed full of contradictions, I now knew why.

For the remainder of that week at work, I found myself treating everyone as a suspect – even Leo and the tuneful Mr Hum.

Is everything wrong? Leo asked me, several times.

Anything, I told him. Is *anything.*

Eh? he said, frowning.

Never mind, I said.

It couldn't be Mr Hum. He never so much as looked at me when he ate his cheesecake, always kept his eyes fixed on his plate.

Tim hadn't been in since last Thursday, not that I was counting.

No one ever flirted with me or made eyes at me or watched me, that I knew of.

There was one rather furtive-looking man who had started coming in since the new deli had opened, but he wasn't anywhere near tall or broad enough to be the stalker.

I spent my lunch breaks in the kitchen with the laptop, reading advice online about how to handle stalkers and harassment. Everything that I was feeling – frightened, destabilised – was normal, given that it was the object of the crime. It was also common for the victim to blame herself.

That didn't come as a shock at all.

In fact, most of the advice was about what the victim ought or ought not to be doing. It was meant to be empowering, yet it felt as though the emphasis was on what the woman was doing wrong. There were pages of advice entitled: 'Common Mistakes That Victims Make'.

Was this the case for, say, armed robbery?

Common mistakes: walking along the road when someone is running towards you with a gun and failing to mind out of the way?

The advice was frustratingly unhelpful. But I recalled Mike's comment about having bigger things to worry about than sexism in legislation, so I kept myself calm and alert – as instructed.

I also kept the rape alarm in my pocket. And I was using a smaller diary, one that I could carry on my person. Now there was to be no forgetting anything.

I was sleeping better too on the second course of temazepam, my body having adjusted to it.

Perhaps, I thought, I could do this.

The forecast on Saturday was sunny so Nicole and I had arranged to take the children swimming. She was going to pick us up and drop us home afterwards. Mike would use the free time to work on our winter-abandoned garden.

We were standing in the hallway at ten o'clock, swimming bags at the ready, waiting for Nicole, when my phone rang.

'I'm so sorry,' she said. 'I have to cancel.'

'Oh, that's a shame,' I said. 'Everything OK?'

'Not really. Zack's just been sick everywhere.'

'Oh no. Can I help? I could bring you some supplies?'

'No, hun. I don't want you to catch anything.'

'Fair enough,' I said. 'But shout if you need me. And give him a big hug from us. Hope he feels better soon.'

'Thanks, Suzes,' she said and hung up.

I gazed at the phone uncertainly, wondering what Mike would say. He halted in front of me, stepping into his wellington boots. 'What's up?' he asked.

'Nicole's cancelled,' I said. 'Zack's poorly.'

'Well, that puts pay to that then,' he said, his mouth a firm line.

'Nooo!' Ruby shouted, stamping her foot. 'Please, Mummy! Can we still go?'

'Have you seen my trainers?' Jake said, not looking up from his book.

I plucked the book from him. 'Have you heard anything that's just taken place?' I asked.

'No? What?'

'Nicole and Zack can't come.'

He looked horror-struck, the way that children do when agreeable plans were cancelled. 'So, we're not going?' he said.

I couldn't bear to let him down, not after all that had taken place of late.

'Shall I drive?' I asked Mike, wondering when I had become so wifey.

Mike was pulling on the old donkey jacket that he used for gardening. 'I don't think that's such a great idea.'

'Why not?' said Ruby, sticking out her bottom lip. 'Mummy's a good dwiver, aren't you, Mummy?'

Jake didn't seem quite so sure about this, judging by his expression. 'Why don't you drive, Daddy?' he said.

'Because I've just put all this on and I'd like to get on with the garden whilst the sun's out.'

'Then why don't we walk down?' I suggested.

Mike shook his head.

I drew closer to him. 'It's a lovely day and it's only a ten-minute walk. And—' I tapped my coat pocket '—I've got this now.' I meant the smart alarm. I lowered my voice. 'We can't live like this, hiding at home.'

'What are we hiding from?' Ruby said.

'Nothing, poppet,' I said.

'From mutant zombies,' Jake said.

'OK,' Mike agreed. 'But go straight there and back.'

''Course,' I said. I was about to say thank you, but then I considered that this was taking the subservient role too far. So, I merely nodded and held my hand out to Ruby. 'Shall we?'

'Yay!' she said, skipping to me. Jake was beaming. I had done something good.

I swam carefully with the children, keeping my head above water, my hair fixed up. But after ten minutes, my hair was so wet I didn't bother trying to keep it dry.

I wasn't much of a swimmer. There was too much about public swimming that I found unpleasant: the urine and saliva in the pool problem, the after-smell of chlorine, shaving my legs in March. But the children loved it and sacrificing my own discomfort for them was just what I had needed that day in order to feel good about myself as their mum.

Afterwards, we went with our wet hair licking our backs to the leisure centre café in search of the overpriced chocolate fudge cake. There was a queue of some ten people and no free tables. However, I found myself saying that yes, absolutely, we would queue for cake.

It was so warm. That was the other thing I didn't like about swimming pools. Why the need for the temperature changes? Freezing water, sweltering changing rooms.

So I was thinking, with Jake and Ruby arguing by my side about who had swum the most lengths, when the table next to us became free.

'Sit down there, Ruby,' I said. 'And you, please, Jake.' I dropped the bags on to the table. They were heavy, full of wet garments. 'I'll stay in the queue.'

I reached into my bag for my purse, only to find it gone.

'Oh no,' I said, spinning round to look at the children. 'Where's my purse?'

There was a man and twin boys behind me. The man eyed me expressionlessly.

'You paid for the pool, Mummy,' Jake said. 'And for the locker.'

Yes, I had. I would have to go back to the changing room. The queue was already thickening behind me, although I seemed no nearer to reaching the counter. I had no choice but to give up my place.

Ruby pouted sulkily as I joined them, taking off my coat. 'We need to go and look for my purse,' I said.

'No, Mummy,' Ruby said. 'We'll lose our table.'

'We can wait here while you go,' Jake said. 'We'll be OK. There are people everywhere.'

That much was true. Someone was pressing up against me as we spoke, kicking the backs of my calves.

Jake and Ruby were looking at me with their backs straight, hands folded on laps, employing their *I want cake and will do anything not to stuff this up* faces.

I hesitated. I didn't want them to become paranoid,

overanxious. What would they conclude if I told them that they weren't safe at the local leisure centre for three minutes on a Saturday morning in a café full of parents and children?

Tough. They had to come with me.

I imagined dragging them through the reception, back to the changing rooms, crying, protesting.

Jake stood up. 'Fine, Mummy. Let's go,' he said. 'Just do what you have to do.' He sounded resigned, weary.

'No,' I said. 'Wait here with Ruby. Don't move. I'll be one second.'

And I took off.

As I hurried away, I thought of my mother's funeral, of how I had felt at the end of the ceremony as though I were moving in the wrong direction, away from all that I held dear.

It felt like that now. I was moving away from my children, should have taken them with me. But I was halfway down the corridor already and would only be gone a moment.

I pushed the changing room door open with two hands and then panicked that there might be a small child the other side of the door who I would have just smacked in the face.

Thankfully, there wasn't.

The changing room was empty. I could hear echoey muffled voices coming from the pool beyond, as though from another dimension.

I pulled open the locker that we had just used. There, at the bottom of the locker, was my purse. I grabbed it, ran from the room.

'Please let this be OK,' I said to myself.

I shouldn't have left them.

At the café, the queue had grown, making access difficult. Two boys were hitting each other; a mother was jigging a crying baby on her shoulder; dads were looking at their phones; a little girl was sobbing.

I made my way through as forcibly yet politely as I could. 'Excuse me . . . Thank you . . . Excuse me . . . Thank you . . . '

But it was all right. There were Jake and Ruby, exactly where I had left them, no harm done.

I arrived at the table and put my hands on it, catching my breath, experiencing a head rush of gratitude.

It took me a moment to realise what was wrong with the picture. It had looked so perfect to my panicked eye.

The children were eating cake.

Ruby grinned at me, chocolate lining her teeth. 'Want some, Mummy?' she said, pronging her fork into thick icing.

'Where did you get that from?' I said.

Jake looked up from his plate. 'From the man.'

I think my heart stopped beating. 'What man?'

'He said you told him to bring it,' Ruby said, chewing.

'What?' I stared at her and then Jake. I looked all around me. I could only see hot faces and parents and children and swimming bags and silver chairs gleaming in the sunshine that was pouring in through the large windows.

'We need to go,' I said.

Jake looked at me in astonishment. 'What? But we just started our cake!'

'No, Jake,' I said sternly. 'We have to go *now*. Come on!'

We pushed our way back through the queue again, Ruby whining, Jake sullen. I hurried them through the turnstile in the atrium, out into the fresh air, blinking at the glare.

'Tell me who gave you the cake,' I said, as we hurried along the narrow concrete track and down the grassy bank to the riverside. Ruby began to cry. I grabbed her hand, held it tightly.

Now we were on the flat, alongside the river. Jake was scuffing his feet in protest, kicking up dust in the gravel. We were going underneath the railway track, through the tunnel. 'Stop that, Jake!' I said.

'What did we do wong?' Ruby said.

I squeezed her hand. 'Nothing. I just need to know who gave you the cake . . . Jake?'

'I don't know,' he said.

'What do you mean you don't know?' I took his hand, pulled him closer. The weight of the swimming bags on my shoulders was hurting me. 'You must know.' I glanced around us in dread – back over my shoulder, the bags swinging.

Was he here?

Was he watching us?

There was no one on the river path. We were alone, exposed.

I thought of the alarm in my pocket, my phone in my bag. I would get the children up to the high street as quickly as possible.

'Come on,' I said. 'Let's run.'

Ruby was already running to keep up with my strides. She began to cry more insistently. 'I don't know what we did wong,' she kept saying.

'Hush, Ruby . . . It's OK.'

'No, it's not,' Jake snapped.

I glanced at him. He didn't look at me. We were running the length of the river. There was a man ahead of us, walking a dog. To my relief, there were two women behind him. And now tourists in colourful anoraks were coming up behind us on hire bikes, chattering in a foreign language. They overtook us and then we made our way up the incline to the high street.

We were behind the deli now, separated from it by the main road. I could see the back of the building – the yard where I put the empty boxes and accepted deliveries.

As we waited for the lights to change at the pedestrian crossing, a group of people amassed around us.

Ed was right, I thought: I hadn't scared the stalker off. All I had done was make things worse.

'Ouch, Mummy!' Ruby said, wiggling her fingers. I was holding on to her too tightly.

'Sorry.' I loosened my grip, looked at Jake. His cheeks were pale, despite the exercise. He still wouldn't look at me, even though I was obviously trying to catch his eye.

I didn't speak again until we had reached the other side of the road and were climbing the hill to home.

I turned to Jake, my voice as steady as I could make it. 'So, this man . . . what did he say to you?'

'I don't know,' Jake said.

'But you said that he spoke to you.'

'I didn't say that. Ruby did.'

'OK. But you must have heard him?' I said, taking his hand.

'No, I didn't.'

'Can you describe him?'

'No.'

'He was smelly,' Ruby said.

'Smelly?'

'He had dirty teeth.'

'I didn't smell him,' Jake said. 'He was old.'

'Was he wearing a dark green wax jacket?' I asked. 'Did he have a beard?'

'Don't know,' Jake said. He pulled his hand away from me, kept it inside his pocket.

'Come on, Jake,' I said. 'Talk to me.' I tried to extract his hand from his coat.

But then he knocked my hand away and glared up at me, his face crumpled with upset. 'Leave me alone!' he shouted. And he took off up the hill.

'Jake!' I shouted.

'Where's he going?' Ruby said.

'Come on,' I told her. 'We need to keep up with him.'

At this, Ruby began to howl. 'I can't. I *can't*! I'm tired.'

Jake was already over the brow of the hill and out of sight. I began to feel tearful myself, wretched. What would he tell Mike?

I shouldn't have left them. Everything had been all right until then.

Except that it wasn't all right. Even if I had taken them with me, we would have still been close to the stalker. He would have been somewhere near us, watching, waiting.

I thought of phoning the police, wondered whether I should have already done so. But the advice was to get us to a safe place before calling them. And I wouldn't feel safe until we were home.

I unlocked the front door, ushered Ruby inside. As I did so, I wondered how Jake had got in. Then I realised that he would have gone around the side of the house to find Daddy in the garden.

I dropped the swimming bags down in my haste to go downstairs and find Mike, before Jake said too much.

Ruby followed me, sticking close behind as we went down to the lower ground floor and then on down to the garden level. She was breathing heavily, sounded scared.

'It's all right, poppet,' I told her, taking her hand.

To get down to the garden level of the house, we had to go through the playroom. The children didn't use this room very often, aside from in the summer when all of us were in the garden nearby. In winter, they were too cut off down here.

'Do you want to play here for a minute, whilst I talk to Daddy?' I asked Ruby, as we crossed the room. She looked doubtfully around her, at the beanbags and stacks of board games, and followed me wordlessly to the door.

'That's OK,' I said. 'You can come with me.'

Outside, Mike was underneath the magnolia tree, beside the wall, digging. When he saw us, he stopped, put his hand to the crook of his back and stood straight.

Jake was squatting on a tree stump, near his dad, face turned away from me. I could tell in one glance exactly what sort of conversation had taken place.

Ruby looked at me cautiously and then all of a sudden – as though a connection had been cut, releasing her – ran to Mike across the lawn, calling for him. He held out his arms to her and scooped her up, her feet lifting high from the ground.

'Hush,' he said. 'It's all right, Ruby.'

She was sobbing. He was smoothing the back of her hair, dancing her in his arms like soothing a baby. Jake watched them, his back still turned away from me.

I stood very still, taking in the scene – the scene of my family without me in it.

I should have said something, but I was stunned.

Besides, it was subtle, what had happened in the last few moments. My nerves were fractured, my judgement impaired. I was frightened and on medication. I couldn't have been trusted to make a judgement either way.

But it felt to me as though something had just occurred, something more significant than the swimming pool incident, the Ethan catastrophe, the stalker himself.

My children had run from me to safety.

28

Mike set Ruby down on the lawn and walked towards me, his trouser legs soaking up the wet. It had rained first thing, before the sun had appeared. All around us, drops were falling plaintively from shrubbery, as though the world were made of ice and melting.

'What happened?' he asked.

I watched Ruby as she gathered fallen magnolia petals, placing them delicately in the bottom of her coat which she had turned up to make a pouch. She liked to collect the pastel petals, saying they were ballet shoes for her teddies. Once amassed she would stash them in her bedroom drawers, where I would find them wizened, browning, and would discreetly dispose of them for her.

I had been doing that my whole life, I felt then; disposing of ugliness, removing it from sight.

'Suzy, if you don't tell me what happened then I'll only have Jake's version of events to go by.'

I glanced at Jake. He was still balancing on the tree stump, picking at a loose bit of rubber on the sole of his trainer. When he saw me looking at him, he swivelled away.

'Jake says that a stranger bought them cake. Is that true? . . . Suzy!'

The children stopped what they were doing, turned to watch us.

My hair was still damp. I shivered, pushed my hands into my coat pockets. 'I only left them for a minute,' I said.

'Bloody hell,' he said. 'Why would you do that, with everything that's going on?'

A robin darted down from a branch on to the sundial beside me. I looked at the simple creature, wishing to trade places.

'I lost my purse,' I said. 'It's got the company credit card in it.'

'So why not take the kids with you?'

I thought about that. I could remember my intense desire to please Jake more than I could remember anything else.

'I wanted to make Jake happy,' I said.

Mike stared at me, confounded. 'Well, look at him! He clearly isn't!'

I glanced over at Jake again, but he was running about now, trying to hit flies with a large stick.

Mike scratched the back of his neck underneath his shirt collar. He had taken his jacket off; it was hung on the handle of his spade. 'Did you phone Ed?' he asked.

I shook my head.

He exhaled, pulled his phone from his pocket. 'Guess *I'll* do that then,' he said curtly.

As he phoned Ed, spoke to him, I continued to watch the robin as it hopped from sundial to magnolia branch to sunhouse rooftop.

Mike hung up. 'He asked if you found your purse,' he said, pushing his phone back into his pocket. 'Well, did you?'

'Yes. It was in the locker.'

He stared at me for several moments, then he shook his head.

Ruby had approached so quietly, we hadn't noticed. She looked at me timidly as though unsure whether to disturb me, before deciding to opt for Daddy instead. She tapped his arm. 'Snail, Daddy,' she said, holding up a snail by its shell.

'Yes, Ruby,' he said. 'Good girl.'

She withdrew, taking her snail with her.

I felt I had to say something to defend myself.

'It was an innocent mistake,' I said. 'It could happen to anyone.'

'No, it couldn't. Not to someone responsible.'

'And what's that supposed to mean?'

'You put the children at risk, Suzy,' he said.

'No,' I said. 'I didn't put them at risk. The stalker did. Why does everyone keep forgetting that I'm reacting like this because of what he's doing to me – to us?'

'No one's forgetting that. I'm doing everything I can to help. I've involved the police. I've organised extra security. I've told you repeatedly to be sensible and alert . . . What else can I do?'

Suddenly Ruby spoke by my side. 'What's a stalker, Mummy?' she said, still holding the snail on the palm of her hand.

'Oh, Ruby,' I said. 'How long have you been stood there?'

'Not long,' she said. 'Why's a stalker putting us at wisk?'

I gazed at her, my mouth falling open. She was so pretty stood there on the grass, holding the snail as though it were made of gold, I couldn't answer her.

I felt overwhelmed, under suspicion by the people I loved the most.

I turned on my heel, running across the lawn towards the house. Ruby was calling after me. 'Mummee! *Mummee*!'

'Suzy!' Mike shouted.

As I ran up the steps, I could see Mike in the reflection of the windows, limping across the grass towards me.

Inside the house, I didn't stop running until I reached our bedroom, at which point I stood by the wardrobe, wringing my hands, unsure what to do next. I put my fingers to my temples and pressed, trying to make myself think, to stay calm.

I realised then that I was due at work that afternoon.

I looked at my watch. It was midday already. I had to be there in an hour.

I hadn't given the deli any thought, hadn't considered the day ahead. I reached into my coat pocket. The alarm was still there. But I didn't have my diary on me, couldn't even think where it was. So much for being more organised.

I sat down on the bed, my head in my hands, rocking myself, moaning.

There was a light knock on the door and Mike entered. He stopped before me, catching his breath.

I looked at his feet. He had taken his wellies off, was wearing old socks, his big toe sticking out forlornly.

I wanted to laugh – at the toe, at myself rocking.

It was pathetic.

Mike put his hand out to still me.

'I'm a mess,' I said. 'I don't know what's wrong with me. I'm falling apart.'

He didn't say anything. He simply sat down heavily next to me, the bed dipping, creaking.

We remained like that for a little while, until I felt strong enough to stand up and get ready for work.

That evening, I lay in a hot bubble bath, my muscles aching, my mood low. It had been an awful day. The deli couldn't have been quiet, but instead had pushed me to the limits with a coach-load of Welsh tourists stopping by. I didn't want to be ungrateful, but the effort had drained me, depleting any energy that I might have been saving for home. The children were avoiding me, or at least had afforded me lots of space. And, for once, I hadn't tried to counter the distance, but had allowed it to stay put. Maybe it was because I needed the space, or maybe I didn't have the strength to do anything about it.

Either way, the children had gone to bed after giving me tiny, cold kisses that felt like snowflakes on my skin.

The bathroom door handle jiggled and Mike entered. I had kept the door unlocked tonight in the hope that he would come in. Sometimes he chatted to me whilst I bathed; sometimes he brought us both a glass of wine.

Tonight, there was no wine.

I kept my eyes on him warily, wondering what his purpose was. For he surely had one, was standing some feet away across our lofty bathroom, hands in pockets, expression sombre.

'I've been thinking . . . ' he began.

His voice echoed around the ceiling. I imagined the words hanging there listlessly, above the steam.

' . . . and I think it might be a good idea for you to move out for a few days.'

I felt myself start in surprise. I sat up, the water cascading around me, the bubbles sloshing up the sides of the bath. 'What?'

He held up a hand. 'Don't overreact. Just hear me out, Suzy . . . You could go to your mum's.'

'But—'

'I said, hear me out. *Please.*'

'You want me to leave you . . . and the children?' I said.

'Not like that,' he said, shaking his head. 'Just temporarily. Think about it: you're still paying the rent at your mum's place. The stalker won't know where it is – you've barely been there for years. But you know the place well. There are people all around, neighbours in close proximity. And Nicole—'

'Wait, wait,' I said, rising. I reached for the plug, the water gurgling away down the plughole. I stood on the floor mat, my body pink and steaming. 'I can't go there. I can't leave—'

'Listen,' he said, pulling a towel from the rack and handing it to me. 'It'll be like a safe house. You're close to the police station there. Nicole's just around the corner. You can taxi to work and back so you're not walking anywhere on your own.'

'But what about the stalker?'

'What about him? Being there is no different to being here in terms of safety. He's proven that he can get to us wherever, whenever. But there's a good chance that he won't know where you are. And by the time he works it out, you'll be back.'

I stared up at him. 'So why go? What will it achieve?'

He hesitated. 'You saw Jake earlier, what he was like . . . and Ruby . . . They were scared. This is too much for them.' He bent slightly to look at me, his knees creaking. 'It'll give you a bit of breathing space. You need a chance to focus on yourself, without worrying about everyone else.'

I was standing there, still holding the towel. He took it from me, wrapped me in it. 'You said you wanted to move on,' he continued. 'Well, how are you going to do that without taking the time to sort yourself out? You won't speak to a therapist. You're working non-stop. How are you going to heal, Suzy, hey?'

I didn't know.

Put like that, it sounded very much as though I wasn't going to.

'I can manage,' he said. 'And I'll be just around the corner. You could clear your mum's things whilst you're there. It's got to be done eventually.'

I looked down at my feet, began to cry.

Mike lifted my chin. 'It isn't as drastic as it sounds. And it might not even work. But it's all I can come up with. So maybe give it a go . . . for all of us. But mostly, for you.'

Sometimes, I was Suzy Taylor, mother, wife, deli owner.

Sometimes, I was Suzy Stone, marketing director, board member.

Sometimes, I was Suzy Faire, six years old, trapped behind that bookcase, unable to help my mother.

I saw then that it wasn't right to be three people in one life. Philosophers could say that we were many people as we journeyed through our lifetime, but that simply wasn't true. We had one soul; and mine had been split, compromised for too long.

'You can do this,' Mike said.

I wasn't so sure. But I knew that I had to try.

THE INFORMATION AND ASSESSMENT MEETING

Wednesday 29 March, 2017

'I want you to relax, if possible. If you feel that things are getting too much, then take a walk around the room. There's an assortment of gadgets over there . . . ' He points to a corner table. 'Personally, I prefer to get a moment of fresh air by pulling up the window and taking in the view. That's acceptable too. It's your time, your choice.'

I look at the table of gadgets in the corner. I haven't noticed them before. There are several stress balls, a black cube of some description, a couple of fidget spinners.

I look back at Dan.

'We'll be talking about whatever it is that you feel comfortable saying. All the decisions will be yours. I'm here to try to fit your needs. This first stage of the process is mostly conversational. If at any point things get out of hand, I may ask you to step outside of the room to cool off . . . Does all that sound clear?'

'Yes,' I say. 'Thank you.'

'Any questions?'

'I . . . I don't think so,' I say.

There is a movement behind Dan then. It's the poster of the stick parent and child, fluttering in the heat wafting from the radiator. It looks as though the stick figures are waving at me.

I take this as a good sign.

'So, what would you like to talk about?' Dan says. 'Anything at all, just to start us off?'

29

We arrived outside my mother's block of flats mid-morning. Mike pulled my suitcase from the boot of the car, extended its handle, set it upright on the pavement for me. There were also half a dozen flat-packed cardboard boxes accompanying me, to help me pack up the apartment.

'Do you want us to come up with you?' he said.

'No,' I said. 'I think it's better that you don't.'

Ruby got out of the car, took my hand, twisting my fingers shyly. 'Are you coming back?' she asked.

I laughed. 'Of course!' I said, my voice falsely high. 'I'm just going to clear Granny Annie's flat. I'll be home in a few days. It won't take me long.'

I glanced into the back seat of the car to look at Jake. Mike knocked on the window. 'Jake, come and say goodbye.'

Reluctantly, Jake got out of the car and came around to my side, dragging his coat along the side of the vehicle. He halted before me, didn't look up.

'Bye, sweetheart,' I said, trying to control the wobble in my voice. I stooped, pressed a kiss on his forehead. 'Look after yourself, won't you? Clean your teeth, learn your spellings, be good for Daddy, don't punch Ruby and I'll be back before you know it.'

In response, he shrugged.

'Jake,' Mike said. 'Tell Mummy goodbye properly.'

'That's OK,' I said, blinking rapidly to stave off tears. The last thing I wanted to do now was cry in front of them. 'I'd better get on. I'm going to try to clear it all today.'

'Well, good luck,' Mike said. 'But if you don't get it done, leave it. Take your time. This is supposed to be a stress-free time, remember.'

'Yes,' I said. I turned to Ruby. 'Goodbye, poppet. I love you so much.' I knelt down, straightened her coat. She smiled bashfully at me, then pressed a sloppy kiss on the end of my nose.

Jake was already in the car.

'I'll call you later,' Mike said.

I watched them leave, the backs of my children's heads gradually getting smaller

'Look back,' I murmured. 'Please.'

The car stopped at the junction. As it turned and began its way down the long lane, I saw Jake's head turn to look at me.

It was something, better than nothing.

I remained standing there until the car disappeared and then I looked at the suitcase on the pavement and the flat-packed boxes.

We are all alone, my mother used to say; we come into this world alone and we depart it alone.

This felt like one such time for me.

I picked up the boxes, took the handle of the suitcase and approached the doors of the shabby block that I had grown up in.

The doors were wooden panelled with criss-cross wiring inside the glass. I wondered how many times I had reached up to that thumb-printed handle to open the door. The pathway was shiny and bowed under decades of footsteps, the welcome mat faded.

There were only twelve flats, yet there seemed to be a lot of people coming and going – women with prams, teenagers in black anoraks. Even whilst I was standing there, two boys appeared, their faces looming beyond the chicken-wire glass.

I stepped back and the door swung open, the acrid smell of marijuana accompanying them.

I waited for the boys to disappear, before pulling on the door handle and entering.

In the lobby, I headed for the stairs, tugging the suitcase behind me. I thought of my mother trudging up these same steps each day, her legs weary after a day's work, cleaning products in her arms, the charms on her holdall jingling.

When I reached our door – her door – I stopped, dropped the boxes, out of breath.

In the flat behind me, a bass was booming. My mum hadn't ever complained to me about the noise here, nor had she indicated that she was unhappy. Yet I had often wondered whether there were times when she had regretted leaving Carlisle. Had it all been worth it?

This question had haunted me all my life, even before I was aware of it. The idea that my mother had lost everything by coming here – status, standard of living, friends, family – had made me work extra hard, with the intention of one day taking care of both of us.

My plan, as recorded in my teenage scrapbook, had been to buy the perfect home; just like 8 Rose Lane, without the violence. But things hadn't worked out the way I had imagined.

My mum had been serene, malleable. She would definitely, so I had believed, agree to my proposal. Yet when the time had come to ask her to move in with us, she had declined the offer.

My life was with Mike and the children, she had told me. I had to live my own life. She wasn't a part of that, would be in the way.

My mother hadn't been needy, weak, but strong. I had already known this on some level, but still I had thought that she would come when I called.

The whole thing had upset me greatly, my big plan foiled.

A sudden noise in the corridor startled me, speeding me back to the present. The door behind me opened, the music blaring. I turned to see a man wearing a ripped hoodie. 'All right, darlin',' he said.

'Well, the music's a little bit loud ...' I said, trying not to sound uncivil.

'Piss off,' he said, before going down the stairs, jumping down several at a time.

'Charming,' I said to myself, and then unlocked the door.

Inside, I peered around the gloomy room. The curtains were half open. I had left them like that as a mark of respect.

I sat down on the edge of my suitcase, biting my thumbnail. Then I made up the cardboard boxes and went through to the bedroom.

There wasn't much to clear away. I wasn't exaggerating when I said that my mother had few possessions. We had moved into the flat fully furnished, bringing nothing with us, amassing little over the years.

In the bedroom, I gazed at the threadbare carpet, the worn eiderdown, inhaling the scent of my mother – the sweet musty scent that was so peculiar to this room that it was hard to say whether it came from her, from the room, or both.

I took a deep breath and pulled open the top drawer of the chest. I had already looked through this underwear drawer since my mother's death, in search of clothes for the burial. The oversized knickers were a kerfuffle of faded prints and ancient grey elastic. I had bought her new underwear over the years; they were still there in the packaging, untouched.

I gathered up the knickers, placing them inside a bin liner. I then did the same with the sock drawer, noting the new items at the back.

I had often teased my mother about her habit of stashing things, telling her that when she one day passed away I didn't want to find perfume in cellophane, clothes still tagged. Yet here I was doing just that. I wasn't going to feel wretched about it though. I had told her how I felt, had told her to stop waiting and start living. But she hadn't heeded me.

I turned hesitantly to the bedside table. I hadn't ever gone poking about in there. It was my mother's personal space, in an apartment that afforded little.

'Well, here goes . . . ' I said.

There was nothing inside the drawer, other than a plastic bag secured with elastic bands. I picked the package up and took it to the window where the light was better.

The bag contained a dozen bottles of pills.

I sat down on the bed, pulled my phone out, looked up one of the medications: *citalopram*. It was an antidepressant, also used for panic disorder. I typed in another: *zolpidem*. Sleeping pills.

I did the same for each of them. They were all for anxiety, depression, sleep disorders.

I sat staring at the bottles strewn on the eiderdown.

I'd had no idea. And yet I should have known that there was no way that my mother could have been settled here, not with the past hanging over her.

Something unpleasant occurred to me then.

Evidently, my mum had been reliant on medication to get through the day. Was I headed the same way?

I remained on the bed, my back against the wall, my knees drawn to my chest. I thought of how my mum had seemed the last time I had seen her – in the weeks and months prior to her death. I wouldn't have said that she had seemed as though she were on medication and yet maybe she had been on them for so long, I couldn't remember who she was without them. Maybe she couldn't either.

I rose, went to the mirror, looked at myself.

I was shocked by what I saw. Perhaps it was because when I had last looked in this mirror, I had been so much younger.

Whatever it was, I looked ghastly, sallow, gaunt. No wonder Mike had sent me away.

I gazed about me at the desolate room.

This wouldn't be my future.

I picked up the pills, tossed them into the bin liner. Then I went through to the lounge and unzipped my case, grabbing the temazepam. There was only one pill left, rattling forlornly inside the bottle. Even still, I flushed the pill down the toilet and threw the empty bottle in the bin.

There. Gone.

I returned to the bedroom, where I opened the wardrobe door and surveyed the clothes within. As anticipated, there were many items with the tags still on. The rest were shabby-looking.

'I'm sorry, Mum,' I said, beginning to cry, pulling the clothes delicately from the hangers, placing them into the cardboard box. 'Thank you for everything that you did for me.'

I came to one of her favourite cardigans and held it to my face, inhaling my mother's scent, closing my eyes.

I felt her presence strongly then. It was the only time that week that I did. But I felt her beside me, loving me, telling me to be strong.

I had arranged for my friends to come over that evening to keep me company. When they arrived, they gathered tentatively by the front door of the apartment. I could smell the pizza through the stack of cardboard trays that Donna was holding.

'Well, don't just stand there,' I said, beckoning them inside.

Their hesitancy was partly circumstantial, partly historic. My mother had never made anyone feel at home here, apart from me.

Nicole slipped off her coat, glancing around as though looking for somewhere clean to place it. Helen and Donna were taking their shoes off, whispering to each other. 'Don't worry about shoes,' I said. 'I'm about to give the place up.'

'Right you are, sweetheart,' Donna said, pulling a bottle of red wine from her tote. 'And is this allowed?'

Helen looked doubtful. 'What about Suzy's—'

'Meds?' I said. 'Not on them any more.'

Donna arranged the pizza boxes on the lounge table. I went to the kitchen for plates, Nicole following me, hunting for wine glasses. 'There aren't any,' I told her.

'No worries,' Nicole said, pulling chipped cups from the mug tree. The cups were bell-shaped, ugly really. My mum and I had bought them from a charity shop some thirty years ago. They had lasted well. We had been delighted, I recalled, to find a set of four.

I lit a few candles, stood them in jam jars to create a bit of atmosphere. But then I realised that we only had two chairs. All these years, I had only just noticed that no one could ever have sat down to eat with my mother and me.

Helen had read my thoughts. 'We can sit here, Suzy,' she said, lifting cushions from the sofa and dropping them onto the floor.

We sat on the cushions, eating pizza, pouring wine into mugs.

'So how are you doing?' Helen asked me.

'Not too bad.' I gazed at the cardboard boxes and bin liners set by the door. 'I didn't stop all day, clearing the flat. It's done, aside from a few kitchen and bathroom bits.' I paused. 'She's gone. I don't think she's here any more.'

There was a respectful silence.

'Why are you here though?' Donna asked. 'I'm not sure that I totally understand.'

'It's not that complicated,' I said. 'It's ... well ... a time out, if you like.'

'When will you go home?' Nicole asked, sipping her wine.

'When I'm ready, I suppose.'

'And what about *him*?' Donna said. 'Do you feel safe here on your own, knowing that he could be out there, somewhere nearby, watching you?'

'Don!' Helen said reproachfully.

'What? I'm just saying. To be honest, I'm surprised at Mike for letting you do it, Suzy.'

'He thinks it's more than likely that the stalker won't know I'm here, that it's a safe house, of sorts. And to be perfectly honest ... it's about keeping the children safe. If I'm away from them, they're safer, if you see what I mean.' I sighed, glanced about me. 'Funnily enough, Mike's right: I do feel safe here. It's a solid building. The doors and walls are heavy, rock solid. And I'm used to it here.'

'You're so brave,' Helen said, placing her hand on my knee. 'I don't know if I could be so brave ... Do you want one of us to stay with you?'

Even as Helen said this, I saw the uncertainty flash through her eyes as she began to think about how that might work with school runs and club drop-offs and homework to supervise and meals to cook.

'No, thanks,' I said. 'I'll be fine.'

'Well, I think we should meet here again mid-week to see how you're doing,' said Helen. 'What say you, ladies? Can we all make Wednesday?'

'Works for me,' Donna said.

'Roger that,' Nicole said.

'Do you always have to say that?' Helen said, tutting. 'It always sounds so—'

'I wasn't aware that I said it very often,' Nicole retorted.

After we had cleared up, my friends assembled by the door, ready to leave. 'You know where I am, hun,' Nicole said. 'I'm just around the corner. Give me a call any time for anything.'

I kissed her on the cheek. 'Thank you.'

We all hugged goodbye.

I opened the door, pressed the light on, listened to it whirring. My friends started down the stairs, their footsteps growing fainter. I could hear voices, a sneeze. Then the front door slammed shut.

There was a little click and the light timed out.

I closed the door to the apartment and stood with my back to it, surveying the empty space.

30

No wonder my mother had never complained to me about the noise; her apartment was extraordinarily silent at night. There could have been a party out in the hallway and I wouldn't have heard. It was like sleeping in a soundproofed cell, except that I had the key to get out. I found myself sleeping so deeply that week, I had to turn my wake-up alarm to its maximum volume on my phone.

I couldn't remember the last time I had showered of a morning without someone banging on the door to ask me a question, or the last time I had got ready for work without one of the children pushing my lipstick up so high on its stalk that it broke off, or asking me why I wore blusher: did I like looking embarrassed?

Experiencing getting ready for work without a family was both luxurious and disquieting.

A black cab took me to work. I had selected it especially in order to feel safe. The same driver would be picking me up and bringing me home every day until further notice. I wasn't fooling myself that I had a chauffeur, but I did feel like the woman who had once commanded a place on a board of directors. It had been too easy – nappy-changing, selling quiche – to forget her.

Despite the fact that the cab felt secure and smelt like the inside of a hair salon, I found myself glancing over my shoulder often to see whether we might be being followed.

The driver seemed to have noticed my erratic behaviour. 'Not in any kind of trouble are you, love?' he said, his eyes smiling in the rear-view mirror.

'No,' I said. 'Just anxious about getting to work on time.'

'Well, I'm going as fast as I can,' he said.

That was on the first journey. By the end of the week, I was no longer jumpy, no longer wide-eyed. Five nights of sleeping alone in my mother's space, of grabbing moments with my children at the deli or over the phone, had fortified me, stiffening my resolve.

I had thought that my past had made me weak, susceptible to harassment, but it was – so this time alone had taught me – quite the opposite.

It was my past that made me so well equipped to deal with this. I knew all about men like him. He could come up behind me by car or on foot. He could bring his worst. This time, I would be ready.

On the Friday morning I was unlocking the deli, trying to keep a look out for Mike and the children who would be passing by on foot at any moment, when Tim appeared.

'You're early,' I said. 'I'm not open yet.'

'I had an early meeting next door. I thought they'd at least have put some toast on for me, but no such luck. I'm starving.'

'Well, we can't have that now, can we?'

'Allow me,' he said, extending his arm to open the door for me.

Inside the deli, the light was dim, the air cool. I was pulling up the blinds when I caught sight of the red of Ruby's coat. Mike and the children had rounded the corner onto the high street.

'Get down behind the counter,' I said to Tim, poking him in the back. 'Quick!'

He stared at me. 'You've got to be kidding . . . '

'It's important!' I said. 'Please!'

He hurried forward, ducked behind the counter. I went to the door, the bell tinkling as I stood on the pavement, waiting.

'Morning,' I said brightly, as they drew level.

To my pleasure, Ruby was smiling at me, but was still gripping Mike's hand. Jake nodded in greeting.

'Hi,' Mike said. He had shaved, had a little nick on his chin. 'How are you?' He stooped to kiss my forehead. It was a slightly stiff, formal gesture. I went on tiptoes to kiss him on the lips instead. 'You look good.'

'I feel good,' I said. 'I'm sleeping really well.' I crouched down to address Ruby. 'And how are you, my gorgeous poppet?'

She smiled at me, revealing a gap in her teeth in the middle of the lower row. 'The toof fairy came,' she said.

I looked at her in surprise. 'Really?' I stood up, frowned at Mike. 'I didn't think they lost them that early?'

Mike nodded. 'They can do, apparently. I googled it.'

'You googled it?' I said. 'Why didn't you *ring* me?'

'Because I didn't think it was important.'

'My daughter loses her first tooth,' I said, keeping my voice low, controlling my annoyance, 'and you didn't think to tell me? I didn't even know it was wobbly! This is exactly the sort of stuff you should be telling me about – the things that I don't want to miss.'

Mike pulled on my arm to move me closer, so that we might talk discreetly. 'Don't make this into something it's not. It's not easy, manning the fort alone . . . Think of the children.'

I was about to reply when I noticed that Jake and Ruby were staring up at me expectantly, wondering what I was going to say next.

Jake had a milk moustache, I saw then. I knew that Mike wouldn't notice the details, that the children would be going to school with sleep in their eyes, wax in their ears.

I went towards Jake, wiped his mouth. To my sorrow, he pulled back from me. 'I was just trying to . . . ' I trailed off.

'Well, we'd better get going,' Mike said.

'Yes,' I said. 'Mustn't be late for school . . . ' I glanced at my watch. I still had a few minutes though. 'How's Narnia?' I asked Jake.

He shrugged.

I looked up at Mike for clarification.

'Finished it,' Mike said.

The moment was bittersweet.

'*The Last Battle*?' I said, astonished. 'You finished the final book?'

'Yes,' Mike said.

Why wasn't Jake talking to me? It was me who had bought him the set of Narnia books; me who had spent countless hours encouraging him to read. Had he somehow forgotten that?

'Well, we'll see you later,' Mike said, shuffling his feet.

'Wait,' I said. I bent forward to kiss Ruby and to button up her coat, smoothing it flat. Then I turned to Jake and kissed the top of his head, the only place he seemed to allow me access to, given that he had withdrawn deep into his fur-lined parka. 'Are you coming by later?' I asked Mike.

He shook his head. 'Sorry. Football training.'

'Oh yes, of course.'

'Morning,' Mike said to a passing father. The man had a daughter in Ruby's class, a son in Jake's. The children began to play tag instantly, giggling insatiably.

'Walking along?' the father said.

'Yep,' Mike said.

'Wait, Mike,' I said, glancing at the man, who with good

grace turned to look in the window of the dry-cleaner's. I gazed up at Mike. 'Maybe you could pick me up tonight on your way home so I can have supper with you and the children? I'm thinking of coming home tomorrow morning. If you could come and get me around ten, we could—'

I broke off. He was shaking his head.

I was distracted then by the children. Jake and the boy had uncovered a dog's squeezy ball, which they were kicking about on the pavement, banging it against the metal shutters of the shop next door.

'I don't think we're quite ready for you to return,' Mike said quietly.

'Hey?' I said.

The man's patience had timed out. He tapped Mike on the arm. 'I'm gonna make a move,' he said.

'Sorry,' Mike said. 'I'm coming now . . . Come on, you lot. Let's get going.' He glanced at me, lowered his voice. 'We'll talk about this later. Call me in your lunch break.'

And that was it. He was off down the road with the man and the four children.

On the corner, Ruby turned back to look at me; Jake did too.

I just stood there, dazed. And then I returned to the deli.

Tim stood up from behind the counter, brushing his suit down. 'Bloody hell,' he said. 'When did you last dust down there?'

'I think I'm losing my family,' I said.

'What?'

The doorbell sounded and Leo entered, frowning – no doubt wondering why the coffee machine looked cold, the pastry baskets empty. 'Good morning?' he said, as though it were a question.

'Hi, Leo,' I said. I was on my way out to the kitchen. The deliveries would be arriving at the back door any moment.

The doorbell rang again as one of my other staff arrived. I

could hear footsteps behind me; Tim was following me through to the kitchen. As I went to unlock the back door, he put his hand on my arm.

'Do you want to tell me what's going on?' he said.

I didn't have long with Tim, not enough time for anything other than a brief explanation. The deliveries were arriving; my staff were putting aprons on, loading baskets, brandishing trays of goodies from fridge to counter. Tim was adept at swooping backwards to avoid large objects so it seemed, one hand protectively on his silk tie.

'I promised your mum I'd keep an eye on you,' he said, as I lifted pains au chocolat with the tongs and dropped them into the counter basket.

'Forget all that,' I said. 'I've got friends. And I don't need the complication of an ex in my life.'

'Don't think of me as an ex. Think of me as a friend too. We've known each other a long time.' He followed me out to the counter. 'Suzy . . . I know it's none of my business, but it sounds like you need to do something about this.'

I stopped. 'Like what?' I said.

Leo was wiping the coffee machine nozzles, tea towel tucked into his back pocket. I could tell from his stilted body language that he was listening in to our conversation.

'I dunno,' Tim said. 'But I suggest that whatever you do, you get on with it pretty sharpish.'

Leo glanced at me then. I raised an eyebrow at him as if to say, *Concentrate on those nozzles, will you.*

'I really must get on with work,' I said.

'Fine,' Tim said. 'But here's my card. I expect you binned the other one.'

I hadn't, but nor did I know where it was.

'Call me if you need anything,' he said.

I followed him over to the door. 'Don't you have a life?' I asked.

He tucked his shirt more neatly into his trousers. 'A life?' he said. 'I've got a *wife*.'

Well, that told me. I nodded meekly.

'You were good to me,' he said. 'When my mum died ... remember?'

I did remember. Tim's mother had died during the time that we were seeing each other. I had held his hand at the funeral.

'You call me,' he said, pointing at me. And then he left.

I put the business card inside the till for safe-keeping. 'He looks like he works out,' Leo said, smirking.

'Oh, wind your neck in, will you?' I said.

'Wind my neck?' he replied in confusion. 'What's wrong with my neck?'

At lunchtime, I went outside to the small yard where the deliveries arrived. It wasn't that quiet there, overlooked as it was by the main road, but it was fairly private. We shared the yard with the other businesses, but mine was the only one that took daily deliveries, aside from the florist at the end of the row. The shop girls were currently unloading flowers from a van. I couldn't hear what they were saying to each other, yet the sweet scent of the flowers greeted me. It was a very blue time, March, I noted: lilacs, cornflowers, bluebells galore.

One of the girls noticed me, shouted out something. I didn't catch it. I called out hello in return.

Then I turned away, my face growing serious. I put one finger against my ear and dialled, holding my breath.

'Mike?' I said, as soon as he answered. 'We need to talk. I'm not sure that doing it over the phone is best though.'

'I don't want to discuss this in front of the kids,' he said. 'And you're at work. So ... '

I didn't want to argue about this of all things. 'OK,' I said. 'Let's talk now.'

There was a long pause. Clearly, he expected me to lead.

'I want to come home,' I said. 'It's time. I miss the children. And I miss you ... I don't understand why I can't, what the problem is.'

'Well, it's Jake, for starters,' he said.

'Jake?'

'This has really affected him.'

'How?' I said, watching a cyclist making his way along the road above. The yard was set below the road, at the bottom of a steep grass verge. The cyclist was puffing away, face gleaming, a long line of traffic behind him.

'His teacher said that he's been acting strangely, that he's subdued, withdrawn.'

'Well, why didn't you tell me?' I asked.

'Because you've got enough on your plate. And it's nothing major. It's just that she was worried about him. She asked me if everything was all right at home.'

'Oh my gosh,' I said, putting my hand to my face defensively. 'How embarrassing. What did you say?'

'Well, what could I say? I just said there were some issues but that we were working hard to sort them out ... And then there's Ruby too.'

I felt my heart shift, twist. 'What's wrong with Ruby?'

'She's been wetting herself. I've been handed her pants in a carrier bag twice after school.'

'That's nothing,' I said, thinking of all the times I had wet the bed as a child. 'She's only four. Accidents happen. And she's missing her mummy. My not being there has unsettled her.'

He paused. 'It was last week, Suzy,' he said. 'Before you left.'

My stomach turned over anxiously.

'It's not happened since you've been gone,' he was saying.

'And Jake's teacher said this morning that he's like a changed person, back to his old self.'

'Oh,' I said. 'So, what are you saying?'

It was pretty clear what he was saying.

'Just that it's not as simple as you moving back home when you're ready ... This time apart has given me time to think. And well, I think that for everyone's sake, especially for the kids, it might be a good idea if we consider temporarily ... '

Don't say it.

Don't say it.

' ... separating.'

I inhaled sharply. A lorry was passing by on the road overhead, hissing through the puddles, exhaust clouding behind it. Everything was rushing at me, all my senses hitting me at once.

'You can stay at your mum's and get yourself together. We'll work out a timetable regards you seeing the kids. And then when things are better, we can review the situation.'

I looked up at the sky. It was one of those spring skies that looked like it had stepped out of a children's paintbox. A seagull was gliding lazily, riding an airstream, the sunshine highlighting its wings.

I wasn't listening to him. He was asking if I had seen the stalker, if I had gone back to the GP, if I was still on temazepam, whether I had thought any more about seeing a therapist.

I was thinking about a poster I had passed that morning on my way to work – a large poster in a plastic frame at a bus stop. The cab had pulled up alongside it at the traffic lights and I had gazed at the image of a woman with blonde hair and red lips who was beaming reassuringly at the camera.

A lawyer isn't just for Christmas, the caption had read.

'I've got to go,' I told Mike. And I hung up.

I typed *A lawyer isn't just for Christmas* into my phone and looked at the page of suggestions, clicking on the first one.

It took me to the website of a firm of family lawyers in central Bath.

I went to the Contact Us page, clicked on the green telephone icon and listened for the click as the call connected and rang.

31

THE INFORMATION AND ASSESSMENT MEETING

Wednesday 29 March, 2017

Today

'OK,' Dan says. 'So, what would you like to talk about? Anything at all, just to start us off?'

I look down at my lap. I can't imagine who will speak first and what about.

'Actually, if I could just jump in and say something,' Mike says.

I glance sideways at him. For the past ten minutes, since arriving late – without apology or explanation – he has been sitting there, statue-like, arms folded, shirtsleeves taut on his biceps. He's wearing a checked shirt that I bought him only last month. He looks very attractive and my heart dips at the thought of this because I'm not certain what the situation is between us.

'Go ahead,' Dan says, holding up his hands accommodatingly.

'Well,' Mike says, shifting in his seat, 'it seems to me that this is about suitability – whether Suzy's suitable to be looking after the children any more.'

'What?' I say. 'Why would you say that?'

But Mike isn't looking at me. He is looking earnestly at Dan, who is sitting in front of us, right in the middle, like the adjudicator that he is.

'She's become too unreliable,' Mike says. 'She's forgotten so many things and has put the kids at risk on countless occasions. I've tried to be patient and supportive, I really have. But when all's said and done, I just want what's best for our children. And I'm not sure that that involves Suzy at the moment.'

I stare at him, astounded.

Dan is nodding cordially as though saying, *Yes, the weather is very mild for March.* 'And how long would you say that this has been the case?' he asks.

'Since the beginning of February,' Mike says.

'Since my mother died,' I say, smoothing my black dress flat on my lap. 'I haven't been myself since then, as you can imagine. But' – I look at Mike – 'everyone needs to be cut a bit of slack now and then, don't they?'

Mike still won't look at me. 'Not when children are involved.' He lifts his chin, addresses Dan. 'I used to be a chief inspector in the police. I know exactly how little time it takes to destroy a life. It can happen in a matter of seconds.'

'Destroy a life?' I say, laughing uneasily. 'That's overstating things a little, don't you think?'

Neither Mike nor Dan are laughing. Mike's chin, if anything, is a little higher, more righteous.

Dan is writing something down on his pad, leather file propped on his knee. 'So, you're not in agreement with this, Suzy?' he says, looking at me.

'No,' I say. 'Not at all. I mean . . . yes, I've been a bit scatty—'

'Scatty!' Mike says, shaking his head. 'It's more than that.' Finally, he turns in my direction but still there's no eye contact. 'You've been all over the place. And it's affected the kids.' He turns back to Dan. 'Jake's teacher reported to me that he's been withdrawn in class. And Ruby's very unsettled.'

'And they, of course, are our primary concern,' Dan says.

'And mine,' Mike says. 'Which is why I'm here. I'm their primary carer. I see what goes on, on a day-to-day basis.'

'You're here,' I say, swivelling in my seat to look at him, 'because I contacted this law firm to get some advice because you can't just overrule me and say that I can't come home, whether you're a stay-at-home dad or not. They're my children too.' I look at Dan in exasperation. 'He's totally shut me down.' I look back at Mike. 'You're shutting me down.'

'Because you're not a fit parent at the moment,' he says.

The tone of his voice is strange. There's an edge to it that I can't decipher. He isn't just angry with me. It's something else.

'Perhaps at this juncture,' Dan says, dangling his arms behind his chair, 'it would be beneficial for us to park this conversation and move on to some basic details of the process instead . . . So, based on the information that I gathered when I interviewed you separately earlier in the week, I believe that you *are* suitable candidates for mediation. I would envisage you needing three to four sessions to iron things out. How does that sound?'

How does that sound?

I can't answer that, not out loud.

'Going to court is the last resort,' he continues. 'Mediation can help you separate without the emotional and financial burden of court . . . '

He is talking about costs now. I am not listening, am gazing at the stick parent and child poster, asking myself how precisely we got here.

Does everyone do that – ask themselves that same question?

Things are moving too quickly for me. Two days ago, on

Monday, I was sitting here in this same room with Dan Cassidy, discussing my options. It was nerve-wracking, but it felt under control since it was at my instigation.

But now Mike is here and we are already agreeing to four sessions at the end of which we will have reached an agreement. To do what? Separate permanently? Divorce?

Where will I be once that point is reached? Where am I in all this? Living in my mother's flat? Seeing my children at appointed times?

I paid for our house. It was my money, the money I saved from my role at JB Alliance during a time when I was earning six figures yet still living with my mum.

I have been supporting us since Mike's injury. I have been the breadwinner. And it is my father's 1.8 million that will be arriving later in the year.

It's my beautiful home. I will not part with it.

I will not part with my children.

'I don't want to do this,' I say impulsively.

Dan stops talking, looks at me.

'I don't want to separate,' I say. 'I just want to be at home with you and our children, Mike. We're a family. We don't need to put ourselves through this. We just need to go home.'

There's a silence. For the first time, Dan looks awkward. Perhaps it's not awkward so much as apologetic.

He turns to Mike. 'And what would you like to say in response to that?'

Mike takes a long while to reply, as though he is thinking about it. I see in this delay a glint of hope. Perhaps my words have affected him and he is arguing internally about the best course of action.

I smooth my dress flat again, thinking of the last time I wore it: at my mother's funeral. I remember the dark shape that I noticed over in the corner by the yew trees that day. I think of the stalker. He seems very removed from this, as though hailing from another world, another time.

I have only seen him once since the swimming pool incident, only once since moving to my mum's. It was on Monday, as I was closing the deli. I was pulling down the blinds when I saw him stood a little way along the high street, leaning against a letterbox, watching me.

I knew it was him. As always, I couldn't see his face. But I knew that it was the same man who I saw at the park that day, the man who bought cake for the children at the pool. I had no proof, of course.

I didn't do anything about it on Monday. I didn't call the police. I just pulled down the blinds as though he wasn't there. By the time I'd locked up and stepped into the cab, he had vanished.

I bite my nail, tears pricking my eyes. But I will not cry here, will only ever be professional, rational. To Dan Cassidy, I will seem just like the woman who once worked for JB Alliance.

Mike is speaking now. I focus on his lips moving. He has turned in his seat and is looking straight at me, at last.

There is no mistaking what he is saying. I could have asked him to repeat it, but it would have sounded exactly the same.

'You initiated this, Suzy. You made this about the law. So, let's do this the right way, with the kids' interests at heart. Anything less than that will be half-baked, messy. And it's not fair on them.'

I open my mouth to reply but then I stall, thrown by his words.

'Well, that's it,' Dan says. 'I'm afraid we're out of time for today. But are you both free next Monday for the first official mediation session?'

Dan sees us out, the corridor seeming too small and narrow to house the three of us, as well as Mike's disgruntlement. Dan holds the white door open for us, and although he says goodbye warmly enough, I sense that he is thinking about his next clients, who are in reception and are standing up in preparation.

I have lost something of the bond that I had with Dan Cassidy, if indeed there ever was one, which I suspect there was not.

Mike is in the loop now, will be at every meeting henceforth. Mike being here has changed everything.

I think of the thin lady in the thin coat, who was so desperately seeking a moment of Dan's time an hour ago. She is no longer in reception, has disappeared. I hope that she is all right.

I understand now why she wanted a word with Dan Cassidy alone, without anyone else to bear witness to her agony or to curdle the truth.

But Mike is striding off, through reception, making for the door; I will have to be quick if I want to speak with him. As I hurry forward, I catch sight of a giant wall poster of the blonde woman with the red lips – the same poster that brought me here.

'Bye for now,' the receptionist calls after us.

'Bye,' I say, over my shoulder. Mike is pulling open the front door. 'Mike!' I call after him. 'Wait.'

But he's not waiting. He is gripping the black railings, going down the steps joltingly. The effort will be hurting his leg, such is his haste to get away from me.

I squint in the daylight. It's not as if we have been sitting inside in the dark, but somehow it still seems too bright. It is lunchtime; the square is busy with a party of tourists emerging from the hotel next door; shoppers are bumping paper bags as they pass each other; workers in suits are spilling down from the steps of the offices housed in Georgian buildings.

Mike is already going along the pavement. That's it? He doesn't want to talk to me, or even say goodbye?

I race down the steps after him, pulling on his arm to make him stop.

'Why are you in such a hurry?' I say. 'Can't we be civil and discuss this like grown-ups?'

'That's what mediation is for, Suzy,' he says gruffly.

I gaze up at him in confusion. Is he even in there any more? How does this happen? How do you go from loving couple to this in the space of, what, a couple of months?

'Mum's funeral was on the first of February,' I say. 'Is that when all this started? It seems to me like that's when it—'

He shakes his head. 'It's not about your mum or your grief,' he says. 'It's everything.'

'Everything?' I say. 'What does that mean?' I reach for his hand. 'Don't you love me?'

He doesn't reply, at least not with words.

Ever so gently, he pulls his hand away.

'Oh no,' I say, dismayed, tears pricking my eyes. And this time I don't have to stop them because Dan Cassidy isn't watching me. 'Mike. Please ... '

But he is looking at something else, has set his eyes on the horizon, on something or on some place other than me.

'I need to get going,' he says.

I sniff, burrow my face in my scarf. 'When will I next see you? When will I see the children?'

He pushes his hands into his jacket pocket, stiffens his back.

I chose that jacket. I went to town with the children on Christmas Eve and bought it for him. It didn't fit into our bag, so we carried it home with it poking out of the top. It was raining, and we were worried about the jacket spoiling, so we ran home, all the way up the hill. When we got in, Mike wasn't there so we lit the fire and hung the jacket in front of it to dry off before wrapping it.

All this I think as I look at him.

There is something on almost every part of him that has touched me in some way or has been associated with me.

How can we separate?

'We'll see you on the school run like we always do,' he says. 'And—'

'That's not enough.'

'If you just let me finish . . . I'll bring them into the deli after school tomorrow.'

'And what then? I'll only ever see them when you say so?'

'No,' he says. 'You'll see them depending on what's agreed in mediation.'

I want to ask him more: why he doesn't seem to love me, whether it's permanent or temporary, whether there is hope, whether the ultimate aim of mediation in our case is not for us to separate but to move back in together and continue as before.

But I don't ask any of this because he is walking away from me and is lost in the crowd.

For a moment, I think that I can't breathe, that I'm going to die right here outside the law firm, stepped over politely by tourists and office workers.

And then I remember someone – three people.

I leave the square and, as I go on my way, I phone Nicole, Helen and Donna. None of them pick up. I leave them all the same message.

'I need you to come over tonight. I don't mind what time, whatever suits. But please . . . Just come.'

As I walk it begins to rain, yet it's sunny too. There will be a rainbow. I look for it. It doesn't happen instantly. But by the time I'm back on the high street in my domain, nearing the deli, I see it there, arching through the sky behind the trees.

I think of the rainbow over the stick mum and child in Dan Cassidy's office – because it's a mum, I've decided. It's not clear, looking at the poster, hasn't been clear to me. But I can see now.

It's a mum holding on to her child.

32

‘This doesn’t seem like Mike,’ Donna says, pursing her mouth sceptically. ‘What’s got into him?’

‘He said it’s everything – my grief, all the cock-ups . . . ’

‘What cock-ups?’ Donna says. ‘So, you’ve, what, forgotten a few diary events? Who the heck hasn’t? What does he want, perfection? Because that’s overrated, big time, believe me.’

‘Do you want me to have a word?’ Helen says. ‘I’ve always got on really well with him.’

‘So did I,’ I say wryly.

Nicole is stood with her back to us, looking out of the window. I used to stand in the exact same spot as a small girl, watching children play at the park. It wasn’t that my mum kept me captive here exactly, more that she always had me home before dark. In the winter, I barely left the flat, given how early the sun fell.

‘What do you think, Nic?’ Donna says. ‘You’re the one who’s been through divorce.’

‘Divorce?’ I say, wincing.

‘Perhaps we shouldn’t be bandying that word around too much,’ says Helen. ‘Hopefully it won’t come to that.’

‘It can happen really quickly,’ Nicole says, turning around to look at us, her face pale, pinched. ‘One minute you’re happy. The next minute . . . *Gone.*’

'Great,' I say, taking a long drink of Merlot.

'How does he seem, Suzy?' Helen asks. 'Upset? Because if so, then you might be better off with a marriage counsellor. He probably still loves you. It's just all gone a bit . . . you know . . . confused.'

'My sister saw a marriage counsellor,' Donna says. 'Said it was a complete waste of time. When a marriage is over, it's over.'

'*Not helping*,' Helen says, frowning.

'He's not acting upset at all,' I say. 'If anything, he's acting robotic.'

'Robotic?' says Donna. 'What, cold?'

'Yes. Sort of.'

'Emotional numbness,' says Helen. 'I learnt about that on a mental health course for work.'

'Now you're the one not helping,' says Donna. 'This isn't about mental health. It's about their marriage.'

'Funny,' I say, tucking my feet underneath me on the sofa, 'I finally get my life back under control and my act together, and I lose Mike.'

'You haven't lost him,' Helen says.

'She has,' Nicole says.

We all look at her. She's wearing a pale-pink long cardigan over a denim dress. She has one arm wrapped around her waist, one hand holding her wine glass. She is still standing by the window, her hair haloed by the street light outside.

'If you're in mediation then it's the end,' she says. 'They're not there to help you get back together. They're there to help you split up. I had to go through it with Jamie before we got divorced. We only had one session though. There was nothing to argue about. It was pretty clear that Jamie wanted nothing to do with Zack.'

There's a silence whilst everyone digests this bitter information.

I am thinking that I wish Nicole wasn't having to relive her own experience on my behalf. I look at her regretfully, remembering how much weight she lost when Jamie left her, how much support she needed.

Donna puts her glass down, looks at me intently. 'This is about custody, Suzes. That's why he's shutting you down. He's going to file for divorce and go for full custody of the kids.'

Helen tuts and frowns at Donna.

But I say something that surprises everyone, including myself. 'I think you're probably right.'

'Oh my gosh,' says Helen. 'Do you think so?'

'Yes. I do. And I have to think that way, even if it's not true. Because if I don't, if I'm sailing along thinking this is going to blow over and everything's going to be all right, then I could find myself waking up one morning to the fact that I've lost everything: my kids, my husband and my home.'

Helen stares at me, mouth open.

'Then you know what you've got to do, Suzy,' Donna says. 'You've gotta fight. Every step of the way.'

'I will,' I say.

'And we'll be there, right behind you. Won't we, girls?' Donna glances around her.

Helen nods, cautiously. Nicole is quiet.

'What's up with you?' Donna says, turning to look at her.

'Nothing,' Nicole says. 'It's just that ... well ... it's not as simple as that. It's horrible. I wouldn't wish it on anyone.'

'Well, you don't have to. Because it's already here, by the looks of things. But Suzy can handle it. Look what she's achieved so far. She's even managed to clear her mum's flat.' Donna gestures about her, pointing to the neat arrangement of boxes and bin liners by the front door. She turns back to me, taps my leg. 'You can do this, girl. It'll be a walk in the park.'

Later, when my friends leave, I see them out and go back into the apartment, closing the door behind me.

Donna's words were rousing. But Helen's caution told another story, one that foresaw heartbreak. And Nicole's silence told another: one of the harsh reality of where I was headed. It took years for Nicole to recover from her divorce.

Was I really strong enough for what lay ahead?

I wake early the next morning, unsettled by a pain in my chest. As I rise and draw the curtains, looking out over the gloomy courtyard beyond, I realise that I am missing my children so much it is physically hurting. I left them two weeks ago this Sunday. That's two weeks too long. I need to be with them; I have to be home.

Now that this seems to be more about Jake and Ruby than anything else, I notice that my attention has shifted from Mike, taking some of my feelings for him with it.

Perhaps this is what happens when we fight for our children. Custodial battles kill marital love by default.

I don't know whether this is true. I don't even know if I'm in a custodial battle. But I do want to know more about the law. So, as it's early, I make a coffee and look up everything that I can find online about mediation, divorce, court orders and child arrangements.

On my way to work by black cab, I gaze out of the window, wondering whether the need for such precautions is still there, whether I can drive now – whether I can ask Mike for the car, or purchase my own. Yet I don't want to make any changes at the moment, don't want to do anything that makes it seem as though I am setting up on my own.

Nor do I want to inadvertently instigate divorce. I have already set the legal system into motion simply by asking for advice. And now we seem to be caught in the wheels of a juggernaut that is thundering ahead, dragging us along with it like roadkill.

I don't know where we're headed, but I need to know precisely what's going on and what my rights are so that I'm prepared, forewarned.

Despite my resolve not to, I find myself glancing behind me again, scanning the landscape to see whether someone is following me.

I tell myself not to do this any more and sit back in my seat facing front again.

I wonder when I will be free, whether that day will ever come.

At work, I get going right away, working at double speed. This will allow me ten minutes for a brief meeting before we unlock the doors.

Leo is the first to arrive. 'Once you've got changed,' I say, 'can you join us for a meeting, please?'

'Sure thing,' he says, eyes shining inquisitively.

When the other two staff arrive, I ask them to sit down at a table whilst we wait for Leo.

I notice the children passing the window then and I jump up quickly, pulling open the door.

'Good morning,' I say. Mike nods mechanically. Jake looks down at his feet. Ruby pulls away from Mike and skips towards me.

'I had a dream about you, Mummy,' she says.

'Oh, did you, Ruby? That's lovely.'

'We can't stop,' Mike says, tugging on Ruby's hand. 'We're running a bit late.'

'That's fine,' I say. 'I'll see you after school then. I'm making *valinna* cupcakes especially.'

Ruby smiles at me, exposing her missing tooth. Jake nods.

And off they go.

I will not be upset by the brevity of the encounter. I am concentrating on the end goal. I return to the deli, sit back down again.

Leo has joined us. I begin. 'I don't want to make a big deal out of this, but I thought a quick meeting would be helpful.' I take a deep breath. 'Mike and I are going through some difficulties. I'm not sure where we're headed, but it could become complicated . . . ' I pause, lay my hands flat on the table. 'There may be times when I'll need to pop out to get things done, but you won't be left in the lurch. And on the rare occasions that you do have more responsibilities, I'll ensure that you have pay packets to reflect—'

I break off. The older of the two women has placed her hand on mine. She has a large hand; it's warm, sun-flecked. 'Suzy,' she says. 'We know you won't take advantage. See to your family. It's important. We can cover for you.'

'Oh,' I say, blushing. 'That's kind of you.'

'Well, you're a good boss.'

Leo shrugs, wags his finger. 'This, I'm not so sure of,' he says. 'Good boss? Hmm.'

I laugh. 'You're horrible,' I say.

'You love me,' he says, going out to the kitchen to fill up the bread baskets. The two women put on their aprons, go behind the counter.

I eye the phone, wondering how early I can phone Dan Cassidy. My research has raised questions that I would like to run past him. I tap my pocket, feeling for my slimline diary; the list of questions is in there. The rape alarm is in my cardigan pocket. I am never without it.

I decide that the phone call can wait until lunchtime. And then I get on with the day, uplifted by the thought that my children will be here after school.

It's a good omen, I think, when I unlock the door and the first person to enter is Mr Hum.

I set my face purposely at neutral, bidding myself not to reveal how upset I am when the children arrive and step timidly into the deli's book corner. Ruby won't touch her beloved red velvet cushions; Jake won't sit down.

Whatever has taken place that day since they last saw me, they have shifted away from me. Ruby doesn't mention her dream about me, won't be drawn into conversation about it. Jake is holding his arm; he knocked it at lunchtime and has an elbow cut.

I eye Mike enquiringly, wondering why the sudden change. He is seated as far away from us as possible, reading a newspaper at a table by the window, glancing intermittently at his phone. He doesn't want a drink, has refused my offers. Taking something from me now means admitting that I am useful or needed, I speculate.

Things are worse between us than I had imagined.

But this isn't about him, or us. It's about the children.

I will not give up.

I kneel down on the cushions and pick up a book about ghosts that I know Ruby likes. The front cover creaks like the door of a haunted house when you open it; on the final page there's a panel that you have to warm up in order for the image to appear. Jake always likes this bit. I am rubbing the panel as fast as I can now and blowing on it, trying to make the ghoulish image manifest itself.

'Look, Ruby,' I say. 'It's coming.'

Jake looks at it critically. 'There's not enough heat.'

I rub even more determinedly.

'It's not working,' says Ruby, sticking out her bottom lip. A small child is behind me, watching closely, dribbling on my shoulder. I stand up, ease myself past the toddler and go to the coffee machine where I press the book against the hot filter jug. 'There!' I say triumphantly, taking it back to the book corner.

I crouch down. Jake, Ruby and the dribbling toddler peer over my shoulder.

'Ogoowah,' the little tot says in awe.

'It's magic, Mummy,' says Ruby, plonking herself on to my lap. She is close to me finally. I wrap my fingers around her waist, watch as she plays with the book. I press my nose into her hair, inhale. I love the scent of her strawberry shampoo. I love her little fingers, warm and sticky from school, speckled with ink. I love everything about her.

I look up at Jake. He is perusing the books on the rowing boat. I think of when he first saw the bookcase in the furniture shop at the top of town. His face lit up, he ran towards it. *This one, Mummy. You have to get this one.*

I pat the cushion next to me. 'Come and join us, Jake,' I say.

He hesitates and then sits down, bringing a book with him. 'What you got there?' I ask, pointing at the book.

'It's about dinosaurs. I've read it at school. I like it.'

'Oh,' I say. 'Well, that's good.'

He presses himself a little closer to me. 'Would you like to read it?' he says.

I gaze at him. 'I'd love to,' I say, taking the book from him. I can smell Marmite. He has a little streak of it on his sleeve. I touch his elbow. 'Is it sore, sweetheart?'

He nods. 'Very.'

'Well, I've got a first aid kit out back. How about I look at it for you before you go?'

He nods again. Then he looks up at me. 'I love you, Mummy,' he says.

I put my arm around him and I kiss the top of his head and my heart swells so much, I feel light-headed. 'I love you too,' I say. 'Never doubt it, not even for a moment.' And I open the book and begin to read.

33

FIRST MEDIATION SESSION

Monday 3 April, 2017

Things went a little better with Mike on the weekend. I asked him to come over with the children on Saturday morning to help me take the bags of my mum's things to charity, plus some to the tip and the remainder home to our spare room. Since our house was the final stop-off, once there, I asked if I could stay for lunch and help the children with their homework, as well as pick up some clean clothes for myself and do some laundry. Part of me resented having to ask; part of me just wanted to be nice. Mike agreed and it all went well. He even told me to take good care of myself when we parted and sounded sincere, affectionate almost.

But today he is sitting next to me with his arms folded and the wall has gone up, a little higher, a little thicker than before.

'So, our goal today and over the course of the next few sessions, is to try to reach an agreement about where your children will live and how they will divide their time with you. We will also be wanting to get down to the nitty-gritty of details, including when contact – such as phone calls – can take place and any other issues that you might have. Some people want to specify food choices, for example.' Dan smiles. 'I've known couples argue over how many doughnuts are acceptable per day . . . I kid you not.'

There is a silence. I can't think of anything that I will want to lay down the law on, given that Mike and I have the same values, have rarely argued over any aspects of child-raising. The mention of doughnuts makes me think of Krispy Kreme's though, which was where Nicole bumped into Tim a few months ago.

I wonder what Tim's wife is like. I expect she is gorgeous.

This is what mediation does, or separation in general. Everything feels like a competition or a judgement. You start to wonder if your legs are too dumpy, your eyes too close together – whether you are being let go because you have let yourself go.

I glance at Mike. I presume, before I study him, that he will be looking even more handsome to me now, with my newly acquired insecurity.

Yet he doesn't. He looks tired, more than I have ever seen him look before. He is holding himself at a funny angle. His walking stick is propped against his chair.

I gaze at him with interest. Perhaps he is cracking under the strain of being a single dad. He thought of himself as the children's primary carer but didn't realise how much I did too.

Maybe it is better to have an unhinged wife than no wife at all.

Well, we are in mediation. If there's a safe place to ask this question, it is here, surely.

I turn to him. 'Can I just say, before we plunge head first into this today . . . ' I glance at Dan. He nods for me to continue. 'Well, I'd like to check whether this is what you really want, Mike. Because if you're in any doubt—'

'I'm not,' he says.

The sharp tone in his voice surprises me.

I look at Dan in embarrassment. He holds up his hands. 'This is a good point that you've raised, Suzy. It highlights the fact that we all need to be very clear about our intentions . . . Suzy, you and I met initially to discuss your needs, shortly after which I met with Mike to do the same. And it seems to me, Mike, from our first private conversation, that you are looking to separate on a formal, permanent basis. Is that correct?'

'Yes,' he says.

I swallow awkwardly – audibly, I fear.

'OK,' Dan says. 'Then let's talk about living arrangements.' He crosses one leg over the other, takes off his glasses and chews the end of the glasses' arm. 'What we agree here won't be legally binding, unless you get a solicitor to draft a consent order for the court to approve. For now, it's informal and just between us . . . So, who would like to begin?'

'I want to live with the children,' we both say at once.

I smile sadly; Mike shifts in his chair, flinching as he straightens his leg.

No one will care for you like I do, I want to tell him.

I held your hand when you were in hospital; I was there when you passed out in pain. I organised your medication, helped bath you, feed you. You leant on me when you first stood again.

'I think I should just come out and say it at this stage,' Mike says, looking at Dan. 'Ultimately, I'll be looking to file for divorce on the grounds of unreasonable behaviour.'

I stare at Mike, and then Dan, and then the poster of the stick figure mother and child on the wall. The poster has been secured down, is no longer flapping. Everything is being nailed down, settled.

I feel faint. My mouth has gone so dry I am worried that I

can't swallow. I look about me for the water cooler, but it has moved, is no longer there.

Intuitively, Dan is pouring me a glass of water from a jug. There's a splash as an ice cube drops into the glass. He hands the glass to me. 'Mike?' he asks.

'No, thank you.'

I drink, my hands trembling. I set the empty glass at my feet, stare at the carpet in mortification.

How can this be happening?

'I don't understand,' I say.

'Suzy,' Mike says, 'you had to realise that we're in mediation for a reason? I've been tolerant, but your behaviour has been unacceptable. You nearly ran a mother and baby over, for Christ—' He stops, modifies his language. 'Well, it's not what I signed up for. I'm sorry.'

I look at him. 'Not what you signed up for?'

I'm about to say that I didn't sign up for a husband with only one good leg, but I stop myself just in time.

I sit up straight, address Dan. 'I just want what's best for the children.'

'Of course,' he replies. 'So, let's get back to where we were: who wants to begin regards living arrangements? Someone needs to kick us off. Clearly you both want to live with the children, but that's not possible. So … what instead? What do you envisage working for you?'

'I'm not moving out,' I say, folding my arms.

'You already have,' says Mike.

This statement cuts the air, hangs there menacingly.

'I haven't,' I tell Dan. 'I'm just … '

'Living away from us because you're too unstable to live with us,' Mike says.

I go to reply and, once more, I choose not to.

I can see where this is going. I will stay quiet as much as

possible today, out of harm's way. I will listen, ensure that things don't go too far. And then I will go home tonight, regroup, work out my best course of action.

At the next session, I will know exactly what to say.

On our way out, I sense that Mike would like to be rushing off through reception and out of the front door as he did before, but this time his progress is slow. He is hobbling on his cane. I follow behind, mutely. Whenever I provoke him, I seem to uncover something that I don't want to hear. Perhaps if I don't say anything . . .

But then when we are outside on the street, he turns to me. 'I'm sorry,' he says. His voice sounds hoarse, strained.

'What for?'

This sounds like one of those things that I shouldn't ask, but I've said it now.

He doesn't tell me what for.

I suppose it is obvious.

He glances around the street, squinting at the sunlight, scanning the horizons.

'I want you to be careful,' he says, looking down at me. He moves me to one side as three ladies come along the pavement wielding shopping bags. He still protects me; he cannot help himself. 'Ed hasn't got anywhere with the case, has pretty much dropped it. It's not his fault. There's just no evidence and he's under pressure. It's tough . . . '

I nod. I know how it works.

'But that doesn't change the fact that the creep's still out there. He could appear at any time. So, you need to keep your guard up. OK?'

'OK.'

'Have you still got your alarm?'

'Yes,' I say, tapping my pocket.

'Good. Keep it on you. And watch your back. You haven't seen him since last Monday, have you?'

I shake my head. 'No.'

'Good. Well, stay vigilant.' He tightens his grip on his cane, shifts his weight. 'I'd better be off now.'

'Are you in pain?' I say, looking up at him.

'I'll survive,' he says.

What I would give to rewind a few months, to be able to reach up and run my fingers through his hair, to go on tiptoes to kiss him. He isn't putting balm on, is getting chapped lips. No one's there to tell him otherwise.

When did he decide that he didn't want me to do that – to kiss him, care for him, be his wife? At what point did he realise that he didn't want to be with me? Was it overnight or a gradual process? Either way, why hadn't he told me what he was feeling so that I could have done something about it?

Maybe he had told me or had tried to at least. Maybe I had missed it. After all, I had missed almost everything else, veering from small lapses in memory and judgement to bigger divorce-inducing errors.

I well up, bite my lip, look away from him.

'Could you get an emergency appointment to help with the pain?' I say.

'I have,' he says. 'Wednesday – a two-hour consultation and therapy.'

'Well, that's good,' I say. 'Do you want me to do the school run?'

He shakes his head. 'No need. It's at eleven. I'll be done in plenty of time.'

'Oh.' I button up my coat. It's still chilly, even though it's April now.

Today is my parents' wedding anniversary, I realise.

The thought makes me feel peculiar, almost like laughing out loud. The day that my husband announces he wants a divorce is the same day that my parents' doomed marriage took place.

The only thing that could make the moment more perfect would be snow falling from the sky, as it had on my mother's coffin.

But life isn't like that, of course. There is no snow today. And now Mike is hobbling away from me, turning the corner, out of sight.

34

Work was exhausting today. It felt as though everyone within a five-mile radius visited the deli, wanting a table or takeout. At one stage I had to go out to the delivery yard just to inhale some fresh air.

For once in my life, I don't like being this busy, not when I have so much thinking to do.

That evening, Thursday, I work into the early hours on deli paperwork and then on research into the law surrounding children and separation.

When I finally go to bed, I am wired, beyond sleep. I flick through some invoices. Yet work doesn't appeal – I'm past it, caught in a neverland of not wanting to work or to rest.

I pick up my phone, yawning, scroll through it, deleting old texts and emails. There are hundreds of photographs, mostly of Mike and the children. I will leave them all there for now. I go instead to the videos, which I rarely ever look at. Sometimes, Jake hijacks my phone; I watch some wobbly footage of a toy car hurtling down our staircase on a ramp made of hardback books. I can hear Ruby laughing in the background, Jake is commentating. The sound of their voices makes me homesick.

I click off it, open another video. I had forgotten about this one. It's the footage that I recorded of the children playing football at the park.

I watch Ruby holding her dress out wide, spinning around. Jake and Zack are trying to tackle Helen's daughter. The video lurches as I turn to talk to my friends, before swooping back to the children again, capturing grass and sky in the process.

And then a dark shape crosses the picture.

I peer closer at the screen. What *is* that? I tap the screen, pause it. And then I clap my hand to my mouth, my heart racing.

There he is, in the background, just beyond the children. I zoom in on the beard, the broken-down boots, the roll-up between the fingers.

All along I have had, in my possession, an image of him.

I look at the time. It's two thirty. I can't disturb anyone yet. I will have to wait.

I replay the video until my eyes grow too heavy to look any more.

When I next open my eyes, it is morning and I am lying there, gripping my phone, my hand aching.

I order the cab to come earlier than usual so that I can get organised. My hands are shaking as I unlock the deli's doors, pull up the blinds; it is partly tiredness, partly trepidation.

When Leo arrives, I ask him to look after things for me. I may be gone an hour, maybe more. He tells me this is fine and I slip away before my other staff arrive. As I leave, Leo winks, wishes me good luck and whilst he doesn't know what I am doing, he can probably tell from my expression that I am not going to have my hair done.

It is quite a walk, across the bridge, past the homeless men sleeping on the steps of the Baptist church, along by the river, past the gushing weir and up the steep hill to the top of town. I am dressing in a more corporate style lately, wearing clothes that I haven't worn since JB Alliance. Today I am in a wool blazer, pink shirt and navy chinos, but I am wishing I hadn't gone for wool now that I am overheating.

When I arrive at my destination, I run up the dozen steps, pull open the door and step inside.

It is quiet and warm inside the station. I approach, smoothing my hair on my shoulders, pulling my blazer straight.

'I'm wondering if someone can help,' I say to the desk officer.

He raises his eyebrows at me. 'All depends what it is that you require help with, ma'am.'

'It's regarding an ongoing case. I have some information. Ed and Brian have been dealing with it. I would have rung them but I've got something that I want them to see personally and urgently. So, I thought it best to bring it straight here.'

'Ed and Brian . . . ' he says leadingly, probing for more information. But I don't have any – no surnames, job titles, identification numbers.

I feel my face redden. 'Oh. I thought they worked here,' I say.

'Wait a sec,' he says. He taps a keyboard. 'Thought so. There's an Ed and Brian based at Hilton.'

'Hilton?' I say. 'Isn't that out near—?'

'Bristol. It's a rural branch.'

'Oh.'

'So how can we help anyways?'

I glance about me. 'Well, it's about a . . . harassment issue.'

'I see,' he says, leaning towards me slightly. 'Concerning yourself?'

'Yes,' I say.

'And you are . . . ?'

'Suzy Taylor.'

He nods. 'I'll buzz Inspector Davies.' He presses something underneath the counter, speaks into a handset. 'He'll be right with you,' he says, after hanging up. 'Lanky bloke. Can't miss him.'

I smile. 'Thank you.'

'You're welcome. Take a seat.'

I perch on the edge of an orange spongy chair, just along from an old man who has his eyes closed and a battered carrier bag on his lap. Within minutes, I hear footsteps approaching.

And then before me is a very tall, lean man. The counter policeman was right: you couldn't miss him.

He clicks his heels together officiously. 'Mrs Taylor?' he says. 'Inspector Davies. Please' – he sweeps his hand towards the door – 'follow me.'

We go down the corridor into a side room, the entrance of which the inspector has to stoop under in order to enter.

It is cooler in this room and unadorned. The walls are white, the carpet beige. In the middle of the room is a table, with a chair each side. It is an interviewing room. I wish it weren't so clinical-looking, but then I am here about a clinical issue.

I sit down, clutching my holdall on my lap, before reconsidering. I do not want to look neurotic, housewifey; I have Tupperware on display. So, I set the holdall down, cross my legs, my hands clasped around my knee.

I notice then that Inspector Davies is carrying a loose sheet of paper, which he begins to read when seated.

'There isn't much logged about this case,' he says. 'But I think I have the gist of it.' He stretches his long legs out, puts his hands behind his head, elbows wide, and gazes at me, scrutinising me. I can't imagine that he could take up more space if he tried. 'Adams and Jones have been dealing with you, in the main?'

I nod, uncertainly. 'Ed and Brian?'

'That's them,' he says. 'Slightly irregular, given that they don't work here. Why not contact your local branch?'

'I wasn't aware that they weren't based here,' I say. 'My

husband contacted them. They're old colleagues of his . . . He was Chief Inspector of Westborne branch near Bristol, before he got injured. He took early retirement.'

'Sorry to hear that,' he says. 'Anyone I know?'

'Mike Taylor,' I said. 'I'm his wife.'

A look of something passes over his face then, but it's too quick for me to decipher. Mike has told me the stories about officers trying to get out of the force early, faking injuries to acquire enhanced pensions. This man, older than Mike, could be someone who's desperate to find a way out, resenting anyone who has done so before him.

He clears his throat, looks at me, elbows still horizontal. 'So, someone's been harassing you, stalking you, breaking in, what not?'

Only a policeman could make terrorising a woman sound as trivial as burger toppings.

'Yes,' I say. 'And although up till now there's been very little evidence, if any, I have some new information.' I pull my phone from my pocket, locate the video and push the phone across the table towards him. 'The man's on here . . . Look.' I sit back in my seat and wipe my hands on my trousers.

I watch as the inspector withdraws his long limbs into a more condensed shape and hunches forward to pick up my phone. He plays the video, pauses it, zooms in. Then he pushes the phone back to me.

'You've no idea who that is?' he says. Out go the legs, up go the elbows again.

'No,' I say. 'Should I?'

He smiles ever so faintly at me. 'That's Craig Carver. A corrupt copper from a bad batch in Bristol a few years back. Got kicked off the force, if I remember rightly.'

'And why would I know him?' I ask, with a warm, uneasy feeling in the pit of my stomach.

'Well,' he says, condensing again, setting his hands on the table in front of him, 'I think that's something you should probably ask your husband, Mrs Taylor. Don't you?'

And he gazes at me then, his expression cool, unreadable.

Outside the police station, I am panicky.

I lean against the sloping wall that runs up the side of the steps, but within minutes a female officer has arrived and is asking if I need assistance.

'I'm fine, thanks,' I say, moving away.

Opposite the station there is a small park with a neat iron gate and high hedges. I cross the road, enter the park, sit down on a bench. I look about me. Nothing seems right. The buildings seem too close, too bright, too tall. The trees above me are too green. Everything smells overbearing, pungent. I press my palms together as though in prayer, trying to breathe deeply.

Once I have steadied myself, I leave the park, heading for the wooden hut down the way that has been there for years, housing a taxi firm.

There is a row of cabs waiting, so I jump in the first one and we take off.

Inside the car, it smells of pineapple and coconut; an air freshener is dangling from the rear-view mirror, swinging rapidly with every turn. The driver doesn't want to make conversation and I am fine with that.

Nearer home, along the high street, with my deli in sight, the traffic thins. We are going up the hill to home now, the engine labouring with the incline, the driver shifting gear with a jarring crunch and a lurch forward.

I feel nauseous. I close my eyes.

The cab has pulled up outside our house and the driver is turning in his seat to look at me expectantly.

'Sorry. I was miles away,' I say, climbing out. I reach into my purse, hand the driver a note and turn away. He is calling after me. I have given him too much, but I don't heed him.

I have only one thing on my mind and, as I get towards the front door, my ears ring with a high-pitched sound, jangling my nerves.

I find my key, put it in the lock. It flashes through my mind that Mike might have changed the locks as a security measure. I hold my breath.

The key turns in the lock, there's a click and the door swings open.

35

'Mike?'

The taxi has gone. It waited for a few minutes outside, engine running, before pulling away. I heard it leave. And now I am standing alone in the hallway.

'Mike?' I call again.

Nothing.

I step out of my shoes, but keep my blazer on; I am cold, and I don't want to stay long. I glance at my watch. It is just gone half past ten. I want to be gone within the hour, back at work.

I walk down the hallway. All the doors are closed. Mike always closes them as a precaution; in the event of a fire, they hold it back. I prefer them open. Because I am not living here, these tiny changes are being made. I remember what Dan Cassidy said about getting down to the details of lifestyle choices.

I prefer our children to be raised in a doors-open environment, Mike.

This makes me smile, but only momentarily. I hold the banister as I make my way downstairs. I can hear something now, soft music. As I descend into the kitchen, I see Mike sitting at the table, typing on the laptop, listening to the radio. He hasn't heard me yet, is fully immersed in what he's doing. I cough loudly, not wishing to creep up on him. He turns in surprise, then pulls down the top of the laptop with a snap.

'Something you don't want me to see?' I ask, my tone pleasant.

But Mike's annoyed. 'What are you doing here?'

'I live here,' I say.

He can't really argue with that. I could remind him about whose money it was that provided the down payment on the property. But I am too full of good grace – at this stage.

I pull out a chair at the opposite end of the table, sit down, set my hands on my lap and my eyes on him. 'Do you want to tell me what this is all about?' I say.

He looks at me blankly. At least, he is trying to look blank. But the effort is killing him and his left eye begins to twitch.

'You must think I was born yesterday ... Announcing divorce, out of the blue. Isn't that a bit harsh? My mum dies and I'm upset, forgetful. But is that really grounds for divorce – for, what was it you said ... *unreasonable behaviour*?'

He doesn't reply, merely rubs his eye brusquely.

'What happened to in sickness and in health? After all, I helped you when you had your accident, Mike.'

This is slightly cheap of me, but still, it doesn't provoke him. He is going to sit it out.

I decide to make the situation as comfortable as possible. 'Do you want tea?' I ask him. He shakes his head.

I fill the kettle, wait for it to boil, whilst admiring the view from the kitchen window. If the thought occurs to me that my time looking at this view may be limited, I don't entertain it for long.

I make my tea and sit back down, glancing at my watch again. 'So ... ' I say. 'Tell me how you know Craig Carver.'

He starts slightly at this. He has been trained to keep cool, not to give anything away. He is very good at it. But I'm his wife and nothing gets past me. Or at least, not any more.

'Who?'

I laugh. 'Oh, come *on*! I've just been talking to Inspector Davies. Know him?'

'Nope.'

'He seemed to think it was funny that Ed and Brian were handling our case, given that they work at Hilton.' I cross my arms. 'Did you ask them to help so that you could control the situation? Did they realise they were pawns?'

'Pawns?' He smirks. 'Don't be daft. You're way off target.'

'Am I?' I say. 'Because I don't think I am.' I take my phone out of my blazer and hold it up. 'I've got footage here of Carver. The inspector said that I'm to ask you what your association with him was. So here I am . . . asking.' I put the phone down, gaze at him. 'Did you work with him? Did you know he was corrupt?' I hesitate. But I have to say it. 'Were you corrupt?'

He reacts then, finally, bringing his hand down heavily on to the tabletop, rattling the crockery.

'Enough!' he shouts. 'You don't know what the hell you're talking about!'

I stare at him. 'Oh my God, Mike.'

'No one has anything on me. You can dig all you like.'

'I don't want to dig,' I say. 'I don't care what you did or what you were. That's on your conscience, not mine. You don't work for the police any more. You're not in a position of trust or responsibility – except where our children are concerned. And that's why I'm here. Because of them.'

I stop talking. The clock is ticking above me. It is almost eleven o'clock. I pull my tea towards me, my hands cradling the mug.

'I know it was Carver, following me,' I say.

Mike is focusing on the laptop, fiddling with a button on the side.

'You got him to do it, didn't you?' I say.

He looks up slowly. His eye is twitching again.

'How?' My voice is hoarse, a whisper. I clear my throat. 'How did you get him to do it? And why? I've been good to you, haven't I?'

He fiddles dismissively with the laptop again.

'Tell me!' I say.

He pushes the laptop away suddenly and looks right at me, his jaw set in a nasty square.

'I want the kids,' he says.

It's my turn to give a little start.

But I'm just as good at hiding it. I have been trained just as well as him to hide things, to give nothing away.

'Well, then we have a problem,' I say. 'Because you're not getting them. The law will side with me.'

He smiles spitefully. 'Don't try to beat me where the law's concerned. You won't win.'

'I will,' I say. 'Because I'm their mum.'

Once again, he smiles. 'That doesn't mean so much these days,' he says. 'Not any more. Equal rights work both ways, you know.'

Not any more?

Mothers never had all the rights, I want to tell him. Not in 1982 in Carlisle; and not now.

But he has missed my point. I'm not saying that I will be awarded the children because the law will deem me more suitable as their mum; but that I will be awarded them because as their mum I will fight for them until my last breath.

He is on a roll now, inspired by his innate sense of entitlement. He straightens his back, looks at me with his chin raised arrogantly.

'Divorce rates are at a record high in the UK,' he says. 'And since 2008, there's been a rise in the number of stay-at-home dads awarded custody in cases where the mother's the breadwinner ... So, you see? You can't stick your men at home doing all your dirty work and then expect to walk away with the kids too.'

'I didn't expect that,' I say. 'I wasn't expecting to get divorced, remember? This is all new to me.'

'Who cares?' he says. 'The only thing that matters is that I'm going to get custody. I've looked after the kids all these years. It's only fair.'

'Fair? I worked because you couldn't! I was paying the bills! There's nothing fair about this whatsoever. I'll fight you every step of the way.'

'And good luck with that. Given your history.'

I react then. I'm not able to disguise it. I am staring at him in abhorrence.

He holds up his fingers, striking items off. 'One: unstable past including a history of violence, which you lied about throughout our marriage. Two: temazepam for mental health issues, including delusion, hallucinations. Three—'

'Hallucinations? You can't—'

'Three,' he says, talking over me, 'you give our son a potentially lethal asthma attack because you fail to pack his inhaler.'

'Lethal? That's—'

'Four: you abandon a kid ten miles from home, almost running a mother and baby over in the process, as witnessed by your son. Five: you leave your children unattended in a crowded leisure centre, despite having been warned by the police to be vigilant ... Shall I go on? Because there's plenty more where that came from.'

'You're twisting everything,' I say.

'Tough luck,' he says. 'The law doesn't care. These are the facts and I've plenty of witnesses and records to attest to them. Who are they going to believe? The chief inspector who was injured in the line of duty, or the medicated nut job who once tried to kill her own father?'

A silence falls as I try to gauge how I feel about his using that intensely personal matter against me, but it's impossible to say. My disappointment in him is immeasurable.

'Why is this so important to you?' I say. 'You love Jake and Ruby, I don't doubt. I know you've spent a lot of time with them. But why go to so much trouble?'

'Supposition,' he says flatly, folding his arms. 'Everything you're saying is supposition. I'd expect nothing less from you.'

'I assume you've been turning them against me. That's why they've been funny with me, especially Jake. I'm guessing you've been laying it on thick behind my back.'

'Again,' he says, almost languidly, almost bored, 'supposition.'

'You even managed to get me out of the family home without my suspecting anything. I'm guessing that was your intention: to declare me an unfit mother and then get the house and the kids . . . How am I doing? Am I close?'

He shrugs, lips tightly knitted. But there's something else on his face and I realise that it is pain. He is shifting position, looking about him for relief. I glance up at the dresser to where his medication is kept – high out of reach from the children – and I decide that if he wants it, he'll have to stand, hobble over and get it himself.

'You knew I'd fight you,' I say. 'You couldn't be sure you'd win, even as stay-at-home dad. So, you had to build a case against me. And who better than you to do that, hey? You had time on your hands and you knew the law. I bet you were kicking the plan around for a while. And then fate threw you a hell of a bone when my mum died. I was vulnerable, so you made your move.'

My voice trembles then, but it is merely through self-pity. He hasn't noticed my lapse in composure – is swaying with pain in his chair as though drunk.

I continue, undeterred.

'I'm guessing that you did what you do best: dig up dirt. Somehow you found out that my father was dead, and you found out about the inheritance, and that he was a nasty piece of work. But you didn't want to just tell me about that. Oh no. It was far more damaging for me to discover it myself and relive it. So, you led me slowly up the garden path to my father and the pot of gold.'

I smile sadly, thinking of Carlisle – the metaphorical end of the rainbow.

I should have known that my father's money would never have brought me joy.

'So, you did . . . what? You got Carver to stalk me in order to send me off the rails, so that you could discredit me? All you had to do then was start divorce proceedings. Everything else had been done for you. My father's money would be split up as assets during the divorce. Job done.'

I sigh heavily.

'You played me really well, Mike. Flawlessly almost. Until one little mistake. Because everyone makes one, don't they? You used to tell me that yourself, Chief Inspector.'

He is staring at me, thinking.

One little mistake?

What mistake?

He is self-possessed again now, righteous. 'You're bluffing,' he says. 'You've got nothing.'

In response, I smile.

It is the warmest smile that I can muster. But I am thinking too. I am thinking about how there is something that doesn't make sense.

I can't understand why he has so little regard for me, why he wants out so vehemently. I have been a good wife. Until recently, I thought he loved me. I have made him happy and have provided for him and for our children.

It is resentment, spite perhaps. He has become bitter, angry, that I can go to work whilst he's stuck at home, impaired, emasculated.

Yet that can't just be it.

What else am I missing?

And I am thinking about this, drinking the last drop of my tea, glancing at my watch – it's eleven thirty and I have to go – when the answer appears before me.

From the floor above, there's a slamming noise. It takes me a moment to decipher it over the sound of running water, since I'm rinsing my cup at the sink. So, I stop, listen. I can hear a voice, someone calling.

I turn to look at Mike. He has heard it too. He is looking at me fearfully, his eyes as round as coins.

'Who is . . . ?' I trail off.

I recognise the voice. I open my mouth in shock.

The voice is coming towards us now, heels clipping on the stairs, rapidly approaching. 'Mike? Mikey, honey? Where the heck are you, you gorgeous . . . Oh my God.'

She stops, stares at me in horror.

There, at the bottom of the stairs, in a pretty violet dress and black leather jacket, is my friend, Nicole.

There she is.

The little piece that I am missing.

36

'What are you doing here?' I ask. I smile briefly, cock my head hopefully.

'I . . . ' Nicole glances about her, her eye settling on Mike.

I place the cup down that I am still holding and wipe my hands on the tea towel.

Mike is getting up, leaning on his cane.

And now he is . . .

I stare in shock, unable to process it. My eyes feel as though they are burning. I blink rapidly.

He is putting his hand around Nicole's waist.

'What the hell . . . ?' I say, looking from one of them to the other. And then I laugh. 'Nic! Is this some kind of joke?'

I'm not sure why I'm laughing. But I continue to do so. Yet neither of them is joining in. They are watching me closely. I realise then that I look insane laughing like this and I stop, fall silent, placing my hand to my cheek.

I am trembling all over. I compose myself. I did not come here today to fall apart. I will not do so now.

'Would someone like to tell me what's going on?' I ask.

Nicole's mouth seems glued shut. She looks very small next to Mike, teeny. I have never seen them stood side by side before.

Mike looks at me squarely, brazenly. 'We love each other,' he says.

'I don't believe it,' I say, my mouth wobbling. 'You're nuts. This is nuts.' I hold my hand out to Nicole. 'Tell him, Nic. It's nuts! We're best friends. We've known each other for ever.' I take a step towards her. 'Tell me this is some kind of a joke. You two.' I point, my finger oscillating between the two of them. 'Come on. You're kidding me.'

I am guessing that this is what denial looks like.

It's not pretty, it's not sensible.

And then Nicole speaks and, as she does, a large tear trickles down her cheek.

'I'm so sorry,' she says. 'I didn't want you to find out like this. I was going to wait until everything had blown over, until you'd finished grieving and the mediation was over. I didn't want to hurt you, didn't want to make it worse than it already was.' She breaks off, begins to cry more heartily, Mike squeezing her waist.

'It's OK, Nicky,' he says. 'It's good that she knows. She needs to know.'

I can't say for sure whether it's his calling her *Nicky*, or the fact that he is consoling her in my kitchen that riles me the most.

'Why?' I say angrily. 'Why would you do this to me?' I am addressing Nicole. 'I've only ever been good to you. I stuck by you when Jamie left. Why would you steal my husband? You were my maid of bloody honour!'

'I know,' she says, sobbing. Her make-up is running. She always wears a lot of mascara. Her tears are black. 'We didn't plan it. It just happened. I'm so *so* sorry. I didn't mean to hurt you, Suzy. That was never my intention.'

She is juddering now, gasping between words. Mike is rubbing her back, looking around for the box of tissues. I can see it on the shelf by the window, but I'm not saying anything.

All I can think is that this is my upset, my shock, and she is the one crying, being comforted.

The thought is so sobering, I pull out a chair, sit down, my hands flat on the table as though I'm a fortune-teller. And in a way, I am. I can see clearly what I have to do.

'How long have you been creeping around behind my back?' I ask.

Suzy is too distraught to reply. Mike has found her some kitchen roll. She is blowing her nose with a honk. She is beautiful, but she has never been good at nose-blowing. Her sneezes are also very loud for someone so small; and she often chews with her mouth open. All of which I think as I look at her, at the person whom I misguidedly used to call my best friend.

I wonder then what Helen and Donna will say, whether they already know. But I doubt this very much. They, I feel, are loyal to the core.

Mike is having to sit down, is easing himself into his chair with a pained expression. 'Just over two years,' he says.

I balk a little at this. 'How? When?'

Mike glances at Nicole, but she is facing away, crying into kitchen roll. It is odd, watching someone whom you cared for so deeply until moments before in such distress because you have to stop yourself from going to them.

'It just happened,' he says. 'We saw each other a lot at football training and in the playground ... '

'While I was at work,' I add.

He nods.

'Nice,' I say. 'Classy. And this took place, where? In our bed? Or the spare room? I'm hoping the spare room and not our bed – that even you wouldn't be that tacky. Or maybe it was a hotel.'

'It was at Nicky's,' he says.

And that's when I lose it.

I push back my chair so forcibly that it topples over with smack.

'*Get out!*' I scream at Nicole. I'm scared to touch her, scared to go near her for fear of what I might do. Instead, I motion with my hands for her to leave, shooing her away. '*Get the hell out!*'

'Nicky!' Mike is shouting, standing up again. 'Wait!'

She runs up the stairs, leaving a trail of kitchen roll behind her. There's the sound of footsteps along the hallway, then the slamming of the front door and then silence.

Mike turns on me, his eyes flashing furiously. 'How dare you?' he says. 'How dare you treat her like that?'

'Oh, get stuffed,' I say. 'You big bullying bastard.'

It is brave. But I don't care any more. I approach him, stop before him, prodding his chest. 'Was she in on it?' I say.

'In on what?' he says, glaring down at me.

'You know exactly what.' I prod him again. 'Did she know what was going on?'

He keeps his mouth firmly closed.

And I know the answer.

'You're welcome to her,' I say. 'And surely this has scuppered your chances in court. You'll never get custody if you're having an affair.'

He leans in towards me, threateningly, prodding me in return, hitting my breastbone. It feels, where I have lost weight, like he is drilling into me. But I grit my teeth and don't flinch.

'That's where you're wrong,' he says. 'I told you not to try to beat me where the law's concerned.' He prods more forcefully. 'In the eyes of the law, infidelity's irrelevant. It doesn't affect custody whatsoever. It just means we're more likely to settle out of court . . . Let's face it, Suzy, you're screwed. You're going to lose in court and I'm going to live with Nicole and the kids. And there's not a thing you can do about it.'

I gaze up at him. My breastbone is throbbing.

Suddenly the pain is too much – him, Nicole, everything.

I turn away, walk numbly from the room, heading upstairs.

As I go along the hallway, my head begins to hurt. I glance at my watch, murmuring in alarm.

I have lost track of the time. It's ten minutes to midday. I shouldn't be here, have to go.

And I am hurrying towards the front door, when the knocker rattles sharply, causing me to freeze.

I consider running. But then instead, I advance.

As I pull open the door, I try not to shrink back at the sight of him stood there in his wax jacket. There's a roll-up cigarette behind his ear; his hands are firmly fixed in his pockets.

On seeing me, he rocks backwards and forwards on his feet and it strikes me that he is so much like a policeman – so much like my husband – that it's a wonder that I didn't notice it before.

I see him into the house without saying a word. He stands by the front door and I retreat to the staircase, where I wait half a dozen steps up.

Now comes the tap tap tap of a stick on the floorboards and Mike appears, stopping some distance from the front door.

It's not the first time that I have watched something unfolding from the stairs: an odious man blocking a doorway, prohibiting anyone from leaving, trapping them in their own home.

Little has changed between now and then, except my name. And the size of my limbs. They are still useless to me though, as a woman. I can't compete, not with my body alone. I have to have more; I need a weapon.

I have given self-defence a lot of thought during my life and it has led me to work hard, harder than everyone else. Not to be rich, not to have more. But to be powerful.

More powerful than them.

‘Where’s my money?’ Craig Carver says, standing with his legs apart, his hands still jammed hard into his pockets.

I don’t think that Mike should be laughing. In my experience, it is one of the worst responses to offer an angry person.

‘I’m not here to muck about,’ Carver says. ‘Pay me what’s owed or—’

‘Or you’ll what?’ Mike says.

Mike is taller, stronger-looking than Carver. But he is leaning on his cane, so I’m not sure whether I fancy his chances.

‘You know what I’ll do,’ Carver says, glancing at me. ‘What I’m capable of.’

‘Oh right,’ Mike says, smirking. ‘So, you’re going to, what? Attack my wife? Attack me?’

‘I’m not going to attack you, you cripple,’ he says. ‘Or your missus.’ He smiles. ‘I’ll go for the kids. You know I can get to them.’

‘No, you can’t,’ I say. ‘No one’s touching my children.’ I look at Mike. ‘Give him what you owe him.’

‘You what?’ Mike says in surprise.

I take one step down the stairs, before stopping. ‘You heard him – he’ll hurt the children. It’s not worth it.’

‘Listen to her,’ Carver says. ‘She’s talking sense.’

‘Stay out of it, Suzy,’ Mike says. ‘This isn’t your business.’

‘Not my business?’ I say. ‘Sounds like it is, to me. You used this man to harass me and now you’re supposed to pay him for a job well done. And as it’s my money that you’ll be using, then I suggest you pay up if I say so.’

Mike is getting cross. He places his cane against the wall and his hands on his hips, his forehead glistening. He can’t stand upright without support, is trying hard to do so. ‘I said, stay out of it.’

‘How much do you want?’ I ask Carver.

He gazes at me, an insidious smile appearing on his face.

'I'll give you whatever you want, if you'll answer my questions,' I say.

'Suzy!' Mike shouts.

'Go on . . . ' Carver says.

'Why did you do this to me?' I ask.

Carver glances at Mike. 'Because he thought I owed him,' he says.

'For what?'

'For this,' Mike says, pointing to his leg. 'For doing this to me, you stupid bitch.'

I recoil at that, stung. In our ten years of marriage, he has never once called me a derogatory name.

Yet he can verbally abuse me all he likes. He won't derail me now.

I look back at Carver. 'What's that got to do with you?'

'I was driving,' Carver says.

'When?'

He nods his head in Mike's direction. 'The night he got injured.'

I turn to Mike in confusion. 'You never told me that. Why didn't—'

'Because I didn't want to talk about it. All right?' Mike says. 'He lost control of the car because he's an arsehole and then he walked away, scot-free.'

Carver looks down at the floor, shuffles his feet. 'I've said sorry. There's nothing else to do except move on . . . And pay up.'

'So, you did this out of guilt?' I ask.

'Something like that,' Carver says. 'But he told me he'd pay me too. And then he never did, did you, mate?'

'I said you'd get paid,' Mike says, leaning on his cane again. 'But I never said how much because I thought you'd know that this was your chance to pay me back.'

'Well, I guess I took it wrong,' Carver says. 'But then communication never was our strong point, was it.'

There's a pause as they stare angrily at each other.

'How could you do this to Jake and Ruby?' I ask Mike. 'How could you put them at risk? I thought you loved them?'

Mike looks up at me, shame registering momentarily on his face. 'I didn't put them at risk. He did,' he says, pointing his cane at Carver. 'He was supposed to just shake you up a bit. He was told not to go anywhere near the kids.'

'But then you didn't pay up,' Carver says. 'How else was I going to get you to give me the money? . . . Why aren't you getting that? Is your brain friggin' useless, as well as your leg?'

But Mike doesn't have the chance to come back at him because at that moment I see the flash of blue lights in the frosted glass panel of the front door. Mike has spotted it too and is looking aghast.

Carver is glancing over his shoulder. 'What?' he says. 'What you looking at?'

'Police,' Mike says under his breath. He is confused, wondering how the police knew to come here at this exact time.

Outside, car doors are slamming.

'What the hell?' Carver says. 'You set me up!'

'No, I didn't,' Mike snarls. 'Why would I do that, you twat?'

'You told me to come here,' Carver shouts.

'No, I didn't!' Mike shouts back.

There's a loud knock on the door, several knocks. Carver sets off down the hallway, startlingly light on his feet, throwing Mike off balance as he goes. Mike is falling backwards, crying out, arms flailing.

I hurry to the door to open it, stepping aside as the police charge through.

Carver has got his floor plan muddled up, has lost his bearings. We are on the ground floor. He is shouting in frustration.

He has seen that he's at a dead end, that there's no exit in the study and is coming back down the hallway, realising his mistake too late.

The police are trying to get hold of him; he is struggling, cursing. It takes four officers to restrain him.

'Craig Carver, I'm arresting you on suspicion of breaking and entering, of intentional harassment, alarm and distress ... '

I watch, my back pressed flat against the wall.

Mike is lying on the floor where Carver knocked him. He is holding his leg, his face creased with pain. I feel nothing for him. Two police officers are helping him up, but he is brushing them off, trying to stand without them – kicking his other leg to try to reach his cane.

'Get off me!' he is shouting. 'I'm a retired chief inspector, for Chrissake.'

'Mike Taylor,' one of the officers says, handcuffing him, 'I am arresting you on suspicion of disorderly behaviour with intent to cause harassment, alarm or distress. You do not have to say anything, but it may harm your defence ... '

The policeman's voice is dwindling as Mike and Carver are escorted out of the front door, along the path. I think briefly of the neighbours, of how this will look. I hope no one is watching. I am glad the children are at school.

I think of something else then, something that Mike said weeks before, when he found out about my past. And suddenly I am running outside in my socks, pursuing them.

'You've got a lot of nerve, Mike!' I shout. 'Saying that I wasn't who you thought I was when you married me!'

I'm not sure if the message reaches him. A van is passing by, engine roaring. Carver is shouting abuse at the police. Mike is being placed into a separate car.

I stand there shivering, my socks lapping up the chill and damp of the flagstones.

Mike doesn't look at me. As the cars drive off, I expect him to turn and look for me, but he doesn't.

And then it's just me, on my own. I glance about me. No one appears to be watching from their windows.

I gaze up at the sky, watching an aeroplane making its way noiselessly through the clouds. Then I go inside the house.

It seems so quiet. I talk to myself, mutterings about how I should change my wet socks.

When I'm ready, I brush my hair and then set off down the hill to work.

*

FINAL MOMENTS OF THE MEETING WITH INSPECTOR DAVIES

Three hours ago

'You've no idea who that is?' he said.

'No,' I said. 'Should I?'

He smiled ever so faintly at me. 'That's Craig Carver. A corrupt copper from a bad batch in Bristol a few years back. Got kicked off the force, if I remember rightly.'

'And why would I know him?' I asked.

'Well,' he said, setting his hands on the table in front of him, 'I think that's something that you should probably ask your husband, Mrs Taylor. Don't you?'

'OK,' I said. 'I will. But before I do ... you need to see this.'

I reached down to my holdall and pulled out a plastic A4 file.

I set it on the table between us.

He didn't move. 'What's that?' he said.

'Evidence.'

He picked up the file, read steadily for what felt like ten or fifteen minutes, maybe more. I waited, tapping my foot quietly on the carpet.

When he was done, he put the documents back into the file.

Then he set his eyes on me. They were grey. I didn't think I had ever seen eyes that colour before: dark metal.

'Do you want to press charges?' he asked.

I didn't hesitate.

'Yes,' I said.

EPILOGUE

On a fair autumn morning, the children and I visit the graveyard where Granny Annie is buried.

It's the first time that I have been here since the funeral. I haven't wanted to come before now, wary of having my grief reopened when I have been doing so well. I also haven't wanted to upset the children. But now seems the right time for us to visit. Jake has made a card for her. I told him that it won't last past the first rainfall, but he insisted. We have laminated the card to protect it. Ruby is carrying a small bouquet of Michaelmas daisies picked from our back garden, the base of which she has carefully wrapped in foil. She has also made a card. I am bringing a bouquet of sunflowers.

The headstone has only just been put into place. When Ifor Owens, the stonemason, showed me the final product back in June, I didn't like it, requested a change to be made. And so, he set to work again.

We are here today to see the headstone. As we pass through the stone columns at the entrance to the graveyard, the wind whips our hair, tugs our coats. I hold Ruby's hand tightly. Jake is whistling a song but goes quiet at the sight of the graves before us.

'There's nothing to be scared of,' I say. 'Granny Annie's over here, at the back.' And I lead them down the gravel path to the left-hand corner.

We stop before the headstone. The grave and its neighbours possess the clean look of a fresh haircut. This row is new in comparison with the surrounding weather-worn graves.

'Is this Granny Annie?' Ruby says shyly, pointing to the grave.

'Yes,' I say. 'It is, poppet.'

Jake kneels down and props his card up on the headstone. Ruby skirts diplomatically around the grassy bump in the middle to place the Michaelmas daisies next to Jake's card.

I gaze at the headstone. I'm glad that I changed it.

In June, when I saw the surname *Stone*, it struck me as a mistake. That wasn't who my mother was born to be, but who circumstances forced her to become. I also didn't like the grey stone finish and the black writing.

And so, I changed her name back to her maiden name and requested that the stone be black and the writing gold, in a final bid to bring a little light to her life.

ANNIE MARIE WALKER
Born 4 January 1956
Died 19 January 2017
Beloved mother
With me always

I like the headstone, if such a thing is possible.

'What about yours?' Ruby asks, pointing to the sunflowers in my hand. 'Shall I do it?'

'Please,' I say.

Ruby takes the bouquet from me and gently sets it next to the other offerings. She smiles in satisfaction, straightening the front of her coat. This is a self-soothing gesture that she has inherited from me. Hopefully when the time comes for me to depart this earth, I will have left her more than that.

'What do we do now, Mummy?' she says, gazing up at me.

'Well,' I say, 'we talk to her.'

Ruby screws her nose up. 'Will she hear?'

'I think so,' I say.

Jake nods. 'OK,' he says. 'I'll start.' And he squats down and begins to tell my mother all about the goal he scored last night at football training.

Ruby is laughing, nudging Jake. 'That's so *boring*,' she says. 'Granny Annie doesn't want to hear about *that*.'

'Hush, Rubes,' I say, pressing my finger to my lips. 'Let Jake speak.'

'So,' he begins, 'there are three Jakes on my team. I'm the best. And I'm calling to Jake Parker to pass to me and he doesn't because he never passes. And everyone's, like, *Pass to Jake Taylor* – that's me . . .'

I smile, my eye resting on the sunflower bouquet. Sunflowers were my mother's favourite. I well up, blink quickly and look at the grave next door. Yet there are few places in a graveyard where the heart can find relief. Instead, I gaze at the yew trees in the corner of the yard and I think of the yews in the garden of 8 Rose Lane.

It was always about my past, I think then. Had it not been for what had gone on in that unhappy home in Carlisle, Mike could not have unhinged me so successfully.

I haven't told him what his one mistake was – the one slip-up that led me to uncover what he was up to.

It was right after our first official mediation session. He was in pain, made a little error that he might not have made were it not for that.

We were standing outside the legal firm, when he asked me whether I had seen the stalker since the previous Monday.

I didn't realise the implications of this at the time – not until later that evening when the force of it all but knocked the air from me.

The thing was, I hadn't told anyone about seeing the stalker that Monday – not the police, Mike, my friends, no one. I deliberately hadn't followed procedure, hadn't reported the sighting. Having met with Dan Cassidy for the first time only hours before, I didn't know what I was getting into, but my instincts were telling me to focus on the children, on mediation, and not on the stalker. So, I had ignored him, in the hope that he would go away.

When I realised Mike's error – what it meant – I didn't call the police because of their link to Mike.

Instead, I phoned Tim.

Mike had told me that he was having a long physiotherapy session on the Wednesday, so I knew that he would be gone from the house for several hours. Even better, when Tim and I went home that day, Mike had left his phone on charge.

IT expert Tim hacked Mike's laptop and phone. Mike had taken a lot of security measures, but Tim, after some minor fuss, was able to gain access.

We discovered a letter that Keith Gunnell had sent me six months ago, informing me of the inheritance. Mike had intercepted it, kept it hidden. It made sense then, the odd way in which Mr Gunnell had greeted me in Carlisle.

I was wondering when you'd show up.

Mike had conducted months of research into child custody law. He had emailed and texted Carver regarding harassing me. It was all there in writing. Carver had been becoming increasingly aggressive with Mike, demanding payment for the job he was hired to do.

We printed off a wealth of evidence. And I texted Carver from Mike's phone telling him to come to the house on the

Friday at noon to collect his money. All that remained was for me to tell the police to be there too.

Mike has asked me several times since how I knew what he was up to. It must be eating him up inside. I will let him sweat it out for eternity.

He has quite a lot of time to think about it. He is currently in prison in Wiltshire. We haven't visited him and we won't be doing so either. The children have mixed feelings about him and are frightened of prisons. I am doing nothing to convince them to the contrary. I won't turn them against him – as he did to me – but when he is out, I will let him see them and they can make up their own minds about Daddy.

It's only fair.

The legal process took several months to play out. There was a trial within the proceedings to decide about the allegations made. Then another hearing at which it was decided that Mike had caused the children and me emotional harm.

It was ruled that the children would live with me full-time in the family home.

Fortunately, there was a new law, introduced in 2015, regarding psychological abuse within a domestic setting. Proof was needed that the offence was carried out *repeatedly or continuously*. The victim must have been *caused serious alarm or distress*. The offence must also have been calculated to cause emotional harm.

Throughout the hearings, I thought of my poor mother – of how little the law had done to protect her, how ultimately her only defence had been to run and hide.

Mike would have been well aware of the flaws in the criminal system regards stalking and harassment. For all his talk of trusting the system, he was counting on it letting me down. So greatly assured of his ability to stand above the law, it hadn't occurred to him that he might get caught. Meticulous and painstaking, by ticking all the boxes required to carry out a harassment crime, he had aided his own prosecution. He could not have done a more thorough job.

'And that's when I booted the ball into the back of the net,' Jake says, jumping up in excitement. 'Boom, it went. Boom!' He kicks his foot into the air, reliving the goal.

I smile at him. 'I'm sure Granny Annie loved hearing that, Jakey,' I say.

The sun is shining, lighting the gold on my mum's headstone. The children are rosy-cheeked, healthy-looking, I am very glad to note.

'Well, we'd better get going,' I say, reaching forward to touch the tip of a sunflower tenderly.

The children are taking the opportunity to examine the graveyards along the row. I pause before my mother's grave. 'You don't have to worry about me any more,' I say quietly. 'You can rest now.'

I go around to the side of the headstone, place my hand there, feeling the smooth granite under my fingertips. 'I love you, Mum,' I say. 'I'll see you soon.'

And then I turn away.

The children are coming back towards me. I take Ruby's hand and we go to leave.

'Wait!' Ruby says, pulling something from her coat pocket. 'My card!'

'Oh, yes,' I say. 'Well remembered. Pop it down by Jake's.' I watch as she places the home-made card on the headstone.

As she steps away, I stare at the image on the front.

It's of a stick mother and child, holding hands.

Later that afternoon, I'm at work. There's a food fair on in town so the deli is quiet. I anticipated this, so have invited my friends in for afternoon tea.

Ruby is in the book corner, colouring in, singing to herself. When the children aren't at school, they split their time between here and Helen's house. Helen's eldest daughter, nearly eighteen, helps with childcare to earn pocket money. It's a system that's working well for now.

Jake is currently outside playing football with Leo in the delivery yard. Every now and then I hear the ball slam against the door. Leo is my assistant manager now. I have made his salary so competitive that he can never leave me. He still surfs job-seeking websites in front of me, but I hope this is just his awful sense of humour.

I haven't seen Tim in a while. His project at the architectural firm two doors down is over. He popped in on his last day there a few months ago, saying that he would be back from time to time. I took the chance to thank him for what he did for me, and he told me that it was nothing. And then he was gone.

I don't know if I am lonely without a man in my life, especially without the husband whom I loved so dearly. Yet if my mother's story taught me anything, it is that it is better to go it alone than go at it in strife. If I will be lonely in years to come, I cannot say. For now, I have my children, my house, my deli and my friends. That feels like quite a lot.

'So, it's finally through, the money?' Donna says, dipping her fork into the top of a toffee cup cake.

'Yes,' I say. 'It's the strangest feeling.'

'How so?' Helen says.

We are sitting at the table nearest the book corner, not far from Ruby. I lower my voice. 'Remember how much I didn't want it at first?' I say. 'Yet I want it now.'

'I'd say that's fair enough, after everything you've been through,' Helen says.

'And it's all yours,' Donna says.

The inheritance wasn't put into the pot of assets during

divorce proceedings, wasn't deemed fair to do so in the circumstances.

The money was my father's earnings – earnings that had contributed towards the pressure that had aided and abetted excessive violence in him. And yet I want it, all the same. I want something good to have come from 8 Rose Lane.

'What are you going to do with it?' Donna says.

'I don't know,' I say. 'Nothing, for now.'

'Just leave it,' Helen says. 'You'll know what to do with it some day soon.'

Then Donna drops her fork with an alarming clatter. 'Oh my God!' she says.

'What?' I say.

Helen is holding her cappuccino mug mid-air, stunned.

In the doorway, looking small, thin, pale, is Nicole.

She edges towards us. Helen lowers her cup. Donna's chin is jutting angrily. I have no idea how I look, am hoping that it's not how I am feeling. I don't want Nicole to know how much the sight of her upsets me.

Helen bends her head forward to whisper to me. 'You don't have to talk to her, Suzy. You don't have to do this. I'll tell her to leave.'

But I decide to stand up and face her.

'What do you want?' I say. I glance about me, but there's only an elderly couple by the window. Still, I keep my voice quiet so that Ruby can't hear.

Nicole is right in front of me now, standing close. I don't think I have seen her with so little make-up on before. I'm not sure if it is purposely so, in order to evoke sympathy, or whether it's her new look. It doesn't look good, whatever the reason.

'To see you,' she says. 'All of you.' She looks past me to Helen and Donna.

'What for?' I say. 'What is there to say?'

'I just wanted to tell you how sorry I am.'

'Well, you've said it. So, you can go.'

She gazes up at me, her mouth quivering. 'Please, Suzy.' She raises her hand towards me. 'I'm really sorry.' She begins to cry. 'I didn't mean to hurt you. I'll always hate myself for what I did. I didn't mean to fall in love with—'

But she doesn't get to finish her sentence because then kind, motherly Helen does something that I will never forget.

She pushes her chair back, draws herself to her full height and glares down at Nicole. 'That's enough! Didn't you hear what Suzy said? She said get the hell out of here and never come back, you nasty spiteful selfish marriage-wrecking bitch.'

Nicole stares in shock. And then she turns on her heel and leaves the deli.

I take a deep breath. We all look at each other, our eyes serious, full of foreboding.

Then we start to laugh.

And just like that, I am free.

ACKNOWLEDGEMENTS

Heartfelt thanks to all at Piatkus Fiction; Little, Brown, including Amy Donegan, Clara Diaz, Dominic Wakeford, and especially to Emma Beswetherick for all her hard work and insight; to all at PFD, with special thanks to Marilia Savvides, and to Nelle Andrew for being the world's greatest agent and a little bit more; to barrister and author Sarah Langford for her invaluable and generous legal input; to my family – Mum, Dad, Nick, Wilfie and Alex, and to my friends for always being there.